CODENAME: MADELEINE

CODENAME: MADELEINE

BARNABY JAMESON

First published in 2022 by Whitefox Publishing

ISBN 9781915036131

Also available as an ebook
ISBN 9781915036148

And audiobook
ISBN 9781915036155

Typeset by seagulls.net
Cover design by Dom Forbes
Printed and bound by CPI

To Firo
and to
Tricia and Briggi

ACKNOWLEDGEMENTS

This book would not have been possible without the guidance and support of four stars of the book world: Philip Watson, Charlie Campbell, Marina Kemp and the ever-generous Joanna Penn. The book was fortunate enough to have a world class editor, Philip Connor, and a world class copyeditor, Jenni Davis. In addition, the author would like to thank those listed below for helping him, in their unique ways, to scale a daunting (and at times impossible) mountain.

Isabelle Bruccianni   L-M Lidén
Liz Campbell   Clarissa Machitski
Catherine Cardwell   Frank Musker
Peter Carter QC   Lucy Peter
James Curran   Maximillian Wakefield
Jessica Dash   Olivia Williams
Mark B. Fuller   Miles Woolcock

'What you seek is seeking you.'
-*Rumi*

PROLOGUE

Occupied Paris, 1943

Noor's pace quickened.

The battered suitcase concealing her Mark II radio transmitter was heavy. Caught with a hidden transmitter-receiver, she would be taken for immediate interrogation at Gestapo headquarters. Even the reinforced walls in the basement of 84 Avenue Foch could not shut out the screams. *In extremis* there was Plan C. Hidden in the button of her dress above her belt was a white pill stamped on both sides with red letters.

DANGER!
KCN

Scientific compound: Cyanide. The words of her handler had a reassuring echo.

It will take about twelve seconds.

On her lapel was a silver bird studded with jewel eyes – ruby, like the letters on the cyanide pill.

She was the last radio transmitter left in Paris. Her predecessor, Denis Rake, had made an emergency stage-exit. Any longer and he would have been sitting, arms clamped to a chair, in 84 Avenue Foch.

Noor exited Le Colisée on the Champs-Elysées, suitcase in hand. The café was approved by London. The coat attendant knew the password. Nothing about the two male contacts she left sitting at the corner table had aroused Noor's suspicion. Their French was convincing, if hard to place. One, perhaps, took more than a passing interest in the reddish tint of her hair, though most was concealed under her cloche hat.

As she walked north along the Champs-Elysées, she noticed a man engrossed in a copy of *Le Monde* fold his newspaper. Another, on the opposite side of the Champs-Elysées, put on a pair of sunglasses. Nothing out of place on a warm October day, even in wartime.

Despite the weeping blister on her heel, a strange euphoria came over Noor as she walked. London would be extracting her within twenty-four hours. She had succeeded, where others failed, in eluding the Gestapo. Gestapo units had been scouring the city for weeks like a plague of black beetles in search of a wireless operator who would vanish, like the tap of Morse code, into the ether. She knew she was London's only remaining eyes in Paris. She had refused orders to leave once before. Now even Georges Morel and the *extrême* fighters of the Paris Resistance said it was too dangerous to stay a minute longer.

Noor noticed splashes of colour returning to the drained Renoir of occupied Paris. The burgundy of a woman's beret. The purple of a bougainvillea entwined around the entrance of a florist. The pink of a ribbon around a box of *pâtisseries*. The weather was still balmy. She felt as if she were back at the Sorbonne, carrying her harp instead of a Mark II transmitter. The following afternoon she and her radio would be clambering aboard a Lysander sent by the phantom RAF squadron used to extract agents. Her inner harp strings, so long taut to the point of snapping, were beginning to release.

She cut through Rue Marbeuf. On the wall of a kiosk, she saw a reward for 200,000 francs for information in connection with the disappearance of a Gestapo officer last seen in the 5ème Arrondissement. Her heart quickened. That day she had jumped through Morel's attic window when she heard the pounding on the *porte d'entrée*. As she walked, she felt a presence. The ruby eyes on her lapel glowed a deeper red. The man she had seen folding his copy of *Le Monde* was matching her pace. The man in sunglasses was visible in the reflections of the shop windows. Was it her imagination? She recalled the last Morse transmission from London. *Be extra careful.*

When a shadow crossed her heart, Noor would think always of her father's words. *In times of strife, Bābouli, always find and follow your breath.* She focused on her lungs and initiated *adhyam pranayama* – upper chest breath. She felt her pulse steady. As she breathed, the same conflict stirred in the ventricles of her heart. Could she extinguish the divine light of life? Next to the transmitter was her treasured book: The Wisdom of Rumi. Her father, Inayat, had underlined one of the Sufi master's sayings:

'With life as short as a half-taken breath, plant nothing but love.'

She reminded herself that if she was caught and taken to 84 Avenue Foch, the Gestapo, in their black leather trench coats, would be planting nothing but hate. There was a saying among SOE agents. *If you are taken for interrogation, smile while you still have teeth.* Her mind spun. What could she use? Her .38 calibre pistol was in the safe house. The curriculum of Special Training School No. 5 also included unarmed combat. Even the peaceable mind of a mystic's daughter had one mantra driven home like a sledgehammer. *Everything is a weapon.*

She could feel the softness of her cloche, so familiar it felt like part of her head. Hats were an obvious precaution. This one had a feature unknown to anyone except the F-Section technician who devised the fast-acting toxin for the tip of the hatpin. It was lodged three inches above her right ear.

Noor moved the suitcase to her left hand. The footsteps behind her quickened. She could feel the brachial nerve in her right forearm twitch.

The gentle hand of a Sufi harpist was ready to sting like a scorpion.

PART
ONE

PART
ONE

CHAPTER 1
'THE MYSTIC'

Moscow, Midnight
31st December 1913

Inayat
Amina
Noor

Snow fell like muffled drumbeats on the frozen crust of the Moskva River and on the circus-striped domes of St Basil's Cathedral. Snow fell on the twin heads of the Romanov eagle glancing east–west above the Imperial Bolshoi Theatre. Snow fell on the waiting *troika* carriages and on the plumes of black *Orlov* horses restive in their harnesses. Snow blew northwards through the jangle of harness bells and gathered, as the Kremlin Clock struck midnight, above the Vysoko-Petrovsky Monastery.

In a vaulted chamber lay Amina, her green eyes clamped shut as she writhed, oblivious to the fireworks. Her long barley-coloured hair was streaked wet at the temples. Her mouth was twisted as she bit into a bloodless bottom lip. Her palm gripped a *subha* of ninety-nine prayer beads. Seven altar candles encircled the bed, flickering in the brass, threading the air with Siberian pine. A nun placed a leather strap between Amina's teeth. The nun locked her hands in prayer, looked up at the red stained glass, and recited an invocation to the Most Blessed Theotokos. Her black *apostolnik*

7

headscarf rocked as she incanted. Twelve rows of icons looked down, their black eyes doleful and expectant.

In the outer cloister, Inayat hugged his woollen cloak about his shoulders and gripped his wooden staff. Beneath his cloak he wore a long golden robe tied at the waist. Around his neck hung a ruby in a gold clasp, radiating a ring of crimson. His black hair was anointed with oil, parted in the middle and falling into curls like a lawyer's wig. His skin was the colour of burnt umber, his features delicate and masculine: an Indian Rasputin. His eyes were closed, his brow rucked, his face taut. Snow gathered on his shoulders like white epaulettes as he clasped his abdomen. He breathed inwards and outwards with a concentration that mirrored the prone woman.

Amina felt a quickening. A tearing. She bit further into the leather. The whole of her life was being squeezed through a ring. Images flickered behind her eyelids. A giant fir tree falling. A landscape cleaving and dividing. A volcano erupting in the Caucasus. As dawn flooded the red stained glass, sticky warmth flowed from her like lava. She heard a distant cry – hungry, urgent – and sank back against the pillows, her mouth now supple and pink.

The whisper of Death faded. The nun unlocked her fingers. An ancient Tartar nurse in a red headdress kneaded the newborn dry with a deftness that belied her coarse square hands. As Inayat entered, she placed the infant in his arms – a downy head in a blaze of embroidered blankets clinking with miniature pendants.

Inayat examined the dormant soul taken from amniotic darkness. Her hair was fine and dark, the fontanels of her head soft as seagrass, her forehead puckered, her eyes closed tight as a kitten's, her eyelashes long and delicate, her lips elegant and parted. Snow fluttered against the stained glass like the infant's heartbeat, quick and strong, as a father held his daughter.

The Tartar lifted the child from her father.

'*Bābouli*,' said the nurse in Old Tartar – 'Father's child.'

The word babbled from Inayat's throat, his heart overflowing.
'*Bāb-ouli.*'

*

Inayat Khan started life not in Moscow, but in a noble house on the banks of the Vishwamitri River in Baroda. When the night jasmine opened in the evenings, the marsh crocodiles would gather in the shallows, their serpentine eyes glowing pink in the sunset. The house bordered the grounds of Lakshmi Palace, three times the size of the Bhadra Fort in Ahmedabad, whose high tower pierced the sky like a shining Bengal lance. Inayat's family were of princely caste, direct descendants of Tipu Sultan, a soldier-Maharajah known to all as 'the Tiger of Mysore'. Tipu Sultan was the first commander to deploy iron-cased rockets against the British. Word of his military prowess reached his enemy's enemy. Napoleon himself sought alliance with the Tiger. It was short-lived. A bullet from a flintlock musket struck Tipu Sultan between the eyes as he defended the fort at Srirangapatna from British attack in 1799. Inayat Khan, despite his princely warrior blood, had a peaceable disposition. His gift, shared with his brothers, was music and his instrument the *surshringar*, a swan-necked Indian lute. As a young man, he became one of the most celebrated players in Gujarat. It was said that in his hands his *surshringar* could summon the nightjars from the sky and silence the chattering temple monkeys. When the strange, plangent cadences saluted the sunset, the tails of the marsh crocodiles ceased to flick.

The path of a concert musician strewn with the garlands of acclaim beckoned to Inayat Khan. Fame, however, could not have foreseen the day Inayat Khan's life changed forever. It was his father's forty-fifth birthday. A table was set for forty-five on the lawn leading down to the riverbank. A sea of ivory damask harboured Wedgwood china, hand-blown glasses from Murano and jewel-studded knives from Tipu Sultan's treasure chest. A stream of servants poured from the kitchens, white gloves fielding platters, sauce boats and serving bowls ringed with elephants marching trunk to tail. Six servants stood either side of the table in turbans of pink or orange, fanning the guests with giant palm leaves.

As lunch ended late in the afternoon, Inayat played a recital that pricked the eyes of the guests and stilled the marsh crocodiles. He bowed and, as the clapping faded, he withdrew, *surshringar* in hand. Something drew him indoors into his father's library. Alone, he ran his fingers along the leather-bound books behind a desk where Tipu Sultan had once fired off his orders. Inayat's fingers stopped on the raised gold letters of a worn volume:

THE WISDOM OF RUMI

He laid the book open on his lap. As the night jasmine exhaled, Inayat was drawn into a parallel world. A world of sun, moon, mountains, shadows, fountains, orchards, sunbirds, dates, pomegranates, peacocks, flutes, and sacred geometric stars that radiated into infinity. One part of Inayat could hear the hum of voices in the garden and the distant clatter of plates. Another witnessed the sword of Tipu Sultan above the fireplace blaze the brilliant white of lightning. Incandescence flooded the room. In the mouth of the fireplace stood a figure. The figure wore a robe the colour of firelight and held a chalice. He gestured to the fireplace behind. Where once there had been a coal-black cavern, a path extended into a hanging garden. A fountain stood in the centre beside a running stream. Trees proffered dates and pomegranates from their branches and shelter to nightingales. The garden was illuminated by a sun that radiated beams of amber into the whiteness of the light. Though the figure's lips remained closed, Inayat could hear a voice.

'As you start to walk on the Way,' said the voice, 'the Way appears.'

Hesitant at first, Inayat took his first few steps along the path.

*

Inayat was found by one of the servants. He was lying motionless on the gold and silver threads of the carpet in front of the fireplace. The servant exclaimed on seeing the prone figure, taking his young master's sleeve and fanning his face. Inayat opened a pair of eyes that, to the servant, seemed to radiate back into infinity. His face looked refreshed, as if he had swum to the surface from a deep sleep. Inayat squeezed the servant's arm and smiled. He looked about the room. The events of the missing interval scattered like the fragments of a dream. Only the figure's words remained.

As you start to walk on the Way, the Way appears.

The first part of Inayat's journey took him, in search of a guide, a hundred miles north to a saint's tomb in Ahmedabad. The guardian of the tomb was the Sufi master Nawaz Ali Shah. To Inayat, the master seemed as old as the gnarled neem trees that Time had bent and twisted in the shadow of the tomb's highest dome. His hair and beard were winter white. His mottled hands trembled as they gripped his staff. His feet, by contrast, were lithe and supple in their sandals. His eyes were only half-full of sight but brimming with radiance.

Inayat Khan cleared his throat.

'Master,' he said. 'I seek a guide for the journey.'

Nawaz Ali smiled.

'There are two journeys. Before making the second, you must make the first.'

'What is the first?' said Inayat.

'The first is the journey into the self.'

Inayat noticed the carved symbols on the old man's staff.

'And the second?'

'The second will reveal itself as you walk on the Way.'

'When can I begin?'

'The present moment is the door to all moments,' said the master, a thousand creases sharpening around his eyes.

The building that sprang from the tomb was an elaborate confection of domes, minarets and arches inlaid with lattice. Nawaz Ali Shah offered Inayat lodging in a room under the central dome, whose interior was painted with the constellations of the heavens.

'But I am a stranger,' said Inayat.

11

'On the path of love,' said the old man, 'friend and stranger are one and the same.'

His eyes creased again.

'And besides, two guardians in this place are better than one.'

So began Inayat Khan's journey on the Way, his master casting a light as the Way appeared. First Inayat learned of the boundary that separated the 'seen' and the 'unseen': the borderline between light and shadow. He learned to distinguish sparks of the Infinite in dreams and imaginings. He learned the hierarchy of shadows under Absolute Light and the dance of shadows to a flame. He learned the hidden speech in the symbols carved on his master's staff. He learned the Sufi's sacred order of the Heavens.

After a week, Inayat sent word back to Baroda requesting a trunk of clothes and his *surshringar*. His prediction that he would return before the monsoon rains did not transpire. Inayat stayed with his master as the season changed and the thunderclouds fulminated. Under the surge and retreat of the monsoon rains, Inayat sat with his master on a carpet woven with fountains and birds of paradise. Nawaz Ali taught Inayat the ninety-nine names of the Form Giver and the order of their incantation in the *Zikr*. He taught Inayat the patterns of sacred geometry and to make the black dashes, curls and dots of the Letters of Revelation. Eyes closed, and with the beat of his staff, he taught Inayat the sacred rhythms and intervals in music.

In the evenings, as the stars opened, Inayat would play his master a lament on his *surshringar* that would summon the nightjars from flight.

Inayat was quick to learn. By the time the monsoon rains had retreated, he was learning to find his third eye, the Eye of Intuition.

'It must never be opened outward,' said the master. 'Only inward.'

While closing his eyes and opening his third eye inward, Inayat learned how to drop to the seabed of his mind and remain in the deep until the chattering of his thoughts was silent.

'It is a still lake,' said the master, 'that reflects the sky.'

With a still lake came lessons in breathing: abdominal breath, mid-chest breath and upper-chest breath. 'In times of strife,' said Nawaz Ali, 'always find and follow your breath.' It was a lesson that, decades later, would come to the aid of one yet unborn when danger pursued her like fast-crawling beetles.

'The Divine Breath pervades the universe,' said the master. 'Through breath, all things receive life. It is nature itself.'

A month after the monsoon, Nawaz Ali Shah presented Inayat with a thin wooden box. The two halves were joined in the middle.

'Does it open?' said Inayat.

The master smiled.

Inayat pulled the two halves apart. Each half was inlaid with a mirror.

'This world and the Divine are two mirrors. Each looks for the other in its reflection.'

Inayat held the mirrors face to face.

'Only one who has lost all traces of self can truly reflect the Divine.'

The master's teaching intensified, as if Nawaz Ali Shah could see a culmination of his own journey. One morning, Inayat entered his master's quarters to find candles alight in all corners of the chamber. Flowers were scattered in a circle around the carpet. In the centre stood his master's staff, as if standing of its own accord. The symbols were familiar to Inayat now: sun, moon, mountain, fire, birds, leaves, pears and pomegranates.

'It is time to move deeper along the Way,' said the master.

Nawaz Ali Shah, seated at the edge of the carpet, invited Inayat to stand, touch the staff and close his eyes. The staff was smooth and the carved symbols precise to the touch. The wood felt warm, as if there was a light from within.

'Close your outer eyes,' said the master. 'Look inward.'

Inayat found himself in a night garden flooded with moonlight. There was a fountain in the centre, fed by a flowing stream. Behind the fountain stood a fruit tree, its leaves silver in the moonlight.

'I am the Garden of the Soul,' came a voice.

Next, Inayat saw the same garden without moonlight.

'I am the Garden of the Heart.'

Inayat gripped the staff. With his third eye he saw the same garden, this time bathed in sunlight: the Light of Essence. On the grass in front of the fountain lay a bowl of dates.

'I am the Garden of the Spirit.'

In the final garden there was only the fountain. On the ground in front of the fountain was a single pomegranate. Inayat looked into the fountain. The veils of light became iridescent. The water changed form, cascading now as if running off a weir. For a moment Inayat saw himself reflected and, in the beat of a butterfly wing, saw a streak of the Infinite. He was no longer standing. He felt the carpet behind his head and under his palms. He felt a powerful heat, as if his mind were igniting. He opened his eyes. His master's hand was firm against his forehead, his eyes radiant, like the light in the fountain.

'Rise, Sufi.'

Inayat rose, first to his knees, then to his feet.

'You have made the journey from self to Self. The mirror of your soul has been purified. Let it reflect the Divine.'

Outside, Nawaz Ali placed his hand over Inayat's heart and poured purified water on the crown of his head. It ran through his black hair and on to the shoulders of his tunic.

*

The following day, Nawaz Ali Shah unveiled a roll of papyrus. Ever expanding circles spread from a central circle, like ripples of water. The circle in the centre was marked 'Earth'. Radiating outward through the planets and fixed stars was the circle furthest from the centre: The Sphere of the Divine Throne. Nawaz Ali unveiled another chart showing a circle with lines radiating from the centre like the spokes of a wheel. Inayat picked out various names and phrases written between the spokes.

'He who Elevates' 'The Light' 'The Wise' 'He who Knows'
'The Third Sky of Mars' 'The Perfect Constructor'
'The Guarded Table' 'He who Invokes'
'The Universal Soul'

Finally, the master unfurled a roll showing the predicted phases of the moon.

'The future is part of the *unseen*,' said the master. 'It is a forbidden realm.'

He smiled.

'Perhaps The Perfect Constructor would allow my failing eyes the narrowest glimpse?'

Nawaz Ali spent the whole day consulting the charts. By evening he looked tired and elated at the same time, as if passing a torch to a fresh runner.

'Your second journey is a quest. It will take you to the edge of the known world. And beyond.'

'What quest, Master?'

'To reveal the path to others through words and music.'

'Where must I travel?'

Nawaz Ali's eyes smiled deep in the creases.

'Only two signs have shown themselves. The third will show itself after the second.'

'What are the signs?'

'They are faint. The first is to find your way to where Master Rumi sleeps.'

Inayat smiled.

'And the second?'

'The second speaks only of an iron watchtower by flowing water. The third sign will show itself in the shadow of the watchtower.'

*

The day Inayat left Ahmedabad the sky was cloudless, stretching into the Infinite. He stood between his packed trunk and his *surshringar*, upright in an instrument case.

15

Nawaz Ali Shah appeared on the veranda, his feet still lissom. Folded in his hands was a woollen cloak. Lying on top of the cloak was his staff. He presented cloak and staff to the young master.

'For the journey.'

Inayat's eyes met his master's, two sparks of infinity amid the creases.

'A final question,' said Inayat. 'What is the secret of all creation?'

The master smiled.

'The creation of the world is the motion of love towards perfection and completion.'

Inayat's last sight of Nawaz Ali Shah was standing on the veranda. The image of a winged heart was visible on the wall behind. Nawaz Ali wore a white robe. His narrow form concealed the heart, as if wings sprang from his shoulders. To Inayat, he looked like an angel.

The apprentice, cloak upon his shoulders, waved goodbye.

The parting words came from the master.

'He who has light in his heart will find his way home.'

As Inayat took the first steps of his journey, Nawaz Ali Shah returned indoors. He lay on the carpet under the dome's canopy of stars. He closed his eyes and set his mind and body free. Then he took a step, without feet, and beat his wings upward towards the Throne of the Divine.

*

The following month, Inayat Khan left the family house in Baroda. His father gave him a purse of gold coins and two rings to sell as needed. His parents and brothers stood on the back steps, flanked by the servants. Tears pricked the eyes of all who waved farewell to the young master. A kitchen boy ran forward to clutch his sleeve. The boy was dumb.

'Please stay, Master,' beseeched his eyes.

Inayat embraced the cook.

'It is a journey I must make.'

Inayat turned to wave goodbye. He wore his Sufi cloak. In one hand he carried his staff, in the other his *surshringar* in a leather

16

case that would follow him by land and sea. On his back he carried a scant array of clothes and a book: The Wisdom of Rumi. He left Baroda with eyes full of hope, his black hair parted, his shirt beneath his cloak ironed to parchment.

So began Inayat's journey as a wandering mystic. A journey under sun and moon, over sand, rock and pasture. A journey on foot, on horseback, on the sawdust of railway carriages. A journey aided by the kindness of strangers, peddlers, thieves, fugitives, holy men, courtiers and princes. Some nights along the way Inayat would lie down with the outcasts in the street. Others he would spend in the gilded quarters of palaces beneath painted birds and trees. Sometimes he would sleep in the open, wrapped in his cloak, staring into the Infinite.

After a month travelling west, he walked over the bridge of thirty-three burning arches straight into the jewel of Persia. Isfahan's main square was the size of a small city, overlooked by the minarets, arches and giant azure dome of the Royal Mosque shimmering with gold lattice. The arches around the square were illuminated. Crowds shifted, singers wailed to the strings of the *dotar* and the *tanbur*. An archer on horseback galloped down the middle of the square, turning to fire a flaming arrow through a pomegranate.

'The saying is right,' thought Inayat to himself as he navigated the crowds, *surshringar* in one hand, staff in the other. 'Isfahan is indeed half the world.'

The next day Inayat looked up into the interior of the dome of the Royal Mosque, gold radiating like honeycomb from the epicentre. Inayat could feel his soul soaring into the dome. The words of his master echoed in his mind. *You are the mirror of divine beauty.* Isfahan could have lured Inayat to stay forever, but his path took him westwards again to the bazaars of Baghdad and onward towards the land of the Ottoman Turks. Through the dust and mountains walked Inayat, his footprints blown away by the wind. The walking made him as lean as his staff, and his dark eyes wolf-like in their sockets. He allowed his beard to grow, like his master's, though his was black as obsidian. Inayat performed his ablutions in streams, washing and combing out his lengthening hair, grooming and oiling his beard. He walked, finding shade where he could, from the fierce Turkish sun.

Entering Anatolia, the outskirts of the town of Konya came into view. Inayat's heart beat like a sunbird. He walked over the cobbles of the ancient city, staff in hand, until he found the walled garden of fig and lemon trees. Overlooking the garden was a stone building with a shallow dome guarded by a minaret. When the sun rose, a tall copper-green tower cast the dome and minaret into shadow. In a courtyard in front of the building, half a dozen men with tall *destar* hats were spinning and chanting, robes flaring. The sight of the whirling dervishes made Inayat grip his staff in anticipation. He removed his shoes and entered. The light, cut into diamonds of silver and turquoise, shone from the main arch. Draped in a carpet laced with silver and gold lay a sarcophagus.

Inayat knelt. A small tear ran down his sun-darkened face. *The place where Rumi sleeps.* Inayat kissed the tomb and looked up at his epitaph.

> '*When we are dead, seek not our tomb in the earth,*
> *but find it in the hearts of men.*'

After Konya, Inayat Khan set sail from Bodrum to a continent where the air had a different feel. His first taste of Europe was the stark island of Patmos. There Inayat entered, head bowed, the Cave of the Apocalypse where the Revelation was once told in a vision, before taking the steep path to the fortress monastery that surveyed the Aegean from the island's summit. The monks, black eyes, black beards and black robes, looked like icons. They made the traveller welcome with a simple bed under a cross of burnished silver. After a few days he had set sail again, waving goodbye to the monks as they stood huddled under the twin-headed eagle fluttering from a standard on the monastery battlements.

From the shadow of the Acropolis, Inayat set his compass for north-west. His quest was the iron watchtower. It had come to him in a dream. He continued his odyssey through the land of Homer and up through the land once called Illyria. With his staff, cloak, and steady brown eyes, people sensed a pilgrimage. Inayat drew offers of fresh bread, gourds of water, honey, pears, pomegranates and dates. Inayat continued north, making his way, week by week, along the Dalmatian Coast and into northern Italy. In Monfalcone, he gave an impromptu concert under the bell tower and stayed as a guest of the mayor. He made his way through the Italian lakes and into Switzerland, where he boarded a train of poppy red. Snowdrops nodded in the train's wind-rush as it hugged the side of the Alps.

Finally, Inayat crossed into the land of the Sun King. He travelled through the lavender fields of Provence, across the Auvergne and north again. The seasons had revolved almost full circle by the time Inayat Khan set down his instrument case in the shadow of the iron watchtower by flowing water. He looked upward, straining his eyes to see the top of the Eiffel Tower, taller even than the tower above Lakshmi Palace. In a modest house on the Left Bank with a commanding view of the iron watchtower, warm hands took turns to embrace Inayat and welcome him to the European headquarters of Rumi's Order of Sufis.

*

Inayat was captivated by the city under the watchtower. He spent a month, staff in hand, woollen cloak about his shoulders, pacing the boulevards, attending galleries, lectures and concerts. The sign above his favourite brasserie in the 5ème Arrondissement always brought a smile to Inayat's lips:

> ON NE PEUT PAS BIEN PENSER,
> BIEN AIMER OU BIEN DORMIR
> SI L'ON N'A PAS BIEN DINÉ.
> *One cannot think well,*
> *love well or sleep well*
> *if one has not dined well.*

In the evenings Paris became a circus of top hats, feathers and taffeta: a pulsing Toulouse-Lautrec as intoxicating as green absinthe. On Sundays, Inayat sat between the bookstalls by the river in the shadow of the watchtower and took out his *surshringar*. Above the spiralling treble of the accordion keys came the strange, plangent cadences that threaded the air above the Seine with traces of Himalayan mist. Paris took the mystic in her stride, barely noticing Inayat's transcendent gaze and the strange symbols on his staff. Part of Inayat Khan imagined staying forever among the writers, thinkers, painters and musicians in the bustling City of Lights.

The constellations, for now, had other ideas. One morning, the master of the Rumi's Order of Sufis called Inayat to his quarters. Over hibiscus tea poured from a silver Arabian kettle, the next step of the journey was revealed. Inayat's eyes widened. His own master's words echoed in his ears.

To the edge of the known universe and beyond.

*

The people of Santa Fe did not know what to make of the umberskinned man with expressive eyes who appeared one morning in the pink desert light. His raven hair was long and his itinerant's beard danced in the wind. He wore a woollen cloak and carried a staff. He carried a book, The Wisdom of Rumi, the way a pastor held a Bible. His only luggage was a rucksack and an instrument case holding his *surshringar*. Some said he was a prophet. Others that he was a horseman of the Apocalypse. Santa Fe, however, was familiar with travellers. There was something about his level gaze, his graceful air and his words of compassion that made him welcome. He was, as they discovered, a disciple of Rumi's Order of Sufis. He had been sent to lecture in Santa Fe and at Rio Rancho. It was in Rio Rancho that a female student with long honey-coloured hair, green eyes and a Mona Lisa smile attended his class.

Her name was Ora. She was nineteen. The words of Master Rumi whistled through Inayat's head.

What you seek is seeking you.

Inayat's future wife was staring him in the face. Ora's future husband was staring her in the face, staff in hand. Both their hearts beat like sunbirds.

The *Nikah* took place a month later under a cobalt sky that stretched, Inayat thought, to the Divine Throne in Heaven. The imam read Rumi's blessing.

> *May these vows and this marriage be blessed.*
> *May it be sweet milk, this marriage, like wine and halvah.*
> *May this marriage offer fruit and shade, like the date palm.*
> *May this marriage be full of laughter, our every day a paradise.*
> *May this marriage be a sign of compassion, a seal of happiness here*
> *and hereafter.*
> *May this marriage have a fair face and a good name,*
> *an omen as welcome as the moon in a clear blue sky.*

Ora took the Sufi name 'Amina', knowing, her parents' misgivings still ringing in her ears, that she had pinned her wedding veil to a wandering mystic. They spent their wedding night in Albuquerque before taking the train to San Francisco. From San Francisco they set sail on a steamer headed north. They were bound for Vladivostok. Inayat held his new bride close as they sat huddled in furs on the Trans-Siberian railway listening to Cossacks in the next-door compartment sing, toast and smash their vodka glasses on the floor. They were destined, via the plains of Siberia and the Ural Mountains, for Imperial Moscow. It was to the city on the Moskva River that Inayat had been directed to establish an order of Sufis who followed Master Rumi.

Inayat and Amina took an apartment overlooking the Patriarshiye Ponds in Presnensky. The furniture, bedecked in crimson velvet, was almost invisible against the crimson walls. Rows of icons framed in burnished silver kept watch over Inayat and Amina in the months that followed their honeymoon. When the samovar boiled, it would make the chandelier above *clink*.

It was a union, as foretold, of sweet milk, wine and halvah. Inayat and Amina became the roots of a single sprig. One evening, in their second month in Moscow, Amina whispered to Inayat that she was with child. Her eyes spoke of wonder and apprehension as the firelight flitted across the samovar. A sound came from Inayat's throat – neither word nor song. It was rapture. He watched over the months as Amina's body swelled like a ripening pear.

Snow fell like muffled drumbeats on the frozen crust of the Moskva River as Amina's rhythms quickened in the dying embers of 1913. Inayat wrapped Amina in bearskins and summoned a *troika*. The carriage tracks vanished into white as the *troika* sped through drifts of alabaster. The horses jangled to a halt outside the Vysoko Petrovsky Monastery.

Inayat and Amina named their daughter Noor – *the light*. Her name reminded Inayat of the veils of light in the final garden revealed to him by Nawaz Ali Shah. When Time turned and darkness threatened to engulf the world, the light would find its power. Depending on the danger that stalked her, Noor sometimes used other names. To Inayat she would always, in truth, be *Bābouli*.

*

Noor spent her earliest days on the Moscow hearthrug in the ring of firelight. The fire hissed and popped while the snow pressed on the windowpanes. At night, Amina wrapped her in a chrysalis of embroidered blankets. She slept to the sound of Amina's song and the rustle of pendants as she moved within her chrysalis. In the mornings she heard Inayat incanting the ninety-nine names of the Form Giver. Each name evoked its own colour behind her infant eyes. The incantations became so familiar she would cry if she had to wait for the *Zikr*.

A visitor came in the spring. The snow from his furs melted by the time he mounted the stairs and entered the crimson rooms. He removed his black *ushanka* fur hat to reveal a head as hairless as Lenin's. His beard, by contrast, was a luxuriant black tipped with silver. Behind his round metal spectacles was a pair of kind, intelligent eyes. In his hand he carried a carved wooden bird with ruby eyes.

He was Count Sergei Tolstoy and he presented the bird to Noor with an exaggerated bow.

'Pteech-ka,' said the count with a smile.

He sat while a flame was lit under the samovar. The chandelier clinked as the samovar boiled. The count drank black tea made sweet with honey and tart with lemon. Inayat took down his *surshringar* and, with redolent cadences, summoned the chattering temple monkeys. The count closed his eyes as Inayat played, the strange plangent cadences summoning the birds from flight. A tear trickled from the count's closed eye. When Inayat set down his *surshringar*, the count clapped and opened a leather notebook. He scribbled in the notebook and rose.

'Until next week,' said the count, with a touch of his *ushanka*.

Pteech-ka, the wooden bird, became Noor's favourite toy. She would stretch out her hands before sleeping to hold Pteech-ka, its surface smooth against her cheek and scented with Siberian pine. Pteech-ka's eyes glowed crimson in the firelight.

Count Tolstoy arrived often. Each time Inayat played a different song on his *surshringar*. The count closed his eyes and held his head back as Inayat played. When Inayat set down the instrument, the count would blink his eye dry, scribble in his notebook and set off, tipping his *ushanka* hat.

Summer came. On the first day of August the sky over Moscow was as blue as Inayat's wedding day in Santa Fe. The trees around the Patriarshiye Ponds chattered with the gossip of chaffinches. That evening, as the sun turned the dome of the Grand Kremlin Palace into running gold, the count arrived unannounced. A trickle of perspiration ran from his head, past his temple. The newspaper he held shook in his hands.

война! – WAR!

Germany had declared war on Russia. The Russian Imperial Guard was mobilizing. The gates of the Tula Arsenal were open. Kegs of gunpowder were on their way to the barracks of the Moskovsky Guards. The streets rattled with the sound of the Imperial Cavalry moving gun carriages into formation.

Inayat felt a tremor on the path of love. The landscape started to cleave and divide under his feet. His heart felt like it had been opened by a dagger. Inayat and the count embraced in sorrow as the boots of the Moskovsky Guards echoed on the cobbles below. On the hearthrug sat Noor holding Pteech-ka. Pteech-ka's eyes shone blood red in the sun.

*

The opening days of war exploded in euphoria. Officers of the Imperial Guard strutted in their red tunics, gold epaulettes glittering. The colonel of the Pavlovsky Regiment opened an imperial ball to the sound of twelve cannon. The mirror-black boots of the cavalry officers spun their partners in arcs of taffeta and silk. Tchaikovsky's 1812 Overture boomed and clashed from every concert hall.

Summer rallied autumn. The euphoria began to tail off with the telegrams falling like leaves on the doorsteps of Muscovite families with curt announcements of death, and the hospital trains bringing the wounded, bandages still dripping, back from the Eastern Front. After the crushing Russian defeat at Tannenberg, Moscow was vulnerable to invasion by forces from Germany, Austria-Hungary and Bulgaria. As the first snow came and the Moskva River began to freeze, Inayat and Amina wrapped their daughter in bearskins. They fled Moscow with all they could carry packed on Count Tolstoy's sled. The *surshringar* stood on the back seat, next to Pteech-ka, ruby eyes shining in the snow. The soldiers at the city gates saluted when they saw Count Tolstoy's livery. The sled, pulled by the count's fastest mounts, cut parallel lines through the snow as the cross-tipped domes of scarlet, blue and ultramarine dwindled into distant orbs of sorbet.

'You will be our light,' Inayat whispered to Noor, as the *Orlov* horses pounded into the night. 'And you will keep away the darkness.'

Inayat held his daughter every moment as the sled forged north, the guns of the Eastern Front audible in the distance. The sputter of rifle fire and rumble of the heavy guns made a canvas of black terror behind Noor's eyes. Each beat of her heart scattered the canvas with fretful silvery dots. Each artillery blast lacerated the black with dashes of silver. She held Pteech-ka, longing for the hearthrug in Moscow, the simmer of the samovar and the soothing incantations of the *Zikr*.

At the town of Klin, Inayat, Amina and Noor boarded a train to St Petersburg and on to Tallinn. In Tallinn they found a berth on a ship bound west across the Baltic Sea. Their destination was more than a thousand miles away: a place where Inayat, Amina and Noor had never set foot. Inayat held his daughter in the crook of his arm. She was crying, her tears falling on to Pteech-ka.

'Hush, *Bābouli*,' said Inayat, kissing her forehead. 'All will be well.'

CHAPTER 2
'LE SERGENT'

Rennes, France,
1914

Morel
Bloch

The Morel brothers, Georges and Fabien, volunteered in October 1914. They walked arm in arm into the recruiting office in Rennes City Hall and swaggered out in red breeches, black boots and blue coats with opposing armies of brass buttons.

'High horse, *bicorne* hat and my name is Napoleon!' said Fabien as he and his brother strode out into the square amid spontaneous applause from strollers in the afternoon sunshine.

The night that followed was a blur of rough Breton cider, toasts, speeches, forfeits, arm-wrestles, tumbling tankards, ill-sung ballads and stumbling salutes. At two in the morning, Georges carried his brother up the narrow flight of steps in the modest *pension* they had taken for the night. He lay Fabien down, wrestled off his uniform and pulled the bedcovers up to his chin. Georges left water by his brother's bedside and an empty vase on the floor should the *cidre* return unbidden.

As the light of the morning pierced the room, Fabien groaned like the hinge of a rusting gate, blocking the sunlight with his hands. Georges placed a small phial of Rousseau's laudanum on

26

his brother's lips, held up his head and ensured all the brown liquid disappeared. Fabien lay back against the pillows, pale and silent. Within twenty minutes he was sitting up in bed ready for toasted baguette, Normandy butter, blackcurrant jam and a pot of fresh coffee.

'Show me the enemy and I'll sort them out single-handed!' said Fabien, holding his baguette like a sabre.

'You and whose army?' said Georges, laughing and throwing a pillow at his brother's raised arm.

After basic training, the brothers were given a week's leave. They returned like river salmon to the sea-swept town of their birth: Saint-Malo. They spent their week before deployment inside the walled granite haven from the Atlantic's fury. The Morel household, a spacious apartment looking over the fortress ramparts out to sea, was infused with excitement and foreboding. Neither Albert Morel, the brothers' quietly spoken father, a prosperous printer from the town, nor their mother, Margot, made any direct reference to the obvious. Margot had been Saint-Malo's most celebrated beauty and refused a line of manicured hands offering marriage. Instead, she chose Albert, whose eyes were kind and whose silences were as eloquent as his words.

At dinner on the evening before their departure, Georges spotted the Pol Roger 1901 served with the velvet crab, langoustines and *palourdes* clams and the dusty bottle of Chateau Latour 1895 with the *coq au vin*. Albert raised a toast to his sons, the rarity of the Bordeaux an unspoken tribute.

That night, both boys packed their belongings in their adjoining bedrooms in the eaves. Among them Georges placed a locket containing a family photograph taken on a trip to see the automobiles in Le Mans the previous summer, a lock-knife, a pocket watch, a silver fountain pen, a small leather prayer book and his St Christopher, for luck. Fabien's packing included a sketch of Delphine, the *notaire*'s prettiest daughter, and all the letters she had sent over the previous six months, tied with crimson silk ribbon.

The family met the following morning over a silent breakfast. Madame Morel was pale, the rims of her blue-green eyes red. Within an hour, both brothers were standing by the front door in their uniforms, cases at their feet. Madame Morel held one son tight, then the other – drawing back each time to look at the striking young man so recently a boy. She tried to say goodbye, but the words would not come.

The printing factory's finest car was sent to collect the brothers. Monsieur Morel sat with his sons as they made their way through the nods and waves of neighbours, over the cobblestones and westwards towards the old station. He felt as proud as any father as he nodded and lifted his hat to well-wishers, though his heart was leaden. Outside the station, Père Morel gave each son a box of cigars and a generous roll of francs.

'Keep away from stray bullets and unsuitable women and you'll be safe as houses,' he said as he embraced both of his sons together.

A sudden whistle went for the Rennes train, unlocking embraces and sending hands clasping for luggage. As the brothers waved back from the window of their carriage, Monsieur Morel, their sturdy, walrus-moustached father, who used to carry one son under each arm, felt smaller, older... and alone.

*

Lieutenant Bloch was a history teacher before the war. An Alsatian Jew with thinning hair, round metal spectacles and a pensive expression, he was not the dashing officer of the recruitment posters. Yet he proved to have a cool head under fire, contempt for officialdom and a bottomless vault of stories from the history books. His men would not have a word said against *Lieutenant Histoire*. The historian now found himself History's witness. He recorded everything. The truth, he reminded himself, is always concealed by the darkest lies. Nothing escaped his attention. One week he recorded every shade of mud in the trenches around Metz. His observations on colour, scratched into his notebook, were exact.

Chestnut-amber
Chestnut brown
Bitter chocolate
Plain charcoal
Charcoal-russet-brown
Charcoal-brown with burnt auburn flecks
Charcoal-brown with grains of black
Charcoal with dashes of ivory chalk
Charcoal-black
Goya black

On days of an artillery barrage he noted additional hues, courtesy of the dead and the dying: crimson, oyster and speckled white.

He noted texture. Mud at the point of freezing. Mud frozen solid after three days. Mud dried by a weary sun. Mud after a day of rain. Mud after a five-day downpour. Mud that gathered in shell craters. 'Crater-mud' mixed with rain that became quicksand. Mud that could just hold a man's footing during an advance. Mud that sent men slipping sideways like drunkards.

The stumps of trees bore the same mud palette. Burnt treacle, charcoal and – where their branches had been amputated – tarry black. Even his officer's red pantaloons had been swapped for forest-coloured fatigues worn under the charcoal folds of his greatcoat. He had become part of the mud-scape, living underground like vermin, surfacing day after day with legions of others to drive manic metal into mud and churning mud into more mud. Added to the picture were the hues of bodies selected at random to join the necropolis of mud.

As 1914 drew to a mud-stuck close, Bloch heard footsteps on the ramparts. He spun round, eyes wide, reaching for his Saint-Etienne revolver. He stilled. It was Sergent Morel, the regimental mechanic. Morel removed his helmet, causing a mound of black hair to cascade forward, replaced it, and saluted. He was young behind the moustache – twenty-two at most, thought Bloch – his skin pale against the well-structured bones of his face. His eyes were framed with straight black brows above and purple smudges below. His lips were crimson with a faint blue outline. He looked like a photograph enhanced by an artist's brush.

'As you were, Sergent!' said Bloch.

Morel stood at ease.

'Requesting a short leave of absence, sir,' said Morel.

Bloch looked quizzical.

'To see my brother. Word came down the line last night. He's with the 5th Army Corps, who took up position three trenches south of us this morning. I am seeking an hour's leave of duty to meet him at 18:00 under Observation Post 9.'

Morel reminded Bloch of one of his better students. The lieutenant looked at his watch. It was 17:15.

'When did you last see your brother?' said Bloch.

'Arras. Three months ago. Just after we volunteered.'

'Observation Post 9, 18:00 and that's an order,' said Lieutenant Bloch, looking away to hide a smile. 'Fall out at 17:30. Thou art thy brother's keeper, Sergent!'

'*Merci, mon Lieutenant!*' said Morel, clicking his boots and saluting.

At 17:30 Morel descended into his trench and pulled out a small, locked crate from under a makeshift wooden bunk. He put a key to the padlock and opened the wooden crate like a pirate inspecting treasure. He extracted a box of Gitanes, a brass hip flask filled with golden Laubade Armagnac 1888 and a bar of Red Cross chocolate.

Fifteen minutes later, Georges Morel was walking down the duckboards of his trench, helmet on, his Lebel rifle slung over his shoulder and a signed chit from Lieutenant Bloch in his breast pocket. His cigarettes and Armagnac bounced beside his hip in a creased leather bag. With a nod from the sentry, he climbed the wooden ladder at the back of his trench and trudged south towards Observation Post 9.

Fabien was already waiting, his silhouette recognizable a trench away. He was younger and slighter than his brother, with the same high-contrast colouring. The two brothers locked in an embrace. Their scent mingled in the mist: an animal recognition.

'Quite the sergent!' said Fabien, smiling and twisting his brother's moustache. 'Not to mention, alive!'

The brothers stood ankle-deep in mud next to a tree by Observation Post 9, two shadows in the dusk. A Nieuport 12 surveillance plane flew overhead, its tail painted with a tricolore.

'I bring gifts,' said Fabien, handing his brother a parcel tucked within his greatcoat. 'It arrived in Metz three weeks ago with mine. Well, go on!'

The parcel contained a letter from his mother, a pair of mittens and some thick hand-knitted socks wrapped with string. Something with a cold, hard surface nestled within the socks – George's hand brought out the object. It was a bottle of absinthe with a label attached.

'*En cas d'urgence – Papa.*'

'Not so easy to get hold of these days…' said Georges, looking at the Toulouse-Lautrec sketch on the 1911 bottle.

'And something I had the pleasure of relieving a German prisoner of last week,' said Fabien. 'Semi-automatic, short recoil, accurate to fifty yards. Souvenir. It's yours.'

Georges examined the Luger pistol and weighed it in his hand.

'Top of the range,' said Georges with a smile.

'*Attention!*' said Fabien. 'It works!'

He handed Georges a full ammunition box. Georges placed the Luger and the ammunition in his bag.

'And I did not come empty-handed either,' said Georges.

He handed his brother the Gitanes and the bar of chocolate. He also opened his hip flask and offered it to Fabien.

'Never too early!' said Fabien with a smile as he placed the flask to his lips and tilted back his head.

There was a piercing whistle followed by a dull ring. In the gap between Fabien's two eyes, a third eye opened. Fabien stood motionless for a moment, as if suspended by the breeze. The hip flask fell away from his lips. His body buckled backwards against a tree. Georges caught his brother as Fabien's legs crumpled. Somewhere, Georges was aware of the distant smash of the absinthe bottle. His own helmet dislodged as he tried to prop Fabien up beneath his arms. As Georges summoned the breath to shout, there was another piercing whistle. He felt the wind of the bullet as it whistled over his head, cracking into the tree, and smelt an acrid burning.

Both brothers lay in a tangled embrace. The Gitanes floated like a child's pale fingers in the mud, next to a capsized hip flask, two unworn mittens, a sealed envelope, some letters bound in crimson ribbon and a broken bar of chocolate.

Georges lay under his brother. He could move his extremities and he could breathe. He put his hand to his head. It was damp and spongy, like the ground beneath. Hair and splinters of bone stuck to his palm. Over Fabien's lifeless shoulders he saw three shadows approaching. He lay his head back into the soft mud and felt the shutters of his eyes fall in three slow blinks.

A Breton beach.

The end of summer.

Fabien stood by the water.

His fishing net was floating in the shallows and he was clasping his finger.

Something was wrong.

Georges came running. He opened his five-year-old brother's hand. Blood was oozing from his middle finger.

'It's just a crab bite,' said Georges.

Fabien was pale.

'Will I die?' said Fabien.

'Of course not, Fab,' said Georges.

'Promise?' said Fabien, his bottom lip trembling.

'Promise!' said Georges.

Georges felt the lightness of his brother's arms round his neck as the warm water lapped around their ankles.

*

It was three days before Lieutenant Bloch found Morel. Bloch had walked five miles in the mud to a school that had been converted into a field hospital. The low rectangular building came into view under the heavy rain of the late afternoon. Its once white exterior was now grey and pockmarked from bullets. The carving above the front entrance was blackened but legible:

'SCIENTIA SIT POTENTIA.'

The rear of the building furthest away had collapsed. Outside, a row of a dozen *noveaux morts* lay still, each with a white cross laid along his body. He entered the dim-lit building. A nurse of about twenty greeted him, her uniform smudged with grime and blood. She wiped her forehead with the back of her hand. Her young eyes looked exhausted. Yes, she believed they had a Sergent Georges Morel.

The nurse led Bloch into the school assembly room. Under a wooden-beamed ceiling, men lay on camp beds under rough black blankets. Towards the middle of the row, facing the once long windows, Bloch spotted Morel. He was sitting up – a good sign, thought Bloch – staring at the wall. His head was bandaged down to his eyebrows. His features had lost none of the fineness, but the high colour was gone: Sergent Morel was marble white. He carried on staring, oblivious to the arrival of his lieutenant. Bloch stood a moment, saying nothing. He knelt. As he was about to speak, a voice interrupted from behind.

'Are you his commanding officer?' said someone well-spoken. It was the chirurgien-capitaine.

'Yes,' said Bloch.

'Can you spare a moment?' said the surgeon.

'Of course,' said Bloch, standing.

The surgeon was a tall, owl-like man in his early forties, his brow lined and his hair flecked with grey. The creases around his intelligent, humane eyes were caked with dust. He looked composed but drained. The two men stepped to one side.

'The bullet missed his brain but removed the top of his skull. He's lucky.'

33

'Lucky?'

'A degree south and he would have been killed outright.'

'Will he recover?'

'He should, though he will be badly disfigured,' said the surgeon. 'The real question is his mind. He has said nothing since he regained consciousness.'

'Does he know about his brother?'

'The head sister broke the news. We believe he understands.'

'Thank you, Capitaine,' said Bloch.

The surgeon opened his palms and raised his eyebrows – the gesture said: 'What can I say?'

Bloch walked out of the building, lit a cigarette against spits of rain, and drew in the strong tobacco. 'KNOWLEDGE IS POWER', he thought as he looked at the school motto and back at the row of men laid under white crosses. He threw the cigarette on to the ground, straightened himself and returned to the schoolroom.

Morel remained still.

'The stretcher-bearers found this,' said Bloch. He put his hand into his tunic and took out a dented hip flask. 'Empty but saved. There was also this.'

Bloch took a letter addressed to 'Sergent Georges Morel' from his pocket. It was mud-spattered and there were traces of blood near the bottom edge. The handwriting was well formed and tidy. It was stamped 'S. Malo', posted some weeks before.

'Would you like me to open it?' said Bloch.

He had not expected a reaction – but Morel nodded.

Bloch opened the envelope and handed the letter to his sergent. His bandaged head dropped as he studied the words.

Mon Georges Chéri –

I trust and pray this letter reaches you.

I think of you and Fabien all the time – you never leave my thoughts.

Life in Saint-Malo goes on but it is sad and empty. The newspapers said the war would finish by Christmas. Now they say by Christmas next.

I pray nightly to St Christopher that he may bring you and Fabien back unharmed. Without you the apartment is so quiet. During the day I hear only silence. Papa puts on a brave face but I know he does not sleep – no matter how many tablets the pharmacist puts in the pill-bottle.

The church is full on Sundays, but mainly of women and old men. I saw Monsieur Rocque, your old science teacher. He said the Morel boys were born survivors – strong in body and mind. He swears you will both come back safe.

Some days I walk on the beach where we have our summer picnics and I think of you and Fabien playing in the water. I want it to be summer again and this all to be over.

Please come back, Georges – you and Fabien.

With love and prayers,

Ta Maman qui t'aime

He held the letter long enough for the shadows to change in the schoolroom. Eventually, he looked up and handed the letter back to Bloch.

'I am sorry about your brother,' said Bloch.

Morel stared, wordless.

'I am going to put the letter in here,' said Bloch, noticing the leather bag at the side of the camp bed. Bloch placed the letter in one of the front pockets of the bag. Like the hospital orderlies, Bloch was unaware of the Luger and the ammunition case concealed in the bag's folds.

After half an hour sitting with his sergent in silence, Bloch placed his hand on his shoulder.

'I must go,' said Bloch.

Morel's eyes narrowed.

'*Je reviendrai* – I shall return,' said Bloch, his hand on Morel's shoulder.

At the door of the school, Bloch pulled his lapels about his face and braced into the rain – a lone figure weaving back to the front through tributaries and islets of mud.

CHAPTER 3
'THE SHADOWS'

London, 1915

Inayat
Noor

Barefoot, hair loose about his shoulders, Inayat Khan crossed the floorboards of a London attic with the stealth of a Bengal tiger. Outside, the night was casting the dawn in marble. He gathered his robe, lit a circle of candles on the floor and sat cross-legged in the middle. He closed his eyes and began the familiar journey into the waveless depths of his mind. His master's words echoed: 'It is a still lake that reflects the sky.' His body calmed, save for the rhythmic sigh of his breath. After a time, a small bell chimed. He opened his eyes and started to incant Vedic hymn-mantras as tranquil and peaceable as Lord Brahmā himself.

As Inayat chanted, the cradle at the end of the room began to rustle. He approached the cradle singing and watched his daughter's eyelids pucker, flicker and spring open. Her eyes were Van Dyke brown and her gaze drank in the world with each consecutive blink. She was the *Bābouli* he held after her first few breaths.

'*Bābouli*,' he whispered, 'I sing to you, but you are music itself.'

*

From Tallinn, Inayat, Amina and Noor found a ship bound for Copenhagen. From Copenhagen, Inayat found a berth on a ferry

36

travelling from Esbjerg to Harwich. From Harwich, the family made their way to the fog and soot of London. Amina's first reaction on arriving at the shabby house at the down-at-heel end of Notting Hill was to burst into tears. Inayat took her by the hand over the threshold. The floorboards, hidden beneath threadbare rugs, rasped like consumptives. The house was cold. It was a world away from the samovars, the firelight and the crimson velvet of Moscow.

Yet in the dimness Inayat's eyes glowed. There was an etching on the wall in the hall. A winged heart. The house had been lent by a Sufi academic.

Inayat held his wife and daughter in an embrace.

'Wherever you stand, says Master Rumi, be the soul of that place.'

At least in London, thought Inayat, they would be safe.

*

The war, predicted to last a few months, was fast becoming a fathomless gash in the side of humanity. Each day of conflict brought a fresh tremor on the path of love and a new fleck of grey to Inayat's beard. The lines around his eyes deepened with each new burst of cannon. As the mud on the Western Front ran red with speckles of white and silver, Inayat opened his own war on two fronts.

The first was a vigil he kept every night. Wearing his gold robe, he sat on a cushion and focused his inner eye on a blue sphere suspended against a canopy of black. The surface of the blue sphere grew closer. A stake was protruding from the side of planet Earth from the fissure of the Western Front. Blood ran down the sphere in crimson streaks. The surrounding planets were crying – or turning their faces away in shame. Inayat focused on the stake. His eyelids flickered with concentration. He held the stake at the base and started pulling, gentle but firm, easing it away from the Earth's pierced surface. Blood gushed free as the stake was pulled. Into the hole Inayat pressed mud, tent canvases, uniforms, spent bullets and depleted shell casings... filling the void, staunching the wound. An invocation rose up from Inayat's throat as he sat rocking on the floor.

The second front of Inayat's war was fought on the strings of his *surshringar*. He formed a quartet, the Royal Musicians of Hindustan, who wore gold robes and turbans and played for Indian troops at the Wigmore Hall. Word of their concerts spread. The War Office summoned the quartet to give a concert in Brighton. It was Inayat's most significant campaign.

On the morning of the concert, Inayat entered the shabby dining room dotted with seaside watercolours. Inayat lifted Noor. Her owl eyes were steady and alert. When Inayat closed both his eyes in a slow blink, she blinked back. Inayat clasped Noor to his neck, inhaling the scent of milk and almonds, and replaced her in the folds of Amina's dress. She reached for her wooden bird, Pteech-ka. Inayat left his daughter holding the bird between her hands, brown eyes staring into ruby.

He took his *surshringar* from the wall and laid it in the instrument case that had followed him to three continents. He snapped the brass locks shut, embraced Amina and, with a twist of his beard, walked into a London spring.

Inayat strode, *surshringar* in hand, turban tied high, the hem of his golden robe trailing jewel-studded slip-shoes. As he approached the Underground, he saw a poster on the wall outside.

TO DRESS
EXTRAVAGANTLY
IN WAR TIME
IS WORSE THAN
BAD FORM
IT IS
UNPATRIOTIC

Inayat declined to notice the quizzical stares of his fellow travellers in monochromes as he entered the lift with his *surshringar*. The lift swelled with passengers. Just as the attendant started to pull the 'Descend' lever, a final passenger – a nondescript man in a homburg – squeezed in as the doors shut and the lift descended to the depths of the Central Line. Inayat stood towards the front, his golden turban buoyed on a wave of black and grey.

Inayat stood in a second-class underground carriage trundling towards Oxford Circus. He held his *surshringar* and smiled into the quizzical looks of the wartime populace moving through the catacombs of London. He closed his eyes and ran through the score of the concert he was about to give. Inconspicuous, a few feet away, was a man in his forties – unremarkable in every way – his face concealed by the shadow of his homburg.

At Oxford Circus, Inayat emerged on to a thoroughfare teeming with horse-drawn and motorized vehicles. He took an omnibus south to Victoria Station, where he was absorbed in the shifting crowds of khaki and navy. At the barrier to the Brighton train, he met the rest of the quartet, each with a golden robe, turban, and leather instrument case. They hurried to the train, which was puffing in an impatient cloud of steam. They sat on the wooden benches in Third Class, chatting as the train pulled away. After an hour, the emerald fields of Sussex rushed past to the train's panting clatter. Onwards to the seaside, the bandstands, the whirling carousels and the distant whistle of artillery bombardment.

On the seat behind the musicians on the Brighton train sat a man engrossed in the *Manchester Guardian*, his homburg now resting on his lap.

From the station, the Royal Musicians of Hindustan took an omnibus towards the seafront, past the elegant Nash crescents, alighting with a jumble of instruments at Old Steine. Outside Steine Gardens, the four men looked in silent awe at the confection of domes, minarets, arches and lattice-shadowed walkways that was the Royal Pavilion. They reported to the entrance, where an orderly in uniform distributed four signed chits. From there they were escorted by an Indian subedar-major to the doors of the King's Music Room.

Two sepoys opened the doors into a room with an internal dome so high it appeared to have been stretched heavenwards by the hand of Shiva. Lotus-shaped chandeliers drooped from the dome's edges under the gaze of four carved wooden dragons.

War had entered the dreamscape of the King's Music Room.

The room was lined with iron beds of identical length and height. In each bed lay an Indian soldier swathed in white, with a white turban. Some turbans, on closer inspection, were made of bandages. Beside each bed was a water jug, a glass and a tin of Brompton Cough Lozenges. Soldiers played *pallanguli* and shared donations of cigarettes, handkerchiefs and spiced guava jelly. Leg amputees declined gifts of new bootlaces with rueful smiles.

Entering the Music Room, Inayat's knuckles whitened around the handle of his instrument case. He and his brother-musicians filed through the middle of the room to a ripple of muted applause. The Royal Musicians of Hindustan mounted a stage built for the concert and tuned their instruments. After three taps of Inayat's jewelled shoe, the Music Room echoed to the mournful sound of the *sitar, surshringar, sarod* and *santoor*. Against a sombre drone, the strings mingled into a chain of maudlin scalic cadences, cloaking the room in the scent of night jasmine and the churring of the Indian nightjar.

Inayat began to sing. He sang of tales of the Ramayana and the Mahabharata. He sang of the Cardamom Hills, the Amber Fort, the seven sacred rivers, the garlanded elephants and the chattering temple monkeys. Some soldiers smiled. As the strains grew faster and more plangent, some wept. There was silence. Then a single clap, like a shot, led to applause from the soldiers. The applause spread to the group of doctors, senior orderlies and local guests standing in a knot at the opposite end of the stage. One of the men tucked his newspaper under his arm to clap – a folded copy of the *Manchester Guardian*.

After the concert, the musicians stepped down from the stage and dispersed among the wounded. Inayat made his way to the bed of a soldier in the far eastern corner, with bandages over his eyes. He sat upright, his hands clasped at the front. He was about nineteen. His skin was pale and flawless, his black hair falling in tendrils over his bandaged eyes. He was slim, with a perfect profile and delicate fingers. He sat motionless. Inayat felt his heart twist. A sepoy arrived with a chair and he sat down next to the soldier. He took the soldier's hand.

'I am Inayat,' he said.

'Sanjay,' said the young soldier.

Inayat could feel the pulse of life moving around the man's young frame. The soldier pressed Inayat's hand. Inayat clasped the boy's palm and closed his eyes. After several minutes, the soldier passed Inayat a letter he had written and rasped his instructions. The envelope was addressed to a family in Jaipur.

Inayat could feel a fissure opening on the path of love and in his own heart. Life was sacred. Did the mother country have the right to draw blood from the Jewel in the Crown? He stood, remounted the stage and took up his *surshringar*. This time he sang a lyric from a pamphlet circulated by the Bengal radicals. He sang of India, the tethered tigress. India, the tigress whose neck chaffed from her leash. India, the tigress who yearned to roam free.

Fierce clapping erupted from the soldiers. Some thumped the sides of their beds. The walls of the King's Music Room were alive after a century. The group at the rear looked down at the floor or up at the domed ceiling. A tall Indian army surgeon said something to the man holding the homburg. The latter frowned, looked again at Inayat, then back at the soldiers. He withdrew to the back of the room and slipped through a side door and down a flight of stairs.

Under the cast-iron palm trees of the Pavilion kitchens, Indian Army chefs were stirring daal and frying chapattis on the giant range, and straining giant cauldrons of basmati. The man carrying the homburg slipped through the kitchens, sidestepping the dark stare of the head chef, who stood in the centre grasping a meat cleaver.

After a dinner of curried chickpea and cauliflower, the Royal Musicians of Hindustan made their way back to Victoria. On the slow, clattering return to London, they sat in silence.

*

As the Brighton train shunted back into Victoria, the man in the homburg was already striding up the steps of an anonymous office building in Waterloo Place opposite the engraved ceilings and vast fireplaces of the Athenaeum. His face was between handsome and plain, his height average, his age indistinct. A porter took his hat and coat, and he made his way up three flights of stairs to an unmarked door whose wooden veneer was beginning to wrinkle. There he signed himself into the register with a nod from the clerk in a small antechamber and entered a room of decidedly faded grandeur.

Detective Rush-Williams of the Metropolitan Police Special Branch was back from the seaside. He sat down at a long, polished table with dark overlapping circles where teacups had branded the surface and leafed through his notes. He straightened his tie, smoothed his black hair, and waited. As he registered the muted hunting prints and the decanter of bloodless Scotch, there was a rap on the door.

Three men entered. Detective Rush-Williams stood.

'Welcome to Five,' said one.

The men sat.

'I am Kell,' said the principal, polishing his monocle. 'Willoughby is to my left, former Inspector of the Gold Coast Constabulary. Cooper is to my right, former District Commissioner of Lucknow.'

Willoughby was dressed in tweeds, as if diverted from a shooting party. Rush-Williams wondered how long before the Great Exhibition of 1851 Willoughby had lain in a cradle. He smoked a heavy pipe and Rush-Williams noticed a thin strand of saliva clinging to the stem. His teeth were small, like a child's.

Cooper was lean, with cropped hair and round black spectacles. His face was angular, his cheeks sallow. He looked like a monk who had known malaria.

'Good of Scotland Yard to pitch in,' said Kell. 'You've been briefed, I understand, on our little... Indian problem.'

Rush-Williams cleared his throat. 'My Detective Chief Inspector has given me the rudiments,' he said, the 'rude' in 'rudiments' resonating. He had come far from his Baptist beginnings in Neath.

'Getting anything out of Berlin is nigh on impossible, as you know, Detective,' said Kell. 'That said, a reliable source a month ago has been able to smuggle information out through diplomatic channels in Copenhagen.'

He pushed a buff-coloured folder across the polished table. Two words were stamped at an angle across the top: 'MOST SECRET'.

Rush-Williams took the folder. He asked a tacit question with a raised eyebrow.

'Permission granted,' said Kell.

Rush-Williams opened the folder. The title, unevenly typed, read:

CONFIDENTIAL REPORT ON THE 'BERLIN COMMITTEE' AND THREAT OF A HINDU-GERMAN CONSPIRACY

Rush-Williams cast his eye over the first page of the report, leafed through the remaining pages, and looked up at Kell.

'We know Special Branch have been watching the India House mob since Sir Curzon Wyllie was shot dead in 1909,' said Kell. 'News from Berlin suggests our friends Messrs Pillai and Chatterjee have formed an Indian-German league inside the enemy's capital. And now the Irish Republicans are shovelling gunpowder into the mix.'

He cleared his throat.

'What we don't want, for obvious reasons, are other Indian agitators stirring things up with His Majesty's Indian Army troops at home. You follow?'

Rush-Williams nodded.

'The Indian needs beating with a firm stick,' stated Willoughby. 'Or we'll have a sepoy mutiny like in '57, right at our own front door!'

A vein in his temple started to throb.

'I think what Willoughby is alluding to,' said Kell, 'is keeping any incitement to disaffection on a tight rein—'

'Or they'll turn their guns on us just like they did on Sir Curzon!'

'For the sake of completeness,' said Rush-Williams, 'a Parsee doctor was shot trying to save Sir Curzon and the Indian Cavalry Corps have been fighting and dying for His Majesty daily since the beginning of this war.'

There was a pause.

'Detective,' said Kell, clearing his throat. 'Nobody doubts the loyalty of the vast majority of Indians, but we need to take certain precautions. I am sure you of all people understand. May we enquire as to your assessment of the target?'

'Well,' said Rush-Williams, looking into three pairs of enquiring eyes. 'Pacifist. Yes. Indian patriot. Yes. But from what I have observed, nothing to upset the apple cart.'

'What's that supposed to mean?' said Willoughby.

'Songs,' said Rush-Williams with a Welshman's resonance. 'He sang songs. Songs of Mother India. Mention of a tigress wanting to roam free in her homeland is some way from incitement to disaffection. And he's quite a respectable bass-baritone—'

'Don't be impertinent!' barked Willoughby.

'Thank you, Willoughby,' said Kell, tapping his foot. 'Detective, we would ask Special Branch, through your good offices, to carry on keeping an eye.'

'Yes, sir,' said Rush-Williams, tugging at his waistcoat. 'Will that be all, gentlemen?'

'For now,' said Kell. 'Yes.'

Detective Rush-Williams closed the door to the Directorate of Military Intelligence Section 5.

He stretched his collar with his forefinger. Our nation safe in their hands, he thought, rolling his eyes as he descended the stairs.

*

The following evening, as the stars opened over London, Inayat Khan held his daughter and looked into a sapphire sky. The warmth of her head flowed into his temple. 'What path has the Divine Weaver paved for you, *Bābouli?*'

It may have been Inayat's imagination, but the stars appeared to brighten. Though his eye was familiar with the Sufi order of the constellations, not even Inayat could have imagined the pattern planned by the Divine Weaver.

He looked east. And for a moment, Inayat Khan's world spun upside down.

The sky was the sea. London lay on the ocean floor. The stars were crests on the waves above. A vast grey shadow moved across the water. It was the shape of a whale. It slowed. Lights fell from the shadow's belly. They exploded into phosphorescence as they hit the ocean floor.

The shadow passed over Noor and Inayat. Inayat looked at his daughter, as if for an explanation. Her eyelids fell and lifted. Two fish swam up from the ocean floor. One swam near the whale-shadow's fin. One near its eye. The shadow burst with light. The first fish burst into incandescence and fell to the depths. The second plummeted, spiralling in a downward arc, squid-red in a haze of ink.

Fish were on fire.

Fish were falling.

London was burning.

Inayat wrapped Noor in her birth-blanket clinking with miniature pendants and raced downstairs. He woke Amina, pressing his finger to her lips as her eyes widened. Inayat took his wife and daughter to the basement. Outside was the echo of distant thunder. Inayat sat on the floor, holding Noor. She looked at him with wide, quizzical eyes. Inayat had expected Noor to cry but there were no tears.

The commander of Zeppelin LZ.38 surveyed the silent city as its whale-shadow passed over Tower Bridge, following the mercury-like current that divided London like two hemispheres of the brain. The airship continued westward towards the dome of St Paul's, then thirty-five degrees north towards Farringdon and the dank streets of Clerkenwell. London slept, oblivious to the silver-skinned incubus, swelling before preparing to strike.

The prospect of an airborne attack on London had divided the German High Command. One Prussian general had stormed out of a Council of War, calling it a breach of military convention as well as the height of bad manners. Another resigned.

For the architect of the plan, Rear Admiral Behncke, it was not a choice but a duty: 'For loyal sons of the Fatherland the destruction of the enemy's capital is a solemn obligation.'

There was no shortage of volunteers. The whale-shadow passed east over the city, hovering over Farringdon Road. The low hum of the airship deepened the dreams of the sleeping populace.

'It's time to light the candles,' said Commander Linnarz.

As he spoke, a biplane came out of the night into the view of the command deck. The aircraft flitted on the air currents. A moth with a propeller, thought Linnarz. It manoeuvred parallel to the front quadrant of the Zeppelin. A cough of machine-gun fire rattled from the plane. Did the enemy really think this contingency was unplanned for? Was the young pilot, thought Linnarz, resorting to his revolver? There were bursts of fire from the deck-mounted *Maschinengewehr*. The plane, canvas skin over a matchbox frame, burst into flames, disintegrating as it fell.

The whale-shadow moved on alone. From its belly there fell more than a hundred bombs, heavy and incendiary, marking a flaming path between Farringdon and Stoke Newington.

Inayat returned to the top of the house. The Shadow of Death had come. Fire raged in the east. The smoke gathered over London like a purple halo. He stood, imagining the people in houses crumpled by bombs, raging with fire. He placed his palms over his eyes. He glimpsed into a future where entire cities were destroyed from the sky. Men attacked each other on land, he thought. Men attacked each other on the water. As soon as they learned to fly, men were fighting each other in the sky. Now they were raining bombs on to a sleeping city. Was there any way back?

He lay on the floor. Tears streaked from his eyes and into his ears. He lost all track of time. He awoke, sprawled on the floorboards, to the sound of starlings. War had unleashed the shadows. London lay charred and smouldering.

*

The shadows returned. Sometimes they came in pairs. Sometimes in schools of six. They passed over the faces of Noor and Inayat. Inayat Khan's heart twisted as they moved. Noor's eyes darkened and blinked. The shadows, she knew, were pain.

Meanwhile, London turned to a handful of pilots. They practised the new-fangled art of flying from a field behind a farm in Hornchurch.

'Welcome to the Suicide Club,' said Squadron Leader Ashworth to his latest pilot-officer. 'Otherwise known as the London Air Defence Squadron.'

'Sir!' said the new lieutenant, remaining at attention.

'Lieutenant... Robinson?' said Ashworth, scanning a report.

'Yes, sir.'

'Formerly with No. 4 Squadron in Saint-Omer,' said Ashworth, reading aloud. 'Right arm wounded by shrapnel over Lille... Mainly flown BE2cs... Recommended for air defence duties.'

'That's the sum of it, sir.'

'And now you're here, lucky chap. How's the arm?'

'Good as new, sir.'

'Any night flying?'

'Half a dozen sorties so far.'

'That's a start. I have lost more pilots crash-landing in the dark than in combat. What do you know about us?'

'Defence of the realm, sir?'

Ashworth gave a weak smile and drew on his cigarette.

'Defence from...?'

'From Zeppelins, sir.'

'Zeppelins, Lieutenant,' said Ashworth. 'When you say Zeppelins – you mean six hundred feet of hardened aluminium wrapped in Satan's bladder flying at high altitude with enough bombshells to wipe out London and the Home Counties?'

He flicked his cigarette.

'You mean airborne fortresses impervious to .303-inch Vickers machine-gun bullets in the unlikely event that anyone gets above twelve thousand feet and close enough to fire?'

Robinson winced.

'Still, it's nothing too much to worry about,' he said. 'By the time the War Office get their pin-heads round the problem, I daresay there won't be a London Air Defence Squadron – and I daresay there won't be a London.'

Ashworth balanced his cigarette on the side of an ashtray and began poring over an enlarged aerial photograph. Lieutenant Robinson sat in the chair, unsure whether the interview was over. As the minutes passed, the cigarette curled into a coil of ash and extinguished. The lieutenant cleared his throat.

'Will that be all, sir?' he said.

Ashworth looked up as if he and the pilot had never met.

'Will that be what?'

'All, sir.'

Ashworth looked again at a written dispatch next to the aerial photograph. He raised his head, stared straight through Robinson, and muttered a calculation.

'They're coming,' he said.

*

Inayat Khan stood alone at the window in Notting Hill. He raised his arms in supplication. Are the shadows to destroy God's entire creation? He summoned all his energy, inhaled, and closed his eyes.

Behind his flickering eyelids he saw a tunnel. At the end of the tunnel was a silhouette of Bhishma, the Archer Prince.

Bhishma pulled the string of his bow so far back it began to shake.
Bhishma balanced an arrow of smoothed wood tipped with iron.
Bhishma shot the arrow upward in a lethal arc.
The arrow climbed, levelled, and started to fall.
As the arrow fell it began to spin, whistling with speed.
The iron tip was revolving like a mechanized tool.
As the arrow spun it began to transform.
Veins started opening inside the wood.
As it approached its mark, the arrow became a flying flower.
A regiment of archers unleashed a volley of arrows.

They fell in bursts of colour over Zeppelin-scarred London.

Inayat breathed Rumi's words: 'Raise your words, not your voice. It is rain that grows flowers, not thunder!'

His invocation was unanswered. The following night, a shadow was cast over London so vast it felt like the apocalypse.

The shadow cast the faces of Noor and Inayat into silhouette. Inayat closed his eyes and recited the *Zikr* – fast, whispered incantations. There was terror in Noor's eyes. It was the largest shadow of them all. As Inayat incanted, a young airman took to the skies. The engine note of his BE2c Night Fighter sharpened as the plane curved upward into the dark. He flew alone. His only company was an air-cooled Lewis machine gun and three drums of phosphorus-filled bullets.

'Why phosphorus?' asked Robinson.

'Go back to your Greek, Lieutenant,' said Ashworth. '*Phos* – light. *Phoros* – bringing. Something that might actually ignite Satan's bladder!'

The only barrier between London and an R-Class Super-Zeppelin was a lone pilot with a single machine gun. The only barrier between Lieutenant Robinson and the unseen ground at ten thousand feet was a thin sheet of metal. The 'E' in BE2c Night Fighter stood for 'Experimental'. The noise of the wings shaking was being outrun by the sound of the propeller. Gusts of cold wind buffeted his goggles as he strained to view the instruments.

Inayat held Noor.

The shadow was shutting out the sky.

Robinson could see nothing, but he could hear a distant hum. The clouds cleared. A tip was visible. It was the hind end of the world's largest Zeppelin. Zeppelin L-21 decreased altitude as it flew over Epping. Cables that ran along the interior keel started to pull and screech as the rudders moved starboard. The airship started to revolve twenty degrees south. The incendiary bombs rattled in their racks – restless and impatient. The Kapitän raised his voice over the drone to address his first officer:

'It promises to be a most interesting evening.'

Nothing, at twelve thousand feet, prepared Lieutenant Robinson for its scale. His training manual referred to the Zeppelin as an 'airship'. It was less an airship, he thought, approaching from above, more an elongated *whale-planet*. Robinson flew along the top, passing yard after yard of silver membrane with ridges at intervals that held the Zeppelin's shape. He passed over the Zeppelin's widest point. He had already flown further than the Royal Flying Corps' longest airfield.

As Robinson flew, he could hear cables pulling. The Zeppelin was beginning to turn, ready to strike. As Inayat held his daughter, he could see a speck approaching the vast shadow. Another plane was about to become a flying funeral pyre. He squeezed Noor as they watched.

The Night Fighter descended and manoeuvred perpendicular to the Zeppelin's underbelly. Robinson opted for a ninety-degree attack on the Zeppelin's flank. The side of the Zeppelin illuminated with sudden bursts of light. Robinson gripped the Lewis machine gun and returned fire. The phosphorus bullets emitted a trail of blue tracer as they whistled towards the Zeppelin. The Lewis gun cut out. It was not, as Robinson first thought, jammed. The ammunition drum was empty. The needle on the Night Fighter's fuel gage was nearing the 'empty' sector.

He had fifteen minutes.

He descended and reduced speed. Yards of the Zeppelin's silver membrane moved forward overhead. He positioned the Night Fighter behind the Zeppelin's engine cars at the rear. He reloaded the Lewis gun. He tried to keep the Night Fighter steady, despite the buffets of wind and the Zeppelin's backdraught.

'*Phos – Phoros.*'

Robinson shouted the two words as he curled his palm around the grip of the Lewis gun and eased the butt into his shoulder. He placed his index finger over the trigger. The Zeppelin's engines were a furlong away, but to Robinson the *thrummm* might have been distant thunder. He closed his left eye. And paused.

Inayat held his breath.

The pilot focused on a single target: a patch of the Zeppelin's underside at the stern between the last engine car and the rear point of the airship. The precise square of membrane was framed in the sights of the Lewis gun.

Behind his closed eye, the dimensions of time and space uncoupled and fell, bending and straightening, into the void. Before his open eye there was just the cross and the target.

Pressure. Squeeze. FIRE!

The bullets chased each other, jostling for the same gap torn in the Zeppelin's membrane until the machine gun started to glow in a halo of phosphorus tracer. The second ammunition drum sputtered to a halt. Robinson loaded the final drum and placed his finger back on the trigger. His right shoulder prepared for the recoil. The Lewis gun burst into life, phosphorus bullets pursuing each other with trails of blue smoke bursting across the night sky.

Robinson stopped firing and looked at the target. A cloud of phosphorus tracer hung behind the engine cars like a blue ghost and evaporated. The shadow approached West London. The Zeppelin was preparing to drop its first wave of bombs.

Inayat clasped his daughter.

Robinson put the butt of the Lewis gun back into his shoulder and re-curled his trigger finger. Final attempt. The ammunition drum thumped and rattled as the coil of bullets were ejected one after another after another and then—

Nothing.

The last drum was empty. Robinson was cut off like an orator in flow. He put his head on the ledge above the instrument panel and closed his eyes. He felt the wind whip around his ears. The plane hovered in the blackness.

London would be destroyed.

A sun ripped through the fabric of the night. The rear quadrant of the Zeppelin was on fire. The first explosion was muffled. Louder explosions followed as the Zeppelin's internal compartments exploded along its body. A vortex of air spun over the Night Fighter. Peeling away, Robinson could hear cables snapping and see ropes on fire.

The observation basket beneath the Zeppelin dropped like a jaw. Two crewmen fell out, like teeth, into the crisp night air. The whale-shadow was in flames. Flaps of skin tore away as it plummeted. The shadow vanished from the sky. And hid in an infant's mind.

CHAPTER 4
'THE SAILOR'

Quiriquina Island,
Chile, 1915

Canaris

Prisoner 95 lay on a narrow straw mattress staring at the bruise-coloured light leaching through a grille-lined opening to the sky. He could hear the shrieks of the storm petrels out to sea. The mattress could have been stuffed with cider apples from his family estate. He imagined lying on his own brass bed, thousands of miles away on a lake of polished parquet. His present kingdom was smaller than his father's gun room.

Wilhelm Canaris, Oberleutnant of the Kaiser's Imperial German Navy, was a long way from home.

'*¡Levántate!*' shouted the guard, thumping the door.

He went through the morning drill: mattress folded, grey flannel shirt buttoned, prison boots laced, metal bucket one pace away from the cell door. The lock turned with a thud. He filed along the landing, bucket in hand. As he walked, he recalled the aroma of fresh coffee and warm *Bauernbrot* drifting from the bright family breakfast room, where cherry blossom circling the Meissen china trailed on to the papered walls.

The prisoners clanked down the metal stairs, buckets in hand, a slow millipede moving through the well of the prison, through the latrine block, through the courtyard always cast in shadow and into the high-ceilinged refectory, where prisoners dined under a statue of Christ more pierced and contorted than the statue in the prison chapel.

'How are you, *marinero*?' said Prisoner 106. It was the aquiline teacher, Álvaro, in prison for debt.

'Could you wish for more than the Chilean breakfast?' said Álvaro, flourishing his hand at the bread and coffee. 'A jar of caramel *manjar* and you'll be wishing you could stay here forever!'

'Seconded!' said Prisoner 59. It was Gilberto, the squat moustachioed horse-thief and legend of the pampas. 'I have been here seven years and for coffee this good I would stay another seven!'

The men laughed. The warmth of the Chileans had touched the Oberleutnant the evening he arrived, handcuffed and shivering. He came to love their bearing, their curiosity, their benign insults, their charged silences... His Spanish was fluent now. It came to him with ease – the roundness of the words, their expressiveness, their melodrama. Were his ancestors once Latin, he wondered? Some thought he even looked Spanish – his olive complexion, dark eyebrows, and the deepening lines that framed his upper lip.

'How could I leave my *amigos*?' said Prisoner 95. 'Even if the prison gate swung wide open?'

Prisoner 59 slapped his back: 'We will make a Chilean of you yet, *marinero*!'

*

The young Canaris had joined the Navy against his father's wishes.

'Well-born men do not ride on boats. They ride on cavalry stallions,' said Herr Canaris senior, a Prussian of the old school.

His son insisted.

Officer training involved an apprenticeship with the North Sea: navigation, meteorology, watch-keeping, ship-handling and rope-work performed in lashing winds under gun-metal skies. At the passing-out parade at the Imperial German Naval Academy in Kiel, Canaris received the Sword of Honour.

His training at the *Marineakademie* was polished with a spell at the Britannia Royal Naval College, Dartmouth, in 1912. His mother saw him on to the overnight train from Dortmund.

'The British will make you our finest naval officer,' she said, holding the nape of his neck. Could it only have been seventeen years since she had held him as an infant?

Her son wore a stiff white collar, a navy-blue suit and his best *Hutkönig* trilby.

'*Danke, Mutter,*' he said, trying to keep his voice from cracking.

*

In his cell, Canaris closed his eyes. The same image returned. The darkening sky and the gun-grey ocean that forged a black line across the horizon.

The line was on fire. Two ships were burning, white like the bones of an X-ray.

He was watching from the deck of SMS *Dresden*. The *Dresden* – pummelled, rivetted, soldered and welded at the Blohm & Voss shipyard – was the pride of the Imperial German Navy. Almost four hundred feet of high-tensile steel, her waterline sagged under the weight of shells and torpedoes. Inside her metal body beat a 15,000-horsepower heart. She flew the white Imperial ensign with a central black eagle circled at an intersection of black stripes.

It was a bitter afternoon in November 1914. Navies that had trained together were now enemies. The German and British fleets clashed above the Antarctic Circle, a telescope's sight from Coronel, Chile. The *Dresden*'s antagonist was the light cruiser HMS *Glasgow*. Of the two, *Dresden* was faster and better armed, spearing *Glasgow* with a trident of fast-loading cannons, L/55 guns and deck-mounted torpedoes. A volley of shells tore through *Glasgow*'s bridge in a hissing Catherine wheel of shards, splinters and sparks. One torpedo came within a sailor's cap of her propeller.

The discipline of *Glasgow*'s crew made the *Dresden*'s Oberleutnant dig his nails into his palm as they fought fire, falling beams and the 'szing' of *Dresden*'s repeated 35-pound shells. Despite her retaliation, *Glasgow* would soon become a floating funeral pyre. Was *Dresden* right to pursue the onslaught to the end...?

Glasgow's bow was illuminated by floating infernos: HMS *Good Hope* and HMS *Monmouth*. While *Monmouth* blistered red against an iron sky, *Glasgow* summoned the last of her strength to carry her out of *Dresden*'s range and into the cover of *Monmouth*'s cremation. As *Glasgow* sailed to safety, the knuckles of the *Dresden*'s Oberleutnant recoloured. Something elusive tinged his fury. He made an inventory of his emotions. Something on the list made the Dartmouth-trained sailor's brows knit. It was elusive, but it was there. Relief.

'A brave fight, Captain Luce!' he shouted at the *Glasgow* in cut-glass English.

The Battle of Coronel saw the Navy of Drake and Nelson defeated. After five hundred years, Britannia no longer ruled the waves. The German victory led to the transmission of the Kaiser's personal congratulations to Admiral von Spee on the German flagship *Scharnhorst*. The German Emperor and King of Prussia expected even greater things in the future.

*

Morning sunlight streamed into the prison refectory. As the Oberleutnant ate the last of his *marraqueta* roll, he caught the eye of Ernesto, the cook. Ernesto stared out from dark expressive eyes framed by a pitchfork beard. The girth he carried under a floor-length indigo apron was that of three men. He was larger than the mightiest stoker of any vessel on which the Oberleutnant had sailed. Yet his hands, as they worked the dough of the *empanadas*, were delicate. It was not the first time Ernesto had sought out Prisoner 95. Everyone had an agenda. What was the man-mountain Ernesto's?

As the prisoners finished breakfast, the Oberleutnant looked up at the statue of Christ. He knew every contour now: the arch of his instep, the rent in his side, the protrusion of his ribs, the thorn-pricked trickle from his temple, the narrow face and the steady, forgiving eyes.

Decades later, the gaze came back to him when his hands were tied behind his back and a proclamation read aloud.

He looked down at his metal mug of half-drunk coffee and thought of his sisters. How their eyes would have widened and their ivory fingers pressed their lips to see their brother sitting in a prisoner's uniform. He looked down at his prison shirt and boots. He would return home to Dortmund if he had to swim the Atlantic. The first challenge was escaping. The second was... he was on the wrong ocean. He looked up again at the statue's eyes.

Turning from the steady, painted eyes, he caught the animated, quizzical eyes of Ernesto. Ernesto's eyes spoke with silence and urgency. 'There is something I need to tell you,' they said. Canaris took his coffee mug back to the servery. As Ernesto poured more coffee into a large metal jug, he said in a hoarse whisper, 'The *consulado* in Santiago has been in touch with some high-up people in the prison...', and rolled his eyes upward. 'I have arranged for you to take a job in the kitchen. Keep your ears open and your mouth shut.'

The Oberleutnant said nothing. Inside, excitement burst.

That evening, he paced his cell like a leopard. Even on a dot in the South Pacific, an officer of the Imperial German Navy was not forgotten.

Lying back on his lumpy mattress, he closed his eyes while his mind skimmed over the grey waves of the South Atlantic. After Coronel, the ships of his squadron had sailed with an air of swagger and invincibility. On the *Dresden*, however, Canaris remained extra vigilant, transmitting intelligence reports with added caution. Victory, his Dartmouth instructor once said, is sometimes more dangerous than defeat.

Dispatches from the German Imperial Naval Office warned of sightings of an expanded British fleet several degrees south of the Falkland Islands. What was Von Spee thinking when he ordered his squadron to chase the routed British ships straight into Stanley Harbour? Vanity? Ill-judgement? Stupidity? Or was it rumour of

the mysterious contact signal in perfect German naval code ordering the Kaiser's fleet to sail straight into an enemy-held position?

The sight that greeted the German admiral made his eyes
bulge and his hand steady himself as if he had stumbled into
his daughter's bedroom on her wedding night. Ships of the
British Atlantic fleet were rearmed and bloated with coal. HMS
Glasgow was there among the colliers, her four funnels puffing
like silver cigars.

HMS *Canopus* was stationed one bay along, as if a butler in
attendance, her 40-calibre guns trained on the harbour entrance.
The German cruisers *Nürnberg*, *Dresden* and *Leipzig*, despite
their formal black-and-white ensigns, were not correct company.
Canopus opened fire from a concealed location, smashing the glass
of the conning tower on the German flagship. Admiral von Spee
continued to grasp at the wheel of *Scharnhorst*. His face began to
colour and swell until it burst into throbbing panic.

Scharnhorst began to turn in an arc, her propellers over-spinning
and clanking under the strain. Immediate orders went to all vessels
in the squadron to make a dash for the open sea. This was suicide,
thought Canaris. The entire German squadron was short of coal
and ammunition. A retreat would be fatal. Why was the admiral not
ordering an attack while the enemy was cornered?

The German fleet scattered. The British light cruisers fanned
out across the ocean, a pod of hunting orcas. *Scharnhorst* was first,
her funnels reduced to stumps on a fingerless hand, before she
groaned and sank with Admiral von Spee himself gasping his last.
Then *Gneisenau*. Then *Nürnberg*, each taking one of the admiral's sons. And as darkness descended, *Leipzig* too descended, to a
watery, silent cemetery.

Only *Dresden* escaped. And vanished into a traceless phantom. The British thought she might have run aground, until a
month later she emerged from the Chiloé Archipelago to sink the
merchantman *Conway Castle* on course to supply wheat to a belea-
guered Australia. Tempers within the Naval Intelligence Division

detonated. The First Lord of the Admiralty, Winston Churchill, was apoplectic.

'FIND AND SINK THE DRESDEN. P. R. I. O. R. I. T. Y,' read the orders to HMS *Glasgow, Kent, Orama* and *Bristol.*

*

The hours aboard SMS *Dresden* were long in the small, window-less signal office. Morale, however, was good among the ship's company and the Oberleutnant's young deputy, Holz, was atten-tive and willing.

'One slip and our war is over,' Canaris would remind Holz over coffee and, in the evening, over schnapps. At the ship's modest mass on Sundays, the Oberleutnant thumbed his rosary and prayed for his ship's deliverance.

On a brisk morning at the beginning of March 1915, the Oberleutnant slammed his coffee mug on to the signaller's table. He swore with such unexpected boom and colour that the officer of the watch, Baumann, came rushing into the signal room. The former was seated at the table, his fingers pressed into his temples. Sitting on his desk was his deputy's transmission of a message sent fifteen minutes before to a Chilean collier.

PROCEEDING TO JUAN FERNANDEZ.
ALMOST OUT OF COAL.

The message was *in Klar* – uncoded – as if the letters were dancing naked. Juan Fernandez was an archipelago off the Chilean coast. *Dresden*'s position had been exposed.

'We must change course immediately!' shouted Canaris.

*

A week later, rays of a March morning sun shone into Canaris's cabin. *Dresden*'s port side clattered with running footsteps and echoed with urgent shouts. The siren went. The Oberleutnant was one of the first on deck, surveying the icy Chilean waters to the south, when he turned thirty degrees and recoiled as if slapped at a dance. The Glasgow sat glowering at eight thousand yards, the whaler's harpoons – Vickers three-pounders, three-inch guns, and mounted machine guns – glinting and calibrating ready to fire. HMS *Kent* appeared alongside, the duellist's brooding second.

'We are in territorial waters!' shouted the Oberleutnant, as if *Glasgow*'s gunners could hear.

Glasgow erupted like an amphibious volcano. Volleys of lava spat from her three-pound guns as she closed on the *Dresden*.

He dashed up to the conning tower.

'Permission to speak, *Kapitän*! We are in Chilean territorial waters. This is a violation of the international law of armed conflict!'

Within ten minutes, *Dresden* raised a white 'parley' flag and signalled to *Glasgow* to receive a boarding party. *Glasgow*'s heavy guns fell silent and its machine-gun fire tailed off like concert applause. A solitary launch was lowered from *Dresden*. Three sailors were on board: the slight, dapper figure of the Oberleutnant and two ratings. The Oberleutnant stood for the duration of the journey. Even Luce, *Glasgow*'s captain, commented on the Oberleutnant's composure.

Minutes later, Oberleutnant Canaris was marching into *Glasgow*'s wardroom, halting and saluting her captain. All *Glasgow*'s officers, including Captain Luce, stood to attention and saluted.

'Do I have the extreme honour of addressing Captain Luce of His Majesty's Ship *Glasgow*?' said the Oberleutnant in flawless English.

A strong protest followed at engaging a ship in territorial waters, but reasoned, and without resort to ill temper. Captain Luce made notes and listened before he delivered the verdict.

'Herr Oberleutnant,' he said. 'The question of *Dresden*'s location is one diplomats and lawyers can argue about for the rest of the century. Your vessel continued to fly its ensign when we engaged. I have my orders – to destroy an enemy ship. I am, like you, a naval officer.'

He beckoned Canaris to be seated. Luce too sat: two enemies from Coronel at the same table, elbows almost touching.

'You are a man of honour, Herr Oberleutnant,' said Luce. 'I am going to offer you an honourable way out.'

By mid-morning, the Oberleutnant stood with his ship's company on a craggy Chilean cliff, many willing back their tears, watching SMS *Dresden* buckle and list from a thunderous explosion in her forward magazine. *Dresden* left her signature in bubbles. The Oberleutnant, now a prisoner of war, felt a piece of himself sink with his ship to the depths of an ice-born ocean.

*

There were two thumps on his cell door.

'*¡Visitante!*' shouted the guard.

The door swung open. Silhouetted against the light was a priest in long black robes and a broad-brimmed black hat. In one hand he carried a small leather-bound Bible. He entered the cell and extended his free hand.

'Which of my flock do I address?' said the priest, his intelligent brown eyes looking straight – it seemed – at the prisoner's soul.

Prisoner 95 scrambled to his feet, patting dust from his shoulders and smoothing his prison shirt. He stood firm, as if to attention.

'*Yo so Wilhelm*,' said the Oberleutnant.

The priest smiled.

'Wilhelm?'

The man clicked prison boots together.

'Wilhelm Canaris, Oberleutnant, *Kaiserliche Marine*.'

The priest nodded. There was a look of approval in his alert brown eyes.

'Do you believe in salvation, my son?' said the priest, looking straight at the prisoner.

'*Sí, Padre*,' said Canaris, eyes lowered.

'Then I would like you to study some of the scriptures before confession on Sunday.'

The priest handed Canaris the Bible, black with a faded gold crucifix on the front.

There were three silk book markers of scarlet, grey and blue threaded through different pages.

'Until Sunday,' said the priest.

'Until Sunday, *Padre*,' said Canaris, bowing.

The priest was gone almost as soon as he arrived.

Canaris moved to the shaft of light in the corner of his cell and opened the page threaded with crimson silk.

It was the Book of Psalms.

A pencil mark drew his eye to Psalm 55, verse 8:

I would hasten my flight from the turbulent storm and tempest.

Then the blue silk at 2 Peter, chapter 2 verse 9:

The Lord knows how to rescue the godly from trials.

Then the grey silk at Luke, chapter 21, with a mark by verse 36:

Watch therefore, and pray always, that ye may be accounted worthy to escape.

CHAPTER 5
'THE MUSKETEERS'

Hôpital Val-de-Grâce,
Paris, 1915

Morel

Morel awoke. He was in the Hôpital Val-de-Grâce. He lay in a surgical gown, staring out of the window. On to the ward walked a surgeon-colonel from the Royal Canadian Medical Service and two nurses in white headdresses, each emblazoned with a red cross. The colonel was a Quebecois and specialist in head injuries who had been drafted in to perform the operation. His name was Boucher – but dark jokes about his name were misplaced. Boucher was a brilliant surgeon and a pioneer. Morel thought him too young to perform the operation. Perhaps thirty? Thirty-five at most. He wore a surgical coat and carried a clutch of X-rays. He smelt of gardens.

'My colleagues have explained the proposed operation,' said Boucher.

Morel nodded.

'The bullet took away thirty per cent of your skull, Sergent. What's left is not much stronger than eggshell.'

He held an X-ray up to the light.

'Left as it is, your brain is not properly protected. And you are susceptible to infection as soon as the bandages are removed.'

Morel looked again out of the window. He wanted to walk away from the building and leave behind his injury. He wanted to go back to Saint-Malo with Fabien. He looked up at the surgeon-colonel.

'Your head has been measured for a tin plate. Your chances of surviving the operation are fifty-fifty. It remains an experimental procedure, but I have had success in the last three months.'

Morel thought of the expression on his mother's face when she first saw him in hospital.

'Of course, the aesthetics are not ideal, but the main aim is putting you back together.'

The surgeon-colonel studied the medical notes handed to him by one of the nurses.

'They say you have spoken little since you were wounded. I need to know you understand the risks. This operation will require your consent, war or no war.'

Boucher's pen was poised.

Morel closed his eyes once again. He rolled his life around in the palm of his hand. What would Fabien have wanted?

'*Je c-consens.*'

*

A week after the operation, the ward was bandaged in darkness. The flicker of street lamps outside elongated the beds' shadows. Morel sat on the side of his bed, feet on the floor, alone among the sleepers. His elbows were on his knees and his hands clasped the sides of his head. The locks of hair that would have trailed between his fingers were gone. His fingers and palms clasped cold metal.

He reached for a leather bag under his bed and removed an object with the cold, unyielding surface of his head. He gripped his most precious possession, allowing the reassurance of oblivion to weigh in his palm. Sergent Morel sat in the blackness wondering what fate had ordained for himself and his last gift from Fabien – an eight-round semi-automatic Luger pistol.

'*Au lit* – to bed,' said a nurse.

*

Morel recalled the day his bandages were removed. His surgeon, Boucher, was delighted – showing off to colleagues the rods, drilled into bone like shorn tent pegs, that held the plate in place. To Morel, the image staring back in the mirror was closer to Frankenstein's monster.

Following the operation, he lay, staring from the window of a room at the Val-de-Grâce as the seasons turned, listless and mute. He relived his boyhood when he was whole and Fabien was alive – the shrimp-fishing, the blustery picnics on the beach, the wigwams made of driftwood, the warmth of the robe his mother wrapped her sons in after swimming.

Pain drew him into the present. Twenty-four rivets around his head. A rivet, he thought, for every hour of the day. When the hospital orderly spoke to him, he opened his mouth to reply but there came only the sound of a man gasping for air. The orderly asked how many phials of morphine he took per day.

'Are you proposing to speak?' he said.

Morel held up four fingers.

Each night, Morel dreamed the same dream. He was a boy in a crowded station. He was in charge of Fabien, holding his hand tight as the swelling crowds buffeted the brothers. There was a piercing whistle from behind. Morel turned to see a black loco-motive erupt in a cloud of steam. When he looked back, Fabien was gone. He cupped his hands around his mouth to amplify the scream. When he awoke, damp pyjamas clinging, he was in a dark room echoing to the same stifled mantra:

'fa-fa-fa-fa-fa-fa-fa-...'

The word never came.

Morel's days started to elide, grains of sand falling through concave glass. Weekdays, weekends – all the same. He could see his life stretching into the distance, small indents on a Breton beach leading to nowhere. Then the pain would return.

A new nurse came to take away his dinner tray early one evening. She paused, put the tray on the floor and walked to his bedside.

She sat down and took his hand. Her eyes were all the colours of a Saint-Malo seascape: wisps of blue, green and grey.

'There is something I have to say.' She took a breath. 'I think you're beautiful, Sergent.'

She left in silence.

That night, Morel dreamed he was in his trench. A full artillery barrage was unfolding under a sky of blistered orange. He looked over the top. The nurse was walking towards the French lines, oblivious to the bullets and shells. She was walking towards him, arms outstretched. The dream changed. He was on the concourse of a crowded station, holding a smaller hand. There was a sharp whistle from behind...

Boucher came to him one rainy morning in the autumn.

'The plate has taken, Sergent. There has been no major infection since you were in theatre. I am able to declare the operation a success. Now we need to get the rest of you working. I have recommended you for speech therapy.'

Morel looked up, doubtful. What was the point? He would only ever be a monster.

'Just an hour a day to start. That larynx of yours could do with a dust-off.'

*

It was an unusual circle that met mid-morning in an anteroom next to the hospital chapel. Morel with his tin head. Jolivet, whose walk resembled the canter of a man at the back of a pantomime horse. Brossard, who kept sheltering under the desk from poison gas and reaching for an imaginary gas mask. Tissier, the doctors' conundrum: physically unblemished, sitting in an invalid chair, his faculties on all-out strike. The circle, it was apparent, was short of words. Its members had all the vocabulary of a dummy without the ventriloquist.

None of this dampened the enthusiasm of Monsieur Eugène, a retired theatre director, who would arrive every day with stage props and an easel holding a wad of paper. Each page had letters in black against a white background, as if the men were at the optician's. When each member of the circle failed to say a word on one sheet, Monsieur Eugène would tear it away and try with the next. The combined sounds that came from the men gave Morel an uneasy flicker of amusement, as four throats dilated before delivering up words that were strangled at birth.

Monsieur Eugène underlined the letters that required emphasis.

SUR LE PONT
D'AVIGNON

There were no takers. Monsieur Eugène tore away the page.

UN, DEUX, TROIS
ALLONS-Y AU BOIS

Nothing – just four mouths that opened and closed like trout.

QUATRE, CINQ, SIX
CUEILLIR DES CERISES

'*Cerises!*' he said. '*B-e-a-u-t-i-f-u-l* word. Think of the cherries you will pick when this beastly war is over! Basket upon basket upon basket!'

The men, as they set their mouths to the first syllable, looked like they were smiling. No words came, only the sound of a line of 'S's being throttled in succession. Monsieur Eugène was undeterred.

'Excellent work, Messieurs. Truly excellent work!'

At the end of the lesson, he would sign off the same way: 'I look forward to the extreme pleasure of your company at the same time tomorrow!'

After the initial class, Jolivet clapped like a child.

Morel's days stopped eliding. Weekdays were defined by speech lessons. Monsieur Eugène was always pleased to see his students, and sorry to see them depart. His enthusiasm bubbled like

Normandy *cidre*. Sometimes he would bring a basket of pastries cooked by Madame Eugène, wrapped in red and white gingham. As the classes continued, Brossard spent less time hiding under the desk and Tissier sat higher in his invalid chair, arms clutching the sides. The lessons, Morel admitted to himself, were the highlight of his day. Perhaps there was a horizon at the end of the shore?

On one occasion, Monsieur Eugène arrived with four cloaks and four hats that flopped like crêpes.

There was a pyramid of words on the easel.

ATHOS

PORTHOS

ARAMIS

D'ARTAGNAN

They tried. None of the Musketeers could say their own or each other's name. Monsieur Eugène remained buoyant.

'Excellent effort, *mes Mousquetaires*! Excellent! Soon you will be sword-fighting and talking at the same time!'

One morning, Morel was sitting with the other mute *Mousquetaires* in the anteroom of the hospital chapel.

Into the vaulted room walked a gerbil-like man in battledress. Above a less-than-prominent chin he sported a small, trim moustache that looked like it had been emphasized with a make-up pencil. He wore a red cross around his arm and the shoulder flashes of a surgeon-commandant.

The men in the room could not speak, but their silence had a quality – expectant, trepidatious. The first pronouncement from the moustachioed gerbil was that Monsieur Eugène had been dismissed. Four mouths opened in protest. No words filled the void – only the sound of four 'N's being massacred. Tissier whacked the sides of his invalid chair with both hands.

'Silence in the ranks!'

An uneasy quiet descended.

'Hereafter your treatment will be administered by a senior medical officer. *Moi-même!* Following my treatment, you men will SPEAK.'

The men looked at one another.

'Those I consider fit to return to the front will do so.'

He glowered at Tissier.

'Believe me,' said the surgeon-commandant. 'You men will speak even if I have to pull the words direct from each of your tracheas.'

The man marched out of the room and slammed the door.

Surgeon-Commandant Daquin, it turned out, was one of the war's more intriguing paradoxes.

By 1914 he had reached a zenith of mediocrity. He lived in a mediocre apartment in the Saint-Ferréol district of Marseille, with mediocre paintings, a mediocre cellar and a mediocre wife. In mediocre rooms in Les Accates he kept a mediocre mistress. He wore a mediocre suit, a mediocre hat and mediocre shoes. He held a mediocre surgery near the Vieux Port where he treated mediocre patients with mediocre ailments. The outcome was almost always... mediocre.

War came. Sensing a life meandering through Seven Ages of Mediocrity to a mediocre death and eternal rest in a mediocre coffin, Docteur Daquin signed up as an early volunteer. He was first attached to the Première Armée headquartered at Épinal. Within weeks, hands that had never handled anything more invasive than a tongue depressor were wielding scalpels, knives and three different sizes of saw.

The outcome of Docteur Daquin's surgical interventions was somewhere approaching... mediocre. Critics classed it as on a par with that of an enthusiastic amateur. The critics, however, tended to be the ones convulsing and fainting on a portable operating table while Docteur Daquin, in a mediocre apron tied with a mediocre knot, learned the basics of battlefield medicine. Other critics were in a zone where body and soul were sitting on opposite platforms at the Station of Life and Death and thereby unavailable for comment. His results were, however, not so scandalous as to inhibit a rapid rise up the medical chain of command. The army was more interested in a medic who kept quiet and followed orders.

Months into the war, he was overseeing the triage protocol for the 14th and 21st Army Corps and both cavalry divisions of the Première Armée. Under his supervision, the constant trail of wounded – some walking, some on stretchers – were divided into three groups:

'Beyond Help.'

'Will Survive.'

'May Survive if Treated.'

As time progressed, Docteur Daquin abbreviated the system in his own mind to 'Red', 'Black' or 'Spin the Wheel'.

By 1915, he was surgeon-capitaine. The following year he was promoted to surgeon-commandant. His habitat was the casualty clearing stations dotted behind the front line, hospital tents and commandeered shacks that became, in time, the outbuildings of Hell. As the metropolis grew, Docteur Daquin was his own Hades, exerting his rule over a scattered purgatory bordered by the Western Front – a River Styx that ran a deep mud-red. His subjects were the Young Damned, men with once hopeful eyes marching row by row into a turbine of flying metal. The ones who staggered out, perforated or un-whole, found themselves under the knife of Docteur Daquin, who, if the other gods were watching, looked very much as if he were conducting a human sacrifice.

Daquin, into whose well of mediocrity were thrown decisions of life and death minute by minute, expanded his underworld, inured to pain and blood. He worked among the splintered bone and the mangled tissue, trimming arms and legs like branches in the garden of Hades.

Outside a commandeered school one evening, stretcher-bearers set down a man with the top of his scalp ripped away by a sniper's bullet. Docteur Daquin looked at the man, another of the legion of the Damned, face the colour of marble, lying on the grass. The stretcher-bearers had left a battered hip flask in the crook of his arm. Daquin could not resist opening the flask. Armagnac and not a bad vintage, he thought with a sniff.

'Last drink for someone,' said Docteur Daquin out loud as he left a 'Beyond help' label on the man's chest. It was only because the man cried out in the night *'fa-fa-fa-fa-fa-fa-fa-fa-fa-fa'* that the night-duty doctor replaced the label with one that gave him one last spin on the wheel.

As time wore on, the Docteur was convinced his underworld was running short of ether. He started to wield his scalpel with half the dose. A month later, he was feeling the path of a bullet through a fainting adjutant's femur.

'Shall I etherize the patient, Docteur?' said the nurse.

'Not yet.'

The nurse went to the portable glass cupboard at the corner of the tent.

'Supplies are ample, Docteur,' said the nurse.

'I said not yet,' said Daquin, anger rising.

'When, Docteur?'

Daquin looked up, aghast, and resumed his sacrifice.

Then something occurred that the Underworld King least expected.

*

Daquin felt four nails dig into the veins of his wrist. They dug with such force his hand went white and limp. He was staring into two eyes so incensed they made him blink and turn away.

'Have you taken leave of your mind?' said the nurse.

The adjutant was lapsing in and out of consciousness but appeared to sense something was wrong.

'How dare you!' said the Docteur.

The nurse picked up a scalpel. Docteur Daquin realized he might soon be lying on the floor of his tent with a label on his chest marked 'Beyond Help'. He left the nurse and the groaning adjutant and stamped out of the tent.

The Docteur's subsequent attempt to have the nurse dismissed backfired. It emerged that she was, scalpel or no scalpel, the daughter of a well-known general. She had submitted a statement. The allegations were serious. There was talk of a board of inquiry. Charges of dereliction of duty.

'I think it's time you took a breather,' said Daquin's colonel. 'Prolonged work at the front takes its toll on everyone. There is a temporary post at Val-de-Grâce loosening the tongues of malingerers who are refusing to speak. It's demanding work. It needs a real doctor.'

Le Traitement Daquin was something Georges Morel would not forget. The treatment started with injections of large quantities of insulin. The doctor gave no reason. The injections sent Morel into a blank, dreamless sleep, sometimes for days at a time. He would sit in the chapel anteroom where he had once eaten *pain au chocolat* dressed in a Musketeer's cloak. There were four words on a blackboard in chalk:

MORT POUR LA FRANCE

Morel sat alone looking at the blackboard. Docteur Daquin pointed at the first word with a paste stick. Morel's index and third fingers were taped together. Wires extended from his fingers to a small, innocuous box with a dial.

'It's quite simple, Sergent,' said Docteur Daquin. 'Say the first word.'

'*m-m-m-m-m-m-m*'

'Try again...'

'*m-m-m-m-m-m-m*'

'Again!' said the Docteur.

'*m-m-m-m-m-m-m*'

'Each time you fail to say the word, the voltage will increase. Do you *understand*, Sergent?'

As the weeks continued, wires were taped to his toes and his thighs, as well as his fingers.

'*m-m-m-m-m-m-m*'

'*m-m-m-m-m-m-m*'

'*m-m-m-m-m-m-m*'

It happened one balmy October morning, as the leaves in Paris began to drop, weary from the summer of war. Morel was propped up in bed. The nurse with the Saint-Malo eyes had just administered a phial of morphine.

The words came, clear and precise, from a man who had lain mute while the seasons came and went.

'*Docteur Daquin est un bâtard.*'

The nurse turned, eyes wide.

Morel looked embarrassed.

'Again!' she said, breathless.

'*Docteur Daquin est un b-b-b-b-bâtard!*'

'Wait there,' said the nurse, as she ran from the room, wiping her eyes.

CHAPTER 6
'EL COMEDOR'

Quiriquina Island,
Chile, 1915

Canaris

Sunlight flashed along the knife as it cut into flesh.

Canaris sliced a side of beef into elegant strips for the prisoners' weekly meat: *charquicán* stew. His hand was practised now, cutting the meat against the grain with precision and speed. The strips were laid on a mammoth wooden board with fine black circles betraying the tree's age. Ever present in the prison kitchen was the strong brooding presence of Ernesto, master of his galley of simmering heat, copper, iron, and sudden hisses of flame. At first, he inspected Canaris's chopping before picking up the tree-trunk board as if it were a saucer and scraping the meat into a giant stew-pot. Now Ernesto took the chopping board without examination – a silent gesture of approval.

Canaris turned his attention to the row of expectant pumpkins, hacking them into quarters and carving away their hard outer layer with a paring knife. He moved on to a pyramid of red *cardinál* potatoes. The hands trained at Dartmouth to rig spinnakers, fasten ropes and palm the tiller back and forth now spiralled the skins off potatoes like a conjurer. Runner beans, stringy and unruly, were topped, tailed, sliced, and put into ordered green platoons.

A sailor's hands were working again.

In the corner of the kitchen was a metal vat almost the same height as Ernesto. The vat itself had a hatch halfway up one side, which fastened shut with two metal bolts. During kitchen hours, the hatch was pinned back on a hook. Canaris and the other kitchen workers threw their peelings of potatoes, carrots and pumpkins through the hatch, along with discarded trimmings of beef and pork. The vat sat on four wheels and was known in the kitchen as 'El Comedor' – the Eater.

The following day, Canaris put on his cleanest prison shirt and attended mass in the prison chapel. The rhythm and lull of the service, the Latin rites, the prayers and responses, the ring of the bell and the incense soothed his nerves. As he took communion, the priest blessed him and said – '*Confesión después* – Confession after.'

The prison confessional was a rudimentary but dignified construction in a side chapel. Canaris entered through the curtain and sat on a worn wooden seat. As he waited, he thought about what confessions the small wooden box had heard. A box of secrets veiled by a curtain and guarded by a priest, thought Canaris. Was he in a place of safety or peril?

There was a rustling and tapping on the other side of the wooden divide as the priest entered and assumed his seat.

'Bless me Father for I have sinned...' said Canaris.

'Time is short,' said the priest. 'Listen to Ernesto and do exactly as he says. Hesitation is the devil. Be ready next Saturday evening when the guards get out the Gran Pisco. Plans are in place here and on the other side. The Lord go with you, my son.'

Confession was over.

The following week, Canaris worked with the same focus as he did when operating from the *Dresden*. He started work in the kitchen before light, kneading the dough for the *marraqueta* rolls and the *empanadas*. Ernesto taught him how to make the *pico* for the *empanadas* – ground beef with chopped onions, boiled eggs, raisins and olives. Canaris ground, fried, chopped, stoned and mixed, filling the pockets of dough and sealing them with his fingers. Ernesto would watch his charge between stints at the range. Sometimes he would sample the *pico* and nod – the highest form of praise from the wordless *maestro de cocina*.

When among the prisoners in the refectory, Canaris would look up at the Christ statue for any sign in his soulful brown eyes. Did he imagine it, or was his gaze softening?

'You are quiet these days, *marinero*,' said Gilberto. 'Too many *empanadas* made you seasick?'

The table erupted with laughter. Canaris smiled and laughed with the others.

On the Friday night, Canaris shifted around his prison mattress. Where would he spend the following night? He had no equipment, no funds and no plan. As his thoughts turned to the world beyond the prison, his cell felt secure. Did he fear his deepest wish? Sporadic sleep scattered his night like the patches on his prison blanket.

He rose before dawn, his body drained but on animal alert. In his pockets he placed his three possessions – the Bible given to him by the priest, a rosary and a small brass compass presented by his navigation instructor at Dartmouth. 'Carry a compass wherever you go, Wilhelm,' he had said.

On the Saturday, Canaris was back preparing *charquicán* stew, cutting the beef as if he had been the *Dresden*'s cook, not Oberleutnant. There was an air of something imperceptible in the prison kitchen – anticipation flavoured with fear.

At the end of the morning shift, Ernesto took Canaris by the elbow and muttered, 'Come back on shift at five. Keep your head down. You will eat early with the kitchen staff. When the prisoners finish their dinner, a chance will arise. You will have a maximum of ten seconds. Follow my instructions.'

'*¡Sí, el Chef!*'

Canaris passed the afternoon in the prison library, watching the black minute hand of the clock above the door move like a reluctant truncheon. He was tired from lack of sleep yet stoked with anticipation.

Watch therefore, and pray always, that ye may be accounted worthy to escape.

He thumbed his rosary, closed his eyes, and prayed.

By five, he was back in the kitchen. Ernesto was adding paprika to the *charquicán*. He looked towards Canaris, then picked up a wooden spoon to taste the stew as if the young Oberleutnant were invisible.

At six-thirty, the kitchen staff ate pork tacos in silence. None would look at Canaris. They stared at their plates, only their jaws audible. Were they part of the plan? Canaris followed and kept his eyes and head down.

The prisoners entered at seven. There was the familiar clatter of trays, scraping of benches and timpani of metal spoons on metal bowls. Canaris helped serve some of the broth, his ladle shaking. His heart felt like it was beating outside his shirt. He looked down at his chest for reassurance.

Dinner started coming to an end with the percussive stacking of bowls and trays. Canaris felt a clasp of his elbow. It was Ernesto, pulling him away from the counter.

'To the back,' he said.

The refectory echoed with prisoners scraping back their benches. The three guards turned their backs, preparing for the evening's canasta over a bottle of Gran Pisco. The kitchen staff huddled into the middle of the kitchen, obscuring the guards' view.

'Inside!' whispered Ernesto, shooting a glance towards El Comedor.

Canaris did not hesitate. Ernesto bent on one knee and made a stirrup with his interlocked fingers. Canaris placed his left foot into Ernesto's palms and his right on the trough of El Comedor's hatch. He jumped inside. Ernesto closed and bolted the door with two metallic thuds.

A second later, an officer of the Imperial German Navy was lying face down on a dark bed of vegetable peelings, empanada crusts, pork rind and beef fat. A dank, animal smell wafted from the depths.

At first, Canaris could only hear the blood pumping in his ears. He sensed Ernesto's movements at the cooking range and in the distance the sound of the prisoners talking in clusters, preparing to return to their cells.

The double doors of the refectory burst open. Into the long room strode Ramirez, the new deputy governor, flanked by two armed guards.

'*¡INSPECCIÓN!*' shouted the larger guard, stamping his rifle butt on the ground.

The din turned to silence.

Ramirez was a former colonel and veteran of the War of the Pacific. His right cheekbone was shattered fighting the Bolivians at Tacna in 1880. His face retained a hardened, dented look under a hairless head flecked with sunspots. He was known to his men as 'The Skull'. He was reputed to have tied naked Bolivian prisoners to wild horses before cracking his whip. The Skull held the blade of a swordstick high, like a conductor's baton.

He walked through the refectory, parting the silent prisoners with his swordstick like ears of corn. The prisoners stood in silence, hands by their sides. Only the Christ statue looked calm. The Skull sniffed the air as he prowled, as if hunting for hidden quarry.

He moved towards the kitchen. The staff moved aside. Ernesto stood by the range, holding a ladle.

'An army marches on its stomach. What are you feeding these wretches?' said Ramirez, tapping his swordstick against the stewpot.

'*Charquicán* stew, Deputy-Governor,' said Ernesto.

'On the Bolivian campaign we were lucky to find squirrels, let alone beef!'

Ernesto said nothing.

'What's that?' said Ramirez, pointing his swordstick at El Comedor.

'The Eater,' said Ernesto. 'Scraps from the kitchen's belly feed the pigs.'

'*¡Abrelo!* – Open it!' said Ramirez.

*

The Skull plunged the blade into El Comedor with a matador's flourish. It sounded like it was piercing a young bull's flank. He retracted the blade and plunged it back. The second strike almost penetrated the left calf of an Oberleutnant of the Imperial German Navy. Canaris, who was small and familiar with confined spaces at sea, was curled into a ball, face between his knees. In his mind he saw the eyes of the Christ statue. The only thing that divided him from The Skull was a membrane of tin. He thought of Christ sitting opposite on a bed of cabbage and pumpkin rinds.

He could hear The Skull breathing.

The matador retracted his blade and executed a long deep stroke following the outward curl of his wrist. It glanced the side of Canaris's left boot. The Oberleutnant sank his face further between his knees and held his breath. Soon the locks would be snapped open and the guards would extract him like a tooth.

'*¡Cerdos afortunados!* – Lucky pigs,' said The Skull, cleaning the length of his blade with a handkerchief.

*

Canaris stayed curled in his verdurous cabin for what seemed the length of his imprisonment. After a time, the refectory emptied and the lights were extinguished. The main doors were locked and bolted. He sat in blackness. He must have slept for a time. When his eyes opened, the refectory was immersed in chrome-grey moonlight. There was something else. He was moving.

El Comedor was being pushed by invisible hands and legs. As the vat was wheeled down an incline, there was a sudden drop in temperature and something Canaris had not felt for a long time – an outdoor breeze. El Comedor was wheeled over some gravel and stopped. Outside, Canaris could hear the faint opening of a metal gate. El Comedor and its passenger were on the move again. It felt like a road underneath, with occasional potholes. There was a concerted push and Canaris felt El Comedor go up a short incline.

What sounded like blocks were placed under the wheels. He could hear voices, Spanish but in a dialect he did not understand.

El Comedor was still, but something underneath was moving. He could hear the clip-clop of a horse. El Comedor and its passenger were riding on the back of a horse-drawn cart. The cart travelled for about three miles, until he could hear gulls and sense the freshness of the sea. The cart stopped.

'*Amigo*,' said a voice in Spanish he understood. 'Time to get out.'

Canaris heard boots climb on to the cart. The locks were unbolted. Canaris clambered out of El Comedor and stood massaging his muscles. Two men stood by the side of the road, one in his thirties, one perhaps in his late teens. Their faces were obscured by scarves.

'Message reached us from the priest,' said the older man. 'It seems you have God on your side.'

Canaris jumped down from the cart and moved to greet the men. The younger man simply turned away, his hand over his mouth to suppress a peal of laughter.

Canaris looked about himself. He had an epaulette of carrot peelings on his right shoulder. Across his chest were coin-size pieces of pumpkin, sitting like an unsteady row of medals. Some pork rind was stuck in his hair. Spinach clung to his trousers like seaweed. His left hand glowed avocado green.

The younger man looked back at Canaris, turned away and continued to convulse.

'Okay, joke over,' said the older man. 'This is for you.'

He handed Canaris a sturdy leather suitcase with metal corners.

'Get yourself cleaned up and changed quickly.'

He handed some banknotes to the driver of the horse and cart. Canaris saluted inwardly to his second ship, El Comedor, as it trundled into the distance.

He set the suitcase down behind a Chilean pine next to the road and unclipped the locks. As he opened the suitcase, he drew back in astonishment.

Moonlight poured over a folded suit, woollen shirts, braces, a fawn and black poncho, a pair of boots, woollen socks, a rabbit-hair *chupalla* hat and rolls of pesos and American dollars. There was also a Colt 1900 pistol wrapped in a flannel. Canaris gave silent thanks to the padre, to Ernesto, to the Christ of the Refectory – and set to work. He emerged minutes later in the dark chocolate-brown suit – oversized, but wearable – and the broad-brimmed *chupalla*. The younger man took the suitcase.

'This way,' said the older man.

He led the others off the road on to a narrow path that descended steeply through some woods. His paraffin lantern elongated the shadows of the trees as they tramped. The sound of the gulls was getting louder. By the time they reached the edge of a cliff, fingers of dawn were beginning to spread across the night sky.

And there, before Canaris, the waves swelled and crashed in a sailor's salute.

The trio descended steep steps carved into one side of the cliff. Sometimes the incline was almost vertical. The men clung to shrub branches as they made their descent. Sea air buffeted them as they reached the bottom. The older guide was the first to jump on to the beach. Then Canaris, followed by the younger man, who jumped with the suitcase.

They made their way over to the centre of a small bay where a group of fishermen were smoking pipes and preparing their nets. Three fishing boats rocked off a pontoon. There was an animated discussion between the older guide and one of the younger fishermen. A roll of banknotes changed hands.

'This is Raúl. You can depend on him. He will land you on a beach near the town of Concepción. When you reach the mainland, head due east for the town. It's an hour's walk at a pace. When you get there, head for this address and ask to see a man you can trust.'

The guide handed him a small piece of folded paper.

'Good luck, *compañero*!' said the man.

Within fifteen minutes, two men set off in a red and yellow fishing boat, *Impávido*. One wore a poncho and a *chupalla*, fastened under his chin. A light spray flecked the men's faces as they sailed, flocked by cheering seagulls.

It was a bright, clear morning.

The *Impávido* skimmed east across the water into a rising sun.

CHAPTER 7
'TREASURE'

London, 1916

Treasure

There was a tap at an entrance that some hinted led to Paradise. The gold epaulettes and gold braid on the collar of the man tapping his cane against the mirror-black door suggested an officer of the highest rank. The door was answered by an attendant in a powdered wig and a velvet coat. The young attendant made a bow, ushered in the officer, and took his gloves and cane.

A woman crossed the chessboard marble floor with the grace of a duchess. She placed her palms around the man's hands and looked at him with the radiance of sunlight after thunder.

'General, how good of you to come,' said Mrs Morgan.

Mrs Morgan had a way of putting those who walked over the threshold at ease, whether it was their first time or they were patrons of old.

'Milton,' she said to the bewigged attendant. 'Be so good as to take General Page into the library and ensure he is made comfortable. I shall be with you shortly.'

She opened her palms in the direction of the library.

'General?'

She gave a smile of such warmth the general thought he could feel its heat. His inner strings, so close to snapping, loosened a sliver.

Ten minutes later, Mrs Morgan opened the door to the library. The general was sitting by a well-stoked fire with a brandy and soda in a room threaded with the scent of cedarwood, leather and fresh tinder. The general moved to stand. Mrs Morgan stilled him with a light finger on his shoulder. Milton placed a chair behind Mrs Morgan, bowed and withdrew.

'Any visit to Balcombe Street should be a pleasure, General. Your first should be one that you never forget.'

The general smiled.

'There is someone I had in mind, but I thought I would take the opportunity of discussing your prerequisites in a little more detail first. As much or as little as you wish. If, of course, General, that meets with your approval.'

There was something about Mrs Morgan that allowed the general to speak frankly over his brandy and soda. The general felt, for a moment, like a soldier in the Crimea unbuttoning his pain in front of Florence Nightingale. The fire popped, on occasion, as he spoke.

'Perhaps I may be immodest about my instincts,' said Mrs Morgan. 'But they are usually good. And I have had a little practice.'

She awarded herself a fleeting smile.

'The one I had in mind is the one I am going to suggest.'

She wrapped her hands together, sealing the proposition.

'She is Treasure.'

*

Treasure sat in bed propped up on a bank of silk, rereading Kipling's *Kim*. A bell went. She heard a familiar clatter of footsteps. It was Milton. He stood with a metal tray bearing a glass set in an ornate brass holder, with a long spoon protruding.

'Who do we have today?' said Treasure.

'General Page, Miss.'

'Doesn't sound familiar. Has he been before?'

'No, Miss. It's his first time.'

Treasure smiled.

'Thank you, Milton.'

She put down her book. Her preparations were second nature. She was ready in half the time it took at the beginning.

Ten minutes later, Treasure heard a pair of boots ascending the stairs – slow and weary, like Sisyphus carrying the rock up the mountain. Treasure opened her doors to a man of forty-five, who looked a generation older. Under his peaked cap his hair was the pigment of discoloured salt, and the bags under his eyes carried the full consequences of his orders. There were still flecks of brown in his moustache, but they were overtaken by the grey. His skin, stretched taut over his face, was a map of trench lines.

General Sir Bertrand Page sat down on the side of Treasure's bed. Treasure knelt and placed her hands around the heel of his left boot. The general shook his head. What had he come for...? Seated, he looked alone, a rusty soldier abandoned from a toy box. Treasure sat beside him on the bed. The general stared into the white and grey of the chinoiserie on the walls at the exquisite herons and plovers perched or in flight. The two sat together on an island of silk, look-ing at the wallpaper. The general offered his hand, which Treasure took. Her other hand rested on the general's shoulder. They sat in silence as the corner clock stuttered out the passing seconds. The general said nothing. Sometimes he would take a handkerchief from his pocket and wipe under his eyes. Then he would squeeze the handkerchief tight in his palm. After almost an hour, the general looked at Treasure, squeezed her hand, and stood.

'Thank you,' he said. He replaced his red-banded cap and left.

The general returned to Balcombe Street whenever he was on leave. He always asked for Treasure. He never asked more than to hold Treasure's hand and look into the white and grey chinoise-rie at the birds amid the silver branches and the white blossom. Over the months, a strange bond grew between the two in the silence of Treasure's room, the pulse of the general's hand beating in Treasure's palm. The general's silences filled the room, rising to a mute crescendo with the whitening of his knuckles around his handkerchief.

Before leaving, General Page pressed a jewellery box tied with ribbon into Treasure's palm. Inside was a silver bird with tiny ruby eyes.

'It belonged to my mother,' said the general.

She squeezed his hand.

'It's now Treasure's treasure.'

Neither Treasure nor the general could have foreseen the bird's migration.

*

Doris Richards was eighteen-and-a-day when the hackney carriage first dropped her outside 75 Balcombe Street, Marylebone. The war was still a glint in the eye of its protagonists. Leaving the orphan house in Stepney, Miss Dingemans said Doris was a lucky girl – she was going to a special place where there would be other girls of her own age. It was, said Miss Dingemans, like a miniature academy for young women of unique potential.

Doris wore her one good dress and hat the day she left. Miss Dingemans tucked a loose strand of the girl's hair behind her ear before she went. 'Make sure you make a good impression on Mrs Morgan,' said Miss Dingemans. 'She will help you if you allow. See everything as an opportunity.'

Doris sat in the back of the carriage clutching a parasol, a present from Miss Dingemans, in her gloves. Anticipation fluttered like a caged bird inside her as the carriage drew to a halt. All her possessions were in one small suitcase, which she set down on the pavement. She straightened her hat and tapped the brass knocker. There was a flurry inside. The door was opened by a boy of about ten, who was dressed like the young Mozart in a powdered wig, scarlet velvet coat and buckled pumps.

'This way, Miss,' said the boy, taking her case.

Doris absorbed the discreet grandeur of the house – a marble floor of chessboard squares, fresh orchids in twin glass vases on a Chippendale sideboard, white Chinese porcelain with blue dragons chasing their tails and still lifes by original Dutch masters.

A polished wooden door opened at the end of the hallway. A handsome woman in her forties, with dark hair curved into a widow's peak and a porcelain brooch at her throat, walked forward, arms extended.

'Welcome, my dear,' said Mrs Morgan.

Doris could think of nothing else to do but curtsy.

As Doris curtsied and straightened, the full beauty of her face, set off by the vermilion of her dress, hit Mrs Morgan like a cuff. In that moment, Mrs Morgan knew without a flicker of doubt that her eyes were on treasure.

She christened the girl on the spot.

'While you are with us, you will be known as Treasure,' said Mrs Morgan, smiling.

Treasure was shown to a large room on the first floor. The walls were papered with grey and white chinoiserie. The same chinoiserie, with perched plovers and herons, echoed across an undulating dressing screen at the foot of a vast bed. The curtains were made from dove-grey organza and mirrored a pale silk rug, grey with flecks of lavender, that extended from the foot of the bed over dark polished floorboards. The doors to the wardrobes were papered with the same chinoiserie; there was enough hanging space inside to house most of the souls from the orphan house. There was even a room *en suite* with strange photographs and sketches framed in black and a deep enamel Armitage Shanks bath that filled with unlimited hot water.

She sat on the side of the bed and took off her gloves. She ran her hand over the sheet. It was silk. She later found out that it came from Yokohama in Japan. She lay back against the duck-down pillows swathed in Japanese silk. The image facing her on the wall opposite made her start. It was a painting of a nude reclining on the crest of a wave with a group of angels circled around her head. The young woman's hand took the place of a fig leaf. As Doris lay against the pillows, she had the uneasy thought of seeing her reflection. She swung her legs back towards the floor and sat, straight-backed, pulse racing. She stood and walked to a bookshelf on the wall opposite the dressing table. There were books bound in leather with their authors in gold on the spine – Fielding, Thackeray, Defoe. There were several books grouped together at one end with just titles:

The Oyster

Beatrice

The Nunnery Tales

There was a knock at the door. It was the boy in the Mozart wig and velvet jacket.

'Mrs Morgan asks if you would join her for lunch at twelve-thirty.'

'Thank you,' said Treasure.

'If you like, Miss, you can call me Milton. Most of the other girls do.'

'Milton,' said Treasure. 'That's an elegant name.'

'I was found in Milton Street when I was a baby,' said the boy. 'I don't have a ma and pa.'

'Neither do I,' said Treasure. She looked away, then back at the boy. The bond between two orphans formed on the spot.

'I hope you stay here for always, Miss,' said the boy.

He withdrew backwards with a bow. After he closed the door, Treasure heard the fading clatter of his pumps on the wooden staircase.

At twelve-thirty, Treasure walked down the wooden staircase, holding the banister, conscious that her new heels might give way at any moment. She was shown into a panelled dining room with a refectory table and places laid for two. Two candles in silver holders flickered, despite the daylight. Mrs Morgan sat at the head of the table.

'My dear,' she said, gesturing Treasure to be seated.

A footman in white gloves pulled back an embroidered chair. Minutes later, cheese soufflés were served in white ramekin dishes. Treasure thought she was tasting ambrosia. After the soufflés, fried lemon sole was served with tartare sauce beaten to perfection. After coffee and *petits fours*, Mrs Morgan put a napkin to the corner of her mouth.

'Do you have any experience, my dear?' she asked.

Treasure sat straight-backed, determined not to disappoint.

'I have skill as a seamstress, Mrs Morgan,' she said. 'I also taught reading and writing to some of the younger ones at the orphan house.'

Mrs Morgan smiled.

'Do you have any knowledge of… the sons of Adam?'

Treasure looked quizzical.

'The sons of Adam, ma'am?'

Mrs Morgan placed the back of her hand against Treasure's cheek. If she was valuable when she walked into 75 Balcombe Street, Treasure was now priceless.

'My dear,' said Mrs Morgan. 'We are a unique house. We avail ourselves to the needs of the Lords Spiritual and Temporal.'

*

On her first night at Balcombe Street, Treasure sat alone on the edge of her bed. What were the needs of the Lords Spiritual and Temporal? Fear clutched her heart. Tears started to roll down her cheeks. Milton entered with a tray of scrambled eggs. He saw Treasure crying, put the tray down and sat next to her with his arm around her shoulder. He said nothing. He just sat with a fellow traveller, the heat of his small body flowing into hers. He fetched a hankerchief from the dressing table.

Mrs Morgan came in later, strode across the floor and took her hand.

'The finest eggs come from happy hens. While I am entrusted with this house, my girls want for nothing.'

She stroked Treasure's hair. 'There are, after all, certain advantages,' said Mrs Morgan with a sweep of her hand. 'In any event, you will not commence entertaining until you are ready.'

Treasure dried her eyes.

'Balcombe Street is a place of dreams, not tears. You are not a captive. You are free to leave whenever you like.'

Part of Treasure felt like packing her bag there and then. The other part realized she had nowhere else to go.

'You have had a long day,' said Mrs Morgan. 'Everyone needs time to settle. What you need is a good night's rest.'

Mrs Morgan placed her hand on Treasure's and left in a whirl of taffeta.

The next morning Treasure woke at six, as she did in the orphan house, and was down for breakfast before seven. Number 75 Balcombe Street was asleep. Treasure sat alone in the dining room at the refectory table, waiting for the clatter of breakfast there was in the orphan house. She wondered whether she had imagined Mrs Morgan and the Lords Spiritual and Temporal. It was not until eight that a footman appeared.

'Ladies of the household normally take their breakfast in their rooms between nine and ten,' said the footman. 'Would you like your breakfast here or upstairs?'

Treasure looked stunned. Breakfast between nine and ten? In her room? She asked for breakfast at the table. Instead of Miss Dingeman's hard soda bread, a thimble of jam and a mug of watery tea, the footman drew back a linen napkin covering a basket of sugared brioches, croissants, and cinnamon toast. He poured amber Earl Grey tea into floral Wedgwood china. As the clock struck nine, she heard activity at the rear of the house – footsteps over marble and the neighing of horses in the street behind. She heard the drum of hooves on cobbles as the wheels of a carriage whisked the top-hatted occupant south towards Westminster.

The house returned to silence. Treasure wandered next door to a small library with leather chairs and a sideboard that hosted a bottled ensemble of whisky, sherry, Armagnac and sloe gin. The library held, among the muscular leather-bound books, *Wisden Cricketers' Almanack*s from 1864 and an entire collection of *Punch, or The London Charivari*.

She scanned the titles of the novels on one shelf:

Robinson Crusoe
The Count of Monte Cristo
Journey to the Centre of the Earth

The Hound of the Baskervilles
The Mayor of Casterbridge

She imagined the books open on the laps of silver-haired men in striped trousers, smoking pipes. At the end of the shelf, she saw a title of only three letters.

SHE

Intrigued, Treasure took down the book and returned to the dining room. She laid it open at Chapter One.

> There are some events of which each circumstance and surrounding detail seems to be graven on the memory in such fashion that we cannot forget it, and so it is with the scene that I am about to describe. It rises as clearly before my mind at this moment as though it had happened but yesterday. It was in this very month something over twenty years ago...

*

In her first week at Balcombe Street, Treasure met the other girls who flitted around the house, each with a different coloured peacock emblazoned on the back of her tea-gown. She learned their sobriquets: White Peony, Fire Opal, Monsoon, Venus and Honeysuckle. Apart from Fire Opal, they came from faraway dots on the polished wooden globe in Balcombe Street. White Peony was from Shanghai, Monsoon was from Jaipur and Honeysuckle was from the Blue Mountains of Jamaica. Treasure learned the one house rule that was strictly enforced: no discussion as to how each girl came to be in Balcombe Street – or when she would leave. There was no mention of the stooped man in a Mandarin collar who came to the tradesman's entrance every month to take payment towards White Peony's family's release from indenture. There was no mention of Fire Opal, a pre-Raphaelite with russet ringlets and cat-green eyes, being loaned to pay off her father's gambling debts. There was no mention of the sum that would one day find its way back to the orphan house in Stepney. The secrets of Balcombe Street remained with Mrs Morgan. Mrs Morgan would allow nothing to interrupt the smooth running of her unique house. It was said that the Balcombe Street Ledger, detailing the weekly fluctuation of house funds, was more securely guarded than the vaults of the Bank of England.

*

Once Treasure had become familiar with the rhythms of Balcombe Street, Mrs Morgan took her aside. It was time for her to start with Mademoiselle Pelletier.

'Who is Mademoiselle Pelletier, Ma'am?' said Treasure.

'You shall find out tomorrow,' said Mrs Morgan.

After breakfast the following morning Treasure was shown into a room that, to her surprise, was concealed behind a sliding book-case in the library.

Mademoiselle Pelletier had, in her twenties, a reputation for beauty and dexterity that catapulted the daughter of a Provençal baker into royal circles extending from London to Vienna. She had been the subject of several infamous duels – one involving a prince from one of Europe's grandest houses. She had been lavished with largesse over fifteen years and lived like a discreet countess. She felt a solemn obligation to pass on a portfolio of rarefied skills to the next generation and gave a charitable amount of her time to Balcombe Street and a house in Paris whose address was one of the capital's most sought-after secrets.

Treasure found herself standing in a bare panelled room with, at its centre, a polished metal table inlaid with zinc, sandstone and Murano glass. On the table was a fruit bowl made of pink glass, high-sided and opaque. Looking more closely, Treasure realized it was not fruit protruding from the bowl, but objects sculpted from ivory or carved from polished wood. Next to the fruit bowl was a large brown-paper parcel bearing a Paris postmark. Adjacent to the parcel was an oversized hatbox, though the gold writing on the top bore the stamp of a saddle maker 'By Appointment' to the King. At the end of the table there was a shoebox and a black velvet jewellery case.

Behind the table, a woman in her mid-thirties stood like a purveyor of illicit luxuries. She wore a watery-pink lace dress edged with silk coral-coloured primroses. A skein of white lace led from her breastbone to a swan-like neck, pinned with a cameo brooch circled by miniature pearls. Her hair was gathered over her right shoulder, just touching the empire line of her dress. Everything about her grey eyes exuded a mix of wisdom and mischief.

'You are Treasure,' said Mademoiselle Pelletier.

Treasure was not sure if it was a question or a statement.

Mademoiselle Pelletier walked around the table.

'Allow me,' she said, eying Treasure from the distance of a dance partner, before taking half a dozen paces away. She walked behind Treasure, gathered her hair, and with a deft curl of her wrist held it over her head. With her free hand she drew out two opposing wisps from her temples. She blinked, then let her hair fall back.

'*Mais oui*,' she whispered, as if to herself. '*Mais oui, mais oui.*'

The only other furniture in the room comprised two leather chairs either side of the fireplace. Above the fireplace was a drawing of a Japanese woman lying back, hair in disarray, her eyes closed as the mouth and tentacles of a giant octopus circled and delved.

Mademoiselle Pelletier walked over to the fruit bowl.

'Pleasure', she said, running her finger along a surface of ivory, 'is like good champagne. It is best when shared.'

She moved towards the brown-paper parcel. With dextrous hands, she tore open the paper.

'Pleasure cannot be shared if one is not properly attired.'

Inside the parcel were layers of pink and white tissue. Hidden in the tissue were folds of silk, satin and lace in whispers of cream, scarlet and black.

Treasure was bashful at first, but she was used to changing in front of the other girls in the orphan house. Within minutes she was standing in front of Mademoiselle Pelletier swathed in silk and lace. Mademoiselle Pelletier passed her the shoebox. Inside, resting in the tissue paper, was a pair of ankle boots overlaid in lace, with tall, tapered heels.

Treasure put on the ankle boots and stood a step taller. The air sharpened.

'The contents of this box you will come to when you are ready,' said Mademoiselle Pelletier, tapping the lid of the hatbox.

Mademoiselle Pelletier opened the jewellery case. Inside was a black silk choker bisected by a ruby. She stood behind Treasure, moved her hair to one side and fastened two small black hooks at the back.

A moment later, Mademoiselle Pelletier stood facing Treasure. She cocked her head, eyes narrowing.

'When it comes to beauty, men tend to see better than they think,' she said. 'In your case, *belle fille*, I fear they will not think at all.'

*

It was, she recalled, six weeks after her first visit to the library at Balcombe Street that she was considered ready for the hatbox placed on her bed with a card secured by a white silk bow.

'For Treasure'

Looking at the hatbox, she thought of a lifetime of birthdays without presents. Now there was an outsized present, a silk bow and a card. She untied the bow and lifted the lid. There were loose layers of tissue paper beneath, pink and white like candyfloss. She delved through the candyfloss. Her hand settled on what felt like a confection of hardened ribbons, stiff on one side, soft vellum on the other. She pulled out the ribbons. They hung in tendrils from her palm. The colour of the leather struck her first. Almond. She noticed the fineness of the stitching, tracing it with her thumb, while her fingers brushed the softness of the suede underneath. At the end of each piece of ribbon was a cuff pierced with a row of holes on each side. The holes were threaded with narrow leather laces, the colour of cocoa.

She closed one of the cuffs around her wrist. She pulled the laces tight. The cuff felt like it was staunching a wound.

The following week, Treasure had another audience with Mademoiselle Pelletier. Mademoiselle Pelletier stood in the same hidden room, behind the table inlaid with zinc, sandstone and glass. The table was bare save for a coffee glass with a graceful handle standing in a lace bronze base. A long silver spoon lay against the rim of the glass. Mademoiselle Pelletier stirred the contents with slow, deliberate circles.

'Before we entertain,' she said, 'we must master the first line of defence.'

She gestured at the coffee glass.

'Two parts olive oil, one part acacia honey, one part Siberian cedar resin.'

Treasure looked bewildered.

'*Ma petite*,' said Mademoiselle Pelletier, 'in the ocean of your womanhood, these are Nature's *fishermans*.'

The word '*fishermans*' would echo in Treasure's head for years to come when the bell in her room announced twenty minutes' notice. There would follow a knock on the door, with Milton holding a tray with a coffee glass in an open bronze bodice. The second line of defence, as she discovered, was a concoction of cloves, Queen Anne's lace, periwinkle and Madeira, drunk at the end of the evening.

Mademoiselle Pelletier placed a demonstration leather cuff round Treasure's wrist. She pulled the laces tight.

'Pleasure without pain,' she said, eyes flashing under their hoods, 'is like *croissant sans beurre*.'

*

It was the aroma of the Lords Spiritual and Temporal that Treasure remembered. Cigars, Armagnac, shaving soap, leather, sandalwood, and Mr Trumper's Extract of Limes Cologne. And their clothes.

Long boots from Lobb & Co., striped flannel trousers, black frock coats with silk lapels, stiff-fronted shirts, starched wing-collars and dove-grey cravats. Silk top hats stood rigid and glistening on Treasure's dressing table.

It was in Balcombe Street that Treasure discovered her true love. Not the sons of Adam – books. Milton would bring armfuls up from the library. They lay scattered on Treasure's bed and on the floor. She read Defoe, Swift, Thackeray, Eliot, Dumas and Salgari. While the Lords Spiritual and Temporal writhed and tumbled in a forbidden sea, Treasure swam through the vellum pages – dissolving into the bazaars of Simla in pursuit of enemy agents, fleeing bandit kidnappers in the steppes of Russia and searching for the lost city of Kôr in a hidden African empire. No self-respecting peer, spiritual or temporal, would attend upon Treasure without a tied parcel from Hatchards, booksellers to the King. The master of one of Cambridge's oldest colleges and senior member of the Athenaeum considered Treasure better read than all his undergraduates and most of his fellows.

*

It was one innocuous afternoon during her third year at Balcombe Street that Treasure's life changed track. The aroma of cigar smoke on the stairs outside made Treasure lurch for the bathroom and hold the sink with both hands as her body shook. The cloying scent of almond shaving soap had the same effect. She developed a strange craving for Colman's mustard. Running her eyes over her calendar and patting a discreet swelling in her belly, the realisation dawned. Nature's 'fishermans' had failed to catch. The moon that governed her internal tides was in repose. She sat on down on her bed, hands folded in her lap. What was going to happen? She confided in White Peony, her closest friend. White Peony's voice was soft but her words were firm. She had to tell Mrs Morgan.

Mrs Morgan received the news with what seemed like regal composure. The options were twofold, she told Treasure. She could call upon the services of Dr Urquhart or she could remain in her current condition. There were those of the Lords Spiritual and Temporal, said Mrs Morgan, who prized such a thing. 'However,' said Mrs Morgan, 'the dreams that are Balcombe Street do not include infants.'

*

It was decided that Treasure would entertain until the baby was two months away. A month away, Mrs Morgan arranged for her to stay in a warm saltbox house on the beach at Whitstable. The night before Treasure left, the two women dined together.

'Balcombe Street is not for everyone, Treasure. But we are a family, and we would like you to stay.' She placed her hand on Treasure's. 'Besides, the edifice of state may collapse in your absence.'

Treasure smiled.

'I am going to make a suggestion,' said Mrs Morgan. 'When I was in a certain condition some years ago, I had cause to place an advertisement in *The Lady*.'

Treasure's eyes widened.

Mrs Morgan put down her fork. 'I knew Lettie would be taken care of, that's all.'

She looked away, blinking. 'It happens to us all, Treasure, and the pain never leaves.'

*

At Victoria Station a fortnight later, Mrs Morgan placed a wedding band in Treasure's palm and enclosed it in her fingers.

'Give your husband a name and a regiment serving overseas,' she said. She whispered something else into Treasure's ear.

In Whitstable, Treasure walked along the shingle at dusk, holding her belly, the wedding band glowing in the evening sun. She felt for the first time the trappings of a normal life. The wind whipped her hair as the tide ebbed and flowed to the rhythm of the life within. She imagined meeting her baby at last, the long-awaited encounter between the soil and the flower.

A week before she was due, one of the country's most eminent physicians, and a Balcombe Street patron, took lodgings in

Whitstable's grandest house on Island Wall. Just short of a week later, a housemaid with a lantern rapped on the door at midnight. The physician threw on his frock coat and reached for his medical bag, initialled *EM*, with no time even to loop and thread his Athenaeum Club tie. In the time it took for the doctor to mount the stairs of the wood-slatted house, Treasure was delivered of a child. Opening the bedroom door, he found the baby – eyes tight closed – in Treasure's arms. Under a puff of cigar smoke, the baby's eyes opened wide.

It was a boy.

'Does he have a name?' asked the physician, placing a pair of surgical scissors on white damask.

'James,' said Treasure.

'And a good many middle names,' said the physician.

'Including Edward,' said Treasure.

The physician drew on his cigar.

'Including Edward.'

Treasure held her son in the firelight. He was perfect. She spent the next day counting and re-counting his fingers and toes. His expression was serene and curious, until the shadow of a frown clouded his face. He suckled hungrily at her breast and fell asleep against her neck, his breathing deep and even. When apart from her, even for a moment, his hands searched for her in the air.

After a week, Treasure wrapped him in a blanket and put a knitted cap over her head. She made a sling from a scarf and placed the baby in the crook of her arm. She carried him on to the beach. The warmth of his little body emanated into Treasure's ribs as they walked. She stood looking out to sea, shielding James from the wind and rocking him, mother and son bound together. There was something in the air, far out to sea. Her intuition could sense it like a beacon. The century was moving towards its teens and her senses told her the old order was beginning to crack. The fracture was almost imperceptible, but it was there. Treasure held her son and pulled the hair away from her eyes as it whipped across her face.

Three weeks later, a telegram arrived from Balcombe Street.

Treasure spent the day sitting, looking out to sea, clutching her son. Her make-believe husband, Captain Kelly, was never coming home, whatever the neighbours thought. The dream of Whitstable was slipping into the waves. That night she lay awake, restless and febrile. Mrs Morgan's words echoed around the bedroom.

'I knew Lettie would be taken care of, that's all...'

A further telegram came. It was specific. A time and a place.

Treasure wore her best vermilion dress and hat when, three weeks later, she walked up the marble steps of Bloomsbury's Great Russell Hotel. In one hand was a carrycot, in the other a handkerchief she had kept since the orphan house. It was three in the afternoon. A solitary couple sat in the tea room. Against the velvet flocking and the marble pillars they looked shipwrecked, the surrounding tables floating in their sorrow. Treasure approached the table. The man half-stood. He had thinning fair hair and an amber-coloured moustache. There was a sheen of perspiration on his forehead. The woman had brown hair parted in the middle. She had a comely face, though her eyes looked hollow, caverns of hushed desperation. There was a carpet bag by her feet.

Tea was brought while James slept in the carrycot. The man was a solicitor, he said, from Guildford. Pritchard & Pritchard. The firm was prosperous. He was soon to become a partner. They had a house overlooking the Surrey hills. It had an empty top floor and a large garden. Treasure listened, though she picked up only fragments. The man gave a quiet cough and gestured towards the cot. Treasure took up James. He still slept. She placed him in the woman's arms. Treasure felt as if she was falling.

The woman opposite held the baby and peeled back the blanket to see his face. She looked down. Then she looked at Treasure. Her shipwrecked look had vanished. Her eyes were bright. She rocked James. Treasure felt dizzy. She stood to leave, gripping the gilt of her chair. The man half-stood again. He held out an envelope and muttered some gibberish about the 'consideration unto the bargain'.

She pushed the envelope away and walked out of the tea room before the marble pillars collapsed.

She walked towards Holborn, still dizzy. She stopped a moment, leaning against a lamp post. She closed her eyes. She was in Whitstable with her newborn's warmth flowing into her body. She felt amputated, as if she had left one of her limbs in the tea room. She turned on her heels and started to run. Passers-by stopped to watch a woman moving like a fast vermilion sail through Russell Square and up the steps of the Great Russell Hotel. The tea room was empty. The corner table was laid, as if it had never been occupied.

CHAPTER 8
'LA CUMPARSITA'

Buenos Aires,
Argentina, 1916

Canaris

Rays of an afternoon sun were beginning to wane as a man in a frayed poncho and worn *chupalla* strode through the narrow streets of San Telmo, carrying a battered leather suitcase. Outside, waiters were polishing street tables. Inside, barmen stood under slow fans, holding glasses up to the light. Young men in black suits with open white shirts and wide-brimmed *norteño* hats were beginning to congregate in knots, smoking and provoking each other's bravado with the imperious passing *señoritas*. The late-afternoon strollers paid little attention to the small, agile-looking man in the *chupalla*, with his nut-brown face and rough mahogany hands. To those who even registered him, he was probably another itinerant *mapuche* from the south, looking to hawk his wares in the City of Fair Winds.

As he turned from San Lorenzo on to Defensa, the man could hear the flights of a *bandoneón* expanding and contracting into the evening, the treble spiralling ever higher above the rhythmic, pumping base. Outside the Café Los Inmortales, a woman with coal-black eyes, plum lips and hair scraped taut was moving forward with a fixed stare… left-heel-over-right… right-heel-over-left... pushing the chest of a young man wearing a tilted *nort-eño*. The man paced backwards, heel behind heel, in time to the *bandoneón*. They halted. Now the man made the advance... left-shoe-over-right... right-shoe-over-left... pushing the woman back. She made a defiant retreat: heel-click, heel-click, heel click... Then both stood facing each other like duellists, the woman flicking and hooking her stockinged calf around the man's leg while the man retorted with a hook and flick of his calf around the woman. The man curled his arm around the small of the woman's back and drew her to his hips. Their heads swivelled ninety degrees as they strutted on to the road together, eyes fixed, led by their interlocked fingers. They stopped. The man raised the woman's hand above her head and plunged it downwards like a *toreador*. The woman cork-screwed in a series of twists, her skirts flaring in pursuit. Then she stopped dead with the last note of La Cumparsita, her face pressed against the man's shoulder, calf curled around his leg. Applause rippled through the evening strollers.

A smile broke under the *chupalla*. A smile that recognized the *duende* of the dancers and the certainty that had the same spectacle occurred mid-waltz at an Admiralty ball, the participants would have been liable to immediate arrest. Beyond that...? The thought gambolled in the man's mind as he moved along Defensa, eager to find his destination before its sleek doors closed for the evening. Number 17 was a colonnaded building with tall windows behind balconies of black-lace ironwork. A column of brass plaques ran alongside the front door. The man ran his eye down the names of companies and qualified specialists. One plaque stood out:

DEUTSCH
GESCHÄFTMISSION

The weight of the brass knocker itself gave an indication of the gravity of the business conducted within. He held the curved brass in his hand, placed his head against the door and said a silent prayer for deliverance. Deliverance from snow, ice, rock, river, jungle and prairie. The journey of a thousand miles – by foot, horse, mule, sled, bicycle, wagon, steam train and lately Oldsmobile – was at an end.

He knocked twice. Nothing. He knocked again. There was a shuffling from inside. The door was opened by a suspicious-looking porter, whose first reaction was to close the door on an unannounced *mapuche* hawker. The visitor persisted. He could not give details but his business was of the utmost urgency. The porter narrowed his eyes. There was something unusual about the man in the faded poncho. He looked like a *mapuche*, but stood ramrod straight and spoke with unmistakable, if quiet, authority. After some vacillation, the porter allowed the man over the threshold.

The internal courtyard was spacious and cool, built around an expanse of black and white chessboard tiles, pivoted from squares into diamonds. A row of butterfly palms against the far wall added to the feeling of airy sanctuary.

On the floor above, hazy sunlight shone through four tall windows, catching the fragments of the chandelier and making prisms of light flicker across the wall. A man sat at a gilt-edged writing table, reading an ironed copy of *Argentinisches Tageblatt*. A swirl of smoke rose from a Cohiba in the man's hand. He turned the pages with languor. A glass of pisco sour stood next to the newspaper. Behind the writing table was a mahogany bookshelf yawning with pamphlets on taxation, mining, forestry and shipping. There was also a collection of maps, railway timetables, sailing schedules, company registers and almanacs.

Franz Tauber, head of the German Trade Legation, found *Argentinisch* life congenial. His wife and daughter enjoyed the social vortex of Buenos Aires. Their sizeable lodgings on Santa Cruz, overlooking the Parque Ameghino, compared favourably with their house in Hanover. Frau Tauber had plenty to occupy herself, entertaining with an enlarged retinue of servants. For Herr Tauber, increases in the price of silver, zinc and copper meant a renewed interest from German mining prospectors. His evenings of pisco and canasta with the mine owners in the bar of the Palacio Duhau lubricated the wheels of commerce. While the mine owners were in the far western province of San Juan, exaggerating their mining concessions to the prospectors, the owners' wives found themselves at a loose end. This led Tauber to rent a discreet set of rooms at the quiet end of Azopardo and to alter his post-lunch arrangements. That afternoon it was the hand of Señora Santana, always in a fingerless lace glove, which rested on Tauber's chest as he lay against the pillows blowing smoke rings from a Turkish cigarette.

The mud and blood seven thousand miles away on the opposing side of the Atlantic seemed, in every sense, a long way off.

Tauber had returned at five to his office, where he sat, calm and relaxed, emanating fresh cologne. It was time for his first cigar of the evening and completion of the newspaper. There was a knock at the door.

'*¡Entrar!*' said Tauber, flicking ash from his Cohiba.

Efraín, the porter, opened the door. Behind him stood a small, dark-skinned man in a *chupalla* and a poncho. Next to him was a battered leather suitcase. Tauber looked at Efraín. Why on earth was a hawker being shown into his office?

'The man said it was urgent, señor,' said Efraín, looking apologetic.

Tauber looked at the hawker. A suitcase of alpaca furs was his first guess. The hawker's eyes met Tauber's with a steady gaze.

'Forgive me if I ask to speak with you in private,' said the visitor with surprising gravitas.

Tauber looked at the hawker, then back at Efraín. He thought of dismissing both and continuing with his newspaper. There was, however, something entertaining about the *mapuche* aping the tone of a patrician.

He gave Efraín a look that said, *just this once*. Efraín nodded and withdrew with a bow.

'Franz Tauber, head of the German Trade Legation at your service,' said Tauber, savouring the irony.

The man opposite removed his *chupalla*, exposing hair the colour of bleached sand.

'Wilhelm Canaris, Oberleutnant, *Kaiserliche Marine*.'

The hinge that held Tauber's well-formed jaw together swung without warning. The Cohiba between his teeth dropped on to his chest, scattering ash over his fresh shirt. Franz Tauber, so suave and impeccable around the señoras of Buenos Aires, stared agog, like his daughter's goldfish. He stood to greet the man, knocking over the glass of pisco sour.

Tauber's verbal response had all the volume of a silent film.

Canaris filled the void. 'I am an officer of His Imperial Majesty's Ship *Dresden* and an escaped prisoner of war,' he said. 'My service number is 16950. I apologize for calling unannounced.'

Tauber located his breath.

'But the *Dresden* was sunk in the Pacific,' was all he could offer.

'I know,' said Canaris. 'I was there.'

The machinations of Tauber's brain were almost audible. What was Oberleutnant Canaris doing here on the Atlantic?

'I was held as a prisoner of war on Quiriquina Island,' said Canaris. 'I escaped via Chile. It's been an eventful journey. With a little help from above...' He gestured to the heavens.

All Tauber could do was sit back in his chair. His world was unravelling. The head of the Trade Legation had, after all, not rushed to volunteer in 1914, preferring to advance German interests from a robust four-poster on Azopardo. His war was fought in the warm Atlantic breeze, pisco in one hand, Cohiba in the other, rallied by the sound of the *bandoneón*. Now a part of the real war stood before him in a faded poncho, courage the colour of mahogany.

Tauber regained his composure. An unexpected caller was rattling the gates of Eden. He had to proceed carefully or the Garden was in peril.

'How can I help?' said Tauber, his suavity returning.

'I still have an ocean to cross,' said Canaris.

*

Tauber moved fast. He led an offensive planned at a gilt writing table under a chandelier that clinked with encouragement in the Atlantic breeze. An observer might have thought the entire outcome of the war depended upon the immediate return of a single escaped officer to the High Seas Fleet.

The first matter was to find Oberleutnant Canaris temporary quarters. An idea led Tauber to spend the following morning overseeing the reconfiguration of an intimate set of rooms with shutters capable of keeping out all traces of daylight. Tauber himself carried away various accoutrements, including a patented contraption, 'The Manipulator'. 'The Manipulator' had arrived the previous autumn under plain cover from New York, promising to deliver '...an oscillating massage efficacious to discerning ladies of rank'.

'Where are you going to put him up?' said Frau Tauber when she was told of the unscheduled escapee.

'I have managed to find a set of rooms at the end of Azopardo, off the beaten track,' said Tauber.

'Clever you,' said Frau Tauber with a stroke of her husband's cheek.

The next mission was to make his new acquaintance look like the Chilean-Danish industrialist in whose guise he intended to travel. This required a visit to Tauber's own Italian tailor, Fabrizio, in Calle Balcarce. Two suits and a dinner jacket were required in a fortnight. Was Fabrizio up to the challenge?

Fabrizio took the needle from between his lips and bowed.

'*Certamente!*' he said.

A visit to Tauber's main contact, Señor Enrique, at the Argentine Navigation Company secured a one-way berth on the *Frisia*, which was due to sail in two Thursdays' time. Tauber wrote out a cheque for a second-class ticket, folded it around several peso notes and handed it to Señor Enrique.

'One first-class *billete* in the name of Rosas,' said Señor Enrique, eyes smiling.

As to procuring a convincing Chilean passport, Tauber had to expand his net wider. Travel documents were scrutinized with more care since the start of European hostilities. Tauber had to ensure his plans did not fall at an early hurdle. Discreet enquiries as to the procurement of 'reproduction' documents produced three names. The first, it transpired, was in prison. The second was dead. The third was more promising, as Tauber knew him by sight: Ugo, the concierge at the Palacio Duhau.

Ugo was a man whose life was carved into his face – prize-fighter, mariner, gunrunner, hustler, and one-time agent of the Coca-Cola Company charged with sourcing the best coca leaves in South America. He wore a gold tiepin, a gold ring on each fourth finger and a gold bracelet. His face was a patchwork of scars, one side numb and motionless with a boxer's palsy. His mane of untamed grey-black hair above the bridge of a nose broken and re-broken during fighting bouts added to the impression of a grizzled, ageing lion – a pride leader at·the point of challenge.

Tauber approached the concierge's desk.

Ugo half-stood, the bulk of his frame hidden under his tailcoat.

'What can I help sir with?' said Ugo, a voice of boots on gravel.

'I have a matter in which I think you may be able to help, but it will require a conversation in private,' said Tauber, opening his jacket to show the tip of a roll of pesos peeping from an inside pocket.

'*¡Sí, claro!*' said Ugo.

Ugo clicked his fingers. An underling with smooth, greased hair slid from a back office into the front-of-house seat.

'*Sígueme* – follow me,' said Ugo, loping towards the velvet curtain at the back of the atrium that concealed a set of steps leading to the 'below stairs' part of the Palacio.

Ugo led Tauber away from the marble, cut glass and mahogany into a subterranean world of rusting pipes, peeling plaster, dank corridors, and steam permeating from the kitchens. Next to the linen storeroom was a wooden door marked:

ESTRICTAMENTE PRIVADO

Ugo opened the door into his basement realm. The faded, sepia-coloured walls held a career of boxing photographs matching the yellowed masonry. A boxing belt from a contest in Montevideo, 1899, hung next to a cabinet crowned with trophies. The shelves below held an entire library of cigar boxes. The cigars, alms for a multitude of favours, lay in state under cedarwood box lids etched in red and gold, spicing the air with dried tobacco and tinder.

Ugo went straight to a cupboard and withdrew a bottle of pisco and two shot glasses. He pulled out the cork with his teeth and poured two shots.

'*Por favor*,' he said, gesturing Tauber to sit at a table that looked like it was constructed from ocean driftwood.

Ugo drained his pisco and offered Tauber a Fior del Mundo cigar. Then he turned his palms to the ceiling, as if to say, *How can I help?*

'*¿Coca?*' he said. '*¿Chicas? ¿Hombres?*'

Tauber shook his head.

'*¿Pistola…?*' said Ugo, taking aim and pulling an air trigger.

'Chilean passport,' said Tauber. 'Ten days.'

There was a pause.

'In your name?' said Ugo.

'Name of Rosas,' said Tauber.

'Argentinian would be easier.'

'It must be Chilean,' said Tauber, having seen Canaris's false documents.

Ugo chewed his boxer's lip.

'There is a man I have used in the past,' he said, like a doctor making a referral. 'He is soon to retire to the *pampas* but he told me he was looking for one last job.'

'What are we talking?' said Tauber.

'Ten days is short notice,' said Ugo, the gravel of his voice milling his words.

Tauber fanned a roll of pesos on the table like playing cards. Ugo looked at the player's flush.

'The price of ink and paper has gone up since the war.'

Tauber added two further aces.

'That will start the ball rolling,' said Ugo. 'Same again on completion.'

Tauber raised his eyebrows.

'*Créame* – believe me,' said Ugo, leaning forward. 'In these matters it pays not to economize.'

*

Light from a tall window fell on to a sloping draughtsman's table. In a crescent lay varying widths of parchment, book-binding string, gum arabic, various Indian inks, silver writing nibs, a box of gold leaf, a Remington typewriter, letter-printing blocks, kitchen weights, document stamps, swatches of dark blue leather, a pair of tailor's scissors, a square pine-block, two small photographs from a Kodak No. 2 Brownie, a quiver of paint brushes and a bowl of diluted coffee.

The neck that pored over the draughtsman's table was thin, camouflaged by a cloud of white curls. The bones under the sagging suit were tired. Yet the eyes that peered through the gold spectacles were bright and the mottled hands steady. The hands started by cutting the parchment into folded squares and ageing the paper with a thin layer of watery coffee. Their ancient owner separated the pages and fed several through the Remington typewriter. He imprinted the other pages with document stamps – some square, some round. He mounted one of the photographs with gum arabic on the top right corner of a parchment square.

He drew a meticulous sketch of an image torn from an encyclopaedia. He placed the sketch over the pine-block and rubbed the back of the drawing over and over with a burnisher. The outline of an image began to appear on the pine-block. He took a gouge and started carving the wood away from the outline so it stood proud. He picked up a needle and sewed the pages of parchment together with book-binding string, like a master tailor. He took the best swatch of leather and folded it in half, trimming the edges with the tailor's scissors. He sewed the pages of parchment into the seam where the leather creased. On a side table, he laid out the letters in the printing blocks:

ELIHC ED ACILBUPER
ETROPASAP

He pressed the printing blocks into gold leaf then into the supple leather. He held the blocks under his palm, as if staunching a wound. After fifteen minutes, he replaced his hand with the kitchen weights. Next, he pressed the carved pine-block into a fresh sheet of gold leaf. He drove the pine-block into the leather between the lines of print. He held it firm until the shadows of the evening stretched across the floorboards.

The following morning, he inspected the leather. In the centre, imprinted in gold, stood an Andean deer facing a crested eagle. Between them was a gold shield embossed with a five-point star. The text above and below was also burnished in gold:

REPUBLICA DE CHILE
PASAPORTE

The old man placed the finished article under his heel. He scooped up an impeccably scuffed passport and pressed it to his lips.

'*¡Viva, Señor Rosas!*'

*

The presence of an escaped Oberleutnant caused an inevitable stir around the elegant dining tables of the mannered Deutsche Volk of Buenos Aires. Invitation cards littered the Taubers' hallway – tennis afternoons, supper parties, theatre openings, dinghy racing and *Doppelkopf* card parties. Letters accompanying the cards from some of the town's highest-ranking hostesses all extended invitations to the dashing naval officer known to have strangled a prison guard, scaled a 100-foot perimeter wall, swum from an island in the mid-Pacific to mainland Chile and walked barefoot over the Andes.

While Tauber was outgoing and expansive, Oberleutnant Canaris was diffident and self-effacing. Throughout his stay he remained a model of quiet, attentive charm towards Frau Tauber and her daughter, Elise. When Fräulein Tauber found out the Oberleutnant was going back to the war, she took to her room, sobbing, and refused to come down for dinner.

The longer Canaris stayed, the sharper the tones of contrast between the Oberleutnant and Tauber's lives were exposed. People were beginning to ask questions. Why was Tauber not fighting like Canaris? Tauber anticipated his friend's departure date as a desert explorer seeks an oasis. He wore off much of his agitation over pisco sours at the bar of the Palacio Duhau, while Canaris went in search of the ancient churches of Buenos Aires. One evening, a small package was set down next to Tauber's drink.

'With the compliments of Señor Ugo,' said the barman.

Inside was a dark blue passport embossed with gold. Tauber's heart leaped. He placed a roll of pesos in the envelope and asked the barman to return it to Señor Ugo.

'*¡Por supuesto!* – Of course!' said the barman, hand on chest.

The approach of the departure date also suited Canaris. He was anxious to return to naval headquarters in Berlin. In any event, the future head of German Military Intelligence had made his assessment of Tauber at the first wave of his cigar. Canaris's discovery of various lace handkerchiefs in his quarters, each with a different monogram, made him lie awake thinking under the canopy of the four-poster bed with unease. Then there was the other matter that was always left unsaid.

Tauber broached the subject on their last evening together. First he made a whirlpool of the wine in his glass.

'As head of the Trade Legation, I am sure you would have gathered I am exempt from fighting,' said Tauber. 'Crushing, really.'

'*Natürlich*,' said Canaris, with a look as enigmatic as the Mona Lisa.

*

Thursday arrived. Canaris was up at dawn, his new suitcase packed, his face closely shaven. He wore a well-tailored charcoal suit of fine Argentine merino and a silver silk tie. A tied package peeped from his pocket.

He ate his last breakfast in South America – warm glazed *medialunas* and several strong *cortado* coffees – at the Café Los Inmortales. A motor car from the Trade Legation collected him at nine. The sailor could sense a change in the air as the car made its way along the imposing tree-lined Avenida Independencia towards the Puerto Madero and the promise of the deep. The vast red-brick warehouses along the Avenida Alicia Moreau de Justo crowded his view: grain vaults of a metropolis expanding faster than New York City.

As the vehicle approached the port, Canaris could see a tangle of mainmasts – some rigged, some bare – of clippers, luggers and whalers. Soon the legation car was engulfed in a termite-like bustle – a speck among the trucks, horses, cargo-locomotives and trolley wagons leading to the cranes and gantries by the water. The eternal migration of cargo was unfolding. Copper, iron, timber, corn, nuts, cotton, oranges and munitions were being loaded on to freight carriers, while wooden crates stamped Sai Kung Canned Fish Company were being unloaded from a Hong Kong-registered steamer under armed guard. Emerging from the car, Canaris was swept into a moving column of shore-bound crewmen, flat-capped stevedores, shipping agents sporting their pencils like rosettes and customs officials wearing wing collars, dark ties, and the frowns of officialdom.

Canaris moved, buffeted by the surge, towards the far end of the port. The sun disappeared. The dock stood in the silhouette of a rivetted leviathan: the *Frisia*. Smoke from her gigantic funnels caught the back of his throat. Men, women and children swarmed next to the ship like ants under a cliff. The steerage passengers carried their entire lives in suitcases, packing boxes and trunks. The first-class passengers were roped off, conspicuous by their hands in their pockets or clutching parasols as if at a garden party while their luggage was being unpacked by the stewards aboard. Canaris arrived at the first-class embarkation area, discomfited at carrying his own suitcase. As he gazed up at the ship, sea spray flecking the air, he thought of the humble *Impávido* skimming the Pacific. Now he was setting sail first class over an ocean that stood between him and the bloodiest conflict since men invented spears.

Footsteps closed from behind. It was Tauber. He wore a light suit and a panama.

'I said I would see you off,' he said.

The men chatted with stilted bonhomie, knowing it was their last encounter.

'*Für Elise*,' said Canaris, handing Tauber the parcel from his pocket.

When Elise opened it that evening, she found a knitted Peruvian doll with a skirt of coloured stripes, a woven baby wrapped in a shawl around her neck.

Tauber handed Canaris an envelope.

'I cannot accept,' said Canaris.

'Don't mention it,' said Tauber, turning away to light a Cohiba. 'A first-class passenger will need some collateral at the blackjack table.'

The wind was beginning to rise.

The two men walked towards the queue of first-class passengers. They stopped and shook hands.

'Good luck,' said Tauber.

'Thank you for everything,' said Canaris.

With that he took his suitcase and, with a wave, walked towards the uniformed member of the ship's company. Canaris presented his ticket. The man looked at the ticket and nodded. Canaris presented his passport. The representative raised his hand with a 'Sir-that-won't-be-necessary' shake of his head.

Within an hour, passenger 'Rosas, W.' was standing on deck, the sea breeze whipping up to embrace an Oberleutnant of the

Imperial Germany Navy. Canaris could make out Tauber in the crowd. He was waving his panama.

The funnels sounded. Canaris looked back at Argentina. Part of his soul was being severed from the land of the Incas and the Conquistadors, of *montañas, estancias*, llamas, condors, flamingos and pink river dolphins.

The funnels sounded again.

'*Danke Gott*,' said Tauber.

*

'What is known about him?' said Mrs Cunningham-Reed *sotto voce*, her eyes flicking towards a dark-complexioned man in evening dress sitting alone in the first-class dining room aboard the *Frisia*.

The woman opposite leaned forward.

'Chilean-Danish,' said Lady Partington with a whiff of conspiracy.

'*Chilean-Danish…*?' said Mrs Cunningham-Reed, as if describing an exotic species from the reptile enclosure of London Zoo.

'Returning to Denmark to take over substantial business interests,' said Lady Partington.

'How substantial?' said Mrs Cunningham-Reed.

Lady Partington leaned forward.

'Substantial,' she whispered.

Despite the destination taking Canaris to Rotterdam via the enemy port of Plymouth, it turned out to be one of Canaris's more congenial weeks of the war. The passengers were a tolerable mix of English, Dutch and Spanish. Passenger Rosas W., the chameleon industrialist, blended seamlessly into the social flurry of the voyage – deck quoits, scavenger hunts, blackjack, and the occasional dinner at the captain's table. The Oberleutnant even found himself making up a fourth around Lady Partington's bridge table.

'Faultless manners and plays an excellent rubber' was Lady Partington's assessment.

Both Lady Partington and Mrs Cunningham-Reed were oblivious to the sailor's eyes that scanned the horizon for meteorological changes and the sailor's ears that detected the slightest alteration in the ship's engine note. As for his 'substantial business interests', Mrs Cunningham-Reed's mind was settled.

That evening, Canaris was sitting at the same corner table in the dining room when Mrs Cunningham-Reed approached with her daughter.

'I hope you will forgive the intrusion, Mr Rosas,' she said. 'This is my daughter, Miranda. Miranda?'

A girl of about eighteen stood in a taffeta evening gown, looking mortified and disinterested at the same time.

Canaris rose. He had to restrain himself from taking her hand to his lips and clicking his heels. Instead, he gave a small bow.

'Delighted,' he said.

The mood on the ship changed during the voyage's final stretch. A blanket of fear spread over the passengers. An alarm went after breakfast at ten sharp. The passengers assembled by the lifeboats, including mothers with crying infants. The captain made an inspection at a fast walk. He blew a whistle.

'U-boat drill OVER!' he shouted.

That night, in his panelled cabin, Oberleutnant Wilhelm Canaris lay awake. If, having come this far, the *Frisia* is sunk by a German U-boat, that would be, without question, 'U' for *Unglücklich* – Unlucky.

Onwards and eastwards sailed the *Frisia* – beyond Plymouth, plotting a course for Rotterdam. The remainder of a well-travelled Oberleutnant's journey lay overland across the German border by train. A week later, three delirious sisters ran across the gravel to meet him, their faces streaked with tears, while a mechanized war was harvesting men like sheaves of corn.

CHAPTER 9
'THE ELECTRIC EEL'

London, 1917

Treasure

Courtesy of a discreet War Office subsidy, Balcombe Street stayed open during the Great War. It remained a house for the Lords Spiritual and Temporal with the addition of officers ranked brigadier and above. It was during the war that something occurred without anyone seeming to notice. Milton had grown up. By 1917 he was lissom and agile, somewhere between boy and man. His colouring was distinctive – loose coppery hair, a broad face with bronze skin dappled with freckles, and cocoa-coloured eyes. Milton, named after the street where his mother had left him, would return to Milton Street whenever he had the chance. One day his mother would walk around the corner. He was sure to recognize her...? He searched crowds of faces every night before falling asleep. Once in a dream he saw two faces together, luminous in the shifting grey crowd. The woman had the shy, freckled face of an Irish colleen, with hair the colour of fire. The man had the broad, noble face of a Red Indian Sioux. The Sioux was an axe-thrower in Barnum and Bailey's circus when one evening a flame-haired servant girl from Kilburn took a seat in the front row...

There was a knock upon Treasure's door. It was late. Milton stood, copper hair loose, almost unrecognizable without white wig and velvet coat. He had decided to volunteer, he said. He was disobeying Mrs Morgan, he knew, but she was not his mother. He had found a regiment with a name he liked – the Artists' Rifles. He would be back by Christmas without a doubt.

Treasure begged him not to go. The recruiting sergeants would never find him in Balcombe Street.

'I'll be safe as houses.'

He gave her an envelope.

'Just in case. You're the closest thing I have to a sis.'

Treasure took the envelope.

The two embraced. Two orphans in the frame of Treasure's doorway.

Milton placed a dark hat over his copper hair, picked up his suitcase and walked downstairs. She heard the front door close behind him and from the window she saw Milton, the boy she had met on her first day, stride down Balcombe Street with the ease of youth walking to war.

A long tear ran down Treasure's face and left an expanding dot on the silk lapel of her dressing gown.

*

The war stumbled on like a determined drunk. Letters from Milton told Treasure of the action at Cambrai and his comrades in the Artists' Rifles. His letters always finished:

> On no account send 'nerve tonic'. Total con!
> Your brother (sort of),
> Milton

Each time a letter arrived, Treasure thanked every star in heaven and placed it in a silver box on her dressing table.

In the coming months, Treasure received a letter from Milton saying he had been awarded a Conspicuous Gallantry Medal and promoted to lance corporal. A major push was planned for the winter. When it was all over, he would return to Balcombe Street and ask Mrs Morgan for the keys to the extensive wine cellar. It would be the party to end all parties.

As the seasons turned, the pavement outside Balcombe Street frosted sugar-white, a telegram arrived. The War Office form was curt. Lance Corporal Milton Smith C.G.M. had been killed in action. The form was accompanied by a mud-spattered letter from a Captain Brody. Lance Corporal Smith had died attacking an enemy machine-gun position. His actions had spurred a major breakthrough of the German lines. Lance Corporal Smith was a credit to his regiment and to his family.

The doors to Balcombe Street stayed closed for a week. When Treasure summoned the courage to open the envelope Milton had given her, she found he had left all the funds in the account Mrs Morgan had opened for him at the Trustee Savings Bank to her, his 'Next of Kin'.

Treasure sat alone on her bed. She remembered the warmth of Milton's body when he sat next to her on her first day at Balcombe Street.

'I want you to stay here for always, Miss.'

When she had no more tears left, Mrs Morgan came to her room. She looked a decade older, eyes hollow and rimmed with red. Both women knew Milton was the closest thing Mrs Morgan had to a son. She sat next to Treasure on the bed and took her hand. The two women sat in silence, hand in hand, as the clock carved grooves into the silence.

*

Mediterranean Sea, 1917

Canaris

Thirty-five metres under the night sea, a blind, black eel was moving through the deep. The eel was metal-plated, slipping through the gloom, alert to the scent of prey. Something in the murk had piqued the eel's interest. The sea, a nautical mile away, held the French troopship *Medie* in her watery palm. The six hundred and twenty-six men on board, many asleep, were oblivious to Unterseeboot-27 closing from the depths at a steady six knots.

Once, U-boats had issued a warning before engaging. By 1917, the Deep was a theatre of Total War. The Obersteuermann called out the range and co-ordinates. Kapitänleutnant Canaris squeezed a rosary into his palm and counted a silent drumbeat – ten seconds that would decide life or death. On zero, he gave the order. Two torpedoes slid down the twin torpedo-tubes and ejected from U-27's bow, speeding towards the Medie like blacktip sharks.

The first torpedo missed the Medie's underbelly, spinning on through the water until its nose started to sag and it ploughed into a bed of sand. The second hit the Medie just above her keel, ripping through her hull and tearing through her inner metal folds into the engine room. The torpedo bored through the chest of the chief engineer into a bank of pistons and pipes before heading for another of the Medie's vital organs.

The engine room was submerged within nine seconds, the bodies of the drowned sailors suspended, eyes wide, like lost phantoms. For the troops in the cabins deep below decks, fate depended on finding a life jacket in the dark and taking a correct turn in the fast submerging labyrinth of passageways. U-27's torpedo signed two hundred and fifty death warrants that night as it rampaged through the Medie, renting her metal body open to the fingers of an enveloping sea.

The Medie sank in the time it took for the young Oberfähnrich to locate a bottle of schnapps, pour out a trayful of glasses, and compose a toast. The officers of U-27 formed a circle and raised their glasses to five thousand tonnes of enemy shipping descending to a silent grave. The crew cheered, returning to their posts euphoric as U-27 made a broad circle and began the journey back to the flotilla base in Pula.

The Kapitänleutnant made his way to his quarters, all hands saluting as he moved through the narrow confines of U-27, the pipes overhead snaking like iron entrails. Canaris entered a cabin that felt like an enlarged coffin. Still, he thought, it was better than being smuggled out of a Chilean prison amid the kitchen scraps. He lay on his bunk staring at the weave of metalwork above. The Kapitänleutnant, despite appearances, was always troubled after a sinking. War, reflected one of the Imperial Navy's most successful U-boat commanders, made killing lawful. It gave its combatants veneration and medals. But could any earthly power confer the right to send men made in God's image – fathers, sons and brothers – to walk the seabed as ghosts? His hand tightened around his rosary as he commended the dead.

Canaris closed his eyes. From the iron core of a metal eel, deep under the sea, a Kapitänleutnant's mind began to roam. A vast expanse of sky opened above, mirrored by a clear lake flanked by palms. Spring water gushed into the lake's far end, skittering over a granite precipice in a haze of spray. Distant mountains divided the land from the sky, their caps glazed with frost. He was on horseback, riding over prairie grass so lush and verdant it was almost luminous. Bouncing next to his saddlebags was a gourd of water and one of *tereré* to sustain the young gaucho rounding up errant heads of shorthorn cattle from the furthest reaches of the *estancia*. The sun had just passed its zenith as the gaucho rode on, the brim of his *chupalla* pulled down to shield his face. The hands that held the reins were the bark-like colour of the *ombú* tree. Zafir, the hardy Criollo from whom the rider had become inseparable, moved through the pampas at a steady pace, strong and intuitive, like an animated part of the landscape.

The Estancia Santa Isabel was one of the first ranches where a wiry young man in a faded poncho had sought work in Argentina. He told the *proprietario* he was working his way to Buenos Aires and was looking for a month's employment. The *proprietario*, Señor Talamantes, looked dubious. The man in the poncho had persisted: he was hard-working and a proficient horseman. What's more, he had skill as a chef. Talamantes looked him up and down.

'*¿Como te llamas?* – what's your name?' said the *proprietario*.

'Wilfredo,' said the man.

His accent was difficult to place. As was his story. Yet there was something about the young man that made Talamantes, who normally turned away strangers, take him on for a week's trial.

'The hours are long,' said Talamantes. 'All I can promise you after a day in the saddle is a hayloft.'

'¡Sí, claro!' said the man, as if a hayloft was heaven itself.

The young gaucho went on to make himself indispensable – riding into the sunrise, a *facón* knife tucked into the sash of his poncho, and returning with the sunset. He was the first to muck out the stables, groom the horses and wax the saddles. On the first Sunday he made *charquicán* stew for lunch after church. The other gauchos clapped and raised their glasses high, though the new ranch-hand did not mention that he acquired the recipe working in a prison kitchen on Quiriquina Island.

In the evenings, sparks from an outdoor grill would float and pop into the sunset as the extended family of the Estancia Santa Isabel prepared for a mixed *parrilla* of beef seared with chimichurri, marinated *pollo* and estancia-made chorizo. The branches of a jacaranda tree weaved a tapestry of purple flowers around the veranda that breathed into the cool of the evening. As Canaris, languid from riding, sat with a glass of cold Torrontés amid the scent of the jacaranda flowers while a soulful voice sang of days in the pampas, he looked into an infinite Argentine sky and made a silent prayer to life.

The next morning, Canaris saddled Zafir for another day rounding up shorthorn cattle. Other gauchos were adjusting their stirrups outside the stable. Canaris rode out with Héctor, a gaucho from Corrientes, known for his ability to tame wild horses. The two men passed a white-fenced pen where a figure in a bolero and black riding jacket was cantering a grey Arab mare in a wide circle. The face under the bolero looked up and in the flick of the mare's hoof Canaris glimpsed a pale, fine-boned face and a pair of solemn brown eyes. The two gauchos lifted their hats. A nineteen-year-old

Elvira Talamantes touched the edge of her bolero and continued her arc around the pen.

The two men rode on. Héctor leaned over when they were at a safe distance.

'Creation of the gods,' said Héctor, cocking his head.

It was late afternoon when the gaucho known as Wilfredo misjudged a low-hanging branch on his return to the estancia. He fell from Zafír and grazed his right shoulder and back. Nothing broken, but enough to earn the rider a second shot of pisco at dinner. As the other gauchos toasted their wounded *compañero*, Canaris was aware of a figure standing alone by the open French windows, the silhouette of her evening dress framed against the light. The others ate and drank into the night. Canaris was the first to rise from the table. He patted the other gauchos' shoulders goodnight and made for the hayloft just visible in the darkness.

Canaris lay propped against the hay. His shoulder made sleep elusive. As he dozed in half-sleep, his ears sensed the creak of a floorboard near the barn door. He reached for his *facón* blade. A lantern flickered as it moved across the floor. The *facón* was poised... The figure holding the lantern trod with the lightness of a cat. A mane of black hair framed a pair of lucent, sombre eyes.

Elvira.

'Vine a ver si estabas bien... I came to see if you were all right,' she said.

Her face vanished as she blew out the lantern.

*

Deck gun – *Armed.*
Torpedoes (bow) – *Loaded.*
Torpedoes (stern) – *Loaded.*
Deck hatches – *Sealed.*
Diesel engines – *Firing.*
Propellers – *Spinning.*

Unterseeboot-34 slid from the flotilla base into a starless night.

Kapitänleutnant Canaris's latest command headed out to sea on a north-westerly course, trailing a black wake tipped with silver.

By midnight, the air inside *U-34* was hot from the six-cylinder diesel engines and humid, like a sea-going jungle. It was also finite. U-boat patrols carried air for seventy-two hours alone. Rivulets of condensation ran down the bulkheads, across the glass of the gyrocompass in the control room, and dropped on to the faces of crewmen sleeping in hammocks. Above the U-boat's galley, wet-skinned bananas dripped on to the floor, making it feel like a cramped, sealed-in rainforest. The smell of diesel was omnipresent, permeating the hair and sweat-soaked uniforms of the thirty-five crew who shared a cavern less than twelve feet wide. Even the drinking water had a diesel aftertaste.

German submariners knew they were living on borrowed time. One in three U-boats would be lost. The perils on the surface – torpedoes and heavy guns from enemy ships – were as nothing to the perils beneath. The submerged U-boat was prey to depth charges, fatal collision, mechanical breakdown and ventilation failure. Depth charges could turn a U-boat into an instant catacomb. If the instruments failed, U-boats could go crashing, blind, into undersea obstacles – including other U-boats. If seawater leaked into the banks of batteries, chlorine gas could escape into the interior. Sometimes, entire U-boat crews would be gassed thirty metres under the sea, the U-boat ploughing on, rudderless, into the deep.

The declaration of unrestricted submarine warfare in 1917 had led, despite the dangers, to a moveable *Fest* for U-boat packs. They prowled the waves with stealth and guile, targeting and tracking – before diving to despoil the naked grey underbellies of their quarry. Ships with a parade of ensigns – British, French, Belgian, Italian, Greek and Russian – felt the whip and sting of the electric eel as ton after ton of Allied shipping plummeted to a growing Atlantis of submerged, broken ships.

*

U-34 was forty-nine hours into her patrol – enough air for a further day. Kapitänleutnant Canaris stood at the bridge, scanning the dawn. It was a calm morning, mist rising off the water. The sea was empty in every direction. The prospect of returning to base empty-handed was unpalatable.

'*Kommen, Schiffe*… Come, ships,' he said to a barren sea.

He continued to comb the horizon, framed by the two black circles of his binoculars. The circles, as he watched the open sea, became the faces of two clocks, ticking as the air inside *U-34* dissipated. His mind wandered back in time. Back to the momentous morning fifteen months before. His boots squeaked at quick march as an Oberleutnant in full dress uniform made his way down Bendlerbloch. Rumours of an imperial naval officer escaping from prison in Chile and making it back to Berlin had reached the Admiralty staff – but had been discounted as propaganda.

Canaris marched into *Reichsmarine* headquarters at nine sharp and saluted the duty officer.

'Oberleutnant Wilhelm Canaris, officer of His Imperial Majesty's former ship *Dresden*, reporting for duty, sir!'

His salute signified an escape from Chilean prison, a winter crossing of the Andes and a circumnavigation of the globe. There was an immediate commotion as the boots of passing officers echoed over the marble to form a small crowd around the slight Oberleutnant. A message went straight to the *Reich-Raum* on the fifth floor. Within minutes, Canaris was standing outside the *Reich-Raum* itself, a black and gold eagle from the war ensign staring out from each of the double doors. The doors were thrown open by two *Deckoffiziers* with swords hanging from their belts. He was in a room of scarlet and black, wood and leather, a gallery of charts and four torpedo-shaped chandeliers. Grand Admiral von Tirpitz himself, gyrating like a walrus, shook the young Oberleutnant's hand after the flash of salutes. Canaris was decorated on the spot with an Iron Cross First and Second Class. His name was mentioned in a written despatch to the Kaiser.

A dinner took place the following week to honour the returning prisoner of war. Canaris was placed next to Rear Admiral Behncke.

'What next, now you have done your sightseeing, Oberleutnant?' said Behncke. 'There is, in my view, only one theatre of war of sufficient challenge for the enterprising naval officer. The war beneath the sea.'

Canaris turned to Behncke.

'It is a matter, Admiral, on which I was going to take the liberty of invoking your assistance.'

'U-boat command courses are heavily oversubscribed,' said Behncke. 'Though with a word in the right direction from the Grand Admiral or even myself, I suspect we might be able to smooth that particular obstacle...'

The rear admiral's eyes twinkled in the candlelight as he drained a glass of *Bärenfang*.

*

Something pierced Canaris's field of vision. The sight, travelling east on a 120-degree bearing, felt like a splinter in his left eye. He pulled his binoculars down and turned away, as if he had caught the sun's glare. He replaced the binoculars. The sight he registered was like nothing he had seen on the water. It was a seagoing vessel – or convoy of smaller vessels – clad in a paroxysm of black and white geometric stripes. It looked as if two rival herds of zebra had clashed on the open sea. It was not clear which end of the vessel was which. Its course and speed were hard to judge given the geometric angles, which jarred and dazzled.

Canaris squinted through his right eye. At one end of the tumult of stripes was a flapping patch of white crossed with red. He adjusted his binoculars. Royal Navy ensign it was.

'*Feindliches Schiff am Hafen Bogen!* – Enemy ship on the port bow! DIVE! DIVE!!' shouted Canaris, taking a mental picture of the vessel's course and speed.

The deck hatches clanked and swivelled shut.

U-34 executed a sharp dive, reaching thirty metres in as many seconds. As she dived, the mechanized shunt of the diesel engines gave way to the hum of two hives of batteries used for underwater power. The lights dimmed and flickered back to life. When the output switched to watts, the eel became electric.

Kapitänleutnant Canaris took position in the control room behind the gyrocompass, flanked by his first officer and navigator. A bank of dials stood oscillating in the confined, windowless space: depth, water pressure, speed, output, fuel, air. The faces of each man, pale from subsea existence, ran with diesel-infused perspiration. The dials gave a basic reading of speed, depth and bearing. Otherwise, *U-34* stalked the deep without eyes.

'The U-boat commander hunts with one thing. Instinct,' the instructor at Kiel had told a class of elite, wing-collared officers of the *Kaiserliche Marine*.

Canaris knew the reality. The U-boat commander had to approximate the speed and course of an enemy ship by eye, dive the U-boat, and plot an underwater course to within strike range. Submerged U-boats travelled slower than warships – a factor the U-boat commander had to evaluate while navigating blind. The U-boat was at its most vulnerable when it rose to strike. Misjudgement risked it being torpedoed first or targeted by a depth charge – the dreaded *Wasserbombe* programmed to explode underwater and shred a U-boat into a kaleidoscope of metal shards.

Canaris glanced at a chart and called out his orders, calm and precise, like a surgeon in theatre.

'*Steuerbord*. Twenty degrees.'

The navigator spun the metal wheel.

'Increase speed to seven knots. Hold bearing.'

The hum of the batteries sharpened as the U-boat increased speed.

Canaris looked at the gyrocompass. He calculated three minutes to target range.

'Torpedo room. Prepare bow torpedoes.'

He looked at his wristwatch.

'Two minutes to target.'

There was silence apart from the *tick-tick* of the control room clock, each second draining down the air supply.

'One minute to target.'

Perspiration from the first officer's forehead dropped into the glass of the gyrocompass.

'Rise. Target depth one-point-five metres below surface.'

The needle on the 'Depth' dial moved towards a hidden sky.

'Up periscope.'

Canaris placed his face against the eye shield and gripped the handles. He moved the periscope clockwise, then anticlockwise.

The sight that greeted him on the anticlockwise turn would remain seared into his retinas for life.

Framed in the grid of the periscope was the prow of the enemy destroyer – a towering striped axe blade – ten seconds away from splitting *U-34* clean in half.

*

The camouflage stripes had lured *U-34* direct into the path of the enemy. The tail of the electric eel was almost clipped by the enemy ship as *U-34* plunged into the arms of the deep. While diving, a *Wasserbombe* hit *U-34*'s conning tower, making the entire submarine convulse. The crew stood, waiting for the three-hundred-pound depth charge to explode. Some prayed. One submariner cried. Canaris gave his rosary a final squeeze. The seconds ticked past on the control room clock – a quick, inevitable march to a tomb on the sea floor.

The interior of the control room ran with its own sweat.

The seconds beat on: *tick, tick, tick, tick, tick, tick, tick, tick.*

After a minute, the crew looked at one another. A realization ran through the men like electricity. The depth charge had failed to detonate! Passing marine life picked up strange sounds echoing from the belly of a giant tin eel – a distant roar of cheering and singing, muffled by the sea.

CHAPTER 10
'THE LOST BROTHER'

London, 1918

Inayat
Noor

On her birthday, Noor awoke to a large box wrapped in gold at the foot of her bed. She tore open the paper. Inside was a child's twelve-string harp. Her heart jumped. She sat in her nightdress and placed her fingers on the strings. Her first random notes plucked straight at her soul. She decided that when she grew up, she would be a harpist. Skipping into the dining room, Noor found a birthday cake on the table iced in a henna pattern with blue marzipan elephants in gold brocade marching around the base. That afternoon, half a dozen girls came in their party frocks to the family's new address in Bloomsbury. Inayat played Happy Birthday on his *surshringar*, made the tails to pin on the crêpe-paper donkey and afterwards told a circle of bright eyes the tale of the Tiger, the Brahman and the Jackal. Noor's best friend, Esme, left a present tied with a white silk ribbon. After the party, Noor opened it to find a box of coral-pink and gold. Inside were three tiers of gold-wrapped chocolates from Madame Charbonnel and Mrs Walker of Mayfair. Inayat said that if the birthday girl ate just one chocolate every day after supper, the box would last for weeks.

Each evening for the next month, Noor lay her head on Inayat's neck.

'Please, Papa,' came the familiar words. 'Just one.'

'*Ple-e-e-s-e-!*'

Pir, Noor's infant brother, thumped the sides of his high chair in support.

'Perhaps just one,' said Inayat, receiving a nod from Amina.

He placed his hand in his pocket and withdrew a closed fist. Noor peeled back each finger. In his palm was a chocolate wrapped in gold that might have been weaved from Inayat's robe. She took the chocolate, kissed her father's beard, and skipped from the room. Inayat imagined Noor disappearing into her bedroom, unwrapping the chocolate and allowing the praline to melt on her tongue. He smiled.

After dinner one evening, Inayat heard crying – muffled sobs from his daughter's bedroom. He knew her cry better than his own voice. Inayat motioned Amina to stay seated and crept up the stairs. He entered his daughter's room, dark save for some dying embers in the grate. Noor was sitting in bed shielding her face with a pillow. Inayat approached. Noor's face was lined with tears.

'What is it, daughter?' said Inayat.

'The shadows, Papa!' said Noor, pointing to the firelight shadows on the wall. 'The shadows want to hurt me.'

Inayat took Noor's hand.

'Come,' he said.

He opened the curtains. He held Noor at the window while Noor held Pteech-ka. Three pairs of eyes looked into a full moon.

'The only shadow is the shadow cast by the chariot of the moon god, Chandra.'

He pointed.

'See how it follows his chariot across the surface of the moon as he rides with his goddess, Rohini?'

Noor strained her eyes. There was a shadow. Maybe it was Chandra's chariot after all? Maybe she was safe? She soothed Pteech-ka.

Inayat closed the curtains.

'Back into bed, *Bābouli*.'

He held his daughter's hand and sang a mantra. Her eyelids drooped. By the end of the mantra, her breathing was even. He squeezed her hand. Pteech-ka lay on the pillow, eyes glowing in the darkness.

As he tucked his sleeping daughter under the blankets, something under her bed caught his eye: a plump Russian doll lying in two halves. What looked like treasure glinted in between. He reached down and picked up an object the size of a thimble. It was a chocolate wrapped in gold. Others were scattered in and out of the wooden doll. They were the chocolates she had prised from his fingers every night since her birthday.

Inayat mulled over the puzzle that evening. Why were the chocolates under his daughter's bed? Why were they uneaten?

At breakfast the next morning, Inayat asked a question.

'*Bābouli*, why did you keep the uneaten chocolates in the Russian doll?'

'Papa,' she said, 'I saved them for the poor Russian children… Miss Fitzgibbon said they had nothing to eat.'

*

They came for Inayat.

Mothers. Fathers. Sons. Brothers. Sisters. Widows.

Noor would take them up the stairs of the house in Bloomsbury and knock on the door of the Sad Room, where visitors came. A man in a gold robe beckoned them into a dark study lined with books on the scriptures and a trace of incense hanging in the air. There was a painting at the far end of a heart pinned with a star and a half-moon beneath, like a smile. Two giant wings fanned out from each side of the heart. Under the painting was a large, embroidered cushion.

They came in grief. Inayat received them without words.

The visitor, rich or poor, sat on the same gold cushion under the winged heart. Inayat drew up a cushion opposite and clasped the visitor's hand in his palms. There they sat, outside time. Sometimes the day beyond the room changed from light to dark and on occasion from dark to light. Inayat's hands were a channel, a conduit. Inayat's face rucked with concentration, his lips still – or moving without sound. No meaning was ascribed, no answer – just the breath of two people and the heat of the joined hands. There were times when an oasis of relief spread across the visitor's face. These were when Inayat's face was at its most taut. With each visit, another groove pressed itself into Inayat's forehead, or another hair of his beard turned to grey. He never accepted money, only token gifts when pushed.

Most visitors left in silence, setting their faces before stepping out into an indifferent crowd. Few noticed the occasional presence of two men under the lamp post opposite, the shorter wearing a homburg hat.

Once a woman reached the bottom of the stairs and sat down with her face in her hands. She gave no first name. Just 'Miss Richards'.

'He was called Milton,' she said of her brother killed on his eighteenth birthday. 'There was only the two of us.'

Tears ran into her palms and down her wrists into the sleeves of her dress.

Noor remembered the nape of her neck, white under the tumble of blonde hair, tense and pulsing. Noor thought her the most beautiful woman she had ever seen. She threw her arms around her and placed her head against her ear. Later, Noor went downstairs to prepare a plate of biscuits.

'Why is the lady crying so much, Ma?' said Noor.

'Because she lost her brother,' said Amina.

Noor set out the biscuits and took them up to Miss Richards. The woman declined the offering with a stroke of the little girl's cheek, dried her eyes, and disappeared into the street – just another hat in the oblivious, shifting crowds. Oblivious save for Detective

Rush-Williams, who had decided to close a protracted, fruit-less investigation for good. In his final report to 'Section Five', he concluded that if there ever was a Hindu-German conspiracy, the Mystic of Bloomsbury was not a party. On the contrary, he observed, Inayat Khan ran an unacknowledged field hospital for those whose wounds were hidden. His report ended with words from his favourite psalm, Psalm 147:

He heals the broken-hearted and binds up their wounds.

As the homburg disappeared into the distance, Noor put on her straw boater.

'Where might you be going, little one?' said Amina, coming up the stairs.

Noor looked round, surprised.

'I am going to find the lost brother.'

*

On the day the Great War ended, Noor was playing her harp to an audience of Inayat and Pteech-ka.

Treasure was lying, swathed in Japanese silk, ears pricked for the next set of footsteps to mount the stairs.

Georges Morel was moving through Paris, hat over his tin head, carrying a suitcase and a metal box containing his most precious possession.

Kapitänleutnant Canaris was standing on the bridge of his U-boat as it cruised into Kiel harbour. He was about to witness the most diabolical spectacle his eyes would ever behold.

PART
TWO

CHAPTER 11
'THE HOUSE
OF BLESSINGS'

Suresnes,
Paris, 1924

Inayat
Noor

Suresnes overlooked Paris. Its broad, leafy streets gave the finest view of Haussmann's architectural master plan: grandiose avenues expanding like trench lines from the iron watchtower by flowing water. The Fort Mont-Valérien, one of the city's strongest fortresses, commanded Suresnes' summit. The grounds of the fort had, after the Franco-Prussian War of 1870, become parkland. Rambling family houses sprang up around the park's outskirts. One such house, overlooking the Tour Eiffel and backing on to the Parc des Landes, was the House of Blessings.

The House of Blessings was owned by Madame Kloët, a wealthy Sufi follower. In the numb and uncomprehending aftermath of the Great War, Madame Kloët gave most of her fortune to the Sufi order in Paris that followed Rumi and the path of love. She bestowed the House of Blessings on a Sufi master whose reputation for compassion was spreading like poppies across the fields of Flanders. The Sufi in question was the mystic and musician Inayat Khan.

135

As the constellations changed, the wandering Sufi returned to the shadow of the iron watchtower. In the House of Blessings, with its generous semi-timbered rooms and large garden, his family prospered and expanded. Noor became the eldest of four.

On the first morning of 1924, Noor awoke to find a large box at the end of her bed. It was tied with a gold bow. She sat, breathless, in her nightdress and opened the box. An arch of polished spruce reflected the morning light. Her heart soared. It was a thirty-four-string harp, almost her own height. It took all her strength to extract the harp and rest it on her shoulder. The wood was smooth and had a faint aroma of mint and fir needles. She thought of the birthday recital she would play for Inayat, her most devoted and steadfast audience.

When she came downstairs Inayat was sitting, eyes closed, on a cushion under the painting of a winged heart brought from London. Inayat opened his eyes as Noor entered the room. For a moment he seemed absent, as if seeing into the Infinite, before he came into the present. He embraced Noor. It was exactly ten years since the Tartar nurse had handed him a newborn in an embroidered Russian blanket.

'*Bābouli* – Father's child.'

A silent tear ran from his face and into his beard. Inayat drew back to look at his daughter. His eyes smiled.

'Once an infant. Now ten years along the path. Ten is a blessed number.'

'Why, Papa?'

'Hold up your hands,' said Inayat. 'How many fingers do you have?'

'Ten.'

'Hold up your feet. How many toes?'

'Ten.'

Noor laughed.

'Ten is the number of Totality. The Sufi masters say we change our structure every ten years.'

That afternoon, Noor gave a concert on her new harp just for Inayat: Debussy's *Reverie*. She played, remembering the words of her old music teacher. *Music is the expression of the movement of the waters.* As her fingers weaved and plucked, Inayat joined her on his *surshringar*, infusing the Debussy with the strange, plangent Indian cadence. Their souls soared upward together. The voice of Rumi, almost inaudible, permeated the room. *Only from the heart can you touch the sky.*

At the end of the piece, Inayat turned to his daughter, his gold robe rustling.

'Now you are ten, I want you to promise me three things, *Bābouli*.'

His daughter's fingers fell from her harp.

'Promise to look again if you are in darkness. You may be the light.'

Noor knew that her father, his beard now pricked with grey, had experience of the darkness.

'Promise to remember the words of Master Rumi. He will give you the wings to fly towards a secret sky.'

'A secret sky?'

'Yes,' said Inayat. 'A secret sky.'

Noor nodded.

'And promise also never to tell a lie.'

A shadow passed over Noor's brow.

'Not even a white lie, Papa?'

'Three things cannot be long hidden: the Sun, the Moon and the Truth.'

They embraced. Inayat rose and lit a candle. Father and daughter sat on opposite cushions in the middle of the room. It was a ritual that sealed the end of day. They closed their eyes. The sounds within the house faded. As they began the familiar journey, the birdsong became distant. More distant still was the sound of Paris shedding her day clothes and preparing for evening. Two minds tumbled in the shallows and fell. They fell away from the light, through the playful surface rays towards the waveless depths of their minds. There, on the ocean floor, their minds began to settle. 'It is a still lake', said Inayat, 'that reflects the sky.' Their minds stayed on the ocean floor, unfolding in the undercurrents, until a small bell summoned them back through the stilts of sunlight up to the surface.

'Shall we walk a little in the garden before dinner?' said Inayat.

Father and daughter walked outside among colours vivid in the gloaming. They sat under the cherry tree. Inayat took an orange from the folds of his golden robe.

'Remember,' he said. 'Everything in life is speaking, despite its silence.'

His daughter looked again at the orange. Inayat unpeeled the skin with his deft, elegant fingers. He arranged the segments like a flower opening to the sun.

'Orange for the monks who follow Lord Buddha, for strength, wisdom and the colour that pervades the Wheel of Life.'

They ate the segments of the orange together in silence then dipped their fingers in a water bowl with a floating blossom. Inayat's daughter rested her head on Inayat's knee and he stroked her hair. Behind the water bowl, a single rose-head had withered brown amid its burgeoning scarlet neighbours.

'Why do we die, Papa?'

'Death is the greatest gift to the living,' said Inayat. 'Without death there cannot be new life.'

He gestured to the blossom in the water bowl.

'Every mortal will taste death, says Master Rumi. But only some will taste life.'

Inayat's eyes smiled.

'And besides,' he said, 'you can only die once.'

'I don't want you to die, Papa.'

Inayat felt his daughter's arms wrap tight around his neck. She was trembling.

'Papa. I don't want you to die.'

*

That night, Inayat sat writing in his notebook in his study. The room was a shrine to his wanderings. His *surshringar* hung from the wall. A silver samovar stood on a shelf, watched by a row of Russian icons. A trail of black obsidian rocks snaked across his desk. The rocks, known as Apache tears, came from New Mexico, where Inayat first fell into the green eyes of Amina. A yellowing programme for the concert he gave in Brighton in 1915 lay on a side table. Still tied to the programme was the letter from Sanjay, the wounded Indian soldier of the 13th Rajputs. Inayat had written to Sanjay's parents saying he had a letter from their son, which he had promised to deliver in person. Each year that passed felt like a rent in Inayat's side.

Inayat found his breath and took up his pen. As the ink began to flow, he heard crying. He looked up from his desk. He knew. He mounted the stairs with his tiger stealth and entered Noor's room. His daughter was in bed holding Pteech-ka. The wooden bird's eyes glowed ruby in the dark.

'It's the shadows, Papa.'

They were back.

Inayat smiled at his daughter's bedside.

'The shadows again?'

She nodded, though it had been almost a decade since the Zeppelins had cast their whale-shadows over London.

As she spoke, another shadow passed across the wall. It was a lamp post in the headlights of a car. She sobbed into the neck of Pteech-ka.

Inayat took Noor's hand.

'Come,' he said. 'Remember it is only the shadow cast by the moon god's chariot.'

She hid her face.

'They are not Chandra's chariot. They want to kill me!'

'On your birthday?'

'Yes, Papa!'

Inayat picked up his daughter and held her in an embrace. He offered no words, just the heat of their joined frames. Inayat closed his eyes and while he imbibed the pain another fleck of white appeared in his beard. After a time, he left Noor asleep under the covers next to Pteech-ka. Pteech-ka lay on the pillow, alert in the darkness. Inayat could sense Pteech-ka's voice. *I will keep watch.*

*

That autumn, Noor was enrolled at the École Moderne des Filles de Suresnes. Assembly fell silent when she entered the school hall. A hundred pairs of eyes looked at the girl with the limpid brown eyes and skin of burnt umber. She spoke little and listened with a strange intensity. The other girls were at a loss what to make of the dark-skinned girl who was collected in the afternoons by a father, not a mother or a governess. A father, moreover, in gold robes with a pendant ruby the size of a dragon's eye. Someone whispered that Inayat was a shaman who could turn a girl's skin into scales or strike her dumb for a hundred years.

Next a rumour went around the school that Noor was an Indian princess, descended from a warrior-king, who kept a young Bengal tiger in her garden. Rumour of the tiger helped Noor to escape the venomous stare of Mathilde, a girl with deep-set green eyes and a threadlike mouth who patrolled the school with a posse of Valkyries. They collected 'taxation': sweets or 'donations' from the junior girls' pocket money.

In class, Noor listened to Madame Vallerand reading about the Old Testament matriarchs in Scripture and Madame Proulx evoking the life of Jeanne d'Arc in History. As the lessons wore on, her eyes wandered towards the woods of Suresnes where she imagined, from Inayat's stories, a conclave of animals. Monkeys chattering in the branches, elephants tramping across the forest floor, nightjars *churring*, the moving stripes and low rumble of the tiger.

She excelled in piano. Her teacher, Mademoiselle Monette, was a recent graduate from the Conservatoire de Paris. The girls looked in wonder at the woman who, unlike the other teachers, wore her hair in a bob. She wore narrow dresses that flattened her line and lipstick of Disapproval Red. She smoked Gauloises between lessons, flicking the ash with unstudied nonchalance. There were rumours she lived 'in sin' with an artist from Madrid. She once attended the school in what resembled a man's trousers rolled above the ankle and a black jumper tucked under a belt. The headmistress, Mademoiselle de Brisac, was unamused but did not capitulate to the chorus of disapproval insisting Mademoiselle Monette should go home and change. Having been in Paris during the Commune of 1871 and in 1914, the septuagenarian *femme du monde* knew there were more dangerous things than a woman in trousers.

Mademoiselle encouraged Noor, once she had learned the notes, to enter the music – eyes open or closed, humming or silent, head straight or tilted. 'The notes are a path,' she said as Noor picked out the notes of *Eine kleine Nachtmusik*. 'A path that was left for you – nobody else. Everyone's path is different. That is why music, when played, is always alive!'

One lesson, Noor stopped playing and started to cry. Mademoiselle Monette drew her sobbing pupil to her neck.

'What's wrong?'

When Noor's tears dried, she whispered something into Mademoiselle Monette's ear.

'Does it make me *impaire* – strange? Different from other girls?'

Mademoiselle Monet smiled and took Noor's hand.

'It is nothing to be frightened of,' she said. 'It's a gift.'

*

The following term, a girl called Falinne came to the school. She was the daughter of a prosperous Parisian financier who had moved into the finest house in Suresnes. Monsieur Blumenthal, her father, maintained a large staff, including a full-time chauffeur – a wordless war veteran who never removed his chauffeur's cap. Falinne was slim with pale skin, dark eyes, a cascade of dark hair and a dramatic profile. She was self-possessed, clutching her schoolbooks to her chest as she walked, though her self-possession masked her shyness.

In Scripture, Falinne sat next to Noor at the front of the class, two pairs of dark eyes in a sea of blues and greens. Falinne carried a wooden pencil case with the photographs of her mother and father sealed on the top. The two girls learned of the Sainte Isabelle and Sainte Bernadette. In one lesson, Madame Vallerand showed an image of a woman with long brown hair kneeling on a stone step with a bowl between her hands. The stone roof of the room was only just higher than the woman's head. The walls left her only enough room to turn. There were no windows. If the woman was in captivity, her expression was beatific.

'Apart from the Crucifixion, you are witnessing the highest level of sacrifice,' said Madame Vallerand. Her eyes settled on Noor and Falinne then flicked away. 'The anchoress. Entombed alive deep within the holy walls of a church to dedicate herself to prayer, devotion and contemplation. Alone, the anchoress kept a vigil for humanity. Many died young on the spot where they prayed.'

A vigil for humanity? Noor looked again at the picture – the upturned head, beseeching eyes, unbending fingers, pale shoulders, bare feet and the suppliant folds of her dress. The image of the anchoress came to her each night. A fortnight later, Noor sat again with Inayat under the cherry tree in the garden.

'What path do you imagine the Divine Weaver is planning for your life, Noor?'

'Papa,' she said, 'I wish to be an anchoress.'

Inayat smiled and embraced his daughter.

'A life of self-sacrifice is the hardest path of all,' said Inayat. 'But as Master Rumi teaches us... *What you seek is seeking you.*'

One afternoon, towards the end of the school day, Falinne walked down the steps of the library carrying a pile of books topped with her wooden pencil case. As she walked down the main corridor, lined with a parade of blue coats on hooks, towards the assembly hall, an open palm sprang from the shadow of one of the coats.

'Taxation!' said Mathilde, her green eyes cold and assured.

'Taxation?' said Falinne.

'Half your pocket money now or you will get it.'

Mathilde was joined by two other girls, one blonde, the other a redhead with buck teeth. The three girls stood around Falinne, arms folded.

'Taxation!' said the girls in unison, palms outstretched.

Falinne could feel herself beginning to shake.

'You can afford it,' said Mathilde. 'Not all of us have our own chauffeur.'

The girls edged closer, the circle tightening. Falinne drew herself up, despite the shaking in her legs.

'Get lost!' she said.

She broke away from the circle, dropping a library book, and ran down the corridor.

'I warn you. You will suffer PAIN!' called out Mathilde.

Falinne ran on.

'*Petite Juive* – Little Jew' came a voice from behind.

In class the next morning, Mathilde stood holding what looked like a pendant.

Two of her Valkyries distracted Falinne. Noor could see Mathilde near Falinne's desk. The footsteps of Madame Proulx were approaching. Mathilde dropped the pendant into Falinne's pencil case and resumed her seat, attentive and demure. Madame Proulx took up her position by the blackboard, lips almost the same hue.

'Today, girls, we are going to learn about Marie-Antoinette, the last queen of France.'

The girls opened their exercise books. Falinne slid open her pencil case. On a pyre of pencils lay a dead baby mouse. A shriek flew across the room like a javelin. The chalk in Madame Proulx's hand dropped to the floor and broke.

Falinne ran out, face streaked.

By the end of term, Mathilde had perfected her ability with a rubber band. She held up her right thumb like a painter measuring the horizon and used the tip as a firing pin. She stretched the rubber band back to snapping point. The rubber band fired like a catapult with an accuracy that ranged between Falinne's neck and the back of her head. For Falinne, the bands were a repetitive bee sting that she pretended not to notice. For work at closer range, Mathilde used a compass.

'*Petite Juive!*' she would say with each jab.

Whenever a teacher came into class, Mathilde clasped her hands on her lap, a paragon of serene attention. The stabs continued until one day Mathilde was sticking her compass straight into an open palm. The skin of the palm was the colour of henna. Noor winced as the blood trickled from her own hand.

'ENOUGH!' she screamed. 'No more!'

Mathilde's lips pursed.

'*Chienne noire* – black bitch!'

Noor could feel the jab into her heart, but she stood immovable.

'You will both die,' said Mathilde as she went back to her desk.

At teatime, the girls sat down to fresh bread and jam. Noor stopped Falinne as she was leaving the dining room.

'Turn around,' said Noor.

Falinne turned around, straining with her neck to see over her shoulder.

The back of her blue smock was running with jam. Blobs of butter floated in the strawberry *confiture* – white corpuscles floating in the lagoon of red. Falinne's wall of defiance crumbled. Her parents would discover. She sank on to the floor, head in her arms.

'It's going to be all right,' said Noor. She offered both hands. 'Come, Falinne, up you get.'

Noor took a soft exercise book and scooped off most of the jam. The butter made streaks across the smock like lines left by a whip. Falinne continued to strain her head over her shoulder.

'Does it still show?' said Falinne.

'Only a bit,' said Noor.

'My parents will find out,' said Falinne, her jaw sunk in her palms. She began to cry.

'I have an idea,' said Noor.

Falinne looked dubious.

'Let's swap dresses!'

'Swap dresses?'

'Yes. It won't take a second.'

'Are you sure?' said Falinne.

When Inayat Khan collected his daughter that afternoon, she was wearing a smock spread with butter and jam that might have been served for tea. Noor explained what had happened as father and daughter walked through Suresnes in the late afternoon light. Inayat turned to Noor as they reached the familiar fountain on the way back to the House of Blessings.

'You acted with a compassionate heart, *Bābouli*.'

Noor looked at Inayat, eyes drinking in the tribute.

'But these things are never so simple. Can you also find compassion in your heart for the perpetrator?'

Noor looked down.

'It's hard, Papa.'

'It is hard,' said Inayat. 'Imagine for a moment if your one precious life was defined by making someone else's a misery. Imagine the sickness in your heart, and the affliction of your mind?'

'Yes, Papa.'

'The anchoress kept a vigil for all humanity, good and bad.'

Noor nodded. Inayat held his daughter in a buttery embrace.

'In any event,' said Inayat, 'a wise man once said: there is no saint without a past and no sinner without a future.'

*

The evening before the end of term, Inayat said to his daughter:

'In life, Noor, only the Divine Weaver can choose the thread. We see the pattern from below. Only the Divine Weaver sees the pattern from above. When life assails us, let these words be a comfort:

The dark threads are as needful in the Weaver's skilful hand As the threads of gold and silver in the pattern He has planned...'

The following day, the girls of the École Moderne des Filles de Suresnes stood as Mademoiselle de Brisac, the veins of her hand prominent upon her cane, entered assembly.

'Be seated, *mes filles*,' she said. 'Before we break for our holidays, I am going to tell you a story. It is a story that has been told before and doubtless will be told again. Some stories bear retelling.'

Noor and Falinne sat together in the same row, eyes looking up at Mademoiselle de Brisac.

'At the end of her days,' she began, 'a woman stood high upon a cliff overlooking the shore. She stood hand in hand with her Guardian Angel, gazing back over her life.

At the far end of the shore, she saw herself as an infant at her mother's breast.

So began the path of her life, two pairs of footprints in the sand, the woman's alongside the Angel's.

The path of her life unfolded in images that appeared, suspended above the shallows, as they traced her days along the shore.

She saw herself – uttering her first words, taking her first steps, her first day at school, her first communion, her first dance, her first kiss, her first day teaching.

She saw her wedding day, her honeymoon, her life with her husband in the warm light of their first home.

She saw herself by a blackboard in the classroom, teaching generation after generation of children, watching her hair change from brown to grey.

She saw an older woman, face etched around wise eyes, arms locked in an embrace with an older man.

She saw herself, her hair now white, at the bedside of her husband, holding his frail, mottled hand.

She saw herself, head in palms, as the family doctor shut the man's eyelids and shook his venerable head.'

Noor took Falinne's hand.

'The woman looked at the shore,' continued Mademoiselle de Brisac. 'She could see the two pairs of footprints, side by side, walking in tandem from the start of her life.

Towards the middle of the shoreline there was only one set of footprints.

Then the lone set of footprints was re-joined by another.

The footprints continued, together, side by side.

At the near end of the shore, they became – for the second time – a lone set of footprints in the sand.

The woman turned to her Guardian Angel, her face riven with pain.

"Why did you forsake me when I couldn't conceive a child?" she said. "Why did you forsake me when my husband died?"

A pair of devoted wings enveloped the woman.

> *At those times in your life,*
> said the Angel,
> *You could not walk.*
> *So I carried you.'*

CHAPTER 12
'THE TIN MAN'

Suresnes,
Paris, 1924

Morel

In an attic room in Suresnes, Georges Morel knelt to light the coal in a modest grate. He unbuttoned his uniform and sat down in a chair opposite the fireplace. On the mantelpiece stood a dented hip flask next to an old, pre-war photograph: two boys in their late teens, arms about each other's shoulders, on a beach with a craggy Breton backdrop. Under his bed was a leather bag within a locked metal box, which he checked without fail every night.

Morel took off his chauffeur's cap and placed it on a small adjacent table. It was his habit, once in private, to palm the smooth tin plate that had replaced his scalp nine years before. The metal became a magnet, pulling open the distant gates of his mind and exhuming the deep-buried thoughts. On occasion, as the thoughts assailed him, he would sit holding his head in his hands by a small fire that failed to exude any warmth – Van Gogh's *Sorrowing Old Man,* not yet thirty, sprung from the canvas.

Morel had left Val-de-Grâce with a tin head, a row of medals worth less than coins of the same size, a small pension, an unpredictable stutter, and a brother without a headstone. Since leaving hospital he had been living, like thousands of *mutilés de guerre,* in the shadows. He hid his head. He cast the silhouette of a man under a constant hat. He moved from lodging house to lodging house, with a small suitcase and a box containing a worn leather bag. He ate quiet dinners in dim-lit bistros and drank in bars where the bathrooms had nail brushes affixed to the sinks as a gesture to the single-armed. He moved from job to job – tram-driver, warehouseman, museum guard – an anonymous *homme-en-chapeau*.

In the Musée Jacquemart-André he stood as a guard on a sea of parquet. He was haunted by the Monet, the serene blue sky above a field of red poppies. In the portrait gallery he exchanged thoughts with the depictions of men and women in their prime of youth, their bodies whole, their thoughts untroubled. He wanted to jump into the figure of the Hussar, his chest swelling with braid, his pelisse hanging loose over his shoulder, his head complete. The rooms echoed with the footsteps of visitors who seldom noticed the guard, hands behind his back, looking up at the portraits.

*

After the war, Morel had noticed an '*À Vendre*' sign in the entrance of his apartment, above the photograph of a motorbike. He knocked on the door number of the owner. It was a man Morel's age called Perliot. Yes, said Perliot, he was selling. He held up his left arm, amputated just under the elbow. Morel did something rare. He removed his hat. Two survivors from Daquin's Underworld. Instant comrades.

'Let's do this over a drink,' said Perliot with a sad smile.

Each Saturday morning, Morel placed the leather helmet over the tin and sped out of Paris to go scrambling in the woods of Rambouillet or to follow the Seine north-west past Giverny to Les Andelys. He drove fast, overtaking carthorses, tractors and the few cars on the muddy country roads, shooting past fields, over bridges and around blind bends. He rode, free and unstoppable, taunting fate. At quiet country auberges he stopped for bouillabaisse and steak haché, dining outside with his leather cap – the nameless motorcyclist.

Père Morel died in 1919. He went to the station every day after Fabien was killed. Among the crowds he stood, waiting for his son. When the crowds dispersed, they left a man alone on the concourse. Waiting. He died looking out to sea, his final image a blustery picnic by the beach, his two sons splashing in the shallows.

By 1920 Morel was able to afford an imported 606cc Indian Scout motorcycle in muted red. He deepened his affinity for mechanics, stripping and reassembling the Scout's engine, ear acute to the engine note, his tin head reflecting his own engine casing. In the moments of speed, Georges Morel found a fleeting freedom and happiness – until the engine slowed at the journey's end and life returned to the slow beat of a funeral march.

His modest inheritance allowed Morel to graduate from two wheels to four. He bought a brand-new Peugeot Type 156, which he used to chauffeur the growing number of delegates who flocked to Paris for a year of peace conferences. The delegates, with their stiff collars, waxed moustaches and manicured hands, seldom took any notice of the silent man with the high colouring, fine features, and his chauffeur's cap pulled low over his forehead.

The following year, he answered an advertisement in the newspaper for a reliable chauffeur, reasonable rates and a room in the finest house in Suresnes. Monsieur Blumenthal liked the wounded veteran on sight.

'When can our new chauffeur begin?'

*

From his attic room in Suresnes, the acoustics were magnified. At six most evenings it would start – the strange, plangent cadences that summoned the chattering temple monkeys and the scent of Indian night jasmine. Morel's employer, Monsieur Blumenthal, was a well-travelled man and thought it was a *sitar*. Whatever the instrument, Morel would listen at dusk as he held his tin head in his palms. The cadences would carry Georges Morel away from Suresnes, away from Paris and away from pain where the tin cut into his scalp. Other veterans sought solace in illicit absinthe. For

Morel, it was the resonant strings and the voice full of longing and supplication.

The music came from a neighbouring address known as the House of Blessings. The head of the household was a Sufi mystic. Some said he was a guru. Sometimes Morel caught sight of him at the school gates, beard flowing over a gold robe. His turban was gold, like his robe. Morel imagined the yards of gold cloth being wrapped, layer after layer, around the head of the wearer.

Morel had worn a turban once, but he was unconscious when it was wrapped. His turban was white, but it did not stay white for long.

*

The year 1924 saw Paris hosting the Games of the Eighth Olympiad. The boulevards were emblazoned with images of athletes drawn like Apollo standing in threes, physiques overlaid, their profiles turning towards a common glory.

Paris marvelled at the Apollo-athletes, hurdling, vaulting and swimming.

Paris wanted to forget about the cornfield of youth mown down to stubble.

Paris wanted the *mutilés de guerre* to disappear.

*

The summer solstice approached while the Games were under-way. Had Fabien lived, it would have been his thirtieth birthday. Georges Morel locked the door of his room, knelt by his bed and removed a metal box. He placed a key in the lock and extracted a leather bag. From the bag he removed a semi-automatic Luger. He laid the gun on the table as if it were black porcelain. He looked at the pistol, an innocuous provider of death, with a weak smile. His brother's last gift. He laid out a cloth and set to work.

He un-cocked the safety catch and removed the magazine. He extracted the bullets and laid them in the shape of a fan. He looked down the Luger's barrel, zeroing in on a single flower of wallpaper. He rotated the locking bolt, lifted out the trigger plate,

151

and slid off the receiver axle. He removed the internal mechanism and extracted the firing pin. He laid out the parts, like pieces of a jigsaw. He proceeded to clean each piece, and to oil the locking bolt and the underside of the receiver. He replaced the bullets in the magazine, reassembled and reloaded the Luger. He was ready.

It always felt strange making a pilgrimage through the streets of Paris with a loaded Luger. Morel felt a familiar sense of calm as his palm reminded itself of the contours of the pistol. With his other hand he pulled the brim of his hat down low, concealing the other metal he carried everywhere.

He crossed the Pont d'Arcole and headed along the Quai aux Fleurs. His hat was pulled so far down he could see only the ground as he walked, nearer and nearer to the destination. He stood with his back to the Seine and looked skywards. The two towers loomed above the House of Our Lady, guarded by gargoyles. The sight never failed to send a frisson down his back. His shoes echoed on the marble floor inside as he walked. He was aware of disapproving looks from people around him for not removing his hat. Morel kept his focus, moving from the nave to the rose window in the north transept, its kaleidoscope of violets and blues fanning out from the glass stamen at the centre.

Morel approached the votive stand where several candles were flickering, dripping on to the sand-tray below. He took a candle and wrote in the sand:

F.M.M. 21-6-94

'*Bon anniversaire*,' said Morel as he lit the candle. '*Repose en paix*.'

The candle wick flared up then retracted to the flame of a matchhead. Drips from the candle started to fall on the sand, blurring the letters and numbers.

Until next year, *mon frère*, he thought as he descended the steps of Notre Dame, palm over the Luger, and stepped into the luminous night.

CHAPTER 13
'THE CHERRY TREE'

Suresnes,
Paris, 1926

Inayat
Noor

Inayat Khan sat in his study overlooking the garden. It was May and the flowers, lissom and supple, were courting the sun. He saw Noor sitting on a rug under a parasol reading a story to her sister, both girls in white on an ocean of chartreuse green. A choir of thrushes sang in the trees, modulated by the tapping of a woodpecker. From the oak opposite came the sound of Inayat's sons playing in their tree house.

He looked at the roses, languid heads on necks of thorn. He saw Amina in a sun hat, training a rose bush along a trellis at the far end of the garden – petals and leaves snaking through the wooden squares. Did the Crown of Thorns once bear flowers? As Inayat Khan watched, the tune of the thrushes intensified, along with the woodpecker's tap. Bees added a base hum. Inayat strained his ears for the minuscule pulse in the veins of the rose petals carried by the stem of thorns. He took a pen from an inkwell and opened his notebook.

'When we pay attention to nature's music,' he wrote, 'we find that everything on the Earth contributes to its harmony.'

He smiled and looked back at the garden, at Amina, at the children, the flowers and the trees. Was his decision wise? He knelt and made the prayer of *Istikharah*, invoking once again the guidance of the Form Giver and Knower of the Unseen. The response was clear – adding to the harmony from beyond the open window. When Inayat first announced his pilgrimage to India, his older son thumped the table and ran from the room. His younger daughter would not stop crying.

'I don't want you to go, Papa,' she said, sobbing into Inayat's breast. Noor held her sister's hand and bit her lip.

When his son returned, eyes reddened, Inayat drew his family around him. His youngest sat on his lap, holding the ruby that hung from his neck.

'I left Baroda as a young man,' said Inayat. 'I have never returned to our Motherland and the opportunity may never arise again.' He stroked his beard, curling the white tip around his forefinger. 'And life's journey must include one visit to Lord Shiva's own city on the banks of the Ganges.'

His children stared at the floor. Amina looked resigned.

'There is a month before I travel,' said Inayat. 'Let us make each day a celebration!'

Inayat's Sunday afternoons with Noor assumed a greater significance. Inayat spoke for longer, as they sat together under the cherry tree or followed the roses around the garden perimeter.

'Why do we breathe, *Bābouli?*'

'We breathe to live?' said Noor.

'Precisely!' said Inayat. 'For most, breathing is passive. It should be active. Divine Breath pervades the Universe. Breathing is the very act of living. And a well-tuned mind has an easy breath.'

Inayat laid a rug down in the middle of the lawn. Father and daughter sat facing each other, cross-legged. Inayat instructed his apprentice in three types of breath:

- *Adham pranayama*: abdominal breath.
  - *Madhyam pranayama*: mid-chest breath.
    - *Adhyam pranayama*: upper-chest breath.

Noor imitated her father, taking deep inhalations – the first series into her abdomen, then into her ribcage, then into the space under her collarbones. At the end of the breathing, Inayat placed his third finger between his eyebrows – 'the seat of the third eye' – and sat as still as a Buddha. Noor did the same. Father and daughter. Two breathing statues.

Inayat rubbed his palms together at speed, generating a sudden and powerful heat. He placed both hands over his closed eyes, the heat evaporating over his eyelids. He sat for several minutes, palms like eyepatches.

Through Inayat, the words of Nawaz Ali Shah echoed from the tomb in Ahmedabad. *In times of strife, always find and follow your breath.*

*

Preparations for the summer solstice started early in the House of Blessings. Noor oversaw Inayat's ceremonial robe as well as the costumes for her siblings. She polished the moonstone to pin at the front of his turban. There was something about the day that was different, a Zeppelin-shaped cloud over the house that neither rained nor dispersed.

At five in the afternoon, Inayat called for his daughter. It was unusual, thought Noor. Five was the teaching hour for Inayat. When she saw her father by the window of his study, he looked as if Time had robbed him of a decade. She saw the old man her father would become, and her heart felt like bursting.

There were three books set out on the table, each bound in leather.

~ *The Wisdom of Rumi*
~ *The Conference of the Birds*
~ *The Vajrayāna Scriptures*

He placed his palm on *The Wisdom of Rumi*. 'For the path of the soul, *Bābouli*.'

He pointed at the book with painted birds on the cover, straining their necks to hear the sermon of a hoopoe bird. 'For the path to self-discovery,' said Inayat.

He pointed to the scriptures with an open palm. 'For the path to Enlightenment.'

He inscribed each book.

'Before you speak, says Master Rumi, let your words pass through three gates. Is it true? Is it necessary? Is it kind?'

Inayat smiled and kissed Noor on her forehead.

'Few in life ever see the master pattern,' said Inayat.

Noor's eyes looked towards the treetops in the garden.

'It is always there for those who seek to find.'

'I will seek the pattern,' said Noor.

Inayat gathered the books and handed them to Noor.

'Of course you will, my daughter,' said Inayat with an open smile.

In her bedroom that evening, Noor put the books down on a table beside her bed. She thought of Inayat's words. Few in life ever see the master pattern. She took the book of Rumi and opened a page at random. There were two lines in the centre.

You, my dearest, are not a drop in the ocean
You are the entire ocean in a drop.

*

The summer retreat finished at the House of Blessings. There was a short respite for Inayat to make his final preparations. The morning Inayat was due to leave, he called Noor to his study. He was sitting at his desk under the painting of the winged heart. The study was different. The books, loose pages of Arabic calligraphy, prayer beads and obsidian rocks were housed in unfamiliar symmetry on the shelves. On the floor sat a copper Ottoman kettle and two glasses on a silver tray. Inayat beckoned Noor to sit on one of the two cushions set out next to the kettle. He took the kettle and poured out two cups of hibiscus tea. Noor took the tea and looked at her father. His beard had been clipped into an elegant point and his eyes, behind the creases, radiated purpose.

Inayat sipped his tea and replaced the glass on the tray. He turned his palms to the ceiling. Noor followed.

'When we find dark threads in the tapestry, remember we see only the pattern from below. But how do we move through the patches of darkness? Look at your palm, Noor.'

Noor looked palm-wards.

'I want you to imagine something that troubles you.'

Noor closed her eyes. She thought of Mathilde.

'Visualize the subject and shrink it in your mind to something that can stand in the palm of your hand.'

She thought of Mathilde the height of a matchstick, standing in her upturned hand.

'Now turn the image into a symbol.'

Noor imaged Mathilde as a miniature playing card – the Queen of Spades.

'Now I want you to place the symbol within a golden bubble.'

Noor closed her eyes, her brow furrowed. It was done. The playing card was suspended in a diaphanous sphere.

'Now let the bubble float from your hand. Float up into the middle of the room and out of the window...'

Noor could feel her palm rising. The Queen of Spades was gone. The room felt lighter.

'Your mind can guide you through anything. It can take you anywhere. It is a canvas that you can fill with any picture. Shall we explore?'

'Yes, Papa.'

'First let us find our breath. Let us close our two eyes and let the third eye see inward. What do we see?'

The words came with a dreamy torpor, petals scattered upon water.

'A mountain with snow...

A mountain without snow…
A pyramid under the sun…
A pyramid under the moon…
A tree with leaves…
A tree without leaves…
A sky with stars…
A sky without stars…
A desert of black sand…
A desert of white sand…
A lake with mist rising…
A lake without mist…
A valley with a stream…
A valley with no stream…
A minaret with a bird circling…
A minaret with no bird…'

As Inayat's words continued, the images flickered in Noor's mind. Her head felt heavy and fell forward, jerking from time to time. She was not asleep, neither was she awake. When Inayat rang his bell at the end, Noor's eyes opened under heavy lids. Inayat's eyes were smiling. He turned to the window.

'Many things in life will fail, Noor,' he added. 'But not your *Sankalpa.*'

'Papa, what is *Sankalpa*?'

Inayat touched the space of his third eye with his third finger.

'Your *Sankalpa*, Noor, is your heart's deepest intention that seeks inception and fulfilment. It speaks to the larger arc of our lives. To fulfil our *Sankalpa* is the rule that must be followed above all rules.'

'The rule that must be followed above all rules?'

'Yes, *Bābouli*,' said Inayat Khan, eyes bright.

On the evening of his departure, Inayat was dressed in his gold robe. He stood outside the house in Suresnes next to an ancient leather suitcase that had accompanied him to England before the war, and his *surshringar* in a long, mottled instrument case. The family stood on the front steps, clutching each other's hands. Noor's brothers looked away to hide their tears. Noor's uncle brought the car round to take Inayat to the Gare de Lyon for the first part of his journey by overnight train to Istanbul. Inayat made a silent supplication for the protection of his family. Noor's uncle fastened the suitcase and *surshringar* on to the roof. Inayat turned to his wife and children, held his hand over his heart and in a flash of gold vanished into the car.

As the car drove off, the sky came out in a mauve-grey bruise.

*

The day after Inayat left, Amina gave Noor a letter.

'Papa asked me to give this to his firstborn.'

She kissed Noor on her forehead.

For Bābouli

She opened the letter.

Under the blossom where we sat and talked lies the Mother of the Universe.
By the time the Navagraha reunite us,
You will have unravelled the knot.

She read and reread the words.

'Under the blossom where we sat and talked.' That was the cherry tree. She had heard Inayat talk before about the Mother of the Universe. What was she doing in the garden? The *Navagraha* she knew were the planetary deities from a painting in Inayat's study. What was the knot?

She went into the garden. Behind the cherry tree was a mound of bare earth. She scooped it away with her hand. She saw a glint of silver. It was a locket. Engraved on the front was Durga, the Mother of the Universe, all eight hands cupping the sky. She opened the locket. Inside was a curled piece of paper. The lines, printed, read:

It is so close you cannot see it.
It is so profound you cannot fathom it.
It is so simple you cannot believe it.
It is so good you cannot accept it.
What is it?

*

Varanasi
India, 1927

Inayat

The Sādhu stood waist-deep in the water. His chest was bare save for a garland of flowers. His forehead, under a loose orange turban, was smeared white with a paste of holy ash and ivory pigment. A bindi, a daub of red, sat above the Sādhu's third eye. From the steps leading down to the river, funeral pyres carried the souls of the dead into the evening air.

'My own funeral took place the year Empress Victoria died,' said the Sādhu, waving towards the funeral pyres. 'I was reborn a Sādhu. I possess nothing, but I am free.'

The man opposite nodded, a mane of grey hair brushing his shoulders.

The Sādhu filled a hollowed-out skull with water and poured it over the man's head nine times. 'Nine for the nine gates of the body,' said the Sādhu as he poured out the spirit of the Ganges. 'The nine planets in the heavens and the nine incarnations of Lord Vishnu, Protector of the World. Peace and blessings be upon you.'

A flotilla of paper boats drifted past the two men, each carrying a thumb-sized candle. Among them a small figure floated, face down, wrapped in a white shroud. A child? The candle-boats continued down the river, buoyed by the chants from the riverbank that weaved through the air into the smoke.

The following day, Inayat Khan finished his tour of the temples of Varanasi. In the morning he stood in awe outside the scarlet Durga Temple, its reflection rippling red in the tributary of the holy river. Inside the temple a statue of Durga, Mother of the Universe, looked at Inayat with assured almond eyes, from astride a tiger. Two of her hands were busy with a bow and arrow, while the other six were poised like wings. In the afternoon he bathed in the rays of the Earth's own sun – the dome of the Kashi Vishwanath Temple fashioned from so much gold it glowed like a molten sunset. Spires and domes, scarlet and gold... Inayat closed his eyes. He could almost hear the trot of *Orlov* horses pulling *troikas* through the streets of Moscow.

From Varanasi, Inayat Khan made his way to Agra and on to the dusty pink of Jaipur. In a village outside Jaipur, Inayat found a grief-aged couple living in a hut of corrugated iron. He delivered the letter, as promised. Sanjay's mother offered Inayat tea and invited him to read it aloud.

Darling Mata and Baba –

I love you both more than there are stars in the Nakṣatras.

Although far from home, I am not scared. My tears fall only because I will not embrace you both again this life, my blessed Mata and Baba...

Inayat read each word. They sat, as he read, in a skein of grief. All three joined hands. Inayat closed his eyes and whispered an extended funeral prayer.

They waved to him as he left. Two small figures, remembering. That evening, Inayat took out his notebook. The ink gave his thoughts life.

My heart has been rent and joined again;
My heart has been broken and again made whole;
My heart has been wounded and healed again;
A thousand deaths my heart has died, and thanks be to love, it lives yet.

*

From Jaipur he travelled overnight to a city he had left as a young man with coal-black hair parted at the side, shaven cheeks, a dark suit and open white shirt, a *surshringar* in a mottled instrument case, and eyes full of hope.

161

The man returning had long grey hair, a beard tipped with white, skin of wrinkled parchment, a long gold robe and eyes still full of hope. He was walking down the familiar street half a mile from the palace gardens, still recognizable, to the house that was once his grandfather's.

Inayat Khan was back in Baroda.

Outside a pair of rusting gates chained with a heavy lock, a weary traveller set down a battered suitcase and a dust-covered instrument case. The gates cast bars of light into a garden over-grown with trumpet vine and goat weed. The veranda was overrun by wild jasmine, bright white stars piercing an evergreen cosmos. Inayat approached the gate and stood on tiptoes. In a slow blink, Time somersaulted.

He could see a table set for forty-five on the lawn, with chairs of crimson velvet and cushions of silk. The feast for his father's birthday. The vision in his father's study… Inayat was brought into the present by the tapping of a stick. An old man with compassion-ate eyes and few teeth was standing like a decrepit sentry. From the strangled sound in his throat, Inayat realized he was dumb. The man pointed his stick at the garden then pointed it up to the sky. Inayat looked quizzical. 'The prince is gone,' said his eyes. 'It is forbidden!'

Inayat smiled and laid his hand on the man's shoulder.

'I lived here once,' said Inayat.

The old man looked at the visitor. With his gold robe and long grey hair, he looked more like a Sādhu than an heir.

'If you wish, I can tell you the layout of the house, including the three secret tunnels leading from the kitchens. I can tell you where the crest of Tipu Sultan is painted in the meeting chamber on the first floor. I can even show you the initials carved at the base of the weathervane in 1894.'

The old man blinked. He stood as if frozen to the spot by Lord Shiva. He turned his palms to the sky.

'You came back!' sang his eyes.

He dropped to his knees.

'Rise, blessed friend,' said Inayat, helping the old man to his feet.

Words came stillborn to the man's mouth. He gestured with his stick for Inayat to stay by the gate. The old man would return. As Inayat waited, he recalled from the recesses of his mind one of the household's tandoor cooks who was unable to speak.

Ten minutes later, the old man came back with a boy of about fourteen. The boy wore a fresh white shirt over trousers that hung with loose folds of cotton. He placed his palms together and bowed to Inayat. Inayat bowed, though inside he felt a twist in his heart. The boy, with his perfect face and tendrils of black hair falling over his eyes, could have been the younger brother of Sanjay.

'I am Tanveer,' said the boy. The boy placed his hand on the old man's shoulder. 'This is my grandfather. He keeps watch over the property though it has been deserted since many years. My grandfather once cooked for the old prince.'

The boy withdrew a rusty brass key from his trousers and opened the lock. The chains around the gate fell open, interrupting a summit of bonnet-macaque monkeys. The monkeys darted from a fig tree overhanging the veranda, scattering broken figs on the ground. The old man led the way, stooping to brush the ground with his stick to flick away snakes. The three stood in the garden, Inayat, the old man and the boy. Nature had invaded every part, but it was still the garden in which Inayat had climbed the pawpaw trees as a child and sipped tea in the afternoons with his brothers under the lazy sway of a palm leaf. Inayat looked up at the house. It stood like an ageing beauty, hair wild, face unpainted – but nevertheless captivating. The twin domes still stood high above the façade, each supported by a ring of arches. Two macaques sat together on the windowsill of his old bedroom. It was, despite the death of his parents, the same enchanted house.

As Inayat looked towards the sun, he realized the light was causing a stabbing ache behind his eyes. Surely, he thought, it was just the brightness. And perhaps, the memories. Tanveer indicated

the house was unsafe to enter. Where was Sahib intending to stay?
The old man stamped his stick on the ground. He made a series
of gesticulations with his hands accompanied by the half-formed
words of a tongue unable to speak. He stamped his stick again. The
boy nodded that he understood.

'If you are willing to enter a poor house, Sahib,' said Tanveer,
'my family can provide you with lodgings.'

Inayat looked at the old man and the boy with radiance.

'Sahib, you are our family,' said Tanveer, bowing.

Through the streets of Baroda there walked an old man with a
stick, a man in a gold robe, and a boy carrying a battered suitcase
and a *surshringar*. It was into a modest but spotless house behind
the market that Inayat was ushered by Tanveer's parents.

'You do us an honour,' said Tanveer's father, placing his hands
together. 'Our house is humble, Sahib, but our house is your house.'

Inayat Khan spent one of the most gratifying weeks of his
pilgrimage in the simple house behind the market. In the morning
he wrote from a window besieged by the scent of cumin, cinnamon, turmeric and garam masala. In the afternoons he went to
his old house with the old man or with Tanveer and stood, goat
weed curling about his ankles, in the wild, hypnotizing garden of
his boyhood. In the evening he opened his *surshringar* and sang
to a circle of bright eyes that were Tanveer's family and guests. As
his stay came to an end, Inayat sewed a generous number of rupees
and one of his rings into a silk bag. He set the bag on his desk
against an inkwell with a card:

Unstitch the weave when I am gone

Then it struck.

Fever.

What first picked up his scent on the train from Jaipur had
stalked him in silence through the streets of Baroda. Now the
fever stepped out from the shadows. It pressed Inayat Khan

prostrate on his bed. It pooled behind his eyes, making it impossible to look into the light. It ran in streams of perspiration across his forehead and into his beard. It circled his heart and crept into his veins. At times Inayat Khan was so hot he thought he was lying on a road in the dust of Rajasthan in the midday sun. Other times he was so cold he thought he was embedded in a block of ice at the North Pole.

Tanveer came to Inayat's room every half hour with fresh lemonade and a damp towel for his forehead.

In the distance, Inayat could hear Tanveer's mother and father speaking in urgent, hushed tones. He heard the guttural attempts of the old man to make words – plaintive and anxious.

On the third day, Tanveer's father moved the marital bed away from the wall. He pulled back some frayed ends of carpet. He took a knife and cut around the outline of a brick. He pulled up the brick to reveal an old leather purse. It contained the family's only savings. He withdrew the purse and replaced the brick.

He took Tanveer by the elbow.

'You must fetch Doctor Kapoor,' he said.

'How will we pay?' said Tanveer.

His father held up the purse.

'Go, Tanveer!' he said.

In twenty minutes, Tanveer returned with Dr Kapoor. The doctor came with his medical case and a deep frown.

Dr Kapoor was shown into Inayat's room.

Inayat Khan was present in shivering body, but his mind was spinning. He was in Moscow... the cloister of a monastery... snow was falling on his shoulders... he was in a room with icons... he was holding a baby in his arms... he was holding his firstborn...

'*Bab-Bab-Bab-Bab-Bab-Bab*...' rasped the voice of Inayat Khan.

Not only is the patient racked with fever, thought Dr Kapoor, he is semi-conscious and babbling. His frowned deepened. He took Inayat's temperature and listened to his heart. From his case he placed a blue-coloured tincture in a bottle on the table.

'Three times a day,' said Doctor Kapoor to Tanveer's father.

'Will he live?'

'Now, it is with the gods,' said Doctor Kapoor, emptying the gold coins into his waistcoat pocket.

The doctor raised his hat and was gone.

Stars bright as white jasmine came out that night, but no moon.

As dawn broke over Baroda, the soul of Inayat Khan left his body, hovered in the room, curled through the window and dispersed on the wind.

*

A beam of light flashed through Noor's head.

She sat upright.

Something had happened.

She heard Inayat's voice in her ear.

It was different. Disembodied.

'Let your sacrifice define your love.'

What sacrifice?

There was something else.

In the night something had *run*.

The next morning, she found her nightdress streaked the colour of pain. Would she die? She washed the nightdress over and over, but the stain remained. When Amina heard Noor crying, she knocked and entered her bedroom. Noor held the nightdress in a ball on her lap. Amina unrolled the nightdress and embraced her daughter. The streaks were sacred, she said. A gift direct from the moon goddess, Rohini. They would bring new life.

A month later, a telegram arrived at the House of Blessings announcing the death of Inayat Khan. The House of Blessings fell silent. In the garden, the cherry tree wept with falling petals. Amina took to her room, drew the curtains, and wed herself to the amniotic darkness.

Noor sat alone under the cherry tree. Her Shadow-Protector was dead. Was this part of the Divine Weaver's plan? What other dark threads were waiting to be woven? Her tears would not stop.

Thrushes gathered in the branches of the cherry tree. One bird tilted its head at the book on her lap. Rumi's words came in the voice of Inayat. *Death, Dearest One, is our wedding with Eternity.*

CHAPTER 14
'THE RARE BOOKSELLERS'

London, 1928

Marks

On the edge of London's Theatreland stood Marks & Company Antiquarian Booksellers of 84 Charing Cross Road. The bookshop boasted something for every taste: ornithology, art history, horse-breeding, hot-air ballooning, archery, heraldry, cryptography, dream interpretation, calculus, numerology, Egyptology, hieroglyphics, ectoplasm, pantheism, Jewish mysticism, and the Kabbalah. Some clients, for whom Mr Marks held up an umpire's single index finger, were allowed up to the first floor – one of the largest international libraries on freemasonry. A few, for whom Mr Marks signed a chit and raised an index and middle finger, were allowed past the rope outside the door on the second floor – a specialist collection of books on symbolism, magic and the occult. There was a corner of the second floor that was curtained off – a select library dedicated to 'anatomical drawings' bound in vellum.

The proprietors were seasoned operators. When a newcomer came for a valuation, they could tell within seconds whether he had any expertise – or just wanted a quick sale, as Mr Cohen put it, '...to take his good lady out for a fish supper and a night at the pictures'.

Once a schoolmaster came to the shop with a copy of what looked like an early edition of *Paradise Lost*. It was from the forced sale, said the schoolmaster, of a country house in Worcestershire and he wanted to know if it was worth anything. Mr Marks showed his coldest *sang froid* as he strummed – antiquarian booksellers never 'thumbed' – the pages. It almost certainly was the first edition. A first edition, moreover, that would lead to a handsome retirement for both himself and Mr Cohen.

'Difficult to say, sir,' said Marks. 'Folio edition by the looks of it, and one of a fair number. But it's in good condition – I'll give you that.' He took off his glasses and held the book up to the light. He opened it quarter- and centrefold. *Blimey*. It was the first edition. His heart was beating like a piston.

'We're in the fifteen- to twenty-pound range, sir, but only if I can persuade my colleague, Mr Cohen.'

The schoolmaster's eyes widened.

'Blow me down!' he said.

'Of course,' said Mr Marks as a trickle of sweat ran down his back, 'you're welcome to take it elsewhere for a second opinion.'

The schoolmaster shook his head. He was off to take up a teaching post in Simla and was leaving from Southampton the next day. A chunk of his salary in advance would come in more than handy. Messrs Marks and Cohen stood to one side, as if discussing cricket scores. Mr Marks returned.

'Persuaded, sir! – But not without a fight.'

He drew a twenty-pound note from the till with suitable veneration and provided the delighted schoolmaster with a leathery note and a receipt. As the bell above the door rang the schoolmaster out, Mr Marks took out a bottle of Scotch from a bottom drawer.

'I do believe, Mr Cohen, that Marks & Company has just acquired a Milton first edition worth five hundred pounds.'

'I do believe, Mr Marks, that your estimate is an understatement.'

The two men linked arms and danced a jig.

Marks & Co. ran to its own rhythm.

✓ Opening up.
✓ Morning coffee.
✓ Elevenses.
✓ Crescendo into lunch.
✓ The long afternoon swallow-diving into tea.
✓ Stacking up.
✓ Cashing up.
✓ Turning the key on another day.

The wiser clients fitted their visits around the timetable. Mr Marks' favourite hour was just before five. It meant closing time was on the horizon, tea was about to arrive and during term time the bell would soon announce the arrival of his son – known to all at Marks & Co. as 'Young Leo'. No one had considered what 'Young Leo' might be called when a boy of eight turned into a man.

The bell above the door rang, followed by a stampede of foot-steps. Everyone had the same thought at the same time. How could a small boy make so much noise?

'Afternoon, Young Leo,' said Frank, the general manager, a pile of books under his chin.

The boy looked up from under a nest of curls.

'Hi, Mister Frank,' said Leo, putting down his satchel and making for the plate of biscuits set out by the till.

Marks senior wandered over and gave his son's curls a ruffle.

'Learn anything today?' said Mr Marks.

'Only that Mr Van Twisk is actually round the twist.'

'Bit 'arsh, Young Leo,' said Marks senior.

'He reckons a prime number is the same as a lucky number.'

'Can't it be both?' said Mr Marks.

'Only if you want an infinite number of lucky numbers,' said his son. 'Then which one would be lucky?'

'What's wrong with an infinite supply of lucky numbers?' said Mr Cohen.

'Well, if you were standing behind someone with an infinite supply of lucky numbers in the queue for the lottery, you would be there... forever,' said Leo.

'Just 'avin' a larf,' said Mr Cohen, pinching Young Leo's cheek.

Young Leo bit into a biscuit with a cross between a sulk and a smile.

On alternate Thursdays, Marks & Co. stayed open late. Mr Cohen made a vat of sweet apple tea laced with enough Jura whisky to set fire to Charing Cross Road and adjoining streets. Other book dealers and selected punters knocked three times on the door before being ushered up to the first floor for a cup of 'Mr Cohen's tea', some shop talk and a game of chess. Mr Marks weaved around the room pouring eighty per cent proof tea into Marks & Co.'s best crockery as if the bookshop was in Prohibition-starved New York.

Young Leo was allowed to play chess, his favourite game, only after his lesson with Uncle Abraham. Uncle Abraham was a semi-permanent fixture at Marks & Co. On chess nights he arrived at six with his long black *rekel* coat, black fedora and violin. He was technically Young Leo's Great-Uncle Abraham, but he was known to all as 'Uncle Abe'. With his long white fork beard, he looked to Young Leo about a hundred, though eyes behind the creases shone and his frame was nimble. He spoke in a rasp, with the elegant fingers of his left hand folded around his right.

While Mr Cohen's tea was being drunk with enthusiasm, Young Leo and Uncle Abe sat opposite each other in a small anteroom warmed by a meagre coal fire. It was in the same room eighteen months before that Uncle Abe had first opened his black leather notebook.

He wrote three symbols:

א

ב

ג

'Are they code, Uncle Abe?' said an even Younger Leo.

'In a way,' smiled Uncle Abe. 'They are the first three letters of our writing.'

'Like a, b, c?' said Leo.

'Just like a, b, c!'

Uncle Abe gave the symbols sounds.

א	'Alef'
ב	'Bet'
ג	'Gimel'

'And these are the last three.'

ר

ש

ת

'x, y, z?' said Leo, excitement rising.

Uncle Abe nodded and gave voice to the symbols.

ר	'Resh'
ש	'Shin'
ת	'Tav'

After months of practice, Leo Marks was reading and writing ancient Hebrew, the enigmatic code coming to life as he sat with Uncle Abe, running his finger across the page and speaking aloud words from the Torah.

'You are turning into a good Hebrew reader,' rasped Uncle Abe, patting Young Leo's curls.

In their most recent lesson, Uncle Abe said something surprising.

'Sometimes, Leo,' said Uncle Abe, 'it is possible to hide a word inside a word.'

172

'How?'

'Supposing instead of the first letter of our alphabet you used the last?'

Leo looked puzzled.

'So instead of writing Alef א,' said Uncle Abe, 'you would write Tav ת instead.'

'And for Bet ב?' said Leo.

'You would write Shin ש.'

'That means Gimel ג would be Resh ר!' said Leo.

'Indeed so,' said Uncle Abe.

'So גבא would be written רשת?' said Leo.

'It would,' said Uncle Abe, 'if you were reading left to right. Remember in the old speech we write from right to left.'

Young Leo took up his pencil.

'So that means אבג would be written תשר?'

Uncle Abe handed Young Leo a sixpence.

'What if you changed the letters *again*?' said Leo. 'So that א becomes ת and then ת moves one letter up the alphabet to become ש?'

'The possibilities are as endless as the stars,' said Uncle Abe, eyes twinkling.

The next chess night, Uncle Abe arrived as usual with black *rekel* coat, violin and fedora.

'I have a challenge for you, Young Leo,' said Uncle Abe, setting down his violin. 'If you can beat me at chess, we can skip a week's Hebrew.'

Excitement burst in Young Leo.

'Seriously, Uncle Abe?'

'Seriously.'

Embers from the coal fire in the room off the first floor glowed as an old man in a black fedora and a boy with a hive of dark curls set up their opposing armies. They agreed five minutes per move on Uncle Abe's pocket watch. Uncle Abe came from a family of chess masters and, though out of practice, he tied an invisible

napkin behind his neck as he prepared to devour a sparrow. Young
Leo chose white and Uncle Abe, with a sweep of his palm, offered
the boy first move.

Two pairs of eyes twinkled in the firelight as Young Leo opened
the game. The boy thought of his hero, Grandmaster Réti, at the
Karlsbad International Chess Tournament in 1923. He chose the
King's Indian Attack as deployed by Réti – aggressive without
being reckless, modest without being dull. It was a solid opening for sure, thought Uncle Abe, as he drew enemy fire with two
initial sacrifices. Uncle Abe had to remind himself to give the boy a
chance. He allowed the boy to mass his ranks in the central squares
while he prepared a sly counter-attack along white's queen-side
flank with two knights and a bishop.

Next door, the party was approaching full swing, fuelled with
Mr Cohen's eighty per cent proof tea. Sudden peals of laughter
erupted along with intermittent applause. In the narrow anteroom,
there was silence save for the occasional tap of a chess piece landing. At one stage, the door flew open and a guest stumbled in like
a cruise-line passenger bursting into the engine room. The man
clambered to his feet and, seeing two pairs of wolf-like eyes look
up, beat an instant retreat. The minutes ticked by, enemy prisoners
of black and white swelling on either side.

Uncle Abe found himself leaning forward on his elbow, his
payots – sidelocks – falling away from his face. He had allowed the
boy to dominate the centre squares without shoring up adequate
defences. The boy had spotted the counter-attack and pounded his
advance guard with a rook and bishop. Uncle Abe's heart began to
thump under his *rekel* coat as the boy rallied his army for an all-out
attack on the black king. The game was at risk. He pushed the
fedora back, exposing tiny specks of perspiration on his forehead.

Uncle Abe grouped the remnants of the black army around
an exposed king, then tried a second counter-attack. More
prisoners, black and white, were taken from an ever bleaker
battlefield. Black had three pieces remaining, white had four.

The tournament proceeded to endgame, each side clinging to its torn flag, until both players declared a stalemate and knocked over their respective kings.

The old man and the boy shook hands. Uncle Abe breathed an inward sigh of relief. Did talent come through the genes? What would he have said if he had lost? The pair emerged blinking into the wall of cigarette smoke and whisky tea vapour. Uncle Abe stood in the centre of the room with his hand on the boy's shoulder. He took the violin from his case and with his long, elegant fingers played the *Golem Tanz*.

*

One sultry morning, the service bell of Marks & Co. announced a visitor. A woman entered wearing a white summer dress and a white cloche hat tied with a cream bow. The hair under the hat was ash blonde. The legs under her dress were sheathed in white silk stockings. She walked in a pair of cream flapper shoes with high heels and a buckle strap. She sashayed over to the desk and stood with one leg flicked behind, like a stork. She pushed her midriff against the desk, exaggerating her most pronounced curve.

She was one of Marks & Co.'s most exacting clients.

'Now, there's a lady who could spot a Thackeray first edition from Cambridge Circus,' said Mr Cohen.

Where the lady in question had gained such an encyclopaedic knowledge of books, she never divulged.

While not in her first flush of youth, she retained her scarlet lips and cobalt stare – and an ability to reduce men to jelly.

There was a time when men in top hats called her 'Treasure'.

There was a time when Mr Marks called her 'Miss Richards'.

There was a time when she told Mr Marks to call her just plain 'Doris'.

It was a standing joke on the shop floor that Doris was anything but plain.

Mr Cohen was always amused to see how Doris could turn Mr Marks to blancmange.

'Well now, Mr Marks,' said Doris, a voice of sandpaper on quartz, 'any progress on the Kipling? You promised me an early edition, Mr Marks.'

'Your order', said Mr Marks, colouring, 'has been given the highest priority.'

'I'm sure it has, Mr Marks. But when will I hold it here?' said Doris, palms open like a book.

'Two more weeks,' said Mr Marks, conjuring up a figure.

'Is there anything I can do to expedite the process, Mr Marks?' said Doris, leaning further forward. 'Anything?'

'Nothing at all,' said Mr Marks, sounding as confident as a young man at his first dance.

'Are you sure?'

'Sure,' said Marks senior. 'Come back in a fortnight and I'll have a package waiting for you.'

'I should be so lucky,' said Doris.

Then, to the amusement of all on the shop floor, she leaned forward and planted a vermilion kiss on Mr Marks's cheek.

Sometimes in the afternoon, Young Leo, playing himself at chess, would look up and see Doris looking in the windows of Charing Cross Road. She held the strap of a white leather bag, which she swung from side to side. Other times she was gone. Then she would be back, swinging her bag in time with the footfall of strangers.

'Why does Doris spend such a long time shopping?' said Young Leo to Mr Cohen.

'She's not shopping,' said Mr Cohen.

'What's she doing then?'

'She's looking for business,' said Mr Cohen.

'What business?'

'Doris, bless her, is what's called a short-term companion.'

'What's a short-term companion?' said Young Leo.

'Never. You. Mind,' said Marks senior, walking on to the shop floor, ruffling his son's curls. 'Never you mind.'

*

Young Leo was sitting on the stool by the till. He had a notebook open on his portable chess set. He was looking at the reverse of a first edition of Edgar Allan Poe's *The Gold-Bug*. The following letters were written in pencil.

'CN/'

The books in Marks & Co. did not have prices – only codes that gave the booksellers a starting price for negotiations. The challenge was breaking the code. At first Leo tried a direct approach. His father would say 'A code would not be a code, my son, if I told you what it was', and ruffle Leo's hair.

Leo opened the back cover. At the bottom right of the page he could see something in pencil. So faint it was almost invisible. He placed the page under the light. The following was just discernible.

'£6.10/'

He wrote in his notebook 'C = 6'. That was the starting point. How did 'N' become '10'?

He stared at the wall, his mind spinning like a fruit machine. He wrote out a dozen possible 10-letter keywords starting with the obvious:

M A R K S A N D C O

He numbered each keyword from 1–10. The penultimate key-word stared back at him.

M	A	R	K	S	**C**	O	H	E	**N**
1	2	3	4	5	**6**	7	8	9	**10**

Under the 'C' was the number 6. Under the 'N' was.... the number 10!

He circled both numbers and sat silent. The bustle of the world went still. The same world that would one day call upon an abacus-mind when everything hung in the balance.

Leo Marks had just broken his first code.

CHAPTER 15
'LE STRYGE'

Paris, 1929

Noor

Noor perched with her harp resting on her shoulder. She placed her fingers in position and inhaled. Her hands began to weave across the strings. Vivaldi's Concerto in D Minor came to life like a Venetian phantom, cloak flapping, mask jutting. The notes came, clear and effervescent, as if soaring into the Basilica di San Marco.

She remembered the words of Mademoiselle Monette.

'The notes are a path. A path that was left for you – no one else.'

She closed her eyes as she followed the path.

Noor had once told her teacher a secret. The secret that drew her apart.

She saw music in colour.

Each note had its own streak. Poppy. Sapphire. Daffodil. Lime. Holly. Fire. Amethyst. A line of notes made a rainbow. A song made a rainbow burst through a prism. A symphony made a rainbow erupt into fireworks. Music gave her the mindscape of an opium eater.

She had had the gift since childhood. She thought everyone was the same. She once asked Falinne what colours she saw in music. Falinne looked frightened. Noor kept it to herself. Sometimes just the clink of a glass or the swing of a hinge produced a trace of colour. When music played, she walked through a meadow that pulsed with changing colour.

It made her feel alone, despite Inayat's whisper.

'Do not feel lonely. The entire Universe is inside you.'

It was not just the music. It was the dreams. The world that opened behind her closed eyelids was beyond Freud. Her dreams unveiled a carousel of painted horses undulating as they circled, their colours changing to the fairground chime as they spun. Her dreams took her to the pink dust of Jaipur, where she found she could speak to the temple monkey sitting on her arm. Her dreams took her to a hidden waterfall where the Mother of the Universe sat behind a curtain of water stroking a Bengal tiger with all her eight arms. Her dreams led her to a poppy field surrounded by mountains, laid for tea with a family of tame wolves. Her dreams led her into flight with Pteech-ka, whose wooden wings had come to life. She and Pteech-ka flew under the bridges of the Seine and soared up between the towers of Notre Dame.

'Dreams,' said Inayat once, 'are the memories of the future.'

That night she dreamed of a long shore lapped with liquid turquoise. Baby turtles moved across the sand towards the moonlight on the water. She saw a young man she did not know. He wore stone-coloured trousers rolled at his ankles. He was walking barefoot in the shadows, a stone-coloured jacket thrown over his shoulder. He carried a pair of moccasins, a finger in each heel. He walked with the grace of a diver. Some of his footprints made an indent in the sand. Others were swallowed by the incoming tide. Flying foxes jumped from the trees along the shore. Pink pigeons nested in the branches. A Mauritian stag watched from the cliff above. The man walked, hair in the wind, along the shore.

The setting changed. He was standing in the hills above Paris. She was standing beside him, close enough to feel his heat. They were squinting at a point in the distance. They were watching the House of Blessings. The garden was full of soldiers.

*

Morel

Morel walked, eyes down, footsteps percussive on the pavement. The ink-blue night was enveloping the evening. Dark streaks began to blotch his hat-tipped shadow. The façade of Notre Dame loomed above, the north and south towers whispering to each other across the void.

'Le Stryge', the vigilant gargoyle that crouched on a ledge beneath the south tower, chin on palms, wings folded, was watching. And, ears pricked, listening. High above Paris, Le Stryge was alert to the movement of a man walking towards the river with his palm moulded around the grip of a Luger pistol.

It was the longest night of the year and Georges Morel was walking back towards his attic apartment on Rue de la Harpe in the 5ème Arrondissement. The front door of his apartment block was ornately carved, though the green-black paint was flaking away. To the right of the entrance was a complex network of doorbells set out like dots on a large domino. Next to some doorbells were names: Savatier, Belmonte, Tailler... Others had initials: B.H., N.W., M.S-P. The bell at the top right had neither a name nor an initial: just a void. Morel had few visitors. The concierge had asked him what name he should put against his bell. Morel shook his head. Why would anyone wish to call upon a man with a tin head and a stutter?

Morel entered the coolness of the building and walked up the staircase, following the cracked plaster of the internal walls. He reached the top floor and turned his door key. The door opened into a bare attic. The plaster inside was the colour of bruised peach, blotches of umber and tan smudged by an impressionist's thumb. Morel placed the Luger on a desk branded with black rings and cigarette burns. He sat down. He picked up the Luger and massaged a catch behind the trigger. There was a click. The magazine slid from the grip into his left palm. He emptied the bullets. He wrapped the Luger in a dry cloth. He placed the loose bullets and the empty magazine in a leather pouch. He placed the gun and the pouch in the metal box and turned the key on another year.

From a cupboard he took out a bottle of Armagnac, poured some into a cloudy glass, raised a silent toast and allowed the golden liquid to run, burning, down the back of his throat.

At the same time most nights, Morel placed his elbows on the ledge of the attic window and watched, chin on palms, the field of lights surge and dim to the city's pulse. The longing in the voice from the House of Blessings would always echo inside his head. As he placed his elbows on the ledge, he began his scan of Paris, looking north towards the river. Faces appeared under the moon. His mother, her beauty unscathed, setting out a picnic on a craggy Breton beach. His father, waving from the station platform in 1914. Fabien turning, smiling before falling limp. The nurse at his bedside with the blue-grey eyes of a Saint-Malo seascape.

As he watched, Morel was unaware of the stone stare of Le Stryge gazing south in his direction. Their line of vision met for an unconscious moment, before Morel turned his head to the east, a lone pair of human eyes staring across a city of millions.

He had worked as a chauffeur to the Blumenthal family for four years before they moved to Geneva. Monsieur Blumenthal had been generous. He wrote a cheque that had allowed Morel a six-month respite and to move into an apartment in the 5ème Arrondissement. The attic on the Rue de la Harpe was the first property he saw, and he signed the lease without further thought. His only luggage was a suitcase of clothes and a metal box, which the concierge noticed he kept close under his elbow.

On his last journey to Saint-Malo, Morel found his mother sitting by the window in a rocking chair, poring over the curled photographs spread out on her lap. There was one of Fabien, aged seventeen, head thrown back. One of Père Morel, sturdy and moustachioed, thumbs in waistcoat, outside the printing factory. One of the family taken on the beach before the war by a resort photographer who stood with a cloth over his head and made his subjects pose for an eternity. Morel placed his hand on his mother's shoulder, curled like the sepia photographs. Her red, rheumy eyes looked up at her son. She died a month later. Morel returned to the town of his birth and stood as the pall-bearers lowered her coffin into the ground in the local cemetery, next to Père Morel. Under his jacket he placed his hand over his heart. The final tie was broken.

Georges Morel was alone.

He walked from the window of his attic to the mantelpiece. At one end were two candlesticks without candles. At the other was a dented hip flask. Under the hip flask was an advertisement torn from *Octane* magazine. It was for a rare chauffeur to help maintain a fleet of unusual cars.

The following day Georges Morel donned his best suit, a pressed white shirt, and a tie his mother had given him and walked into the summer sunshine. He walked past the Jardin du Luxembourg, his panama tipped over his eyes, unable to quell the anticipation that surged through his veins. He sensed change. He inhaled deeply, picking up the scent of freesias and fresh-cut grass. He rehearsed a single word, remembering the encouragement of Monsieur Eugène. He was not going to stutter. He planned to make a vanished family proud.

At nine-fifteen, Georges Morel stood on the Rue Théodore de Banville looking through the windows of the grandest car showroom in Europe. The Garage Banville was new, a beacon of art deco, with a vast frontage of glass interspersed with coiled steel columns. Behind the glass were rows of polished Bugattis. Their headlights implored like unopened toys waiting to be held and their wheels spun on the ground. The Bugattis came in all colours – dove grey, sapphire blue, ivory edged with black, pale lime and tricolore red. Raised on a plinth at one end was a replica Type 35 in British racing green.

Morel walked through a revolving door. A woman behind a reception desk rose and clicked across the floor on elevated heels.

Morel tugged the front of his panama and nodded. The woman had dark hair coiled like twine over her shoulder and green eyes that reflected the veins of the marble. She wore an ivory-coloured summer dress that clung to her shape. She walked Morel to the lift and pressed the button.

'Fourth floor,' she said. 'Turn right. First door on the left. *Bonne chance.*'

A handsome addition to her morning, thought the woman. Yet his eyes looked sorrowful. As she walked back to the reception desk, she turned for another glance at the high-coloured man. Morel felt breathless. Then the familiar blanket closed in – under the straw of his panama, his head would always be plated silver-smooth like a dolphin. On the fourth floor he exited the lift and found his way to the door marked:

DIRECTEUR

Morel knocked.

'*Entrez!*' came a voice from within.

Morel opened the door into a modern office of steel and chrome, with mirrors etched in geometric lines. Behind a desk sat a hawk in man's clothing – alert brown eyes, taut skin, prominent cheekbones, beaked aquiline nose, and hair brushed back from a low hairline. On the desk were metal models of racing cars and biplanes. There was a gold racing trophy on its own plinth. The man stood to greet Morel and extended an agile, supple hand.

'*Bonjour,*' said the man. 'Robert Benoist.'

'Georges M-m-.'

He took a deep breath.

'Georges Morel,' he said.

'Please?' said Benoist, extending a hand towards a chair of chalk-white leather with polished-steel arms.

Morel sat. Then he performed an action he had practised over and over in his apartment.

Right hand raise, grip, retract.

Right hand raise, grip, retract.

Right hand raise, grip, retract.

In one symbolic move, Morel removed his hat.

The silence in the room deepened. Benoist stared at Morel. Morel looked back through wounded, defiant eyes.

'Shrapnel?' said Benoist at last.

'Sniper. Western Front. 1914.'

Benoist did something Morel did not expect. He pushed back his chair, walked around his desk, and knelt with one knee on the floor, facing Morel.

Their eyes drew level. Benoist placed a hand on Morel's shoulder.

'*Armée de l'Air*,' said Benoist. 'I used to fly Nieuport 12s. Here you are among friends.'

With those words, a bond forged between the two men that never broke. Never, that is, until fifteen summers later, to the day, the sky above one of their heads turned from Monet blue to Goya black.

Benoist resumed his seat and took out a sleek metal pen.

'So,' said Benoist. 'They say you know about cars.'

Morel's knowledge was encyclopaedic – Bugattis in particular. Makes. Models. Engines. Speeds. Brakes. Quirks. Races. Times. He also held a clutch of excellent references as a chauffeur.

'We garage and sell some of the highest-value cars in the world. There is a track from the basement to the roof. There is a practice track on the roof itself. Ettore Bugatti himself hand-picked the cars in the showroom. We are looking for a man we can trust to move priceless metal around the building and to put the cars through their paces with their new owners. Some skill with a spanner would not go amiss.'

Morel was a modest man, but the excitement that rose in his voice was irrepressible. Mechanics were his métier. His skill as a driver dominated his references. Cars were an extension of his hands.

'Besides,' he said, 'I am part m-m-metal.'

Benoist looked up and smiled. He set down his pen and pressed the button on a telephone system sleek enough to compete with a Bugatti Type 35.

The calm voice of a secretary came over the intercom.

'*Oui, Monsieur Benoist?*'

'Could you check if WW is in his office?'

'*Oui, Monsieur.*'

Moments later there was a muted rap on the door. A dark-haired man entered. He wore a well-cut charcoal suit, ivory silk shirt and striped club tie. A dash of white edged from his top pocket. Mirror-black brogues extended from the turn-ups of his trousers. His dark Mediterranean eyes were at odds with his English features.

'*Bonjour, Robert,*' said the man, nodding at Benoist. His French was accentless.

'*Bonjour, WW,*' said Benoist. '*Je te présente Monsieur Georges Morel.*'

The man approached Morel and extended his hand. He looked straight into Morel's eyes as he stood, appearing not to notice his tin head.

'*Enchanté,*' said the man. 'William Grover-Williams.'

It was the British racing driver 'WW', right there in the flesh.

'I saw you win in M-M-Monaco,' said Morel.

'More luck than skill,' said Grover-Williams with a throw-away smile. 'My opponents had an off day.'

'All fifteen?' said Benoist, eyes smiling.

'Must have been the sea air,' said Grover-Williams.

The men sat down and discussed further details of Morel's application. After coffee, Benoist rose.

'Monsieur Morel,' he said, 'would you excuse us for a couple of moments?'

Morel stepped into a corridor with a stone-coloured carpet edged on both sides with geometric black lines. He paced up and down. A minute later, Benoist opened the door.

'Welcome back, *mon confrère,*' he said.

A look was exchanged between Benoist and Grover-Williams. Benoist's nascent smile bloomed on the lips of Grover-Williams.

'We would like to offer you this position, Monsieur Morel,' said Benoist. 'How could a pair of racing drivers refuse a man with a built-in crash helmet?'

There was flicker of a pause. Then the laughter of the three men echoed off the art deco furniture.

'Congratulations,' said Grover-Williams, extending his hand.

'There is a race on Saturday starting from the basement garage, going round the building's interior track and finishing with twenty-five circuits of the roof,' said Benoist. 'As a veteran, perhaps you would do us the honour of firing the starting pistol?'

Morel stood holding his panama hat. He swallowed and blinked. All he could do was nod.

CHAPTER 16
'SHE'

London, 1929

Marks

Leo Marks sat by the till in Marks & Co., elbows on the table, palms pressed against his temples. A pocket chess set was open on the table by the till. His eyes inspected the opposing forces at ground level, each piece polished and ready. He looked at the battlefield from above. He closed his eyes. He imagined the opposing armies invisible on the eve of battle.

He surveyed the terrain like a field marshal. He drew an 'x' and 'y' axis in his mind's eye. He inserted co-ordinates under the invisible pieces.

8	a8	b8	c8	d8	e8	f8	g8	h8
7	a7	b7	c7	d7	e7	f7	g7	h7
6	a6	b6	c6	d6	e6	f6	g6	h6
5	a5	b5	c5	d5	e5	f5	g5	h5
4	a4	b4	c4	d4	e4	f4	g4	h4
3	a3	b3	c3	d3	e3	f3	g3	h3
2	a2	b2	c2	d2	e2	f2	g2	h2
1	a1	b1	c1	d1	e1	f1	g1	h1
	a	b	c	d	e	f	g	h

Then he imagined an empty, featureless battlefield – a blank tableau on which to practise The Art of War.

Leo Marks blinked at the empty grid, taking a mental photograph. He imposed the scenery: knolls, crags, woods, streams running down to the green field of battle. He pictured rival armies assembling on the battlefield, each part delineated into unseen squares. He fired the first cannon shot as the White General, then responded as the Black. He tested and retested his battle tactics:

- ○ Frontal assault
- ○ Flank attack
- ● Pincer movement
- ● Siege
- ○ Attrition
- ○ Stealth incursion
- ○ Subterfuge
- ● Supply-line disruption
- ● Tactical withdrawal
- ○ Counter-attack
- ○ Endgame

By the autumn, Leo Marks could see ten moves into the future, sometimes twelve. Afterwards, he could reverse each move in sequence back to square one.

Young Leo had drawn up a chair opposite Uncle Abe on eight occasions over the summer. The pieces were woken from a wooden box and deployed on the terrain of squares. The boy used different openings: the King's Indian Attack, the Queen's Gambit, the Albin Counter-Gambit, the Catalan Opening, and the hypnotic Black Knights' Tango. He began one game with his own variation on the Spanish Opening, destroying Uncle Abe's pawn defences and neutralizing both his bishops at once.

In the small anteroom a young mind was free to range, watching the grid from above then weaving among his pieces on the ground. His mind was airborne again, working out permutations at a depth of a dozen moves. Uncle Abe rolled up the sleeves of his *rekel* coat, tipped back his fedora and entered the fray, all pretence of giving Young Leo the advantage having long evaporated. Uncle Abe's skill was returning as he galvanized his troops to parry the attacks and capture ground at every instance. Yet as the games wore on, Uncle Abe had the unsettling feeling that the boy was reading his battle orders – infantry, cavalry and artillery – and had foreseen every variation of skirmish.

Of the eight games played over the summer, Uncle Abe had knocked over his own defeated king in seven. The eighth ended in a draw. Young Leo had heard Uncle Abe whisper the word 'prodigy' into Mr Marks's ear.

'My son,' said Mr Marks, ruffling Young Leo's bird's nest of curls.

The Hebrew reading continued. Young Leo would place his finger on the Torah scrolls and follow the words from right to left, reading the Hebrew aloud.

Uncle Abe closed his eyes as he listened to the rhythmic, mesmerizing sounds.

Vay-omer Elo-him yehi or-r-r
Vay-ehi o-r-r...

Part of Uncle Abe delighted in being beaten at chess by a nine-year-old. Another part of him wanted to let the boy know he still held secrets.

Uncle Abe opened his eyes and placed his elegant fingers on the table.

'Sometimes,' he said, 'the letters in the old speech can be hidden in numbers.'

Leo Marks looked up, eyes bright.

'Does that mean that numbers can be hidden in letters?'

'It does,' said Uncle Abe, taking out a notebook. He licked his index finger as he leafed through the pages.

On a clean sheet of paper, he numbered three glyphs.

$$1 \quad א$$
$$2 \quad ב$$
$$3 \quad ג$$

He continued until 10.

'It is, of course, possible to combine glyphs to make higher numbers,' said Uncle Abe. 'Some combinations are fortuitous.'

He wrote a pair of glyphs:

$$ח \quad י$$

'What is the word?' said Uncle Abe.

'*Chai*,' said Young Leo, gargling the first syllable to make the sound: '*h-h-h-high*.'

Uncle Abe repeated the sound: '*h-h-h-high*.'

'In Hebrew, *Chai* is *life*,' he said.

The boy nodded.

'What number does each symbol represent?' asked the old man.

The boy looked at the list.

'Eight and ten,' he said.

'Which makes?'

'Eighteen,' said the boy.

'Which is why we Jews see "eighteen" as a lucky number,' said Uncle Abe. 'It is the code for life.'

On the Saturday before Young Leo's term started, a man stood outside Marks & Co., tapping the shop window with his cane. He was dressed like Oscar Wilde – flaccid bow tie, opera cloak and wide-brimmed Borsalino hat. The tapping on the window was a way of communicating that the door of the shop required opening. Frank, the general manager, opened the door with a caricature of deference. The man walked in to the middle of the shop and struck his cane on the floor.

191

'Inform Mr Marks that the Laird of Boleskine is in attendance.'

He removed his hat. He was bald. With his staring brown eyes, Young Leo thought he looked like a sinister Humpty Dumpty.

Mr Marks entered the room with Frank. Mr Marks nodded, but kept his hand behind his back.

'The usual request?' said Mr Marks.

'The usual,' said the laird. 'Please ensure that I am left undisturbed.'

Mr Marks took out his book of chits. He entered the name 'A. Crowley' and the date. He held up a brace of fingers at Frank.

'Please admit the Laird of Boleskine to the second floor,' said Mr Marks. 'And ensure he is left in peace.'

Frank led the man towards the stairs at the back of the shop, the lean figure of Frank followed by the thickset laird, cape flowing.

The disappearance of the man – together with his decaying aroma of valerian – led to a strange feeling of relief, as if a throbbing tooth had been extracted.

'There are some uncommon folk in this world,' said Mr Marks to Young Leo. 'But none more cockamamie than Aleister Crowley. Still, he's been a client since Cambridge.'

An hour later there was a noise on the stairs as if a medium-sized elephant was descending. It was the Laird of Boleskine. He held an envelope with the letters 'BOY' on the front. He gave the envelope to Young Leo and strode towards the door of Marks & Co., cloak flowing. Leo Marks opened the envelope before he could be stopped. Inside was a calling card. It had a symbol and words beneath.

With the compliments of The Beast

Young Leo studied the symbol. Was it another code? He looked on the reverse. Some words were written in ink:

'When your boyhood is gone let no one stop you to
Do What Thou Wilt.'

Treasure

After the Laird of Boleskine's cloak was seen retreating down Charing Cross Road, the bell above the door rang. A woman stood framed in the doorway, in silhouette, the curve of her line unmistakable. She sashayed across the floor on heels sharp enough to leave a trail of full stops on the floorboards. She walked up to Young Leo, who was sitting on the stool by the till. Her scent hung from her, floral and feral, her most pronounced curve within reach.

It was Doris. She walked, heels clicking, to a far shelf on the ground floor. It housed early editions of nineteenth-century novels. She ran her eye along the shelf. Three gold letters caught her eye.

SHE

Taking the book down, she opened it on the first page.

> There are some events of which each circumstance and surrounding detail seems to be graven on the memory in such fashion that we cannot forget it, and so it is with the scene that I am about to describe. It rises as clearly before my mind at this moment as though it had happened but yesterday. It was in this very month something over twenty years ago…

Doris Richards was back in Balcombe Street. It was her first morning and she was in the small library with leather chairs and a sideboard that hosted a bottled ensemble of whisky, sherry, Armagnac and sloe gin. At the end of a row of books by Dumas, Verne, Melville, Conan Doyle and Hardy was a title of only three letters. She took the copy of *S H E* and wandered into her new life in Mrs Morgan's unique house.

*

Doris closed the book and replaced it on the bookcase in Marks & Co. A tear ran from her eye, which she caught with her index finger. She composed herself with a sigh and took a pink-and-white striped packet from her handbag.

'These are for you, Master Marks,' she said, placing a bag of sherbet lemons in his hand.

She searched his face, as if looking for someone else, then smiled.

Leo Marks went the colour of pimento.

Doris left. She walked twenty yards along Charing Cross Road and stopped at the front door. There was a myriad of bells to the right, some with names underneath, others without. She opened the door and made her way up the well-worn stairs to the top. From the gloom of the stairwell, she opened the door into a bright top-floor flat that could be cast into cool darkness with a single swish of the damask curtains. Reflected in various mirrors on wheels was a row of decanters – Scotch, Armagnac, Gin, Sherry. The bedroom of her place of work was dominated by a brass bed. In the chest of drawers by the wall she kept some of the accoutre-ments from Balcombe Street. The almond leather cuffs lived in the top drawer on the right.

She sat down at her dressing table. The same thought always returned when she was alone. Where was James? Her son would have left his boyhood behind. Her growing fear was that in time he would be one of the nervous undergraduates ringing the top bell of the infamous black door on Charing Cross Road. Surely, she would know if it was him? Surely.

She sat at her dressing table. She winced at the mirror, trac-ing the crow's feet around her eyes with a finger and examining the emerging creases around her mouth. The cobalt of her gaze remained, but the grip of her beauty was loosening. There was still time, she thought with an inward sigh, but it was not unlimited.

Images of the pantomime-painted faces of the older vamps on the patch nearer Leicester Square made her closed eyes tighten.

She composed herself. It was time to prepare. She adorned herself with a mix of silk and lace that would have impressed Mademoiselle Pelletier and dusted her cheek with her best blusher. She curled her eyelashes round a mascara brush and blinked several times.

'I think it's time to make an honest woman of you, Treasure,' she said aloud.

On the sofa by her dressing table lay a copy of *The Times*, the headline making ominous pronouncements about the spiralling descent of the US economy. It was the 'Appointments' section at the back of the newspaper that had drawn her attention. She marked it with a circle of vermilion lipstick.

The doorbell rang from below. She glanced at her watch. He was always punctual. She pressed the intercom and listened for his steps on the stairs as they grew louder. She knew his footsteps like a voice.

It was the general.

A tea gown of amber silk trailed Doris as she glided across the room. She opened the door to a man with badger-white hair and the skin of deep-etched parchment. He wore a charcoal civilian suit and held a grey trilby. In his other hand was a small package tied with a bow. The general never attended without a book from Hatchards. She planted a kiss on his cheek and wiped away the lipstick. He wore the same cologne, West Indian Extract of Limes, as when he had first walked up the stairs at Balcombe Street.

'Lovely to see you,' she said. 'Come in.'

*

Balcombe Street closed with the old world.

A year after Armistice, General Page, through a quiet word with the butler at the Athenaeum, traced Treasure to a lodging house off the Tottenham Court Road. The building belonged to the Salvation Army and the saying above the front door read **BLOOD AND FIRE**. Treasure met the general at the nearby Lyons' Corner House. Patrons looking up from their stewed tea and Victoria sponge would have presumed Treasure was the guest of a concerned uncle.

'You held my hand when it trembled,' said the general. 'You never judged and you never chased the silence.'

The general asked if some spare funds from a family trust would help.

'Just until you get settled,' said the general, who was due to take a seat in the House of Lords the following year.

The general noticed the silver bird with ruby eyes on Treasure's lapel and smiled.

'Treasure's treasure,' said his companion, stroking its silver body.

The general's funds allowed her to buy the flat on Charing Cross Road. And a small stipend for clothes, shoes and accoutrements. When in London, the general would allow himself a necessary excursion along Charing Cross Road. The stairs seemed steeper each time, but it was an escape from the increasingly irritable Lady Page, and he was always enraptured by what lay at the top of the mountain.

The damask curtains were closed. Treasure lay among enough duck-down pillows to rival Balcombe Street. A grey trilby hung on one of the bedposts. As she recovered her breath, she turned on to her side and ran her finger down the spine of the older man lying on his front.

'Bertie,' she whispered. 'I need to ask a favour.'

*

On an autumn afternoon in 1929, Mr Marks walked through the door of Marks & Co. with the *Evening Standard* under his arm. The headline announced Black Thursday in America and the Wall Street Crash. Leo Marks heard his father discussing matters with Mr Cohen in hushed voices. Would orders from the US be affected? Cancelled even? Leo Marks stared at the grid of his pocket chessboard and tried to imagine Wall Street crashing. How did a street crash? Did the whole street collide with something else? He imagined the street in the aftermath of a crash, cars upturned, buildings collapsed, firefighters hosing down the blaze...

*

Doris extinguished the strawberry blaze by the window on Charing Cross Road a week later and put on her flat shoes. She walked down the threadbare stairs and out into the early evening hum. Under her arm was a stiff-backed envelope with three letters signed 'PAGE'. Outside Charing Cross Station, the No. 11 bus came into view. She stepped on to the platform as it started to rain. She found a seat downstairs and, smoothing her skirt behind her knees, sat down. She rummaged past the books in her handbag and pulled out a packet of Craven A. She looked out of the window into the headlights of cars reflected in the watery sheen on the road and up at the blur of electric lights that streaked past. She looked down at her fitted skirt and thought of arriving at Balcombe Street in a corset and a dress that trailed the pavement.

As the No. 11 moved along Whitehall into Parliament Square, she thought of the Lords Spiritual and Temporal swathed in ermine, and smiled. The bus continued westward through Victoria towards Sloane Square. Then further west along the King's Road, past Chelsea Town Hall and the artists' quarter either side of Beaufort Street. Beyond that was World's End, the poor cousin of Chelsea's poor cousin, its terraced houses overflowing with Italian ice-cream vendors, art students, kitchen porters, office clerks, and the occasional resting actor.

She turned the key on Number 31 Limerston Street, walked through the shabby hallway, and let herself into her first-floor flat. She switched on the lights. The main room looked more like the warehouse of Marks & Co., small islands of floor space shoring their defences against a sea of books. She kicked off her heels and went to turn on the taps of a bath. After her bath she put her Remington typewriter on her dressing table, lit a Craven A, and began to type.

29th October 1929
Leonard Frobisher M.A.
Chief Librarian

Chelsea Library
King's Road
London SW3

'I write in relation to the position of Assistant Librarian advertised in The Times on 14th inst...'

The following week, Treasure walked up the steps of Chelsea Town Hall in a tweed suit, pearls and borrowed lace-ups. Mr Frobisher M.A. was Treasure's idea of what a librarian should look like: pale with dark thinning hair, black round-framed Le Corbusier glasses and a reedy voice. Around his meagre frame sat an ill-fitting suit and a limp tie. However, he had intelligent eyes and a tender smile. He begged her to be seated and one of his staff to bring tea.

There were papers spread out on his desk, including a letter with a gold imprint at the top.

'According to Lord Page, you have been assistant librarian at the House of Lords since 1922?' said Mr Frobisher. 'And you have also archived the library at Massingham Castle.'

She tried not to blush.

'Your references are, of course, impeccable, but do you think you might find working here a bit of a backwater?'

Treasure explained she had an aged aunt in World's End and wished to work nearer home.

'I see,' said Mr Frobisher. 'And may I ask what type of books you like?'

'Where to begin, Mr Frobisher?' said Treasure, eyes widening in wonder.

The teapot set down on the desk was drained and refilled several times as Treasure started to unpack her knowledge of books, an encyclopaedic repository of its own, that threatened to engulf the shelves, trolleys, index cards and archives of Chelsea Library and its surrounding buildings.

On Guy Fawkes Day, an envelope dropped on to the door-mat of 31 Limerston Street. Treasure opened a typed letter signed 'Leonard Frobisher M.A.'. The contents blazed like a Catherine wheel. The position of Assistant Librarian was open to her with immediate effect. He had taken the liberty of enclosing a Contract of Employment.

'Who'd have thought it?' Treasure said to herself.

She looked at the Contract of Employment as if it were in hieroglyphics. The labyrinthine document, with elaborate clauses and subclauses, seemed to be calling for her signature. Her first thought was what to do with a lifetime collection of silk, lace and saddle maker's leather?

The doorbell rang. Standing in the door frame was a young man in a worn silk dressing gown. Doris tended to regard men outside working hours as a doctor regards patients at his dinner table, but she never failed to be struck by the man's Apollonian beauty. It was the resting actor who lived in the basement.

'Yes, Percy?' said Doris.

'My dear,' said Percy. 'Could you find it in yourself to spare a sprinkling of sugar and dash of milk?'

Doris smiled.

'My agent seems to have set fire to all my royalty cheques.'

Doris navigated a path through the molehills of books and fetched some milk and sugar.

Percy beamed.

'When my ship comes in, dear Doris, I'll buy you a sugar plan-tation and a dairy.'

CHAPTER 17
'THE LEAGUE'

Kiel, Germany
1931

Canaris

In the chapel of the Kiel Naval Base, Kapitän Wilhelm Canaris knelt in silent prayer. The Kapitän had greying temples and sharp lines that ran across his forehead. The grooves that ran from his nostrils to the corners of his mouth were deeper, emphasizing his upper lip. Canaris sat back in the pew. The trace of incense was fading. Sailors were leaving. They saluted the immaculate Kapitän of the *Schlesien* as they passed.

The outer lines on Canaris's forehead reflected the inner battle lines. The battle between the old order and the new. Prussia was part of an empire that died with the German surrender in 1918. During his voyage from stiff-collared Prussian boy to Kapitän of the *Schlesien*, the old order had crumbled. While Prussia had been forged from a cannonball and spawned the House of Hohenzollern and the Electors of Brandenburg, the new order was bloodless. Canaris's fealty, once sworn to the Kaiser, was now sworn to a pale, anaemic republic.

The boy who grew up to be a sailor set his inner sexton to a poem taught by his father:

Üb' immer Treu und Redlichkeit
Bis an dein kühles Grab;
Und weiche keinen Fingerbreit
Von Gottes Wegen ab.

Practise fidelity and honesty always
Until your cool grave;
And stray not the width of one finger
From the ways of the Lord.

Canaris's highest fidelity was to his country, but now a different type of cannonball was being forged in Germany. Its metal was sported by a new breed of Teutonic knight. And the new knights, heads shaven, hands on their flame blades, were on the rampage. Would they be part of Germany's God-given destiny? Or would they turn the sun black?

Canaris looked up at the Christ statue nailed to the cross above. He knew every contour. The arch of his instep, the rent in his side, the protrusion of his ribs, the thorn-pricked trickle from his temple, the narrow face and the steady, forgiving eyes.

He closed his eyes and thought of the Christ statue in the prison in Quiriquina. Kapitän Canaris's exploits had gone down in naval folklore. Some said his journey was on a par with the *Odyssey*. Others said the staunch Catholic officer must have had some help from above. A few wondered whether half the stories were true.

*

For an officer who crossed the Andes alone in winter to rejoin the Imperial Navy, Canaris's war ended in a way he could never have imagined.

In the first week of November 1918, orders from the *Reichsmarineamt* were transmitted to his latest command, a new Type III U-boat: *UB-128*:

ALL UNDERSEA BOATS RECALLED
TO KIEL IMMEDIATELY

Kapitänleutnant Canaris stood on the bridge of his submarine. It was a crisp, blue November morning. *UB-128* cruised on the surface at a steady twelve knots, its commander savouring the whip of the clean autumn wind. He was heading back to Kiel, his genesis as a naval officer. There was light in his heart as he scanned the sea's horizon.

When he sailed into Kiel harbour, he saw patches of blood. Not on the water. In the sky. The crimson flags of revolution were flying from the Kaiser's warships. For a son of Empire, and a Catholic, it was like witnessing the desecration of the high altar of Dresden Cathedral.

The High Seas Fleet had mutinied. The empire that shimmered with gold four years before was now in peril from an even more dangerous enemy: the godless Bolsheviks.

*

Canaris remained in the Navy after the German surrender. He and his brother officers swore loyalty to the new Weimar Republic – a kingdom without a crown. As the infant Republic became a stripling, a bored naval officer found a letter waiting for him in the officers' mess. It was addressed: 'To a German Patriot.' His eyes narrowed. The recipient was invited to attend an evening meeting the following Tuesday in a private room at the Hotel Zur Mühle. Under no circumstances was he to tell a third party about the fact of the meeting or any matter discussed. The future of Germany was at stake. Secrecy was paramount for reasons the recipient would understand.

Canaris turned over the contents of the letter in his mind. He was not an admirer of the Republic. The threat of anarchy or worse, revolution, was real. But there were risks. A naval officer of the Weimar Republic should not be dabbling in politics. That, he thought, was for others.

At seven sharp the following Tuesday, a slight figure in a well-cut civilian suit, with hair greying at the temples, walked up the steps of Kiel's oldest hotel. Two young men, also in civilian clothes, were waiting for him in the lobby. Canaris sensed that they, like him, were not civilians.

'You do us an honour, Kapitän,' said the first. 'Please, this way.'

The two men led Canaris up two flights of stairs to a door marked:

Privatgelgnde

The second escort knocked. The '*Komm herein!*' bellowed was military to the syllable.

The door opened. Canaris entered. It was not what he expected. The room was dark save for a bright anglepoise lamp beaming into his face. Behind the lamp there were figures, seated and standing in darkness. Canaris's U-boat service had taught him about dark spaces – and the anatomy of fear. He stood straight, unflinching.

'*Danke fürs Kommen, Kapitän,*' said a voice from behind the light. 'Please excuse the theatricals. The identity of the men in this room must, at present, remain secret. Some of them you know. Some you do not. We do, however, have one thing in common.'

There was a pause.

'We are all loyal sons of the Fatherland.'

The light in Canaris's face was now replicating before his eyes like phosphorescent orbs.

'My name is not important,' continued the voice. 'Nor is my rank. What is important, however, is the future of Germany.'

Instinct told Canaris that the voice – calm, assured, commanding – belonged to an officer of the highest rank.

'The Republic is weak,' said the voice. 'The country is bankrupt. The *Reichsbank-Direktorium* prints five-million-mark notes worth less than the paper. Our crumpled industries are kicked before they can stand. Yet war reparations take priority. We face two barrels of a shotgun. Communism or anarchism. Either way, we stand on the brink of oblivion.'

Canaris clicked his heels in wordless affirmation.

'That is why a small number of officers have formed a group – the League of German Patriots. A league based on a profound love of the Fatherland and a desire for Germany to rise from the ashes. We seek men whose loyalty to Germany – and to each other – is unbreakable. I am given to understand you are such a man, Kapitän.'

Canaris faced the light direct.

'The men in this room are, like you, of the highest calibre. They are the sons of Empire that look forward to the rise of a new Reich. A Reich that will see a Germany of such strength and power the world will stand back in awe. If I have assessed you correctly, Kapitän, you are invited to remain and stand with us united. If I have assessed you incorrectly, then you will about-turn and quick march out of this room with your mouth shut forever. We are all quick thinkers in this room. You have, by my watch, one minute.'

Canaris remembered standing around the gyrocompass with his officers in the U-boat as he counted down the seconds before launching a torpedo.

Tick-tick-tick-tick-tick-tick-tick-tick-tick

He stood rooted to the spot. After a long minute, the lights went on. Canaris looked, blinking, at the array of faces. He was staring at the highest echelons of the Weimar Republic's Navy. The grand admiral rose. Canaris and the grand admiral stood opposite each other, hands raised in a mutual salute. There was a ripple of applause. A junior officer poured out a tray of schnapps. The grand admiral raised a toast.

'To the latest member of the League,' he said.

Glasses were drained. The admiral took Canaris aside while the room became an impromptu party.

'I never had a shred of doubt, Kapitän,' he said. 'Never a shred.'

*

The League met on the first Tuesday of every month. The evenings were good-humoured, though underneath there was always the frisson of a far-reaching secret agenda developing at the highest level. There were no minutes and members of the League undertook to destroy all notes or other evidence of the League's meetings.

'Secrecy is paramount,' said the grand admiral. 'Anyone who betrays the secrecy of the League betrays us all. Sloppiness will not be tolerated.'

A League member was appointed to deal with all matters of 'internal security'.

After six months of gatherings, an extraordinary general meeting was convened on the first Tuesday in September. The grand admiral addressed a packed room of senior naval officers dressed as civilians.

'Gentlemen,' he said. 'The Allied Powers have sought to obliterate Germany and to extinguish the spirit of the Fatherland. Our Navy is a husk. Fifteen thousand men. A tenth of our wartime strength. A handful of rusting destroyers. Twelve torpedo boats barely capable of firing a *Bratwurst*. Six light cruisers to patrol the entire North Sea and the Baltic. And, of course, no submarines.'

Murmurs of assent rippled around the room.

'The time has come,' said the grand admiral, 'for Germany to reclaim itself. To rise from the ashes. It is time for Germany to RE-ARM!'

He thumped the table, unleashing a barrage of applause.

'However, re-armament cannot take place openly. We all know the venom that runs off the pages of the Treaty of Versailles. Re-armament will take place in total secrecy through a network of front companies in Germany and in the Netherlands. A number of loyal patriots known to some around this table will be channelling funds into the various companies for certain corporate expenses.'

There were nods of approval around the table.

'The League,' said the admiral, 'is looking to expand the German naval fleet on the water – and below. We are, as you know, prohibited from maintaining submarines. That, gentlemen, is about to change.'

A hush fell.

'The League has long tentacles. They extend as far as Japan. Certain officers of the Imperial Japanese Navy have made overtures to one of our attachés in Tokyo. The Japanese are ostensibly supporters of the Allied Powers. There is, however, a rising military faction seeking to strengthen the power of the Imperial Japanese Navy as a force to serve Japan – and support certain new allies – rather than the unholy cabal behind the Versailles treaty.'

An electric charge passed through the gathering.

'The Japanese require expertise on submarine construction. We, of course, require submarines. Funds are accruing in the League's various accounts to purchase four Japanese-constructed submarines for little more than cost. This initiative – which we will call *Projekt Barrakuda* – will be overseen by one of the League's finest officers and a wartime U-boat commander with an unrivalled number of sinkings to his name.'

The men in the room looked at one another. Among them, a pair of modest eyes glanced at the floor.

'*Projekt Barrakuda* will be overseen by Kapitän Wilhelm Canaris.'

*

The month before Kapitän Canaris was due to travel to Japan, word reached him of an officer so unpopular with fellow officers and ratings alike that he had become a curiosity in his own right. Canaris took aside Leutnant Falke, a well-liked officer with sound judgement. Falke asked if he might speak freely? Canaris nodded. The man in question, said Falke, was frankly detestable.

'He has all the attributes one would look for in order to construct the very antithesis of an officer,' said Falke, with the expression of a man whose coffee had been stirred with salt. Canaris drained his own coffee, curiosity piqued.

'Go on,' he said.

'Where do I begin, sir?' said Falke. 'Prissy. Capricious. Highly strung. Self-important. Cunning. Promiscuous. Supercilious. Sarcastic. And in dealing with those below decks, not a little sadistic.'

Falke reflected a moment.

'And that's on a good day.'

Canaris chortled.

'And on a bad day?'

'The single-handed cause of a mutiny.'

The following week, Canaris requested a certain midshipman to report to his office. There was a knock on the door.

'*Komm herein!*' said Canaris.

The door opened and a young officer entered the room and saluted. The officer in question was thin, with a long, taut-skinned face, a sharp nose, and a pair of sensual lips at odds with the rest of his features. His eyes were small and beamed with intensity bordering on arrogance. As Canaris was about to learn, his voice had the pitch of a self-important whine.

'Midshipman Heydrich with the most distinct satisfaction of reporting for duty, sir.'

Later in life, Canaris often asked himself what had drawn him to Heydrich. An innate sense of fairness? A desire to pull a man from a vortex of unpopularity? Wanting to refashion him as an officer in the Prussian mould? A shared Catholic view? A detestation of the godless Bolsheviks?

It was, on reflection, two things. The first was his unswerving loyalty to Germany. The second was what happened when he placed a Winterling violin under his chin. Reinhard Heydrich was a violinist of superlative ability.

It was not just his virtuosity but his compassion for the music. In his hands, the violin sang as if the player was subsidiary, a midwife guiding the melody to life. His preferences had an obvious German slant – Beethoven, Brahms, Mendelssohn – but he was not above champagne cork bursts of Vivaldi and Paganini. His rendition of Massenet's 'Méditation', played with such tormented yearning, brought some senior officers, including Canaris, to tears.

It was Kapitän Canaris who set about knocking the corners off the young midshipman – schooling his protégé in mess etiquette, conduct befitting an officer, comportment below decks and rules of engagement off duty. Under Canaris's patronage, Heydrich was tolerated with a little less hostility by the officers, though he remained prone to outbursts of anger that culminated in him screaming pike-faced, falsetto-pitched at the ratings. His standing below decks remained somewhere below the bilge pipes.

Under Canaris's influence, however, the career of the young Heydrich began to prosper. He bobbed through the ranks – midshipman, ensign, Oberleutnant – each promotion stoking an inner fire of self-aggrandizement. Rumours spread that he was heading for the very top, though they often emanated from Heydrich himself. A degree of respect replaced the hostility of other officers, though a number maintained his arrogance was unspeakable.

It was his protégé's conduct off base that Canaris had never been able to curtail. Reinhard Heydrich, despite his rake-like frame, had a gluttonous appetite for women. Many wondered how a man with the face of a death's head hawkmoth had such success with Fräuleins of the officers' circle. It was, confessed one, the sheer scale of his attentions. Heydrich would bow, click his heels, raise a Fräulein's hand to his lips and gaze into her eyes as if she were the last woman alive. Over dinner, he marvelled at every aspect of her life down to her tiniest whim, his focus never straying from her face. Every fact about the woman's existence was archived in the repository of his mind, ready for instant or later recall. As his gaze intensified, it seemed as if an invisible strand of ivy were winding around the woman's wrist, crawling up her arm and around her neck.

If capitulation still remained elusive, Heydrich would reach for his Winterling, take up his bow and release the longing of Schubert's 'Ständchen' serenade.

Few resisted. And Heydrich's nocturnal absences did not go unnoticed.

A clique in the officers' mess, however, found Heydrich's promiscuity an affront. One evening over schnapps, Oberleutnant Brandt smoothed back his mane of golden hair and addressed a cabal of fellow officers.

'Gentlemen,' said Oberleutnant Brandt, 'the reputation of our mess is under threat from a man who spends more time horizontal than vertical. I would, of course, feel less strongly about matters if it wasn't for the fact that our brother in arms has an unfortunate secret.'

The other officers leaned forward, closing the circle.

'Oberleutnant Heydrich is, as I am sure you know... a descendant of the Semite race.'

There were smiles of satisfaction that came from learning that the god of arrogance had feet of Yiddish clay. The rumour was never substantiated but it followed Heydrich like a dark shadow until, years later, peril stalked him in Prague wearing a cloak of an unexpected cloth.

It was Canaris who took Oberleutnant Heydrich and told him the season for sowing wild oats was over. He and his career stood to gain from a respectable wife and some upright sons and daughters of the Fatherland. Heydrich, ever mindful of his next promotion, stepped up to the plate. His current infatuation was a woman he called Mimi – an attractive girl from a good family who held Heydrich in high esteem. She was not intellectual, but she kept the attention of Heydrich with her sweet and dedicated nature, and a deep desire to marry and raise children. A fortnight after his conversation with Canaris, Heydrich put on full dress kit, metal sparkling, leather shining, and called upon Mimi's father. He stood in the doorway of a prosperous house on Olshausenstrasse and, hand upon sword, asked for Mimi's hand in marriage. The question was answered with a handshake and a tear from the father, who had wanted this polished officer for a son-in-law from the beginning.

The next day, Heydrich removed his cap, took Mimi's hand and went down on one knee, his officer's sword jangling in its scabbard. They planned a spring wedding. Mimi chose a wedding dress and outfits for the bridesmaids. She imagined walking down an avenue of raised swords, arm in arm with Reinhard, and butterflies threatened to fly from her ribs. The family pastor read out the banns with singular pride the following Sunday.

A week later, Heydrich decided to dine in the mess. Few guests were expected, and he was happy to spend a quiet evening before turning his mind to some tedious but urgent administration. He changed into mess kit and drifted down to dinner. A small gathering of officers and guests was chatting beside the bar. Heydrich bowed to his superior officers and joined the circle. It was as he raised the cocktail glass to his lips that she came into sight.

At that moment, Planet Heydrich spun clean off its axis.

Her name was Lina. She was nineteen. She was fair, with a beautiful, open face and jade-green eyes. A poised, athletic figure moved under her grey silk evening dress. The black seam of her stockings ran behind two perfect calves, tapering into ankles criss-crossed with grey silk. She blinked through long blonde lashes like a cat waking from sleep.

Heydrich was entranced. The officer to his right stepped forward to make the introduction.

'Oberleutnant Heydrich, it is my honour to present Fräulein Lina von Osten.'

Heydrich clicked his heels and drew her hand to his lips.

'*Erfreut* – delighted,' said Heydrich, looking upward with the eyes of a desert traveller finding an oasis.

'The pleasure is mine,' said Fräulein von Osten, with the hint of a curtsy.

As luck would have it, the two were placed next to each other at dinner. And on this occasion Heydrich felt as if he had put his boots on the wrong feet. It was she who shone the torch. She wanted to know everything. His musical upbringing. His father's operas. His violin. His reputation as a swimmer and fencer. His naval career. His remaining ambitions. Heydrich began to feel what his prey must have felt: ivy creeping across his palm, around his arm and winding around his neck.

When she did speak of herself, Heydrich was rapt. She was part of a new political movement, she said. A movement that would rid

Germany of impurity and make the Fatherland strong again. Her brother was a member. She had been to a rally the year before. Now she was a member. The force would, in time, become unstoppable.

'We are always looking for men of stature and calibre to drive the movement forward,' she said, dragging on a cigarette, slow-blinking in the smoke.

She brushed her hand against Heydrich's sleeve. The ivy had penetrated Heydrich's chest and started circling the ventricles of his heart. As the women were about to withdraw, Oberleutnant Brandt pulled up a chair opposite.

'And when do the happy couple intend to marry?' he said.

Lina von Osten turned to face Brandt.

'Your question might be considered premature, Oberleutnant,' she said, smiling.

'I was not referring to you, with respect, Fräulein. But to Oberleutnant Heydrich's fiancée.'

Lina stiffened. Heydrich made a mental note that once he became grand admiral, he would have Brandt keelhauled.

'Thank you, Oberleutnant Brandt, for your concern,' said Heydrich, aware he was colouring. 'But plans remain at an early stage.'

Cold composure returned. Heydrich leaned forward.

'A good officer, Oberleutnant Brandt, must be willing to respond to new events.'

Within a week, Heydrich had called off his engagement to Mimi. Her cries were heard the length of Olshausenstrasse. It was of course unfortunate, Heydrich wrote in a letter to his own mother, but these things could not be helped. Admiral Raeder was furious. What was the meaning of this? How should he respond to the letter received from Mimi's father? Was this conduct becoming of an officer?

Raeder was an admiral who knew his own mind. He dismissed Heydrich from the Navy on the spot. Canaris sought to intervene but to no avail. And besides, Canaris had to accept – the admiral had a point.

One of the rising stars of the Weimar Republic's Navy found that in April 1931 he was *sans* rank, *sans* prospects, *sans* everything. Perhaps not everything. There was one consolation as the good ship Heydrich plunged into the depths.

He was now engaged to Lina von Osten.

On the last Saturday of summer, 1931, a small band of men stood on the deck of the private cruiser *Köln*. They wore long white trousers, blue blazers and striped ties. They looked like members of a weekend sailing club. On closer inspection, they were a hand-picked selection of men from the League. A briefing had already taken place below deck. It was now time to wait for the launch that promised to arrive at noon.

Canaris was among the group, his sailor's eyes locked on the harbour.

The launch appeared in the distance. As it approached, Canaris counted five, maybe six men. The crew of the *Köln* stood by with ropes. The launch drew up alongside. There were five. Four wore brown uniforms with red armbands carrying a distinctive black insignia in a circle of white. The paramilitary uniforms made some on deck feel uneasy, but this had been predicted in the briefing. The fifth man wore a civilian suit and a moustache that looked like a black nosebleed. He was hatless, with black hair shaven at the sides. A long comma of black hair slit his forehead.

The five men boarded the *Köln*.

'*Willkommen, Alles,*' said the rear admiral.

The crew served Asbach sodas. The boarding party commended the elegant lines of the *Köln* and the views of Kiel harbour.

After an agreeable lunch of asparagus soup, *Wirtshaussalat* with *Laugengebäck* and *Obatzter*, and a 1912 Mosel, the *Köln* sailed further out to sea, far from any other vessel, and dropped anchor.

'Shall we begin?' asked the grand admiral. The group, seated and standing, turned to look into the clear blue of the grand admiral's eyes.

'What I am about to tell you', he said, addressing the boarding party, 'is, and must remain, at the highest level of secrecy. Any breach of security will threaten our *Programm* – an ongoing scheme to rebuild the German Navy away from prying eyes.'

'*Natürlich*,' said the man in the civilian suit. There were nods from the shaven heads of the paramilitaries.

'The Navy does not live in a vacuum. A force is sweeping Germany that will restore and purify the Fatherland. That force can hasten our resurrection. We can hasten that force. Divided we are weak. Together we are strong.'

A ripple of applause spread through the crowd on deck. The grand admiral gave a summary of a secret programme of German naval re-armament over the previous decade. The man in the civilian suit listened with black, squirrel-like eyes.

'The current number of torpedo boats?' he asked.

'Nineteen,' said the grand admiral.

'How long would it take to bring that figure to ninety?'

The grand admiral raised his eyebrows.

'Four to five years,' he said.

'What about submarines?' continued the man, skimming his moustache with his forefinger.

The admiral hesitated.

'Submarines are, as you know, prohibited by the Treaty of Versailles.'

'*Und so?*' said the man.

'The most sensitive part of our *Programm* is code-named Barrakuda. *Projekt Barrakuda* has been overseen by an officer with a network of contacts from Buenos Aires to Osaka. Our very own Kapitän Canaris.'

Canaris rose. He had been scrutinizing the civilian from the moment he boarded. He was from the same physical mould as Canaris – small, spare, agile. There the similarities ended. Canaris was a naval officer of the Prussian school. The civilian was no officer. Canaris spoke with the cut-glass tones of a northern Hanoverian; the civilian spoke with the squashed vowels of a provincial southern Bavarian. Butcher class, thought Canaris. Yet he had *something*.

The alert squirrel eyes took in everything. They blazed when he spoke, fists clenched, of the dawn of a new *Reich*.

Canaris gave a summary of *Projekt Barrakuda*. It was the first time the civilian smiled.

'How many attack submarines currently operational?'

'Eleven,' said Canaris. 'Scattered across secret locations in the Pomeranian islands.'

The civilian followed with a series of questions on range and strike capability – each question betraying unusual and penetrating insight. The questions impressed Canaris – and it showed. The civilian was also impressed. He considered that in time Canaris might be an officer of considerable value.

The naval contingent glanced at one another and nodded. The occasion was becoming a notable success. Before the boarding party left, the civilian wrote in the ship's visitors' book:

'In the hope that I can help with the reconstruction of a fleet worthy of the Reich.'

Before the man descended into the launch, the paramilitaries split into facing groups of two and raised their arms, as if saluting Caesar. The man gave the same salute, turned to wave at his hosts on the *Köln*, and was gone.

CHAPTER 18
'THE CHARMER'

London, 1932

Marks

Uncle Abe set another riddle. He wrote the following letters on a piece of paper.

A B R
 A B R
  A B R
   A B R
    A B R
     A B R
      A B R
       A B R
        A B R
         A B
         A

'Are you following the number and line of the letters?'

'Yes, Uncle Abe,' said Young Leo. 'Towards the bottom, each line diminishes by one letter.'

'When we meet again, I want you to think what letter comes next.'

'There will be eight of them,' said the boy.

'There will,' said Uncle Abe. 'But only a true charmer will work it out.'

That evening, Leo Marks made lengthy computations. He looked up at the moon each time his pencil came to a halt. Uncle Abe said the Hebrew month began with each new cycle of the moon. 'While other nations count by the sun, says the Talmud, Israel counts by the moon.' The Hebrew moon was not helping. Young Leo came up with the same answer each time. Gobbledygook.

He closed his eyes. He remembered what Uncle Abe had said once, over the summer. *The key to any lock... is the key.* He said the words to his bedroom wall. But what was the key? Then he recalled Uncle Abe's exact words on the last visit. 'Only a true charmer will work it out.' He laughed out loud and picked up his pen.

```
A B R A C A D A B R A
 A B R
  A B R
   A B R
    A B R
     A B R
      A B R
       A B R
        A B R
         A B
          A
```

He completed the sequence.

```
A B R A C A D A B R A
A B R A C A D A B R
A B R A C A D A B
A B R A C A D A
A B R A C A D
A B R A C A
A B R A C
A B R A
A B R
A B
A
```

His eyes followed the diagonal lines of letters. He started with the lowest 'A' at the bottom point and read up the right-hand side of the triangle. He blinked.

'ABRACADABRA.'

The word stared back at him twice.

Was there some magic after all...?

He thought of Uncle Abe sitting by the fire, his long fingers curled together, eyes twinkling.

During the next lesson, Uncle Abe took out a ruler, drew a blank grid and populated it with numbers, starting with '6' in the top left square.

6	32	3	34	35	1
7	11	27	28	8	30
19	14	16	15	23	24
18	20	22	21	17	13
25	29	10	9	26	12
36	5	33	4	2	31

Young Leo started looking for patterns as soon as the numbers were written. The single figures, he noticed, were all adjacent to another single figure, save '3' and '5'. The numbers in the third row were the closest in range. The numbers in the first and sixth rows were the most divergent.

'What does each row and column have in common?' said Uncle Abe.

Leo Marks could sense the blurred outline of an answer, like the contour of a ghost.

There was a pause.

'What shall we do to each row and column?' said Uncle Abe.

'Add the numbers together?' said Young Leo.

'I'll race you,' said Uncle Abe.

The little boy and the old man each scratched their sums on a separate piece of paper. Young Leo added the numbers of row 1 together. Then row 2. The square was beginning to reveal its pattern. Marks junior tested it on the first column. By the time he ran his eye over the second column, the pattern was exposed.

'Each row and each column adds up to 111,' said Young Leo.

'It does,' said Uncle Abe.

'That makes a combined total of 666,' said the boy.

'It does indeed,' said Uncle Abe. 'The cornerstone number is "6". It has 6 rows and 6 columns. It has 6 times 6 squares. In the Tree of Life, the Sixth Emanation is the sun. That is why we call it the Sun Magic Square.'

Leo Marked looked at the Sun Magic Square and smiled.

'The pattern is there,' said Uncle Abe. 'For those with the eyes to see.'

*

As the bell above the door at Marks & Co. rang just before 11 a.m., twelve-year-old Leo Marks was creeping up the stairs to the second floor. As he passed the milestones of maturity, he found himself drawn to the hidden second-floor section on 'anatomy'. The books were bound in vellum and as he took a copy from the shelf his heart fluttered like a hummingbird. He turned the handle of the door and entered the library of the occult. He tiptoed across the floorboards towards the anatomy section in an alcove veiled by a velvet curtain. He drew back the curtain, expecting to find only bound volumes. The sight that greeted him made his right hand spring to his mouth.

Leo Marks stood face to face with a woman perched on a stool behind the alcove curtain. She had ageless features and long black hair streaked with silver. She was slim and her eyes had the alertness of a Manchurian hare. In a distant life she had been called White Peony. White Peony had, moments before, been sketching in charcoal on thick drawing paper. The surprise of the interruption caused her to drop her sketches on the floor. She knelt down, closing the fan of papers. Leo Marks knelt to help her, though her hand gestured him away. Looking at the sketches, it was clear why the woman was so anxious to hide them against her chest. She placed a finger to her lips. Leo Marks nodded. There was a tacit agreement. The incident would fall through life's floorboards and rest, forgotten. Flushed, Master Marks crept downstairs as if nothing had happened.

It was a Thursday. There was something about Thursdays that made young Leo Marks pick up a pattern. Every alternate Thursday, Marks noticed the same man at the same bay: nineteenth-century literature. He breathed heavily for a man in his twenties, and there were stains on his Old Etonian tie. Just before closing time, another man always joined him in the bay. There was something about his face that was not English. Marks watched them out of the corner of his eye. They stood close together but never spoke. Once, Marks was sure the man in the stained tie dropped something into the pocket of the other man. Each alternate Thursday, he would look out for the pair. Each alternate Thursday, he was sure something was being secretly exchanged. He told Mr Marks senior.

'Could be anything, my son. Could be anything.'

*

Suttill

The polished floor of the Great Hall, Lincoln's Inn, echoed as diners stood for the procession that walked in twos to the Benchers' Table. The hall's vaulted ceiling and stained-glass windows gave the impression of a cathedral nave. Those standing for the Benchers wore evening dress, the white of their starched collars weathering the scrutiny of bewigged judges peering from the vast portraits that hung between the windows.

Master Treasurer said a solemn grace. The hall echoed to the clatter of Benchers, barristers and students sitting down to dinner. On a table in the centre of the hall sat a well-scrubbed Bar student, gown over his dinner jacket, in a 'mess' of four. He was the evening's mess junior, seated to the right of the mess captain. His name was Francis Suttill. Had he not decided on a career at the Bar, he might have been Errol Flynn's screen double. He had honey-coloured hair swept back from a clear brow, animated green eyes and a perfect profile. In a future life, he would find himself in a contest far more dangerous than a courtroom joust. A single slip would be fatal.

The mess was buzzing with news of the decision in *Donoghue v Stevenson*. Mrs Donoghue, the case went, had visited a café in Paisley and drunk a sinless bottle of ginger beer. She took scant comfort from seeing, in the bottom of the bottle, the decomposing remnants of a snail. Later, the impecunious Scots widow 'not worth the sum of five pounds' fell into a delirious illness. A local lawyer took pity and funded a lawsuit against the manufacturer, Mr Stevenson. Did she have claim? There was no contract between the parties, protested Stevenson. The case leaped from appeal to appeal. At last, it came before five 'Lords of Appeal in Ordinary', the highest court in the land. The judgement was portentous. Lord Atkin did not think a more important problem had preoccupied their Lordships in the court's entire history. After vexed consideration, the majority upheld Mrs Donoghue's claim. Mr Stevenson had failed in his duty of care. Negligence was born. Barristers who read the judgement looked like cave-dwellers who had discovered fire.

Rees, a teetotaller from Aberystwyth, sat in the mess with his wine glass turned upside down. He was exercised about the judgement. His cheeks were flushed, despite drinking only water. He banged the table, making the cutlery jump.

'I am with the dissenters,' he pronounced.

'Pray tell?' said the mess captain.

'You tell me where the contract is between Donoghue and Stevenson?' said Rees. 'The court has conjured one out of the *e-e-ether*.'

'Not a bit,' said the mess fourth. 'Why should the manufacturer avoid liability? I'll bet there was nothing on the label about a dead snail chaser!'

'What?' said Rees. 'So Stevenson was supposed to go *round* his factory shining a torch into every single opaque bottle of ginger beer? It's madness, I tell, you. Absolute *b-linking* madness.'

Suttill looked up at the vaulted ceiling as the debate raged. He thought of the snail slithering, eyes on jellied stilts, into a dark brown bottle, far from the madding crowd, only to drown in ginger beer and change English legal history forever. In a future incarnation, he had time, while held in the House of Black Beetles, to mull over *Donoghue v Stevenson* in more detail than any in the mess could ever imagine.

CHAPTER 19
'THE MONKEY BRIDGE'

Paris, 1934

Noor

From a distance, it looked like a baby elephant moving through the 5ème Arrondissement. Closer scrutiny revealed a slim figure leading from the front wearing black culottes, black pumps and a black linen chemise. Around her neck was a locket engraved with the Mother of the Universe. Inside the locket, a riddle remained hidden. The figure was fine boned, her hair cut short *à la gamine*. Her eyes were rich henna brown. Her skin was dark and shone with an inner light. Her face was beautiful and threaded with compassion. Some thought she was Persian, others Italian, even Brazilian.

Noor Inayat Khan, psychology student at the Sorbonne, was wheeling a monumental black instrument case down the Rue Saint-Séverin. Inside, encased in crimson velvet, lay a Salzedo harp, wincing in silence with every bump. She was wheeling her harp back from orchestra practice in the church of Saint-Séverin and decided on a shortcut. She turned into an unfamiliar street, which seemed even taller and narrower than others in the 5ème. The cobblestones were smoother, affording temporary relief to the stringed

222

prisoner in the instrument case. Noor reached the end of the street and looked up, curious to memorize her new route.

The street sign stood high and immutable:

RUE DE LA HARPE

Her dark eyes twinkled.

Drawn by the unfamiliar noise, a man in an attic above came to the window. The edges of his trilby were visible to anyone looking up from the street. From his attic, Georges Morel watched the petite figure pulling the giant instrument case. Something about the sight made him smile. He returned to his table. Spread out were stripped parts of a Luger: trigger plate, receiver axle, locking bolt, firing pin. Sitting down in a hat and shirtsleeves, he poured a small amount of liquid on to a rag and carried on oiling the receiver axle.

Noor would one day return to Morel's *rue* carrying an object more dangerous than a Salzedo harp. For now, she was a harpist walking down Rue de la Harpe under the gaze of a man with a tin head. Noor reached place de la Sorbonne. She decided to stop at the café on the corner. She sat next to her towering harp case. A young waiter came over, handsome to the point of impudence, and took Noor's order for a *citron pressé*. Then, pen poised over pad, he turned to address the harp.

'*Et pour Monsieur...?*'

'Nothing for the moment,' said Noor, eyes smiling.

Noor Inayat Khan did not have quite the same confidence with men as some of the girls in her year, but after almost a year at the Sorbonne she was finding *les garçons* less mysterious, some even intriguing. They were eclipsed, however, by her musical dreamscapes.

She took out her harp transcription of Bach's Cello Suite No. 3 and followed the melody line as she sipped her *pressé*. She could feel the strings under her fingers as she followed the ardent, disciplined path of the notes. The colours opened in her mind on the wings of a butterfly – orange, red and purple with dots of lime. Nothing, she thought, articulated the soul's longing more than the colour of Bach. As the piece lingered and dived into a crescendo, she felt a ripple across the strings of her heart. Onward went the notes, deeper, more plangent. Faster flapped the wings of the butterfly.

Tears came into her eyes. She put down the *citron pressé* and sat blinking. She took a handkerchief to her eyes. Mascara smudged the white cotton. The waiter returned. The amusement in his face was replaced with concern. He offered her white linen and water from a carafe. Noor dried her eyes.

'*Je m'excuse*,' she said.

It was the waiter who pulled the harp case across the square to the door of the imposing building on the corner. He offered to take it up the stairs. Noor hesitated. There were rules about allowing men into the building. Yet some of the girls on her floor had taken their new-found *liberté* to studious lengths. Sylvie, a lithe blonde medical student from Cahors, decreed her *voyages* after dark were anatomical 'practicals'. The pristine sheets on the bed of another undergraduate, Anne-Sophie, were sometimes as taut and unruffled in the morning as they were the previous evening. Anne-Sophie's night had been elsewhere.

Noor looked at the waiter's eyes. They were willing and sincere. Surely it would be all right? Sylvie's voice came into her head. 'Always allow men to demonstrate their strength. Not so long ago they were defending us from *les mammouths*.'

'Are you sure you wouldn't mind?'

He looked elated. He picked up the harp case and carried it up four flights of stairs, straining to make the task look effortless. At the top he rested the harp case against her door. As Noor said thank you, he gave her a piece of paper and disappeared downstairs before she had time to protest. Written inside a folded sheet was his name, 'Philippe', and an invitation to see Marlene Dietrich in *The Scarlet Empress*. Noor smiled. *La vie Parisienne!*

She turned the key and opened the door of her modest room in the eaves of the building in place de la Sorbonne. She took the harp from its case and set it down by the window. Hanging from the wall opposite was her father's old *surshringar*. The door was framed by shelves crammed with books – some in French, some in English – on philosophy, psychology, anthropology, religion, symbolism and music. Above her bed was the painting of the winged heart from her father's study in Suresnes. On her bedside table were three books.

~ *The Wisdom of Rumi*
~ *The Conference of the Birds*
~ *The Vajrayāna Scriptures*

Lying on her pillow was a wooden bird, Pteech-ka.

*

The New Year brought snow. Noor herself had hauled a sack of hardwood and kindling up the stairs to her room. The fire radiated heat within a head's radius. Further away and the room felt like January in Davos. At night, the shadows from the fire would dart across the wall and Noor felt the familiar squeeze of fear around her heart. The words of Inayat came.

'Fear nothing, *Bābouli*. The shadows are Chandra's chariot.'

In the mornings, when the grate was cold ash, she had to blow warmth into her fingers before making coffee. Then she sat by the window and placed her harp upon her shoulder, filling the room with the hues of Bach, Pachelbel and Debussy. Some of the notes escaped through the rickety window frames into the air above place de la Sorbonne. Passers-by would sometimes look up, straining, as if there was a gathering of the city's angels.

To Noor, everything in the city felt so *moderne* – art, design, music, dance, photography, cinema. Even the metro trains felt like sleek silver arrows of the future. She loved the chic. The season's silhouette for *femmes à la mode* was ruffle sleeves, flying collars, belted waists and long hemlines. The designers – Chanel, Vionnet and Schiaparelli – were at their zenith. Each atelier sought to outmanoeuvre the others.

In the less obvious fashion house of Molyneux on Rue Royale, Noor stood and gazed at the dresses, which might have been painted by Matisse. The interior was a cocoon of grey velvet walls and virgin white carpet. The lines of the furniture were as graceful and modern as the lines of the evening gowns for which Molyneux was famous. Life at Molyneux ran under the pristine tick of the Sèvres mantel clock that eyed the comings and goings on the expanse of white carpet with watchful disinterest.

The urbane and discreet manager of the house was half French, half English, known as 'Tommy'. Noor watched him pressing his fleshy hands together as some of the best-heeled women in Paris sashayed into the Molyneux cocoon. As for Tommy, a hand gestured in one direction and a velvet-backed chair would appear. A hand gestured in another and a tray would appear, with Pernod and water.

One day, Noor decided to stop observing and step into the cocoon. She ran her fingers over the silk prints of peacocks and tigers. At her side, the manager appeared from nowhere, as if soaping his fleshy hands.

'For shoulders of such elegance,' said Tommy, 'might I suggest a V-neck wrap dress or an opera cloak?'

Noor smiled. 'Just an accoutrement for a party.'

They settled on a silk lapel flower. Noor had no idea that she was speaking to the White Rabbit. Time had not yet christened him the White Rabbit or placed a bounty of two million francs on his head. For now, Tommy was just 'Tommy', the manager of a fashion house with a staff of modish women. A lone male atoll, thought Noor, in a sea of mermaids.

That evening, Noor went with Anne-Sophie to a reading at Shakespeare and Company by an American writer who had once driven ambulances on the Western Front. The bookshop was packed, some guests spilling into the cold. They were able to slip into the main room where the American owner, Miss Beach, was supervising the wine and chasing her cat, Lucy, off the table.

Between the bookshelves were photographs of her 'regulars', some of whom she had fed when they were penniless and others, like Joyce, she had published. There were posters advertising *Ulysses* and a framed quotation:

LOVE LOVES TO LOVE LOVE

Miss Beach, immaculate in a black dress and white collar, welcomed the two women, squeezing their hands.

'Sorbonne?' she said. 'Always welcome. Just be careful of Lucy. She has a terrible reputation for eating ladies' gloves.'

There was applause as the reading ended. Lucy, the cat, sat on a stool watching as the crush of people in the room expanded and contracted to the echo of popping corks. Noor and Anne-Sophie noticed a man with a dirty collar and tie drinking as if he had never experienced liquid before and putting vol-au-vents in his pockets. He introduced himself as a New York journalist named Miller. He had the look of a dented, hungry tomcat. Would the two like to accompany him to a dive he knew in Montmartre?

At the end of the evening, as Lucy moved between the bottles on the table, licking flakes of vol-au-vent, the American, known just as 'Ernest', kissed Miss Beach goodbye. He shook the last remaining hands farewell and stepped into a Paris night.

The author walked towards the river. He walked along the Boulevard Saint Michel, turned right then left, cutting through Rue de la Harpe. As he took the turning, he saw a man walking towards him wearing a hat pulled down low. He stopped to ask the time. The man in the hat brought his wristwatch up to the glow of the street light. He said nothing. The author caught a pair of lucent, injured eyes. A veteran? The man's air was unmistakeable. He caught a sense of his pain, even though the latter's tin head was concealed. As the author walked on, a phrase echoed in his mind. *You are so brave and quiet I forget you are suffering.*

*

Tommy turned the key of Molyneux. When the colour of the silks was leached by the monochrome fog that sometimes descended on his mind, he would throw a bag over his shoulder and head for a particular door in Montmartre.

The Daisy Bar sat at the foot of a flight of worn stone steps in a side street off the Boulevard Clichy. The silhouette of a woman was visible under a street lamp opposite. She was smoking with studied nonchalance. Other women stood shivering at intervals further along the street. The door to the Daisy Bar led into a smoke-filled room crammed with expatriates from Dante's *Inferno*. The *mecs* sat at their tables, pimps in pinstripes, patting their cigarillo-thin moustaches with linen, the oil of their hair almost dripping under the lights. Amid the *mecs* sat the *poulets*, compact mirrors open, lips pursed as they stained their mouths scarlet. Every so often, a *poulet* pushed away her chair from the mountain of *moules* shells and stood, arranging her hair. A *mec* administered a pat of simultaneous encouragement and dismissal as she sashayed, handbag on elbow, towards the door. The *mec* ordered another bottle of wine, turned to the other *mecs*, and from the folds of his pinstripes pulled a pack of cards. Between rounds of bezique, one of the *poulets* might reappear, lipstick smudged, dress creased, and press a palm-shaped item into a *mec*'s hand. If the *mec* was ahead at cards he might pour her a glass of wine, then shoo her back towards the door while he turned to open another round of bezique.

There was a disused safe beside the piano at the back of the Daisy Bar for apprentice safe-breakers. Above the safe was a fairground dartboard for throwing flick knives. From time to time someone would enter the Inferno, kitbag over shoulder, and weave between the tables of *mecs* and *poulets* to the stairs at the back. There was a sharp aroma when one approached the first floor. And the rhythmic beat of leather on leather.

Dum
Dum
Dum

Then a half-beat.

Dum-Dum

Then back to the regular beat.

The first floor was an uninterrupted space. Industrial metal lights hung from the ceiling. Shadows fell in slats on the walls from the wooden climbing bars. Four of the larger lights hung over the corners of the boxing ring, one over the centre. To the left of the ring were two punchbags. One was in use. A young Italian fighter was hammering out the jabs. A small crowd of men stood by the other punchbag. At the centre was a black-skinned Canadian fighter in vest and shorts. The stark lights made his skin look silver. Ernest, the American, was introducing gains to the coach. In the ring, the American was known as *Le Stylo Puissant* – 'The Mighty Pen'.

On the other side of the ring, men were jumping to the wasp-like buzz of skipping ropes or lying on the bench press pumping dumbbells. One, whose hands spent the day swathed in silk, gripped the metal bar and pushed upward into the lights.

The coach gave two short claps.

'*Chut!*' he said. 'Okay. Tonight, we're going to start with some sparring. The winner gets a friendly round with our heavyweight guest from Canada.'

A ripple went through the crowd.

'Okay, *Stylo*,' he said, pointing at the American.

'And you, Tommy,' he said. 'Get your gloves on.'

Minutes later, Tommy stepped into the ring, lips pursed over his gumshield. His feet danced as he semi-circled his opponent. He held up his right glove, palm over face.

He lowered his head and with his left glove made the first jab.

*

Despite the cold, Paris was simmering. Simmering from the flames of ideology that were ripping through the city. Nowhere were the flames hotter than at the Sorbonne. Noor enrolled in a class on history and philosophy. The professeur giving the course was the Sorbonne's most celebrated historian.

229

He wrote a proposition on the blackboard.

> THERE ARE CAUSES WORTH DYING FOR
> BUT NONE WORTH KILLING FOR

He turned. There was a twinkle in the man's eye behind the round black spectacles. The man's face told a story of what he had witnessed. Men drowning face down in the mud. Men whose heads had enjoyed a liaison with a sniper's bullet. Men with holes in their chests so large they exposed the sky behind. It was also the story of a man who, having seen the apocalypse at first hand, had decided to embrace humanity. There was, after all, still much to learn.

He seldom mentioned that he was a recipient of the Légion d'honneur and known to his platoon as 'Lieutenant Histoire'.

He was Professeur Marc Bloch. The same Lieutenant Bloch who had waded through different shades of mud to find his wounded Sergent, Georges Morel.

And his lecture theatre was erupting with the force of an artillery barrage. There was an impassioned diatribe from the Communist faction. A new world was being forged in the flames, shouted one. Capitalism would be amputated, and its oozing stump cauterized by the fire. Noor's friend Jean-Luc slammed the desk, stood and hailed imminent revolution. There were roars of approval.

Noor closed her eyes. The noise was making an angry impressionist painting behind her eyes. Reds, oranges and yellows were pulsing with rage. The rage was burning. She craved a dreamscape. She took her pen to her notebook and started sketching. She sketched a hare, a deer and an elephant. Jean-Luc looked over her shoulder. His face was thunder. After the lecture, a group went for coffee in the Café des Siciliennes on a corner of Rue Thouin. The debate continued. Jean-Luc thumped the table three times.

'Enough is enough!'

He turned to the group, which included Noor.

'Do you know what's happening in Vienna? I will *tell* you what! Barricades are going up around Karl Marx-Hof where the tenements are being shelled. Children are being thrown from burning balconies as right-wing militia open up with machine guns. Why? Because the people inside refuse to conform to the *petit bourgeois* values of a bankrupt fascist dictatorship!'

There were nods.

'It's all very well to draw pictures of animals when the world is on fire!'

He was staring straight at Noor.

'How naïve do you need to be?'

Noor could feel herself blushing. She was about to speak when the doors to the café burst open.

Five men entered the café. They wore regulation fascist dark shirts, dark ties. Their heads were shaven at the back. Two had coshes. They were members of the '*Jeunesses Patriotes*' – Young Patriots.

'Jews and Italian scum – OUT!' shouted the ringleader.

The others stood behind him, arms folded. Everyone froze. Except Jean-Luc. He put down his pastis and walked over to the ringleader.

'Leave now or I will rearrange your face.'

The ringleader laughed. A crack echoed.

'*Gratuit*,' said Jean-Luc, kneading his fist. 'On behalf of the international proletariat.'

The young fascist stood wiping the blood from his nose.

'You will be DEAD by Mass on Sunday!' said the fascist, pointing a juddering finger.

The other students rose. The Young Patriots were outnumbered and, with their ringleader holding his nose, they beat a retreat. Jean-Luc came back to the table and resumed his seat amid back-slapping. Noor was shocked.

'Have compassion' came the echo of Inayat's voice.

In her room later that night, she cried for the ringleader.

Two nights later, the Young Patriots converged *en masse* in the Place de la Concorde. Jean-Luc stood arm in arm with a hasty alliance of socialists and communists, eyes aflame. They jeered the mob of armed fascists, holding an unsteady line on the second step of the Assemblée nationale. Police moved into the middle. A group of fascists surged forward. One of the police horses reared. A pistol discharged. A communist student defending the Assemblée nationale fell backwards. The bullet had struck his neck, piercing his windpipe.

Jean-Luc lay dying.

His funeral attracted every self-respecting radical at the Sorbonne. Jean-Luc's parents stood, numb with shock, as their son's coffin was wheeled past, draped in a red flag.

*

Noor sat in her room in the place de la Sorbonne. Pteech-ka's eyes glistened with sorrow. Noor had spent half a day making a card for Jean-Luc's parents. It was a procession of animals with their heads bowed in sorrow. Why was there so much hatred? She opened *The Wisdom of Rumi.*

We are born of love. Love is our mother.

She placed a notebook on her knees and took out a pen. What better way to remember Jean-Luc than a story about love? Her pen began to move.

'The Monkey-Bridge'

A giant-like monkey once ruled over eighty thousand monkeys in the Himalaya mountains. And through the rocks where they lived streamed the river Ganges before reaching the valley where cities were built. And there, where the bubbling water fell from rock to rock, stood a magnificent tree. In the spring it bore tender white blossoms; and later it was laden with fruit so wonderful that none could be compared to them, and the sweet winds of the mountain gave them the sweetness of honey...

CHAPTER 20
'ACHILLES AND PATROCLUS'

Berlin, 1935

Canaris

Canaris was on manoeuvres in the Baltic Sea when two letters arrived in quick succession. The first was from the *Reichsmarine* headquarters in Berlin, announcing his promotion to admiral. The second was in an envelope bearing the stamp of the office of the German chancellor. The Führer had the pleasure of appointing Admiral Wilhelm Canaris head of Germany's military intelligence, the Abwehr. There was a personal note from the Führer himself, congratulating the admiral on his promotion and expressing confidence in his unswerving devotion to the Third Reich. The man with the squirrel eyes, thought Canaris. Fate had brought them together. How would Fate play its hand now the tin Weimar Republic had crumpled in the face of a new empire – the Third Reich?

'The Third Reich,' declared the Führer, 'will establish a New World Order.'

There were rallies in Nuremberg, with columns of uniformed Nazis chanting and hailing a new Caesar. The swastika flew from red banners everywhere. Germany was being reborn, read the propaganda in *Der Stürmer*. The New World Order would first

identify enemies of the Reich. Any individual or group threaten-
ing the purity of the Fatherland would be severed from society
with *Flammenschwerte!* – flame blades! For Canaris, however, there
was something pagan about the black swastika stamped on the red
banners. Something unsavoury about the shaven heads of the party
faithful and talk of a Master Race. And the Führer, for all his manic
devotion to the Fatherland, was hardly an Elector of Brandenburg.

Canaris snapped himself out of a malaise. He was an admiral now
and the chief of German intelligence. His duty to the Fatherland
was paramount. His mind turned to the months ahead. There was
work to be done.

'The Abwehr will become the most efficient military intelligence gathering machine in the world,' he told his staff on the
first day. 'No heights will be too high to scale for the chosen
Abwehr few.'

One of his first meetings was with his opposite number in the
Abwehr's tenacious young cousin, the Sicherheitsdienst or 'SD'.
The SD was the intelligence wing of the Waffen-SS. The SD, it was
said, was the closest thing Hitler had to a blue-eyed son.

The head of the SD entered Canaris's office. He was dressed in
the black uniform of an SS-Brigadeführer, with gold epaulettes and
a swastika on his left arm.

SS-Brigadeführer Reinhard Heydrich.

The face of the death's head hawkmoth was beaming.

'Admiral Canaris, may I be the first to congratulate you on
your double promotion,' said SS-Brigadeführer Heydrich. 'Most
richly deserved.'

The Brigadeführer exuded all the bonhomie of a man whose
star was ascending into the Nazi stratosphere at rocket speed. His
sensual lips were twitching under the sharp, narrow nose.

'I look forward, Admiral, to forging the closest working rela-
tionship between our agencies.'

There followed a detailed discussion on departmental co-
operation and information sharing. The heads of the Abwehr and

the SD, it went without saying, would be the Achilles and Patroclus of the new regime.

At the end of the meeting, Heydrich clicked his boots and saluted. As he marched away, he failed to mention one small matter. His personal order to tap all Abwehr telephones.

CHAPTER 21
'THE SWAN KINGDOM'

London, 1938

Marks

Young Leo was nearing twenty when Marks senior asked him to cash some cheques for the bookshop at Lloyds Bank on Charing Cross Road. Marks junior placed a trilby over his unruly curls and, cheques in hand, made his way to the bank. He tried to saunter, but his stocky frame made him look off-balance. He entered the bank and was directed by a liveried staff member towards a cashier. As he stood in the queue, he became aware of the man standing in front. It was the astrakhan collar of his overcoat, the pinstripe of his trousers and the timbre of his voice.

'Good afternoon. Buckley-Chubb's the name,' said the man to the cashier. 'Anthony Buckley-Chubb CB.'

He sounded like a peer who had just stumbled out of the Athenaeum. The cashier, in a dress with a velvet collar, looked inquisitive.

'CB,' he assured her. 'Commander of the Bath.'

'Well, it's an honour,' she said.

'I was in touch with the manager this morning about cashing a cheque for five hundred pounds,' said Buckley-Chubb CB.

'I see, sir,' said the cashier. She was about nineteen, with pearl-white skin and black eyebrows shaped into a permanent quizzical look. 'I'll have to fetch Mr Bagshot.'

Marks had keen eyesight and saw a cheque resting on the cashier's station. It was drawn on the account of the Burmah Oil Company in favour of Anthony Buckley-Chubb CB. The cashier was gone some minutes. People in the queue made their displeasure known. A quiet cough here, a tap of an umbrella there.

Buckley-Chubb stood with his arms folded, the paragon of a wealthy client who detested waiting. He rumbled like a portentous volcano. In time, Mr Bagshot arrived with his cashier. The bank manager himself looked like he had been sent straight from a casting agency – thinning pate, half-moon spectacles, double chin, fob watch and an air of weary respectability.

'Mr Buckley-Chubb, I must humbly apologize for keeping you waiting.'

'It's just not good enough!' said Buckley-Chubb.

'We have had to move funds from our safe and the procedure takes a little time.'

Buckley-Chubb CB looked a fraction less irate.

'Would you mind waiting while Miss Buchanan counts out the notes?' said the bank manager.

He directed waiting customers to a till next door, just unfurling its blind.

Marks was first at the adjacent till. He could not help noticing Miss Buchanan counting out the notes as if she were trying to break a record for sloth.

There was a sudden commotion. While Miss Buchanan was still counting the cash, Anthony Buckley-Chubb CB made a sprint for the exit. His fawn overcoat streamed behind him as he ran, pinstripes a-blur, towards the door. The only obstacle that prevented him leaving was the brace of uniformed constables standing in the door frame.

'Lionel Redknapp, also known as Anthony Buckley-Chubb,' said the taller policeman, 'I am arresting you for forgery and attempting to obtain property by false pretences. You are not obliged to say anything...'

Good grief, thought Marks. Commander of the Bath indeed. Still, he had to admire the man in handcuffs. Superlative effort on the voice.

*

Suttill

Francis Suttill stood outside Court 4 of the Old Bailey. The space felt like a mausoleum for one of King Midas's brothers whose touch turned everything to marble. The vanishing expanse of marble underfoot crept up the walls like oversized varicose veins. There was nothing to do except pace, heel-toe, heel-toe, causing an upward echo loud enough to vex the statues crowded under the dome above. As Suttill paced, his gown billowed and the trails of horsehair from his wig bounced against the back of his starched wing collar. Under his arm were a set of papers and two bound volumes of the Criminal Appeal Reports. The indictment inside the brief was headed *The King –v– Lionel Redknapp*.

Suttill's instructing solicitor, a stooped individual from Pritchard & Pritchard, remained in the cells ensuring the client's instructions were signed. Mr Redknapp had seen barristers come and go during his career and theirs. His first barrister was now an Assize Court judge. Redknapp considered Suttill a young counsel who knew his onions. Studious he was, thought Redknapp, studious. Suttill advised that the cheque was indeed a top-notch forgery. Unhappily, it was covered in the defendant's fingerprints like German measles. His address in Bromley-by-Bow was, for want of a better expression, a forgery factory. And his antecedents showed numerous appearances before the Recorder of London for forgery and related misdemeanours. Counsel was courteous but firm. To avoid imprisonment with hard labour, a plea of guilty looked the only option.

'I'm sure you'll do the necessary if I plead,' said Redknapp in an accent more Aldgate East than Athenaeum. 'I don't wanna be dredging the Royal Dockyard again.'

'I will do everything I can,' said Suttill. His eyes flashed with such sincerity and calm that Redknapp considered he had picked a lucky brief.

'God bless you, sir.'

Suttill entered Court 4 and took up position in what felt like an undersized church pew beneath the dock. As prosecuting counsel outlined the facts of the case, the judge's face looked sterner and sterner.

'The forgery was expert, My Lord,' said Travers for the Crown. 'The bank would have cashed the cheque had the manager not become suspicious of a customer hailing himself Commander of the Bath. As My Lord knows better than I, CB stands for *Companion* of the Bath.'

Once prosecuting counsel resumed his seat, Suttill rose. The lesson he had been taught on his first day as a pupil barrister echoed like the mausoleum outside. Grasp the nettle. Present the rose.

'My Lord,' said Suttill. 'May I first grasp a handful of thorns on behalf of the defendant, Mr Redknapp. He has come before My Lord on other occasions for similar offences. The cheque in question suggests a man for whom forgery might be considered a vocation. The defendant, I concede, made every attempt to flee the scene. That is, however, far from the entire picture. There are aspects of Mr Redknapp, and of this offence in particular, that may drive the court to take a more merciful course than would other- wise be the case...'

As Lionel Redknapp was taken down to the cells, he thanked each lucky star for sending Mr Suttill. He had avoided hard labour.

*

Paris, 1938

Noor

Noor sat in bed, writing. Everything about her apartment spoke two words: *Quartier Latin*. There were books everywhere. On bookshelves. On tables. On windowsills. There were invitations to photography galleries showing the opposing '*f*' holes of a cello transposed on to a woman's back. There were invitations to experimental films by Man Ray and Duchamp. There were flyers for a series of philosophy lectures by Simone de Beauvoir at the Sorbonne. Next to her wardrobe, acting as a hatstand, was her harp. The clothes inside her wardrobe tended towards Rive Gauche black, but with occasional blazes of dreamlike colour, as if Matisse himself had painted her scarves.

There were newspapers scattered in French and English. No one in France was unaware of the blood flowing in neighbouring Spain. Noor read with horror about neighbour killing neighbour during the doom-laden afternoons. Fathers and sons had stabbed each other to death over allegiance to opposing flags. Refugees were pouring over the border into France. How was such inhumanity possible? Noor saw her father's eyes looking down on the world with pity and despair.

Noor took up her pen. Could her words help stem the bleeding? Could they provide a balm? She would write for the ears of children, but the allegory would not be lost on their parents. The stories were, after all, weaved from the previous animal lives of Lord Buddha. She wrote a title across the top of the page.

Banyan

Then an opening line.

Whose are those jewel eyes, piercing the shadows of the forest?

She looked out of the window at the Paris skyline and closed her eyes, delving down for words. She continued.

Watch, my children, how swiftly those pearl hoofs pass through the bushes...! Have you not heard about the

golden deer, my little ones? 'Banyan' the king of the deer
he is called...'

She wrote as the sky darkened. She switched on a small electric light
by her bed and continued writing until the story of the golden deer
was finished.

Love, the story ended, had entered into the heart of the
King. And he reigned with love over his people, and all the
living creatures of his realm...

Other evenings, when she was not out at galleries or listening to
lectures, Noor sat in bed and wrote. A small stipend left by Inayat
allowed her a degree of independence. This enabled her to do what
the rest of the Latin Quarter was doing by day and night. Write.
Her knees acted as an easel for her notebook, as she closed her eyes
and fished in the lake of her mind.

She wrote down a new title.

The Fairy and the Hare

The opening words came.

A young hare once lived in a small forest between a mountain, a village and a river. My children, many hares run
through the heather and the moss, but none as sweet as
he. Three friends he had: a jackal, a water-weasel and a
monkey...

Into the story flew Sakka, a tree-fairy with butterfly wings and hair
woven from the light of moon rays. By the time Noor's eyelids
were falling, Sakka had struck a mountain above the forest with
her wand. The essence of the mountain gushed into a stream from
which Sakka painted a picture of the hare on the side of the moon.

241

Just as she was falling asleep, a shadow from the headlight of a car in the street below moved across the ceiling. A second shadow chased the first. She could feel her heart begin to quicken. Then came the words, gentle and calm.

'Hush, *Bābouli*, the shadows are just Chandra's chariot.'

The following week, Noor started her most ambitious story to date. She took her notebook and pencil case to a café on the corner of Rue Valette. She entered an inviting room of dark wood, low lights, red leather, black and white tiles, and a tobacco-smudged ceiling. She ordered a *café crème* and wrote a title on a blank page in her notebook. Others in the café were aware of a woman in a black polo-neck with black culottes and a scarf painted with tropical flowers. She took up her pen.

The Swan Kingdom

Many lakes there are in the world – blue lakes, green lakes, some with white lotuses, some with white swans sailing through, but none as beautiful as the Lake Manasa, for its water shone with all the colours of the sky. Miraculous flowers with large red cups of honey grew around its margins, and each day they dropped a little of their beauty in this lake.

In this kingdom lived sixty thousand swans, governed by King Dhritarashtra and Sumukha, the commander of his army. The swans were as beautiful as mermaids, and their army chief majestic and strong, but none could be compared to the King, for his feathers were of shining silver, and as he floated along in the night it was as if the moon were on the lake.

The courtiers in every palace spoke to their lords of this kingdom of swans. Many monarchs praised the wonderful nation and marvelled at their governors Dhritarashtra and Sumukha. But above all Brahmadatta, the King of Benares, thirsted to see them.

So it was that one day he gathered his courtiers and said:

'Wise and faithful ones, your King will never be happy until a certain wish is accomplished...'

Noor heard a chair scraping and looked up from the page. A man with an armful of manuscripts was taking a seat at the adjacent table. He looked at her and raised his eyebrows as if to apologize for distracting a fellow writer. Noor had never seen a man with the same attributes: stick-thin, prominent cheekbones, hair that stood vertical as if conducting electricity, a beak-like nose pivoting a pair of round black spectacles. His eyes were glacier blue. He wore a tattered herringbone overcoat and a polka-dot scarf. The dots, she realized, were moth holes. The man could not have been more than thirty, but his brow had the furrows of a man of sixty. Such intensity did not come without attraction and Noor could feel her eyes wanting to retrace the contours of his strange, striking face.

In days yet unborn, Noor would meet the same man again. He was known within his group as L'Irlandais. His work for the group drew death out from the shadows but he weathered the risks, as Noor discovered, with taciturn indifference. At present, the man, whose name was Sam, survived hand to mouth running literary errands for James Joyce. Noor looked beyond the man's profile towards the world unfolding on the street outside and resumed her pen.

Shadows on the pavement began to extend. As dusk descended over Paris, Noor took her notebook under her arm and her pencil case and returned to her apartment. The man at the next-door table was there when she left, squinting into the distance. He was still wearing his overcoat.

She sat in bed that evening, notebook on her knees. The final lines arrived with the midnight chime of Saint-Séverin.

It was a joyful homecoming for all sixty thousand swans and they all lived together happily ever after.

*

As the weeks passed, the pile of manuscript papers on her desk grew. A dozen stories based on the life of Buddha, first weaved by Inayat when Noor was a girl. Then twenty. When the last full stop was added to the last story, Noor took out a calligraphy brush and painted a cover.

Twenty Jātaka Tales

At the bottom of the page, she drew a line of animals: a tiger, a hare, a horse, a swan, an elephant, a monkey and a deer. She tied the manuscript together with string and placed it on her desk. She sat with her hands on her lap. She felt Inayat's hand on her shoulder – tender and proud. She cried tears of joy. And relief. And sadness.

Her friend Sylvie came to her apartment for dinner the following week. Sylvie saw the cover of the manuscript and asked to look inside. Candles burned their entire length that evening as Sylvie read each of the tales. After reading the last tale, she embraced Noor and gave her three kisses.

'All you need now,' said Sylvie, 'is a publisher.'

'A publisher?' said Noor, as if she didn't understand the word.

'Leave it with me,' said Sylvie.

A week later, Sylvie returned with a list of six publishers. Noor chose the London firm George G. Harrap Ltd because it also had an office in Bombay.

Noor spent the next fortnight typing an edited version of *Twenty Jātaka Tales*.

She took up a pen and with a hand that trembled wrote a cover letter.

'Dear Sirs –

I attach respectfully for your consideration a collection of children's stories known as *Twenty Jātaka Tales*...'

Sylvie went with Noor to the post office on the Boulevard du Montparnasse.

That night an Aéropostale pilot took to the skies above Paris, heading north towards the Channel. Rattling in the back of the monoplane, under a heap of letters, was a brown paper parcel destined for the office of George G. Harrap Ltd.

*

Two months after Noor posted her manuscript, a letter arrived. Noor had her harp at her shoulder when the post boy rang, asking for a signature. The letter had a London postmark. She opened it with every expectation of a polite refusal. She had to reread the letter twice for the news to percolate. The letter was from a Mr F. G. Winstanley, managing director of Harrap Publishers in London. The letter began with an apology for the delay in responding. As to the manuscript, the editorial board considered *Twenty Jātaka Tales* a charming collection with the prospect of attractive sales in England and India. Harrap was a small house with a limited budget, but the firm would be pleased to offer £250 for the publishing rights with the usual terms as to royalties. If the proposal was amenable, the firm's solicitor would send a contract. The editorial board wanted *Twenty Jātaka Tales* to head their children's list the following year. The letter was signed in purple ink. Noor sat on the edge of her bed. She was speechless. Her own publisher! The top corners of her harp appeared to rise into a smile.

CHAPTER 22
'RADIO TOUR EIFFEL'

Paris 1939

Noor

A voice on Radio Tour Eiffel announced the next programme.

'*Maintenant, c'est avec grand plaisir que je présente Mademoiselle Noor Inayat Khan.* Now it is with great pleasure that I introduce Mademoiselle Noor Inayat Khan. She will read for us one of the charming stories from her recently published *Twenty Jātaka Tales*.'

There was a crackle-filled pause. Then a clear, well-spoken voice reading in French into the microphone.

'*Le Royaume des Cygnes* – The Swan Kingdom'

'*Beaucoup de lacs il y a dans le monde...* Many lakes there are in the world... Blue lakes, green lakes, some with white lotuses, some with white swans sailing through, but none as beautiful as the Lake Manasa, for its water shone with all the colours of the sky.'

When the story finished, there was a simple '*Merci*' from Noor.

'Our thanks', said the announcer, 'to Mademoiselle Inayat Khan for coming into the studio to read a story of such charm and animation.'

*

Twenty Jātaka Tales had exceeded expectations. Sales were so buoyant in India there were two additional print runs. Messrs George G. Harrap also found themselves negotiating the rights for the *Tales* to be played on national French radio. The royalties began to accrue. Cheques were arriving from London with increasing regularity. Noor decided to take her mother, Amina, frail though she was, on a trip to the Riviera. Then on to Switzerland and the Italian Lakes.

On a Saturday morning under a sapphire Parisian sky, Noor and her mother walked together along Platform 1 at the Gare de Lyon. The train was destined for Nice. Noor wore a navy-blue sailor dress from Molyneux. Amina wore a light summer veil that matched her sage-green frock. Behind them, one porter was wheeling their suitcases while another was wheeling a vast instrument case caging a Salzedo harp. Once on board, Noor insisted on wheeling the harp through the carriage. The two women found their seats. Amina asked where the harp would be spending the journey. It was at this point that a man seated on the other side of the aisle stood. He wore a pale suit and a pale silk tie. He was in the dying embers of his thirties and his brushed-back corrugated hair and elegant, pencil-thin moustache gave the impression of a matinée idol, albeit past his first flush of youth. If Noor was not mistaken, his bottom eyelid had faint traces of a make-up pencil. The man asked in French if he could help with such an extravagant *pièce de baggage*. He strained every sinew to make lugging a harp case into the seat opposite Noor and her mother look effortless.

They made an unusual pair, thought the man. The older woman wore a veil and spoke in a muted voice with a hint of American. The younger woman looked like she might be Italian or even, with such fine features, Persian. She had a radiance about her, and dark forgiving eyes. He thought her one of the most exotic-looking women he had ever seen.

The trio began chatting. The man turned out to be a man of the stage after all. He introduced himself as Denis Rake, an actor, whose eyes misted over as he told Noor and Amina he had once played the lead in *No, No, Nannette* back in 1928.

'I played opposite the *divine* Percy de Vere. Perhaps you have heard of us?'

Noor and Amina tried not to look blank.

Rake confessed he had been having rather a dry patch of late, but things were looking up. Ivor Novello had seen him playing the butler in *The Importance of Being Earnest* and had asked him for an audition. Someone he referred to as his 'Uncle Nigel' had sent him for ten days on the Riviera to spruce himself up for the big day.

Amina commended Rake on his perfect French. Rake smiled.

'Would you believe I was born in Belgium of all places?' he said. 'Feels like rather a long time ago. But that, ladies, is a story for another time.'

With that he lifted his trilby, bowed from the seated position, and placed it over his face.

'Time for a doze,' said the hat.

A whistle blew. The train shunted away, puffing breaths of steam into an indigo Paris sky. It was destined for palm trees, the curve of the Promenade des Anglais, the dazzle of the Mediterranean and the sugared almond folly of the Hotel Negresco.

*

Morel

As the summer of 1939 stumbled on, Georges Morel put on a panama hat and bought a solitary ticket to see a film at Le Champo cinema. He sat in the back row so his hat did not obstruct. He watched the Pathé News broadcast through a haze of cigarette smoke. German troops were amassing on the Polish border. European leaders were, according to the breathless report, '...working tirelessly to avert conflict'. There were pictures of the British prime minister, Neville Chamberlain, dressed like an undertaker. The credits faded and the cinema curtain swung to a close. The curtains reopened. There were isolated claps. The film began. It was about a little girl and dog called Toto. The girl was on a search. During her search she met a strange group – a scarecrow who was looking for a brain, a lion who was searching for courage and a tin man who wanted a heart.

Morel watched. The Technicolor from the screen lit his face. Due to the angle of his hat, and his seat, no one could see the tears follow each other down his face. What of the man who had a heart – a red beating heart – but a tin head? What of him?

He walked back, hat low, to the Rue de la Harpe. He carried a bunch of keys on a chain. He entered the cool of the building. It felt like a tomb. He had taken over as concierge when the previous one retired. It meant a larger apartment on the ground floor. The work of a concierge suited him well. He could stay in the shadows. There was the occasional exchange with an occupant of the building. And Robert Benoist would stop by once a month. Otherwise, it was just him and the canary that fluttered from perch to perch in his cage. Morel bought the canary the day he became concierge. He called the bird Fabien.

An enigmatic trio became the watchers of Paris. Georges Morel, Fabien the Canary and Le Stryge, the gargoyle crouched high on Notre Dame. They watched. And listened. They listened to the rush of air as a gas lamp was lit... To the distant trundle of the Métro... To the bread ovens swinging open before dawn... To the click of a *poulet*'s heel... To the fading lament of a saxophone.

September came to Paris, clear and blue. September came also to the Polish-German border. In the grey drizzle of a Friday morning, German tanks rolled into Poland. Morel listened to the announcement on Radio Tour Eiffel. Germany had been given until eleven a.m. on the third of September to withdraw its tanks. The ultimatum passed. The tanks remained. France and England had no choice but to support Poland.

France and England were now at war with Germany.

Morel sat in silence. He leaned forward, elbows on his knees, holding his metal head. He saw his brother's face just before it was struck by a sniper. He saw Lieutenant Bloch's expression in the field hospital. He saw Dr Boucher's face looking down as Morel was wheeled into theatre. He closed his eyes. No sooner had mankind staggered out from the abyss, mankind was falling back. Was this another world's hell? He opened his eyes. Fabien stopped fluttering. He turned and looked straight at Morel. He tilted his yellow head, concerned.

*

On the day war broke out, Noor was finishing the last orange stripe of an illustration for her next book, *The Song of the Tigress*.

Young Leo was finishing the *Times* cryptic crossword at record speed.

Suttill was tying pink ribbon around his papers in the Robing Room at the Old Bailey.

Doris was stamping a copy of *SHE* at Chelsea Library, her flat black lace-ups giving no indication that she had once been known as Treasure.

Canaris was attending a Council of War at the German High Command.

And Heydrich was flicking non-existent dust off his SS-Brigadeführer uniform.

PART
THREE

PART
THREE

CHAPTER 23
'DOT DASH'

Harrogate,
England, 1941

Noor

Aircraftwoman Second Class, Service No. 42595, sat cross-legged on the floor. It was dawn. Others in the Nissen hut were asleep. Only a pillow separated her from the draughty floorboards. She gathered her service greatcoat around her shoulders. The familiar words came to her as she started her descent.

'It is a still lake that reflects the sky.'

Noor closed her eyes. She began the familiar journey through the rays of light skipping on the surface down to the sea floor of her mind. There she came to rest, in the stillness and the silence. An occasional current moved on the sea floor, slowing the parade of thoughts. When it was time to finish, she would ascend from the depths, back towards the light on the surface and the churn of foam on the waves. As she opened her eyes, other members of the WAAF, the Women's Auxiliary Air Force, were stirring. Noor made her bed with Air Force precision. She polished the hard black lace-up shoes until she could see her reflection. She polished the buttons and belt of her uniform. She stood ready, hands by her sides, heels together, for a kit inspection by the section leader. The roll call, the marching and the undrinkable tea were a long way

253

from her Paris attic, her harp and the *Twenty Jātaka Tales*. They were a long way from the Swan Kingdom and the flowers of Lake Manasa that dropped a little of their beauty into the lake each day.

*

When war erupted, Noor and her mother fled the House of Blessings with a suitcase apiece. Noor managed to squeeze in three books, but she had to leave Pteech-ka on her pillow. Pteech-ka's ruby eyes glistened with sorrow. Noor and Amina boarded an overcrowded train from the Gare du Nord. The train carried them north to Calais, where they caught a ferry to Dover with only space on deck. When they arrived, cold and seasick, the cliffs of Dover looked grey, not white. From Dover, they made their way to Oxford, where a Sufi family threw open their doors.

Oxford was full of pensive undergraduates, their black gowns matching the blackout curtains in the colleges. As they pedalled down Carfax, they thought of those who had left for war, the ink of fear pumping beneath their diffidence. They were next. Noor watched the Pathé news films in the smoke of the Ultimate Picture Palace. As Europe plunged into chaos, the newsreels were upbeat. The narrator sounded like an excited cricket commentator. She saw the faces on the legions of the Third Reich. The enemy cricket team would soon, she knew, be playing away. And they would not be coming with wooden bats and a leather ball. England was preparing for invasion. And the odds were dire.

Noor sat one evening with her gas mask on her lap. She imagined tanks rolling into Oxford. She imagined Nazi flags streaming outside the Ashmolean and the echo of jackboots under the spires. She shuddered. She sat cross-legged on a cushion, closed her eyes, and began the familiar descent. She sat in silence on the sea floor, alert to the currents and the calm. Something was different. Sitting cross-legged on the sea floor was a man in a gold robe. A ruby hung from his neck and there was a red *bindi* daubed between his eyes. His hair and beard were white, both following in the swell. His eyes were closed, his brow rucked, his face taut.

'Papa?'

The old man opened his eyes. They were focused and blurred at the same time, twin apertures radiating back into infinity.

'*Bābouli*,' came a voice, though the old man's mouth was still.

Noor stretched out her arms to touch the figure, but they passed through a sculpture of water.

'Naraka is empty and Vishnu the Protector sleeps.'

The words drifted in the currents. Noor knew *Naraka* was Hell.

'You must do everything possible to stem the tide.'

She was about to say she was volunteering as a nurse.

'It is enough? Listen to your *Sankalpa*.'

Sankalpa – the heart's deepest intention that seeks inception and fulfilment.

In a blink, the figure was gone. Noor ascended from the depths. As she surfaced, she felt no fear. Only an opiate suffusion of calm.

From her room in Oxford, Noor Inayat Khan typed an application for the WAAF. Their cause, she thought, was noble: they defended the realm. Her application, however, was rejected. She had been born in Moscow, making her ineligible to serve. She wrote to the War Office direct. As the holder of a British protected person's passport she was entitled, moreover duty-bound, to serve. A reply came back a fortnight later, signed by the Director of Military Operations in person. The War Office owed Miss Inayat Khan an apology. An overzealous cog in the wheel had jammed the works. Her spirit was exemplary. If Miss Inayat Khan wished to reapply to the WAAF, she would find the flight path clear.

During basic training, Noor and other recruits were summoned into a freezing drill hall. The air commandant was every inch the headmistress she was before the war. She spoke about the regulations. Then regulations governing the regulations. She finished her address with an unexpected question.

'Do we have any knitters or pianists? Or better still knitters who play the piano?' The recruits looked at one another. A variety of hands went up. Noor played both piano and harp, and Amina had taught her to knit as a child. *Listen to your Sankalpa.* She put up her hand.

'All those with raised hands, see the Assistant Section Officer afterwards. Company dismissed!'

To Noor's surprise, those who raised their hands were selected to become trainee wireless operators. 'Can you think of better criteria?' said the section commander.

Noor was introduced to a new type of music. It was a-tonal, with a contradictory, uneven rhythm. It sounded like some of the *avant garde* concerts she had attended at the Sorbonne. She closed her eyes. She saw background dots of grey with masculine strokes of black. The image was an impressionist's painting in monochrome.

'I am a dot,' said the teacher, Mr Stevens.

He was a retired engineer from Marconi, with twinkling eyes and pens that peered from his top pocket like periscopes. He turned to the blackboard.

'I am a dot, a small-shot   .
I can hop atop another dot   :
I can hijack a comma   ;
And exclaim   !
How I tail away into a mystery…'

He lit his pipe and continued.

'I am a dash, nothing flash   _
I can lead you up the garden path.

_ _

                  _

                  _

                  _

                  _

                  _

'I can make stairs that go up.'

Or stairs that go down.'

—

—

—

—

—

—

The WAAF recruits looked quizzical.

'Once a dot danced with a dash and we made Morse _._. _ _ _
_.. '

The women laughed.

'Let's start learning Morse code by tapping out three emergency letters. A dot is one beat, a dash is three. Don't forget to leave a pause between letters.'

· · · _ _ _ · · ·

The women tapped out the code with their index fingers on wood.

'Again, ladies. An SOS must come to your fingers without even thinking!'

A roomful of fingers tapped out SOS in unison. Noor and the others moved from tapping messages with fingers on wood to the transmission arm of a telegraph key. She sat with her codebook open on the desk. Mr Stevens wrote on the blackboard:

'The Owl and the Pussycat went to sea.'

Noor began transmitting.

_ ···· · _ _ _ · _ _ _ · _ ·· ·_ _ ···· · _ _ · ·_ ··· ··· _·_ _ _ · _· ·_ _

When she looked up, the other women were still hunched over their codebooks. Mr Stevens came over to her desk.

'Have you done this before, Aircraftwoman Khan?'

'No, sir.'

'Well, let's see how quickly you can finish the poem.'

She worked with her eyes open, then closed. She remembered the lone dot was 'E' and the lone dash was 'T'. 'I' was double dot.

Four dots made the four corners of an 'H'. 'S' and 'O' she knew were the triple dot and triple dash.

Her favourite was 'R', the last letter of her name, because it looked like a face.

· _ ·

Mr Stevens returned, pens peering from his pocket.

'You're having me on. You have done this before.'

'No, sir, I promise.'

That night, Noor dreamed of the garden in Suresnes. Her sister was lying next to her on the lawn. Amina, in a straw hat, was threading roses through the trellis. Her brothers were climbing in the trees. Inayat was watching the family from his study. She heard the percussion of a woodpecker. Short taps, interspersed with longer taps. It was a message.

· _ _ ···· · _ _ _ _ _ _ _ _ _ _ ·· _ ··· · _·_ ·· ··· ··· · · _ · _ · _ · _ _· _·_

W H A T Y O U S E E K I S S E E K I N G Y O U

After basic training, Noor was posted to No. 34 Balloon Barrage Group in Edinburgh. She slept in a bare dormitory with nine other WAAFs. Under the floorboards, the east and the west wind quarrelled, their tails darting up through the gaps in the wood. Noor slept, shivering, in her service greatcoat. By morning, the water around the communal sinks had frozen into boomerangs of ice.

The Balloon Barrage Group was an anti-aircraft battery operating from a gaunt school building in the Corstorphine district. Behind the draughty neo-Jacobean windows, the commanders debated, with a vast wall-mounted map, the points around the city where the balloons would be deployed. The east of the city was most vulnerable from the air. Noor herself witnessed the launch of a barrage balloon over Leith. She watched the strange, elongated grey balloon take to the sky, straining as it reached the end of its tether. Trailing beneath it hung explosive cables like the tentacles of a Portuguese man o' war. When enemy bombers tried to attack the city, they became wrapped in the stinging tentacles, making orange-blue Northern Lights flash against the sky. Some bombers would plunge like comets around the city's fringes. Noor said an incantation every time she saw a falling comet, each one a funeral and a cremation.

The barrage balloons were the city's guardian angels. Yet there was something unsettling about their vast rugby-ball silhouettes against the sky. The strange shadows they cast over Edinburgh. *The shadows*. They waited in the alcoves of her mind. Until they escaped and distended. An old fear gripped Noor's heart. She heard Inayat's voice.

'In the blackest moments, says Master Rumi, be without fear.'

Noor put her fear away in her WAAF locker. Her greatest contribution to the war, she decided, was to work her Morse up to concert level. She imagined the dots and dashes as quavers and crochets moving across the stave. She made a Morse orchestra in her mind – dots struck by the timpani, dashes responding from the strings. Dot. Dot. Dash. Dash. Dot-Dash. Dash. Dash. Dash-Dot. She practised the notes like a musician – *allegretto, allegro, presto*. Monochrome impressionist landscapes flashed behind her eyes. Her finger tapped out the messages as if it was a devolved part of her that spoke its own language.

Noor became the fastest Morse transmitter within the Barrage Balloon Group. She was selected to transmit from headquarters to the barrage sites around the city. When enemy planes came into range, it was Noor's index finger that tapped out emergency transmissions to 603 Squadron, the Spitfire base at Turnhouse defending Edinburgh and the Firth of Forth. The notes were a path for the Spitfires.

When on leave, she allowed Edinburgh to seduce her – the cobbled streets, the glow of the tea shops and the silhouette of the castle brooding against skies that turned from hazy blue to thunder-black as she walked along the Royal Mile. In one of the boutiques, she bought a kilt with a kilt-pin and a tartan sash. A date had been set for an evening's reeling at the Caledonian Hotel with airmen from 603 Squadron and tartan was a priority for the unattached WAAFs.

One Friday morning, Noor was called in to see the commander of No. 34 Group. She stood to attention and saluted.

'At ease,' said the commander from behind his desk.

He glanced at a piece of paper on his desk.

'Do you want the good news or the not-so-good news?'

Noor looked concerned.

'The not-so-good news, sir.'

'The not-so-good news is that you are going to miss the dance. The good news is you are now Aircraftwoman First Class.'

The commander handed her the insignia of a horizontal propeller.

'That can be worn on your arm with immediate effect.'

Noor saluted.

'Well done, A/C First Class Khan.'

'Thank you, sir.'

She hesitated.

'May I ask, sir – does it prohibit my going to the dance?'

The commander smiled.

'It's not that. You are my fastest wireless operator. You are needed closer to the action.'

'Sir?'

'I have put you down for transfer to Number 6 Group, Abingdon. But I daresay they have dances out Oxford way.'

'Number 6 Group?' she said, eyebrows raised.

By the time the commander finished his words, all the colour had drained from Noor's face.

'Bomber Command,' he said.

That night, Noor dreamed she was transmitting co-ordinates to the navigator on a Lancaster bomber. Behind her eyelids, the hum of the aircraft engine was purple. The crump and crackle of the anti-aircraft fire oscillated between red and orange as the plane flew low over the River Elbe on its approach to Hamburg docks. It unleashed its seeds of fire and devastation. Were dreams indeed memories of the future?

Noor awoke at dawn. She placed a pillow on the floorboards and began the familiar journey into the amniotic ink until she reached the sea floor. Images from her dream crowded her mind – falling masonry, the hiss of fire ripping along wood and the smouldering aftermath. Were these the consequences of serving Bomber Command?

She heard a familiar voice and opened an inner eye. She saw a figure in a gold robe sitting cross-legged, eyes closed. Words echoed through the currents.

'The choice is impossible, but did not Lord Rama confront the demon king Ravana?'

Noor arrived at the headquarters of No. 6 Bomber Command, her WAAF uniform pressed, her belt polished, shoes mirror black. In a gloved hand she held a battered leather suitcase. Inside were three Air Force issue shirts, undergarments, two cardigans, a wash-bag with minimal make-up and three books. Her new commanding officer, Group Captain Pinker, gave a weary but welcoming smile. His eyes, she thought, were far away, until she learned how many pilots under his command had taxied down the base's runway and failed to return. On her first day, she was shown to her quarters – another draughty hut with a corrugated roof, shared with three other WAAFs – and ordered to report to the Operations Room.

The Operations Room was the largest single room on the base. Personnel on duty spoke with the hushed, businesslike calm of surgeons in theatre. There were four clocks on the walls, giving the times in London, Paris, Brussels and Berlin. Under a giant wall map sat a bank of desks. In front of each chair lay a pair of head-phones. In the centre of the floor was a giant square table. The table depicted a map of England and northern Europe. No. 6 Group's base at Abingdon was circled in yellow. WAAFs surrounded the table like nurses. Their patients were models of various aircraft – Lancaster and Blenheim bombers, Spitfire and Hurricane fighters – moved as the wireless operators dictated their courses in real time.

Her induction phase would be monitoring Spitfire pilots undergoing training. She had seen some of the young airmen wandering about the base in unzipped flying jackets, their hair greased, with the studied nonchalance of young men who knew their days might be counted in weeks or – if the gods were smiling – months. Noor noticed one airman with Apollonian blond hair, who wore a white silk evening scarf under his bomber jacket and would lie almost horizonal in a deckchair next to the runway. A one-time resting actor called Percy was now Squadron Leader Percy de Vere and one of No. 6 Group's most revered bombers.

Noor was introduced to the T1154 wireless transmitter. She sat in silence with her notebook open as a male engineer showed her the rudiments: the radio screen with its various frequencies fanning out in a semi-circle under the needle, the tuning dial, the meter deflection dial and an aural sense switch that could be set to 'L' or 'R'. The engineer turned the tuning dial. The radio picked up one frequency and moved through the brambles of crackle and hiss to the next frequency. If voice communication was lost, said the engineer, the radio operator had to be able to transmit and receive in Morse. Noor's index finger familiarized itself with the Morse key, tapping out practice dots and dashes.

Her second week was night shifts, receiving and transmitting messages to pilots training to fly Lancaster bombers in the dark. To Noor, the Lancaster's four propellers made the sound of blurred purple as the plane taxied down the runway – a giant green bird with a Browning Mark II machine gun protruding from its tail. Her sense of relief was palpable when she heard the aubergine of the propellers as it migrated back to base. The end of the night shift was usually marked with tea from the NAAFI so strong it was almost un-swallowable and toast with a full butter ration. She would return to her hut as the sun rose, place a pillow on the floor, sit cross-legged and begin the familiar descent.

Early in her deployment, she was jolted from the sea floor by someone pulling her arm. Another WAAF, Joan, was looking at her, concerned.

'Are you all right, dear?' said Joan, with eyes of amazement. Joan looked into a pair of dark eyes that looked pulled from the deepest sleep. Noor gave two slow blinks and smiled.

'It's nothing to worry about,' said Noor. 'A habit, that's all.'

Joan looked relieved. 'For a moment I thought you had gone into a trance!'

Noor smiled. It marked the beginning of a friendship.

Joan, with dark brown hair, green eyes and an impish nose that wrinkled when she smiled, was the mess pin-up. Her manner was airy and fun and Noor noticed, as their friendship grew, just how many airmen would approach them when they were together. Notes were often slipped under the door of their hut, which Joan would read and place in a shoebox with all the others. The first time Noor and Joan had leave that coincided, they borrowed two rickety black bicycles from the base, secured a couple of exit passes, and cycled into the countryside with a wartime picnic that included the luxury of two hard-boiled eggs. They cycled north, past St Leonard's Church in Sunningwell, through Bayworth and up to Boar's Hill, where they found a field with a commanding view of the Oxfordshire countryside. Joan set out an RAF blanket, which acted as a rug, and the two drank tea from a thermos and ate their hard-boiled eggs with their bread ration and some salad leaves collected from the allotment behind the NAAFI. They tried their teeth on some of the hardest Scottish shortbread ever baked and collapsed laughing when neither's teeth could make any headway. After lunch, Noor lay on the blanket, shielding her eyes from the sun.

'What do you want to do after the war?' said Joan, sitting, hugging her knees.

'I want to have children. As many as I can.'

As the sun set, a Blenheim bomber was flying low along the River Elbe towards Hamburg docks. The crump and crack of anti-aircraft fire exploded around the Blenheim's nose as the golden-haired pilot flew. An anti-aircraft shell whined past the cockpit. The pilot held his hand steady at the controls and began his descent. The bombs rattled in the undercarriage, restless and impatient. The pilot's white silk evening scarf was visible under his flying jacket as he manoeuvred the plane directly over the target.

*

After two months at No. 6 Bomber Command, Noor had become an integral part of the Ops Room: calm, reliable and with a Morse proficiency of twenty-five words per minute. At the beginning of the third month, Group Captain Pinker called her into his office. Noor marched in, saluted, and stood to attention.

'At ease,' said Pinker.

Noor stood with her feet apart.

'I now see why Edinburgh sent you. I would like to send you for further training. An advanced Signals and Wireless course. It will mean revisiting a bit of trigonometry, but a wireless operator of your aptitude needs pushing. The course is held at Compton Bassett in Wiltshire. There is a fresh course starting in a week. And I am sure we could find you a few days' leave in the meantime.'

Noor stood to attention and saluted.

That Saturday, she took the train from Oxford to Paddington. From Paddington she took a taxi through grey, bomb-damaged streets to Bloomsbury. She ascended the stairs of a block at 150 Southampton Row, popular with Indian students from the London School of Economics. Under her arm was a wrapped parcel. She reached a door in the eaves and knocked. It was opened by a slim Indian with a mop of black hair and concerned eyes. The state of his flat behind suggested the recent passing of a tornado.

Noor presented the parcel.

'Happy birthday!'

Brother and sister embraced. It was a biography of Nehru. Her brother had just received his commission in the Royal Navy. It was his last weekend before going to sea. That evening they went to an impassioned lecture at the India League on the Strand. 'This is not our war!' shouted the speaker. 'Indians are not colonial cannon fodder. No, no we are not!' The audience shouted back the words 'No we are not!' At the end of the address, the speaker's fist came down on the wood so hard it caused the entire table to collapse.

After the lecture, Noor and her brother, Pir, went to a curry house on Fleet Street. There were nods of approval from Indian diners at their uniforms, though a diner at one table scowled. 'Not our war, apparently,' said Pir. 'The lecturer should try looking through the right end of the telescope. The war against the Nazis is everybody's war.'

Noor leaned forward. 'It *is* our war. If Lord Rama did not confront the demon king Ravana, there would be nothing left. And Papa has given his blessing.'

Pir held his sister's hand. He knew enough not to ask how the blessing was sent.

The course at Compton Bassett tested Noor to the edge of her limits. While others fell away, Noor received top marks at the end of the week. Before she left, a small bespectacled man approached the leading student.

'If I were to ask you to transmit Morse messages in French, A/C First Class Khan, would that be a problem?'

'*Aucun problème,*' said Noor. '*Je parle le français aussi couramment que l'anglais.*'

*

On a drizzly Oxfordshire morning, an anonymous-looking letter arrived at Bomber Command. It was addressed to Leading Aircraftwoman Noor Inayat Khan. The envelope was marked with the words 'Inter Services Research Bureau'. Noor, back from Compton Bassett, had been on duty all night. She opened the letter over breakfast. It had the word **'Restricted'** in red at the top. The letter was a request to attend for an interview in Northumberland Avenue, London, on account of certain 'sensitive work' that would allow her to utilize her French and her skills in wireless telegraphy. On no account was she to discuss the interview with anyone. It was signed 'Captain S. Jepson, R.N.'.

The interview was in two weeks. Noor could feel a current of anticipation pulse through her body. Work that would allow her to use her French... She obtained a pink chit to travel off base to London.

'Keep out of mischief, Leading ACW Khan,' said her commanding officer with a smile.

Group Captain Pinker looked wistful. She was his best radio operator, and it was only a matter of time before other departments came on the hunt.

On the day of the interview, Noor went to a hairdresser off Oxford Street and spent some of the money she had saved on a shampoo and set. She placed her WAAF cap on top of her waves of hair, straightened her tie, and walked into the West End bustle.

She caught a bus to Trafalgar Square. She offered a coin to the bus conductor.

'Air Force don't pay on my bus, ma'am.'

From Trafalgar Square she turned into Northumberland Avenue. She moved with a half-walk, half-march until she found herself at one of the largest front doors in London. She pressed the bell and a catch went. She entered the hall, still overflowing with unopened letters, and swung the lift's criss-cross brass gate to one side. She pressed the button for the third floor. The sinews of machinery cranked into life. She pulled back the brass gate on the third floor and stepped into the gloom. A door opened. Swathed in light was a man in naval uniform with slicked-back hair and darting, intelligent eyes.

'*Enchanté*,' he said. '*Soyez la bienvenue*.'

Noor saluted.

'*Enchantée*.'

Captain Jepson ushered her into the boardroom of what was once an influential shipping firm. The room was panelled and still had paintings of some of the company ships on the wall. The chandelier was bandaged in a dust sheet.

Captain Jepson shuffled the papers on the desk. There were various copies of the Official Secrets Acts and some loose papers unconnected to the interview. They were, in fact, the outline of his next book, *Man Running*. Selwyn Jepson had been, in civilian life, a detective novelist of some repute. As he put a match to his pipe and sucked alight the tobacco, he looked the archetypal bookman. There were other aspects of Jepson that were singular. He had studied at the Sorbonne and spoke accentless French. He also had a sixth-sense ability with people. It was as if they appeared like characters mid-flow through one of his books and he could tell how they would fit into, or disrupt, the narrative. His judgement was accurate to the point of uncanny. He had never, as it happened, served in the Navy – the letters 'RN' were an officially approved fiction.

'I hear good things about your radio work with Bomber Command,' smiled Jepson. 'What is your speed in Morse?'

'Twenty-two words per minute transmitting. Twenty-five words per minute receiving.'

'Impressive,' said Jepson, his pipe glowing. 'Could you envisage yourself operating your radio in a less controlled environment?'

Noor looked quizzical.

'A less controlled environment, sir?'

'Occupied France, for example?' said Jepson.

He put down his pipe.

'Perhaps it would help, Leading ACW Khan, if I came to the point. Before I do, I am going to need you to sign some documents.'

Jepson spent the next twenty minutes telling Noor about a newly formed clandestine organization. It was called the Special Operations Executive, otherwise known as SOE. Radio operators were of particular value. Noor sat, knees together, in her immaculate WAAF uniform. Her eyes drank in the information as he spoke.

Jepson noticed a glow from her face that seemed to intensify. He also noticed her beauty. It was inescapable.

'Special operations are not for everyone. The work of radio transmitters is particularly hazardous.'

Noor nodded. Jepson knew instinctively that she grasped the significance of his words. His novelist's mind was mapping her character traits. There was no doubt, he thought.

Heroine material. The lamp of her soul burns with a rare bright-ness and will lead her through the darkness.

He decided to test her mettle.

'May I ask what your Sufi father, if he were alive, might think of you going to France a combatant in a secret war?'

Noor met Jepson's gaze.

'I believe my father would support anyone seeking to uproot evil and end suffering.'

The dust particles in the air stopped. Jepson picked up his pen.

'Yes,' he said. 'Yes, I daresay he would.'

He ticked a box on a restricted form. He handed her a card.

'I would like you to think things over for a week. But you cannot tell anyone about the fact or subject matter of this inter-view. If you are interested in pursuing this line of work, perhaps you would write to me at this address?'

Noor stood to attention and saluted.

'Of course, sir.'

She made an about-turn and marched to the door. She marched beautifully, thought Jepson, although it was one skill an SOE agent would not need.

A week later, a letter was delivered to Captain Jepson RN, c/o the Inter Services Research Bureau.

'Dear Captain Jepson RN

I accept gratefully the privilege of carrying out the work you suggested.

Thanking you, sir, for asking me.

Yours faithfully
Aircraftwoman First Class, N. Inayat Khan'

When Joan entered the hut she shared with Noor and two other WAAFs one Saturday morning, she put her hand to her mouth. Noor's bed was stripped. The blankets and sheets sat in a neat pile. The wardrobe next to her bed was empty. The books she used to keep under her bed were gone, as were her music manuscripts. There was no note. All traces of Noor Inayat Khan were gone. It was as if she never existed.

CHAPTER 24
'THE BISHOP'

Wanborough Manor
Hampshire, 1942

Noor

The Bishop punched.

Noor blocked.

The Bishop punched.

Noor blocked.

The Bishop punched.

Noor blocked.

'The Bishop' was SOE Special Training School No. 5's unarmed combat instructor. A lean man in his mid-fifties, with close-cropped hair and black-framed spectacles, he looked to Noor like an older, harder-bitten version of George Orwell. She noticed the scars on his hands and forearms when they first met.

'Fairburn's the name, ma'am. Ex-Royal Marines and Shanghai Municipal Police. Black belt in judo, ju-jitsu and kung fu. Boxer. Wrestler. Inventor of my own unarmed killing system. People call me "The Bishop" on account of my peaceable nature.'

Noor offered her hand. No sooner had The Bishop squeezed her palm than he twisted her wrist, spinning her away like a dance partner. Before she could blink, Noor was in a half nelson, head bowed, nose pointed at her knees. A voice came from above.

'First rule of unarmed combat. Never extend your hand to a stranger.'

Their next session covered self-defence. The Bishop's punches on the croquet lawn came from different angles. Swing. Jab. Uppercut. Hook. Each time, Noor blocked with her forearm, the leather pad absorbing the blow.

'To block a swing, turn your wrist as if you're telling the time.'

Noor turned her wrist.

'Jabs can be parried. For uppercuts, you need to lunge forward with your arm at right angles. Stop them before they happen. Hooks are your worst enemy. They can dislocate your jaw. You have one second to strike in advance.'

Noor paused for breath, hands on her knees.

She stood straight, ready. For the next twenty minutes, the garden at Wanborough resounded to a metronome of glove on pad.

Punch-Block.

Punch-Block.

She imagined herself blocking in time to her harp arrangement of 'The Arrival of the Queen of Sheba'. Each block was another accented note plucked *molto forte*. The greens, yellows and blues of Handel vied in her mind. She began to sense the genesis of the strike, her blocking hand rising in anticipation as if hoisted by an invisible string.

'Now let's work on counter-attacks,' said The Bishop.

He taught Noor to move forward into the opponent's punch, blocking with her left and striking with the palm of her right.

'Imagine you are pushing a door shut,' said The Bishop, gesturing with an open palm. 'Now imagine the door has grown a nose. Your job is to make the door flat again.'

The harpist's hands were becoming a weapon.

'Use the heel of your palm to make first contact,' said the instructor, tapping the bottom of his palm just above his wrist. 'All the energy of a palm strike should pulse through the palm's hardest part.'

Each time Noor struck with her palm, The Bishop would block or move his head. As the practice went on, he noticed Noor's palm strikes becoming stronger and faster. At the end of the session, both let their hands fall loose by their sides as they caught their breath. They talked about the rhododendrons coming into season and the birds.

While Noor was distracted, a blow came from nowhere. It was a right-hand swing. Noor blocked the punch without thinking. Had The Bishop not dodged his head at that moment, his nose would have been flattened by a female palm moving at the speed of an express train. It was the first time she saw The Bishop smile.

'Let's make this more interesting.'

The Bishop drew an object from his back pocket.

'Don't worry, it's retractable.'

He swung at Noor with the knife. Her wrist-block was already in place. And her right palm was heading straight for The Bishop's nose.

'Good,' said The Bishop.

Next, he lunged, knife-hand extended. Noor's instinct was to stand aside and parry the thrust.

'Good instinct. Let's refine it.'

He taught Noor how to stand aside, parry the blow and clamp the assailant's wrist with her left hand – while shooting her right palm towards his nose.

'A strike to the nose will make most people drop the knife. If not, help them with a knee-strike to the solar plexus.'

The Bishop lunged. Noor moved aside, clamped his wrist, sent her palm towards his nose. As he moved his head, the knife fell to the ground. He nodded.

'Again.'

Noor disarmed him, this time prising the knife from his fingers.

'Good. Small piece of advice,' he said, retrieving the weapon. 'The most dangerous part of the knife is not the blade. It's the handle. If you're in a tight spot, grip the handle in a tight fist –

blade pointing away – and use the blunt end to cave your opponent's temple like the shell of your breakfast egg.'

Noor nodded, trying not to shudder.

That evening, The Bishop wrote up his report.

'Gentle as a dove. Fierce as a tigress.'

The one other student who had impressed him to the same degree was a broad-shouldered Mauritian named Joseph Antelme. Antelme had been his star pupil. Gentle manner, like Noor, but with the power of a nine-foot wave. There were rumours he was a millionaire. The major said Antelme was to be dropped into occupied France under the next full moon.

'One man who can look after himself,' reflected The Bishop over tea in the garden.

*

Unarmed combat was accompanied by lessons in marksmanship. Noor remembered the day she first handled a pistol – an innocuous piece of metal capable of taking life in less than the blink of an eye. She imagined how many blinks there were in a lifetime before the final blink halted by a bullet. Could she use a pistol if she had to? The voice of Inayat interceded.

'*What is your Sankalpa, Bābouli?*'

'*My Sankalpa is to shorten the war, Papa.*'

When Sergeant Bannerman, the wiry Scotsman, gave Noor her first lesson in marksmanship, he was surprised by her confident grip of the pistol. He taught her two firing positions, one with feet equidistant, the other with feet positioned like a runner.

'The first stance is best for female agents,' said Bannerman. 'You can hold the weapon with two hands around the grip to lessen the recoil.'

Noor took the pistol and stood feet apart. Bannerman noticed a strange calm that came over Noor as she took aim. *It is a still lake that reflects the sky.* She curled her index finger around the trigger the same way she plucked a harp string. She fired six shots, the pistol barely recoiling. Noor left a cluster of full stops around the target's bullseye.

Bannerman gave a wry smile and entered a comment on the assessment form.

'Natural shot.'

They arranged a follow-up session.

'Next time, the target will not be paper,' said Sergeant Bannerman.

When Noor reported to the range the following week, another trainee agent was being put through his paces. Noor stood silent at the back, watching Sergeant Bannerman with a man of average height and greying corrugated hair brushed back. In profile he looked like a matinée idol rather past his peak. There was a nagging familiarity about his face. And, when he spoke, his voice.

'Ever shot a gun before, Lieutenant?' said Sergeant Bannerman.

'Only on stage,' said the man.

Of course, thought Noor. The actor on the train! How could she forget? The rake called Rake. *How strange the pattern of the Divine Weaver.* It later transpired they were both training as radio operators.

The actor took aim. When the gun went off, Rake stifled a shriek. The bullet flew wide of the target.

'Let's give it another go,' said Bannerman.

Rake's hands were shaking as he raised the pistol. He closed his eyes as he prepared to fire.

'How do you think ye will hit the target with yer eyes closed, sir?'

'I am not sure guns are my thing,' said Rake.

Bannerman signalled for Noor to approach.

'Have a watch, Lieutenant.'

A plywood figure was wheeled into position.

Sergeant Bannerman loaded an Enfield No. 2 revolver and handed it to Noor.

She took the pistol and moved into the feet-apart position. She closed her left eye. The harpist's finger curled around the trigger. She took three breaths into her diaphragm and prepared to fire.

Rake closed his eyes. He heard six shots, each in time with his heartbeat.

When he opened his eyes, the target's head looked like a sieve. One of the shots made a hole between its black-painted eyebrows. Noor half-cocked the pistol and handed the Enfield back to Bannerman.

'Good shooting, ma'am.'

'Thank you, Sergeant,' she said with a smile.

'Now then, Lieutenant,' said Bannerman, turning to Rake. 'If she can do it, so can you.'

*

The following Friday, there was a buzz around the manor. The trainees had been given Saturday off – not even PT in the morning. The French contingent was already planning to introduce the weekend on a wave of '75's. Wanborough Manor had, after all, the best-stocked bar in England. As for Noor, she had been intrigued by a discreet written invitation for a glass of sherry in the library for women agents only before dinner on Saturday.

At six in the evening, Noor made her way down to the library, following a trail of clicking heels. The library was flooded with early evening sunlight. On a side table were open bottles of sherry and white wine, and a tray of sausage rolls. The library had been arranged so that the sofas and chairs formed a loose circle. To one educated agent, it felt like the graduate common room at Girton.

Amid the chatter was an older woman pressing a drink into each newcomer's hand. In her right hand was a Craven A with a precipitous length of ash. She wore a simple black dress with a white collar and three rows of pearls. Pinned to her breast was a silver bird with ruby eyes. The skin around her neck had loosened with the years but her eyes were still cobalt, her lips still full and her cheekbones, if anything, more pronounced. Everyone at SOE Special Training School No. 5 agreed their librarian was beautiful.

'Welcome,' she said with a smoker's rasp. 'Has everyone got a drink?'

She lit another Craven A. There was an air of warmth about her, threaded with mischief.

'Shall we take the weight off our heels?'

She sank back into one of the larger chairs. Someone brought over an ashtray.

'Thank you, my dear,' she said. She drew on her cigarette. 'And thank you all for coming. The major thought it would be an idea to get us gals together without interference from the rabble outside.'

She pointed out of the window at a number of male agents who had started the weekend early, trying to leapfrog each other in the garden after several '75' cocktails. Each leapfrog attempt ended in both men collapsing on the grass in convulsions of laughter.

The amount of gin in a '75' was said to mimic the power of a French 75 mm field gun.

'May I bore you all with a little personal history? Some of it, at least, you may find rather intriguing.'

The women leaned forward, eyes bright.

'I come from the old world. The world of the *Titanic* and the Suffragettes. When I was born, I was given the name Doris. When I was young and beautiful like you, I was given the name Treasure. Now, on account of my imminent demise, people call me Dodo.'

The women smiled as she patted her lungs.

'Too many of these,' she said, holding up her Craven A. 'But there's steam in the old pipes yet.'

She looked around the room.

'What I am about to say must not be repeated. You will understand why in a moment. One thing war does is strip away pretence. And there can be no pretence about the challenges that await you overseas. My modesty, or lack of it, is small beer indeed. Some of you will judge me, others will not. So here's to stripping away pretence.'

She raised her wine glass and drained the contents.

'In the whirligig of life, I have not always been a librarian. When gentlemen still wore top hats and carried ivory-tipped canes I was a member of a profession older, even, than yours. Not by choice, I should add. But if spies are the second oldest profession, I spent time in the oldest.'

A frisson went around the room. Some agents tried to hide their shock. Others broke into wry smiles.

'In some ways I was lucky. No one harmed me. Those I entertained came from the very top of the tree. Some of them have remained friends to this day, though they are soon to be added to the fossil collection of the Natural History Museum.'

There was a ripple of laughter.

'Gentlemen who sought out my company in the old days knew I liked reading. So they brought me books. I dreamed once that the number of books they brought me built a staircase from the Earth to the Moon. One helped me to become a librarian. It amuses me sometimes to remember the eyes of men when they came to see me swathed in silk... and the eyes of men who came to see me behind the desk of the chief librarian.'

She stubbed out her cigarette and lit another.

'How many of you, may I ask, are married?'

A minority of hands were raised.

'And how many of the unmarried know anything about the sons of Adam?'

A few doubtful hands half-raised.

'The challenges you will face in the field cannot be predicted. To that end, the major thought the female agents might be assisted with a user's guide to men. They can be useful. You just need to know what makes them tick. Not only the obvious.'

Noor could feel herself blushing.

'Well,' said Treasure, 'in the words of Prince Hamlet: *what a piece of work is a man!*'

*

Forty miles from Wanborough Manor stood a thatched barn. It was called, inventively, 'Thatched Barn', and it was the size of a small metropolis. The building was 1930s mock Tudor, its white exterior intersected by faux black beams. The dark thatch sat low over the eaves like a sinister hairpiece. In the summer of 1939, Thatched Barn was in the process of being converted into a hotel. At the outbreak of war, it was requisitioned by the War Office. The conversion was completed in total secrecy by the works department of the Ministry of Economic Warfare. Thatched Barn became SOE Station XV – Camouflage Section.

Camouflage Section was unusual even by SOE standards. It was populated by film and theatre cognoscenti, props handlers, and at least one stage illusionist. Camouflage Section produced ever more inventive paraphernalia: incendiary briefcases, gas-expelling fountain pens, Sten gun silencers, plastic explosives disguised as horse droppings, and one prop director's tour de force – a dead rat that would explode on contact.

The clothing department was headed by the Neumann sisters, formerly of the Molyneux fashion house in Paris. They would cut clothes in the French style, age them with dust and mothballs and add frayed French labels. Belts, buttons, zips and shoes all had to match the clothes of the war-weary civilians of France. There was even a dentist who could refit crowns the French way.

At the back of the building, overlooking the grounds, was a room with low-hanging lights, deep butler sinks and tables with photographic paper and pools of sepia developing fluid. At one end of the room was a large printing press that gave every impression of underground pamphleteering. Sitting at a draughtsman's sloping desk, among the discarded remains of false French passports, identity cards and driving licences, was one of SOE's top forgers. He was a visiting instructor from the larger forgery department, Station XIV, at Roydon in Essex.

The junior forgers at Camouflage Section treated him like a living Rubens.

He was Sergeant Forger Redknapp.

*

Lionel Redknapp had been lying on a straw mattress staring at the ceiling of his cell eighteen months before when he heard a key turn in the lock. The cell door swung open. Two prison officers stood in the doorway.

'Guvnor wants to see you.'

'Why-*zat?*'

'You'll find out soon enough,' said the older guard.

Redknapp rose to his feet, brushing down his prison uniform. The trio walked along the prison landing, the chain between Redknapp's ankles trailing behind and echoing in the stone atrium. Within ten minutes he was standing in the prison governor's vast office with arrow-slit windows overlooking the exercise yard. The governor, Captain Myers RN (Retired), looked up from his desk. His eyes were Atlantic blue. Redknapp stared back, standing between the two prison officers.

'I'll come straight to the point,' said Captain Myers. 'You can stay in here and rot or you can sign this form and do your bit.'

The document looked official. Redknapp could make out the words 'Official Secrets Act'. One of the prison officers presented Redknapp with a pen.

'Two gentlemen from an undisclosed government department will collect you at six this evening. If you keep your head down and your nose clean, we will not be seeing you again.'

That evening, the prison gates swung open and Lionel Redknapp was ushered into the back of a black Austin 8. There were two men in the front, a driver in military uniform and a front seat passenger with his trilby pulled low. The men said almost nothing. The car drove north through Ponders End, following the lonely roads of blacked-out London. After an hour, the car was moving through a tree-lined labyrinth of country lanes east of Waltham Abbey. As the branches beckoned the car deeper into the evening, Redknapp wondered where on earth he was being taken.

The car slowed and turned down a private road until it reached a pair of gates. There was a sentry box by the right-hand gate. The driver signed a document on a clipboard and was waved through by a uniformed corporal. The car drew into a gravel drive with an assortment of civilian and military vehicles. As he got out, Redknapp could just take in the shape of the house looming red-brown against the fading light. Had Anthony Buckley-Chubb CB, his alter ego, existed, he would have lived in a Georgian pile with bow windows overlooking an extensive deer park, just like this. The driver set Redknapp's case down in a hallway high enough to remind Redknapp of the atrium of Wandsworth Prison. He was given a mug of tea. It was china, not metal.

'The major will see you now,' said the driver.

Redknapp was led through the interior of Briggens House, which felt like a cross between a stately home and a barracks. Between the portraits and hunting prints were typed military notices concerning duties and inspections. Redknapp was led into a wood-panelled drawing room that had been converted into an office. Behind a desk sat a studious-looking man who, before the war, had been a schools' inspector. Major Knowles looked up and removed his glasses. Behind the black circular spectacles was a pair of alert, approachable eyes. He had an air of businesslike decency.

'Lionel Redknapp?'

'Yes, sir.'

'I gather you have come to us from Wandsworth.'

Redknapp looked awkward. He presumed the major knew it was Wandsworth Prison. The major smiled as if reading his mind. He offered Redknapp a seat. To the latter's amazement, he was given a glass of sherry.

'If it puts you at ease,' he said, 'we have chaps here from Wandsworth, Brixton and Pentonville. It rather goes with the territory.'

Redknapp nodded.

'We are the forgery section of the Special Operations Executive. SOE agents, as you will hear, are waging clandestine war in Europe. Not under their own names – obviously. We forge everything they need: passports, identity cards, travel passes, driving licences, ration cards, petrol coupons. Everything. For our agents, the difference between good and bad forgeries can mean the difference between life and death. We have had our eye on you for some time. According to Special Branch, you are one of the best cheque forgers in the country.

I have seen the Burmah Oil Company cheque you forged, and I thought it was undetectable. That is the standard we aim for here.'

Redknapp looked up at the chandelier and wondered if he really was discussing the zenith of his forging career over sherry in a requisitioned stately home.

'Most take well to their new surroundings,' said the major. 'We have only had to send one back. And if things go well, His Majesty might find himself able to write out a chit to say all is forgiven.'

An official pardon for forgery? Redknapp beamed.

'Although our warfare is unconventional, this is a military establishment and you are subject to military law,' said Major Knowles. 'Tomorrow you will receive your private's uniform and find out your rate of pay.'

The major rose.

'Private Forger Redknapp,' he said, 'welcome to SOE.'

That evening, Lionel Redknapp sat down to a late dinner in the Sergeants' Mess. A group of sergeant forgers were just leaving. They looked like the technical staff of an engineering firm – black-framed glasses, Brylcreemed hair and pens protruding from their top pockets. Redknapp wondered if he recognized one from his wing at Wandsworth. He was given roast pork with parsnips and spotted dick with custard. He licked the last of the warm custard off the spoon. Whatever the SOE were about, thought Redknapp, their weekday fare was better than Christmas dinner. Afterwards, he was shown to his quarters, an airy room that overlooked the deer park. There were no bars on the windows. He lay on a mattress that may have been made from goose feathers and, without removing his prison shoes, fell into a deep, dreamless sleep.

The following day, Redknapp, now in a private's uniform, attended an induction course. It was given by a Captain Majewski, a member of the Polish Resistance-in-exile. The room was darkened, and a projector flashed various images of forgeries on to a screen. Captain Majewski used a ruler to pinpoint the facets of a particular forgery on screen. That afternoon, the new recruits were given various forgeries to handle – and compare them with an original. Redknapp felt like an artist reunited with his lost brushes and canvas. His fingers could read the age and texture of the various documents like Braille. His eyes sought out any anomalies in the official print and he looked at the confidence of the signature. He scoured the mounting of the photographs and the detail of the official stamp at the bottom of each page.

The forgeries were all right, thought Redknapp. But were they going to pass inspection in the field? He looked at a forged *Carte d'identité*. The texture of the paper was on the smooth side, he thought, running his thumb across the top. The ink of one of the official stamps – '*Police Régionale d'État de Lyon*' – was on the thick side. Also, it was the same thickness as the date stamp. The two should be faded to different degrees. The pinkish background to the '*13 francs*' payment stamp was half a shade too dark. The ink of the Commissaire's signature was too bright. And he thought the central fold in the *Carte* was not sufficiently creased.

Each member of the new intake was asked to stand in turn and give a critique of a particular forgery. Lionel Redknapp stood. He had a feeling his words would influence his future. He chose them carefully, giving credit for the forgery insofar as it went – but with some detailed and penetrating suggestions for improvement. He fielded questions with aplomb. One of the sergeant forgers assisting Captain Majewski took notes on a clipboard. At the end of the session, Redknapp was asked to remain. He was not sure if he was being singled out for praise or punishment. The sergeant forger whispered something into Captain Majewski's ear. The captain nodded. Redknapp was assigned straight to the 'Fourth Floor'. For those in the know, the Fourth Floor was 'Procurement and Development'. He would be working under a well-known art forger on loan from HMP Dartmoor.

In the aristocratic confines of Station XIV, Redknapp's star rose – and went on rising. He had, like any master of his art, unique powers of concentration. He would sit searching draft forgeries for faults with a magnifying glass, oblivious to the clock hands. His eyes had the focus of a surgeon or a diamond cutter. He joined a committee that procured a specialist array of papers, cards and inks. He disassembled genuine French and Belgian passports to analyse the faux-leather covers and the shade and thickness of the binding thread. He cannibalized a range of continental typewriters for their type-heads and put together an extensive letterpress library.

Within three months, Redknapp went from Private Forger Redknapp to Corporal Forger Redknapp. Three months after that he became Sergeant Forger Redknapp. He took on all the most challenging assignments, sometimes remaining on his draughtsman's stool until the shadows elongated out of recognition. The station's kitchen was on standby to send up sandwiches if he needed lunch or dinner by his desk. For jobs with an urgent deadline, a camp bed was moved into his office. When members of Station XIV asked if a forgery had been 'Lionized', it was a reference to Sergeant Forger Lionel Redknapp.

The former inmate of HMP Wandsworth now wore a row of service medals. Major Knowles considered him indispensable. The major took a great deal of persuading to let Redknapp go on loan to Thatched Barn. The matter was settled by direct orders from SOE headquarters in Baker Street. Thatched Barn was expanding to meet the demands of an increasing array of forgeries for F-Section agents destined for France. Sergeant Redknapp was needed to ensure the offshoot moved decisively off the blocks.

It was while Redknapp was at Thatched Barn that a rush job came in from Baker Street. An F-Section agent's *Carte d'identité* had been stolen and a replacement was needed within the week. Most recent examples of the *Carte* returned from occupied Europe showed there was a new section that included two fingerprints. There were other more subtle changes in the format. It was a document that needed Lionizing. Redknapp sat down at his draughtman's table and opened the buff envelope marked 'On His Majesty's Service'.

The name for the *Carte d'identité* was 'François Desprées'. There were two recent passport photographs of a man with fine features, honey-coloured hair, and an Errol Flynn moustache. Redknapp jolted, almost spilling his tea.

'Well, I'll be blowed,' said Redknapp out loud.

He was looking at a photograph of his counsel, Mr Suttill. He gathered his paper, inks, letterheads, scalpel, glue and stamps – and took a deep breath.

'This, sir, will be my finest.'

*

Noor's training at Wanborough Manor ended as abruptly as it began. Captain de Wesselow called her into the library. She was nervous. The captain looked up from a table of reports.

'You have given every ounce of yourself to your training here. You have even impressed The Bishop.'

She stood tall, hands by her sides. Was the captain about to let her down gently? The captain, however, knew what Noor did not. SOE was flying blind in occupied Paris.

'It's time for the next phase. Somewhere else scenic. I am sending you on another specialist course for wireless operators.'

She was given forty-eight hours before leaving Wanborough. Her two days' leave were spent walking in the garden at Wanborough, and in the library. One of those she sought out before leaving was the librarian. The two had struck up a friendship. Sometimes they walked among the rhododendrons and Noor recited the stories from *Twenty Jātaka Tales*. There was something familiar about the writer of children's stories.

Noor found Dodo in the late afternoon light, cataloguing French detective stories.

'I came to say goodbye.'

The librarian turned. As she embraced Noor's hands with her palms, the librarian's cobalt eyes looked straight into the expressive brown eyes of the trainee agent.

'My dear sweet child,' said Dodo, once known as Treasure. She wondered how on earth such a sensitive girl was going to survive in occupied Europe. Still, SOE must know what it was doing.

Dodo was wearing the same set of pearls and the same silver brooch. She could feel her fingers reach for the latter. How could it be otherwise? She unclipped the silver bird with the ruby eye and placed it in Noor's palm.

Noor looked up, uncomprehending. Dodo wrapped Noor's fingers around the brooch.

'If you are ever in danger, you will always have a friend.'

*

That night, the librarian closed her eyes. Faces paraded in front of her before she fell asleep. Mrs Morgan, White Peony, Fire Opal, General Page, Marks senior and junior from the bookshop. And the face whose features she always tried to fill. Where was he? As she slept, Captain James Pritchard of the 1st Special Air Service had moved into position with other members of the raiding party concealed outside the battlements of Benghazi. He was a tall, lithe officer with cobalt eyes. At Oxford, he had been a Blues cricketer. He had courage, even by SAS standards. Captain Pritchard gave the order to attack. He led the charge himself, bolting forward to the base of the battlements. Under the battlements, he pulled the pin from his grenade with his teeth. As he threw his bowler's arm backwards, his head, swathed in Arab headdress, was framed in the sights of an Italian sniper rifle. The bullet struck Captain Pritchard above his left ear, spinning him ninety degrees. He was dead before he hit the Libyan sand. The grenade detonated, making an instant burial. He died not knowing he was the illegitimate son of a duke whose infant life changed tack one Edwardian afternoon in the tea room of the Great Russell Hotel.

A pair of cobalt eyes sprang open. Something, somewhere had broken. Treasure could not say what or how. But pillars had fallen. She sat up and put her hand to her heart. She forced her breathing to slow. She lit a Craven A in the dark.

Perhaps, she told herself, it was just a bad dream.

*

The same night, Noor dreamed she was flying under the bridges of the Seine with Pteech-ka. She was being pulled up. Not by wings.

By two Gestapo officers. She was dragged into a windowless room. The room was empty save for a chair under a naked bulb. The first Gestapo man tied her hands to the back of the chair. The second bent down and drew his eyes level.

'You will talk,' he said. 'Of that I can assure you.'

The nightmare was real. They left her tied to the chair for more than an hour.

The Gestapo men returned. They untied her.

'Stand on the chair!' shouted the first.

She looked blank.

'STAND ON THE CHAIR!'

Noor stood on the chair.

'Get down off the chair,' shouted the second.

As soon as she got down, the first officer screamed:

'STAND ON THE CHAIR.'

She stood back on the chair. Something about the first officer was familiar. If she was not mistaken, he had the face of SOE's F-Section head.

His name was Maurice Buckmaster.

CHAPTER 25
'MIDDLE EARTH'

Thame Park,
Oxfordshire, 1942

Noor

After interrogation training, Noor was driven to Thame Park, twenty miles south of Oxford, which had once housed Isaac Newton's library. Now it had a different role. On each column around Thame's periphery gates sat a stone lioness, eyes alert, observing the comings and goings at SOE Special Training School No. 52. There was a sentry box at the centre gate. The driver gave his and Noor's names, signed a visitor's chit and returned it to the sentry. The sentry waved through the vehicle.

Noor alighted in the courtyard of Thame Park. She looked up at the classical lines of honey-coloured stone. She patted down her WAAF uniform and, leather suitcase in hand, walked up the front steps. As she reached the top, a Lancaster bomber roared overhead. She realized how close she was to Bomber Command in Abingdon and felt an unexpected pang.

Moments later she was in a cool interior that might have felt more in place on a hill overlooking Florence. Standing amid the cool pink marble of Thame Park, she could see why SOE was some-times called the Stately 'Omes of England. A uniformed sergeant came over and saluted.

'Leading ACW Khan?'

Noor closed her heels and gave her best WAAF salute.

'Welcome to STS 52, ma'am.' He took her suitcase. 'Let me show you to your quarters.'

The sergeant led Noor through the Italianate rooms hanging with tapestries of light greens and grey-pinks. She was shown to an airy room with lemon silk curtains, overlooking the park. She held a clutch of the silk in her hand. It was heavy and slippery, like a pale eel. Such luxury seemed almost indecent amid the blackouts and the rationing. She opened the window and inhaled the Oxfordshire air. It felt almost like the first day of a holiday.

In the afternoon, Noor entered an ornate drawing room in which two chandeliers hung like vast, shimmering earrings. The room was filled with two columns of school desks. At each desk, a man was hunched over a radio set. At the end of the room, at the invigilators' table, sat two older men, with an array of radios and radio parts. Noor felt as if she had entered a practical exam. The click of her heels echoed around the room. Every man looked round, a flock of greased heads turning in unison. Expressions ranged between surprised and haughty. She was the only woman. The invigilators rose. She recognized one. He smiled and ushered her to an empty desk near the front.

Mr Stevens turned to the class, the pen-periscopes in his top pocket scanning the room for any signs of disrespect.

'We are joined today by Leading Aircraftwoman Khan, formerly of Bomber Command, and if any of you think you can transmit faster than her in Morse, I will eat my own transmitter. She's also trained in unarmed combat, lest any of you ruffians get the wrong idea.'

Noor could feel herself blushing.

'Leading ACW Khan, welcome to SOE's advanced radio opera-tor's course.'

Thame Park, it turned out, was no holiday. The first thing trainee wireless operators had to learn was how to strip and reassemble their Type A Mark II radios, to diagnose faults and carry out ad hoc

repairs. Then there was advanced instruction on atmospherics, wave-
lengths and jamming. Towards the end of the week, agents were
taught how to conceal their radios and how to set up and dismantle
aerials. There was the increasing realization that the training was a
rehearsal for a live performance in which there was no smiling Mr
Stevens on hand to assist. In the field, agents would be on their own.
Capture would lead only to hospitality provided by the Gestapo.

The final part of the course was coding. Trainee agents were
taught 'double transposition' – a cipher system involving a set of
numbers coded according to a keyword. The plain text would be
written under the numbers in a grid. The coded text would form
groups of seemingly random letters read in columns under each
number. The same or a different key could be used to transpose the
message letters a second time. The message would be broadcast in
code, but the slightest error could make the entire message indecipherable. The receiving party would require the keyword. The
method relied on a key lodged in the agent's head.

Noor was also taught about using security checks in their
messages. A 'true' check meant the message was being transmitted
freely. A 'bluff' check meant the agent was captured and transmitting under duress. Looking out for 'true' and 'bluff' checks was the
sole responsibility of overworked SOE transmission receivers.

On her final night at Thame, Noor heard a familiar voice. *The
river that flows in you also flows in me.*

She looked for Inayat, but the room was empty. She felt an
opiate infusion of calm. The sheet around her felt like a skein of
serenity. She lay back on the pillows and smiled.

From Thame Park, Noor continued her stately home tour to
the final destination. She was ordered to take a train from Oxford
to London and from London to Southampton. She stood at
Southampton station amid the shifting khaki and navy of troops
in transit. Few paid attention to the WAAF with polished shoes,
a look of faraway determination, and a leather suitcase containing the writings of Rumi, the manuscript of a Bach harp toccata,

and a 'restricted' manual on the operation and repair of a Type A Mark II radio.

A military vehicle was waiting outside the station. A corporal alighted.

'Leading ACW Khan?'

'Yes, Corporal.'

Both saluted.

'This way, ma'am.'

He helped Noor into the passenger seat and placed the suitcase in the rear.

The corporal drove west out of Southampton. Noor knew enough not to ask any questions. Then the vehicle changed tack, moving south through country roads canopied by trees, dappled sunlight flickering over the bonnet. The countryside unfolded like Middle Earth, an Elysium of shaded emerald fields scattered with ponds rippling with armadas of ducks. Wild ponies and deer grazed under the protective arms of oak, beech and willow. Some tree trunks were the width of the jeep. Noor imagined their hollows were home to entire families of Hobbits.

They moved deeper into the New Forest. The sudden appearance of a fortified gate, a perimeter wire and a sentry box made all thoughts of Hobbits vanish. The vehicle was entering a restricted area. Signs protruding from the verdant grass were all headed by the crossed swords of the War Ministry. Noor was entering one of the most secure areas of wartime England. In the duck ponds inside the perimeter, she could see different types of landing craft fastened together, and armed frogmen emerging from the shallows. In other ponds, she could see trials of raiding canoes for silent nocturnal demolition of enemy ships at anchor.

The corporal drove to a sentry box guarding an inner perimeter fence. The sentry inspected both the corporal and Noor's military passes and a letter signed by one Colonel Buckmaster. The vehicle drove forward into the grounds of Beaulieu, the Montagu family seat since the sixteenth century. Beaulieu was another SOE architectural gem, springing up around the medieval gatehouse to Beaulieu Abbey. The estate comprised a number of outhouses, many reflected in their own ponds encircled by a séance of weeping willows. It also housed SOE Special Training Schools 31 and 36.

The Beaulieu training schools were arranged like a university campus. The main site was Palace House, where agents could unwind in the high-beamed ancestral drawing room amid the decanters, portraits and wall-mounted antlers. Agents lived and trained in the estate's various outbuildings: Boarmans, Clobb Gorse, Warren House, The Rings, Needs Oar Point and The House on the Shore.

Agents destined for France were housed in Boarmans and Clobb Gorse. On the east bank of the river stood Inchmery House, converted into a commando training school for Polish and French troops and paratroopers of the Free French Combat Parachute Company. Middle Earth was yielding its own crop of spies and special forces.

Beaulieu was one of SOE's two finishing schools – centres where the final gloss was applied to agents before deployment in the field. Agents were taught about recruiting and building Resistance networks and about 'circuit' structure and security. There was advice on surveillance and counter-surveillance and passing clandestine messages via dead letter drops. Lock-picking and covert entry was taught by one of south London's most prolific burglars, who had shared a cell with Lionel Redknapp. There was specific instruction for saboteurs targeting the French railway – the spinal column of Reich domination of France. Agents were trained to disable trains using lubricant mixed with grinding material and, for more obvious demolition, to hide plastic explosives in locomotive boilers, disguised as coal. Other saboteurs were trained to use SOE 'time pencils' – pencil bombs that could be activated by crushing a vial of acid that would eat through the device to cause a delayed explosion.

For agents to be inserted by parachute, there was an introduction to the secret RAF 'Moon Squadrons', who would drop agents from Lysander aircraft into remote French fields relying only on moonlight and, if lucky, torches from reception committees. Agents were taught to bury their parachutes and how to approach – and later arrange – reception committees themselves. All F-section agents were given a crucial rip cord – not for their parachutes, but for proving authenticity in the field. The wartime BBC would broadcast an evening bulletin on the Radio Londres service in which the announcer would read out a series of apparently random messages:

'*La chaise est contre le mur*' – 'The chair is against the wall.'

'*Jean a une longue moustache*' – 'John has a long moustache.'

'*Les dés sont sure le tapis*' – 'The dice are on the carpet.'

'*Il y a un incendie à l'agence d'assurance*' – 'There is a fire at the insurance agency.'

Some messages were random foliage. Others had coded meaning. They might inform a Resistance group, for example, that an arms drop was imminent. SOE agents needing to prove their authenticity to networks on the ground would agree a coded message. The agent would radio the message to SOE, who would pass it to the BBC and have the message broadcast the following evening. Sometimes, when the agreed message came over the airwaves after breathless anticipation, it triggered a barrage of twisted metal into cork and toasts of *liberté* until dawn.

At Beaulieu, Noor was given a refresher course on the geography of Paris and a compass hidden in a hairbrush handle. The hatpins were tipped with a substance provided by Station XII for use as an emergency weapon. Another blade was concealed in one of her shoelaces. As a wireless operator, she was given specific instruction on setting up an aerial in an urban environment.

'Remember,' said Beaulieu's chief instructor, 'wireless operators are our eyes and ears. Without you, SOE is blind as a mole. *Never* transmit without a watch. For the first fifteen minutes you transmit in relative safety. After that you become a pip on the enemy's radar. If you transmit for more than twenty minutes you may as well hand yourself straight to the Gestapo. Try to avoid transmitting from the same position more than once.'

The comment stayed in Noor's mind when she had to learn the uniforms of the German Army, the German Field Police and the Gestapo. The silver *Totenkopf* skull pinned to the Gestapo cap stared back at her through hollow, expressionless sockets.

As the weeks prior to departure began to vanish, exercises became more practical. Theatre designers from Camouflage Section constructed a segment of a mock French street at Beaulieu, complete with French cars, French traffic lights, a café and a *bar tabac*. F-Section agents were required to cross the road, enter the bar and order a coffee. One agent was almost failed for stepping into the road and looking right, not left. Another was reprimanded for entering the café and ordering a '*café noir*'. The only coffee available in France was *café noir* and ordering anything other than *un café* would have aroused suspicion. Agents were also tested on receiving a telephone call in the *bar tabac* where the caller was asking to speak to the proprietor. English politeness '*Tenez la ligne*' – 'Hold the line' – was a giveaway. Agents had to use the more abrupt: '*Ne quittez pas.*'

As the Moon Squadrons were preparing for the next full moon drop, all agents' main focus was their cover story. It needed to be as seamless as one of Sergeant Redknapp's forgeries. Some of the film and stage directors from Camouflage Section were brought in to help agents 'become' their part. They had to eat, drink and breathe their new identity and wear it like an unseen cloak. They had to dream their new identity and wrap it around their shoulders at night. When their parachute opened, their old identity would dissipate on the breeze. When Francis Suttill hit the ground in a muddy field in Ferté-sous-Jouarre, east of Paris, the man to stand straight from his parachute roll was not Francis Suttill. He was François Desprées. And in his pocket was a forgery by one of his former clients.

*

The head of F-Section, Colonel Buckmaster, was pacing around his office in Baker Street. The bells of St James' murmured the muted chimes of midnight. He walked with his hands behind his back and his head down, as if counting the threads in the carpet. There were bags under his bright, pensive eyes. Sometimes he felt like Atlas, carrying the world on his back. He did, in fairness, carry a profound weight. It was Buckmaster who had the final say on whether an agent was ready to go into the field. And it was Buckmaster who, more often than not, accompanied the agent to RAF Tangmere, where Lysanders of the Moon Squadron waited in silvery light on the runway.

Sometimes his agents met triumph. Sometimes they met disaster. Buckmaster had known triumph and disaster long before being poached from Intelligence. At seventeen he was a fine sportsman and prominent classicist at Eton, destined for Oxford and a world of gilded opportunity. His world imploded one dismal afternoon when he was summoned to his housemaster's study. Judging by his housemaster's look, he thought there must have been a death in the family. It was worse. His father had gone bankrupt.

The gilt around Buckmaster's world melted. The dream of Oxford vanished. Buckmaster took the train to a Hampshire home crawling with bailiffs, a mother in tears and a father locked in his study. There was something his housemaster said before he left.

'We are at our best, Buckmaster, when our backs are against the wall.'

He gave him a copy of the *Odyssey* in Greek.

'Your journey will be difficult, but you will emerge the stronger for it.'

Leaving Eton, Buckmaster discovered the meaning of the word 'resourceful'. First he turned to teaching, helping to cram less gifted former schoolfellows for their university exams. He saved up enough money for a boat ticket to France. He made his way to Paris, where he presented himself, in faltering but enthusiastic French, to the editor of *Le Matin*. Buckmaster's linguistics gave the impression he had critical journalist experience. In reality, it was a short report on a house cricket match in the *Eton College Chronicle*. The bemused editor, coaxed by a letter of introduction from a family friend, gave him a job as a cub reporter. It was when Buckmaster's copy started coming in that the editor took off his glasses. There was something about the diffident Etonian with the stumbling French that made people's outer casing crumble. Criminals confessed to crimes. Wives exposed their husbands' lovers. Politicians revealed the real destination of the campaign funds. After six years on *Le Matin*, Buckmaster's steely indifference remained but his French was no longer faltering. His accent was undetectable. And he knew Paris like a Parisian.

From journalism, he moved into banking, taking on the account of the Ford Motor Company. Ford were so impressed they poached him to run Ford France. He shuttled between Paris, Lyon and Marseille in a black-and-white 1929 Ford convertible roadster. His journeys took him into the deep heart of the Auvergne, its lush valleys, slumbering volcanoes and red-roofed villages etching themselves into Buckmaster's soul forever. When Germany invaded France, he viewed it as a violation of his own mother. He jumped on one of the last ferries out, volunteering to fight as soon as he landed at Southampton. After some rudimentary training he joined an Infantry division in Northumberland. Intelligence poached him from the Infantry. SOE poached him from Intelligence. As the war entered its darkest hour, the canny Francophile Colonel Maurice Buckmaster became the head of SOE's F-Section, the department assigned to France. It was an inspired choice, but one that weighed heavily on the mind of a man who rolled agents' lives around in the palm of his hand.

As Buckmaster was pacing his office, there was a knock on the door. His assistant, Vera Atkins, stood in the doorway, elegant in a narrow skirt-suit, poised and alert whatever the hour.

'Just delivered by the Beaulieu courier,' she said, handing over a sheaf of reports. Her voice was clipped but there were traces, almost hidden, of an upbringing in Romania. 'Atkins' was an adopted English name.

The papers included reports on the next batch of agents coming up for final selection. Atkins had already placed them in order of importance for Buckmaster. The two had the air of a long-married couple, at ease in each other's company in an almost empty building at midnight. Atkins lit a Senior Service cigarette.

'I'll put on some tea.'

She returned with a tray of tea and biscuits. It was Buckmaster who poured the tea, eyes narrowing as the liquid rose to the top of each mug. She could read his mind.

'You're worried about the Khan girl, aren't you?'

The reports on Noor were divided. Some instructors thought she would make a first-class wireless operator. Others worried that she perceived the world like a child and that sending her into the field was out of the question. Atkins was unofficially in charge of the welfare of F-Section women agents. She knew the consequences of things going wrong in the field. When Buckmaster was not holding up the world, it was Atkins. She drew on her cigarette.

'Can we send her, Maurice?'

Buckmaster frowned as he stirred his tea. The ventricles of Buckmaster's heart were twisting. Did SOE have any choice? He gave a faraway smile.

'She'll be fine.'

CHAPTER 26
'THE IRON HEART'

Berlin, 1942

Canaris
Heydrich

Admiral Canaris ruminated under the ornate ceiling of the director's *Büro*. The grooves in his forehead were deepening. When he ran his finger along his brow, he could trace the ravines. The ridges that framed his upper lip sat like deep-etched parentheses. On his desk were pictures of his wife, Erika, and his daughters. On the wall opposite was a painting of the *Dresden*. Above the painting was a portrait of the Kaiser. The compulsory image of Hitler was exiled to a far wall, behind a telescope.

While he sat, immaculate in his full admiral's uniform, he could feel the accelerating tension. The pull one way towards victory in a chivalrous contest. The pull the other way towards blind despair. Despair in the form of a paranoid king cobra whose venom was penetrating the very veins of Humanity.

In the opening sequence of the war, the Reich's forces swept through Europe like blazing tar, pitiless and unchecked. Poland was first. Polish soldiers had, after all, made the singular mistake of crossing the border and attacking the German Sender Gleiwitz radio station. They burst into the studio mid-broadcast. Radios all over Germany crackled and ripped with the sound of gunfire and breaking glass. Except that the incident, dreamed up and orches-trated by Heydrich, was a sham. Jewish prisoners were forced into Polish army uniforms, drugged, and driven to the radio station's grounds. There they were scattered, unconscious and slumped over Karabinek rifles, around the transmitter tower. The studio 'invasion' was carried out by the SD, helped by the station's sound effects department. The same members of the SD then machine-gunned the Polish 'soldiers' beyond recognition.

The next day, Hitler invaded.

Other countries fell in a domino sequence. Czechoslovakia followed Poland. Then Denmark, Norway, Belgium, Holland and Luxembourg. Followed by the most valuable domino of all: France. The swastika replaced the tricolore above state buildings in a stunned Paris. As for the British, their army had to be plucked, humiliated, from the beaches of Dunkirk by an armada of fishing boats. Guernsey and Jersey fell, two stepping-stones on the inevi-table path to England. Had it not been for a few irritating Spitfire pilots in 1940, Britain would also be a province of the Reich. It was only a matter of time, said Hitler, before Nazi colours would fly from Buckingham Palace and the Houses of Parliament.

Canaris sat at his desk in readiness for a meeting that he knew would test his nerves. A maelstrom of conflicting thoughts writhed in his mind. Was the thrust east towards Stalingrad audacity or outright madness? Opening a war on two fronts had not gone well for Napoleon... For how long would the United States remain a slumbering giant? There was also the thought, nesting in the pit of his stomach, that plagued him with increasing constancy.

'*The duty of a patriot is to protect his country from its government.*'

He also had a duty as head of German military intelligence.

There was a knock at the door. It was young Klasing, his aide-de-camp. He entered the room and saluted.

'Heydrich has arrived, sir.'

'Has he, indeed?' said the admiral, turning the page of an intel-ligence report. 'How long should we keep him waiting?'

Klasing looked down, smiling.

Ten minutes later there was the sound of boots on parquet. Klasing threw open the door and announced Obergruppenführer Heydrich. Heydrich stood in the threshold of the door and hailed the Führer.

'Welcome,' said Canaris. He half rose and gave a naval salute.

Heydrich was, as ever, beaming. Whatever the Nazi doctors were injecting, he looked a picture of health, as if a death's head hawkmoth had acquired the cheeks of a baby. His hair, cropped even higher at the sides, looked a shade lighter.

'My dear Admiral, so good of you to see me.'

Canaris felt a frisson across his back.

'Likewise,' said Canaris. 'And how is Lina?'

'She is in the greatest of health, Admiral. And I hope the same can be said for Erika.'

'Well enough, thank you. And we both join in congratulating you on your new appointment.'

It was a reference to Heydrich's promotion to Reich Protector of Bohemia and Moravia.

'You are too kind, Admiral,' said Heydrich, taking a seat. He crossed his legs and removed his gloves. He made the chair seem like a throne.

'I look forward to my formal inauguration in Prague,' he continued. 'I have, I should confess, always considered the Czechs to be lower than vermin. Such a preponderance of Jews and Gypsies. But I shall cleanse the protectorate of dirty blood. Personally, if necessary. I have given the Führer my word.'

'Is that why he calls you the Man with the Iron Heart?' said Canaris, with a distant smile.

'Perhaps,' said Heydrich, flicking his gloves across his palm.

Heydrich leaned forward.

'I came here to issue a warning, Wilhelm.'

Canaris could feel himself bridling.

'A man was picked up in Amsterdam last month. He was carrying false identity papers, a large sum of money and a sleeve pistol. In his suitcase was a portable wireless. He said nothing to your

Abwehr interrogators. Until he was handed over to us. It seems that in our care he said more.'

'Your people and my people will always be different.'

Heydrich coloured. Rumours that he was Jewish had never been scotched – even when the Nazi's expert on racial purity certified him 'free of Semite blood'.

He gathered himself for the riposte.

'It seems your friends the British are up to something.'

'I remind you, Reinhard, I was engaged fighting the British in 1914 when you were still in short trousers.'

Heydrich shifted.

'And I remain,' said Canaris, raising his voice, 'fighting the British to this day.'

'Well, if that is the case you will want to know that they do not always box using Queensberry Rules. The man in Holland was a Dutchman working for the British. The British are sending armed agents into Reich-occupied territories. We did not ascertain the full name of the organization before this individual... succumbed to our hospitality. The Special Operations Something or Other.'

'We know more about what is happening in England than you might imagine,' said Canaris.

'These people are a threat to the Reich. They must face the same fate as the Jews.'

Canaris could feel the ink of contempt flood his veins.

'Thank you for your concern, Obergruppenführer. The SD's methods and the Abwehr's will never be the same. Was there anything else?'

Heydrich rose from his chair with his fencer's spring.

'Nothing whatsoever,' he said, striding towards the door.

He turned.

'Except this, Admiral. I wonder, sometimes, whether the Abwehr is a little too squeamish when it comes to the more distasteful sides of war? And I wonder also,' he added, looking to the half-hidden image of Hitler, 'whether your priorities are in the correct order?'

He swivelled on his heel and was gone. Silence descended. It felt like the crackle and hiss of a radio had been eliminated. Klasing brought in coffee.

'I would like five hundred Abwehr identity cards printed,' said Canaris. 'Names left blank.'

'Yes, sir,' said Klasing, placing the coffee on Canaris's desk.

After coffee, Canaris put on his greatcoat and went to St Hedwig's Cathedral. There was bomb damage to some of the outer buttresses, but the church was still standing. He entered the church. A thin ray of light pointed to a pew. He entered the pew and knelt. He looked up at the stained glass and closed his eyes.

'*Wachen sie über mich*,' he said to the gloom.

*

Prague, 1942

Heydrich

Heydrich sat alone at the breakfast table of the Lobkowicz Palace. The polished mahogany glinted like a dark mirror. Reflected in the sheen were the faces of angels from the fresco above. Candles flickered in two imperial candelabra, their flames almost invisible in the morning light. Laid out on antique silver was a breakfast befitting the Reich Protector of Bohemia and Moravia: six different cheeses, duck eggs, smoked trout, liver sausage, *Schlackwurst* salami, Black Forest ham, quince jelly, peaches, apricots, almonds, *Laugenstangen* rolls and the finest *Krönung* coffee.

There was a knock. Two footmen pulled open the double doors. A young Obersturmführer clicked his heels and extended his arm in salute.

'*Komm herein!*' said Heydrich, the pitch of his voice unmistakable.

The Obersturmführer marched up to Heydrich and saluted again.

'At ease, Obersturmführer. It's still early.'

'Sir, I have had your orders from yesterday drawn up for signature.'

The Obersturmführer handed Heydrich a rolled document. A trace of red ribbon hung from the seal like a forked tongue.

Heydrich spread out the vellum among the angels' reflected faces. Were the quotas accurate? He looked at the figures. The face of a death's head hawkmoth broke into a smile.

The Obersturmführer presented a pen. Heydrich signed with a flourish.

'Thank you, Obersturmführer. I wish your unit a productive day.'

It was an order for the execution of Jews and Gypsies in Southern Moravia. It was regrettable that women and children could not be spared, but eradication had to include the mother-plants as well as their poisonous seeds. Otherwise the mandrake weed regrew and the poison cycle continued.

There was something about signing a mass death warrant so early in the day that had an aphrodisiac effect on Heydrich. He shifted. He could still feel the heat from the previous night's chastisement, each movement in his chair bestowing an exquisite sting. Such a legacy could come only from someone well practised with a cane. Someone had to step in while Lina was pregnant.

As the spring flowers opened across Prague, Heydrich could feel his own career blossoming. At the beginning of the year, he had chaired the Wannsee Conference in Berlin in which the Reich minsters and SS generals formalized the final solution to the Jewish question. The minutes spoke of populations of Jews being 'evacuated east', though all delegates knew the true meaning of the words. Indeed, such 'evacuations' had already started in Russia and Poland and more camps were being built inside and outside Germany to help speed the process. When Heydrich finished his closing address, the applause went on for a full five minutes. Heydrich gave a deep bow. As he bowed into the applause, he felt like the concert violinist he might have become. His horizons, however, were now bigger than he could ever have imagined.

He was first violinist in the Nazi world orchestra and a virtuoso of racial purification. As Reich Protector of Bohemia and Moravia, he did everything in his power to live up to his name, 'the Man with the Iron Heart'. Eradicating the Reich's enemies, real or perceived, became Heydrich's obsession. As a result, wherever he strolled in Prague, crowds parted like the Red Sea. Whenever his motorcade came into view, all the cars would scatter. As Heydrich swept past in the chauffeur-driven Mercedes 320 Cabriolet, the Reich Protector would smile, reclining in a seat of cream leather as he slapped his palm with his calf-skin gloves.

Approval from Hitler came in the form of divine reciprocity. With each passing week, the grip of the SD tightened. And Heydrich was pleased to see that the reverse was happening to the Abwehr. A small unit of the SD were now watching the Abwehr as closely as enemies of the Reich. Canaris and the other Prussian dinosaurs who attended the old Emperor's funeral in 1941 would soon be extinct. There were increasing rumours about Canaris's loyalty to the Führer and such dissent would not be tolerated. There was something else about Canaris that made Heydrich's upper lip quiver with fury. He had arranged for Abwehr identity cards to be given to Jews in Holland to stop their 'evacuation' by the SD. Worse, he persisted in suggesting that Heydrich was 'of Semite blood', despite formal certification that his blood was true Aryan. And for that he would never forgive his old mentor.

A far door opened, snapping Heydrich into the present. It was Lina, pregnant and as radiant as Heydrich imagined a Norse goddess. Heydrich stood, clicked his heels, and pulled back a tapestried chair. Lina sat, smiled, and placed her hand over Heydrich's. Heydrich tucked an immaculate linen napkin into his tunic. He waved like a conjurer at the imperial breakfast floating on polished silver.

'*Bitte...*'

Afterwards, as the Heydrichs withdrew to the palace apartments, a tear ran from the eye of one of the painted angels. Or was it, as one footman suggested, a leak in the ceiling that was never fixed?

*

303

In an attic apartment in the Uzavřená district of Prague a man was
kneeling, spreading out items on a rug. His name was Gabčík. He
might have been setting out a picnic. The delicacies were intriguing:

- Steel barrel
- Cocking bolt
- Breech block assembly
- Receiver
- Trigger pin
- Narrow metal butt
- Magazine cases (x4), each with 32 rounds

Reassembled, the ingredients made a Mark II Sten sub-machine
gun. There were two other men at a table poring over a map of
Prague. They were Kubiš and Valčík. They were all agents of SOE's
Czech Section.

*

Each had spent two months at the SOE finishing school at
Arisaig, west Inverness-shire. In the craggy, medieval beauty of
the Highlands around Loch nan Uamh, they underwent the final
and most intensive stage of their training. Training to track a rare
human specimen: a Man with an Iron Heart. Once the Iron Heart
was found, the agents had clear instructions how to proceed.

Their mission was named Operation Anthropoid.

As part of their preparation, the three spent a fortnight with the
head gamekeeper of Arisaig House, Hamish McCulloch. They set
off into the early morning mist over peaty tracks and wild heather,
climbing up through the glens high enough to see the peaks of
Eigg and Rùm. The agents had been anxious whether they would
understand Mr McCulloch. Their apprehension was unfounded.
McCulloch said almost nothing. Camouflaged in green-brown
tweeds, he was a wordless part of the landscape. Moving over the
ancient crags, he used the moss to mute his footfall, pausing every
so often to turn his ear to the wind, frowning in concentration. He

scanned the horizon like a bird of prey. Mid-morning on the first day, he stopped dead. He turned to the others, put his finger to his lips and pointed. On the opposite mountainside, a piece of rock sprang to life. It was a stag. The animal looked up, ears pointed, antlers tilted. A pair of fathomless brown eyes searched for danger. It skittered away, sending a buzzard flapping into the horizon.

By the end of the fortnight, the agents had relearned, in the watery highland light, the art of moving, hearing and seeing.

Gabčík went on to Sten gun marksmanship. He learned to strip and reassemble the weapon – in the final test, blindfold. When aiming, he learned to prop the weapon with his left hand under the barrel sleeve while the right index finger curled round the trigger. His trigger finger became as sensitive to movement as the twitchiest highland stag. The thin metal butt caused an almost permanent indentation in his right shoulder. In the end, he could pepper a wooden figure in the face and chest whether he fired standing, kneeling or lying.

Kubiš moved on to explosive projectiles. For Operation Anthropoid, an SOE scientist modified a No. 73 anti-tank grenade. The grenade was made lighter, for ease of throwing, and fitted with an 'all-ways' fuse that would detonate however it landed. Over and again Kubiš practised throwing a dummy grenade at a rusting Austin 16 as it rolled down a ramp in the field behind Arisaig House. As for Valčík, he remained with the gamekeeper for advanced lessons in navigation, tracking... and silence.

*

For the past fortnight, the Czech trio, with the assistance of urban partisans, had been studying Heydrich's movements. On Friday afternoons, Heydrich's car would leave Prague for his 40-acre estate in Panenské Břežany. Normally, Heydrich's chauffeur drove the Reich Protector back into Prague on Monday mornings, leaving Panenské Břežany at eight sharp. One aspect of Nazism was helpful, the agents agreed. Nazis were *always* on time. The men spent a week scoping the route at dusk, avoiding

German patrols, looking for the best vantage point. They settled on the tram stop at the bend in Holešovičkách Street near Bulovka Hospital. The bend would force Heydich's car to slow its approach.

Having decided on the vantage point, it was then a question of checking and rechecking their weapons, playing poker and back-gammon and trying to put matters out of their mind. By the week-end, the atmosphere in the apartment was beginning to sharpen. The final grains of sand were gathering at the aperture of the hour-glass. On the Sunday night, the men sat around a steaming pot of goulash. Kubiš broke the bread.

'The Last Supper. Not for us. For the Obergruppenführer!'

The men laughed. They would have raised a toast but there was only water at the table and toasting water was unlucky. After dinner, Gabčík re-stripped his Sten gun and oiled each part, taking extra care with the inside of the barrel. He left the parts unas-sembled. Kubiš selected three grenades and checked the pins. The three retired to bed with silent prayers.

They rose at first light. Before leaving, Gabčík opened a leather suitcase and placed it on the table. Inside were hard-to-acquire vegetables, packed in straw. He hid the components of the Sten gun under the hay, between the vegetables, and closed the suitcase. If searched, he would admit to being a black marketeer. He carried a roll of banknotes to deal with any summary fine.

Kubiš placed a grenade in each pocket and hung one behind his waist where his spine met his belt. Valčík ensured his SOE sleeve pistol was strapped to his forearm. With the gun in place, he collected a hand mirror and a pair of binoculars. It was time. They descended the stairs like mice. They went to a pre-arranged meeting point outside a café on Čimická Street. A partisan stood alone under a lamp post. On seeing the other three, he gave a low whistle. A battered Renault came out of the mist. The three agents entered the vehicle. They sat, adrenaline surging, as the car crawled through the waking city.

Gabčík and Kubiš took up position on either side of Holešovičkách Street. Valčík took up position further east along the
road, where it moved into a slight upward incline. Kneeling in
some bushes between two buildings, Gabčík opened the suitcase
and assembled his Sten gun. It was as natural as making breakfast. He slid the magazine into place. There was a reassuring click.
Thirty-two bullets lay in coffin darkness, each wanting to be the
first to pierce the ventricles of an Iron Heart.

*

It was a perfect spring morning. Heydrich could feel the air caressing his face – warm but still fresh. There was something about
travelling in an open-top Mercedes that appealed to Heydrich.
Protection was unnecessary. He was untouchable. As the car
cruised along Holešovičkách Street, he could feel the familiar
glow from the seat of his trousers and revelled in the darts of
pain. As he slapped his gloves against his palm, he wondered
about fate – whether he was the instrument of a divine force
sent to purify humanity. Perhaps he was, in fact, God's architect?
His mind started to float. He saw himself in imperial robes high
above bowing masses as the crown of a New World Order was
placed upon his head.

The Mercedes slowed as it approached an S-bend. There was a
flash from Valčík's mirror. Gabčík saw the glint. He picked up the
sound of the engine. With every rotation of the Mercedes' wheels,
Gabčík's heart accelerated.

Come on, come on.

The grille of a Mercedes 320 Cabriolet came into view.

*

Lina Heydrich sat at her dressing table. She took time brushing
her hair with a silver brush. Her father had told her fairy tales
as a girl. About a beautiful princess with long blonde hair who
married a handsome prince and they went to live in a castle where
everything they touched turned to silver and wherever they
went people bowed. She and the prince went on to have strong,

307

flaxen-haired children, rulership of vast dominions, riches unlimited, and they all lived happily ever after.

*

Gabčík jumped into the road. The butt of the Sten gun was wedged into his shoulder. His finger encircled the trigger. The car stopped dead. He had a clear shot at both the chauffer and Heydrich.

*

As she brushed her hair, Lina Heydrich could feel the kick of her fourth child. Her unborn baby kicked like a boy. She patted her belly and smiled.

*

Gabčík pulled the trigger. It was rigid. Gabčík might have been squeezing stone. The Sten gun had jammed. A blade of grass in the barrel had altered fate. Heyrich was on his feet now, reaching for his Luger. Gabčík looked round. Kubiš was now on the road, grenade in hand. Kubiš had seen the gun jam. There was no time to think. He pulled the pin from his grenade, took a breath, and hurled it at the car.

Kubiš turned away. The shock waves from the blast pulsated through his body. A grenade fragment entered the back of his thigh. As the smoke cleared, he heard coughing. His insides almost dissolved. The grenade had fallen short. The blast had damaged the Mercedes' back wheel and rear door. But otherwise the car was in one piece. As, for that matter, was Heydrich. His fencer's agility remained. Heydrich jumped from the car, led by his pistol. The Man with the Iron Heart would not be cowed by a pathetic assassination attempt.

He ran after his assailants, firing with each step. The chauffeur was now out of the car, adding to the firefight. Heydrich ran further, firing. One of the bullets glanced an assassin's calf. Then something happened that no one expected – least of all Heydrich. His legs buckled. He collapsed on the roadside. His stomach was wet. He put his hand over his tunic. His palm was running with blood. As the adrenaline receded, he realized he had been hit by fragments of the grenade – and fragments of the car. He felt limp. And sick. The sun was blinding.

'I will survive for the sake of the Reich and for my family,' he told himself.

His uniform was becoming wetter.

He gave himself an order. 'Stay conscious.'

The chauffeur was supporting his head. There was someone else. A woman. She held his hand and spoke in Czech. Soft, comforting words. He made a mental note to ensure she received a medal from the Reich. A passing van was flagged. The van driver and the chauffeur placed Heydrich in the back. A bleeding Nazi. The pain was excruciating. Shards of glass felt like they were sticking out of his abdomen. The population would pay.

'You are NOT going to bleed to death in the back of a van,' he whispered as his tunic started to drip. 'You were made for higher things.'

The van stopped at the steps of the Bulovka Hospital. Orderlies carried Heydrich inside on a stretcher. News spread through the hospital like typhus. If Heydrich died, the consequences would be unthinkable. The surgical team was assembled. It included some of Prague's leading surgeons. The orderlies lifted Heydrich on to the operating table and a nurse cut away his uniform. There were deep lacerations to his abdomen. Some metal fragments were protruding from his skin. Blood loss was severe. The lead surgeon put on his mask and took up his scalpel. Through force of will, he held the blade steady. He began the incision.

He was bound, he knew, by his oath to do everything in his power to save the patient. His scalpel moved with accuracy and skill as he opened the body of the Man with the Iron Heart. It turned out his organs were as pink, purple and delicate as anyone's, with one collapsed lung clinging to life from a heart that was anything but iron.

There was agreement among the surgeons that the patient's lung would need to be reinflated and his badly damaged spleen removed. First, he needed an immediate blood transfusion. A theatre nurse performed a blood test. Heydrich was blood group 'O'. O for Ordinary, thought the surgeon. Just an ordinary sadist. There was a pause while the theatre sister left to issue instructions for immediate delivery of four pints of blood group O.

The lead surgeon excused himself from the circle of surgeons. He caught up with the sister just as she was walking down the corridor leading from the operating theatre. He put his hand on her shoulder. She looked round, startled.

'I apologize, sister,' he said.

'Time is short, doctor,' she said. She was pale.

'I am going to ask you to do something for me. I can't make you. But I am going to ask.'

'Yes, doctor.'

'I want you to obtain four litres of blood group A. But labelled blood group O.'

The sister's eyes widened as the consequences registered.

'But doctor—'

'There are times, sister, when we are answerable to a higher authority.'

She looked away. Then direct into the surgeon's eyes.

'Group "A" as in Aryan.'

The surgeon nodded.

'You must excuse me, doctor. I have some blood to collect.'

The patient was prepared for the transfusion. The lead surgeon addressed the nursing sister.

'The patient is blood group O. Can you confirm, sister, we have four pints of group O?'

'I can,' said the sister, clear and firm. Certainly, her writing on the label said the same.

Life-giving blood was pumped into Heydrich. His heart started to regain its strength and his organs were becoming plump and firm. Only two people in the operating theatre knew the reality. Heydrich had just been given a large dose of slow-acting, untraceable poison.

The surgeon went on to remove the patient's spleen as if he were handling Ming china. The other surgeons stood in silent awe as the lead surgeon went about repairing Heydrich's perforated diaphragm. He closed the incision with stitching that would not have been out of place on Savile Row.

*

The pair had managed to get back to the safe house. As they bound their wounds and rearmed, the captured son of one of the partisans was having the soles of his feet burned by the Gestapo. He refused to talk. That was, however, until the lead Gestapo officer pressed the boy's head against the glass of a fish tank in which his mother's severed head was floating. As an SS armoured car skidded to a halt below, the pair managed to escape over the roof. They dropped on to the pavement and tore through the streets of Prague. A passer-by gestured to a side door at St Cyril's Cathedral. The men entered the House of God. At least, thought Kubiš, the SS would think twice about attacking a cathedral. The firestorm that followed was to prove him the antithesis of right.

*

The machine-gun fire came in bursts. Then stretches. A storm of bullets ricocheted off the cool stone of the Cathedral of St Cyril and St Methodius. The bullets left a trail of fuming pockmarks on the exterior wall around the main door. The image of Christ on the high stained-glass window fell inwards, breaking into a thousand shards. Christ's body lay on the flagstones in a kaleidoscope of mutilation. The wooden frieze above the altar was reduced to matchwood.

Gabčík and Kubiš, surrounded by a hundred SS soldiers, had a telescopic view of the future. Murder in the Cathedral. But neither was going to die without a fight. Gabčík upended two pews against the wall. Kubiš helped him climb. Once up, Gabčík knelt. Jags of coloured glass jutted from the window's edge. He placed the barrel of his Sten gun where Christ's feet had been pinned to a cross of stained glass. The barrel rested between two fragments, facing the courtyard outside. He pressed the butt into his shoulder and found the trigger.

Gabčík pulled the trigger. This time, the barrel was clear. He felt the punches to the shoulder as he opened fire. First target. The sniper in an attic opposite. Gabčík hit him in the throat. He fell back in an arc of blood. Then the soldiers in the cathedral court-yard. Gabčík had the advantage of height. He pointed the Sten almost perpendicular, raining down bullets on the helmets and torsos below. A number fell, some still, some writhing. Each bullet, he knew, was another letter on his death warrant. From another window, Valčík was adding to the onslaught. Sparks flew from the cathedral as if God's own wrath had been ignited.

Gabčík could hear shouting. It was Kubiš. He had found a stepladder in the vestry. He was almost as high as Gabčík. Kubiš's arm was outstretched. In his palm was a grenade. A final offering. Gabčík placed the grenade in his pocket and carried on firing. Kubiš could hear movement at the back of the cathedral. He approached the rear door from the side. He could hear wheels. Then silence. He crept towards the middle of the door and put his eye to the keyhole. He was staring into the barrel of a field gun. The entire cathedral shook as the rear door was blown inwards in a maelstrom of wooden darts. Kubiš wondered if anything on Earth was sacred as he lay on the ground, his body lacerated like Christ. He pulled the pin from his grenade. He had just the strength to throw it at the crowd of soldiers who were advancing into the cathedral.

Gabčík looked round. He saw Kubiš dying. He heard shouts to surrender. Valčík responded by placing his sleeve pistol against his heart and firing. Gabčík threw the grenade from the window. As it detonated, he placed his SOE-issue Colt to his temple. His last thought was of Heydrich – his eyes when he pointed the Sten gun in the road. The Man with the Iron Heart had the eyes of a frightened stag. Gabčík's body fell to the floor, cracking on the flagstones.

*

In the days that followed, Heydrich started to regain his strength. Heinrich Himmler's own physician, Dr Gebhardt, was sent to attend to Heydrich with a team of German surgeons. Dr Gebhardt found Heydrich in good spirits. He examined the medical notes and the fragments removed from Heydrich's body. Yes, the Czech surgeons had done a creditable job – particularly in removing the spleen. The stitching, he had to admit, was admirable.

The main thing was that the Man with the Iron Heart would live to finish his life's work: the purification of humanity. Lina came to visit her husband with the children. They presented him with a Bundt marble cake in a box with a red ribbon. The strain on Lina's face had started to lift. Now that her husband's survival was assured, she looked radiant. More radiant, thought Heydrich, than she had ever looked.

*

Reprisals had started. In the village of Lidice, an SS death squad had already murdered most of the inhabitants. As Heydrich patted the heads of his offspring, children executed holding their parents' sleeves were being thrown into mass graves. Gestapo intelligence had suggested the assassins' safe house was in the village. The Gestapo gave orders to spare nobody. The intelligence turned out to be wrong. By that stage, the village had been razed to the ground. More than ten thousand Czech graves were dug, many only a few feet long, in revenge for the attack on the Man with the Iron Heart.

*

After a week, Heydrich developed a high fever. Himmler's physician was baffled – and worried. The Man with the Iron Heart would not die on his watch, end of story. He went back over the medical notes. He pored over the radiologist's images. All the surgeons present at the operation were interviewed. It was a mystery. One of the German surgeons hazarded the suggestion that upholstery from the Mercedes had entered Heydrich's bloodstream. Heydrich's blood was going septic. Heydrich realized, staring from his hospital bed, that his work would remain unfinished.

He was going to die.

The death's head face began to look like a funeral mask. Beatific, said one.

Before he lapsed into a coma from which he would never awake, Reinhard Heydrich clutched the sleeve of Dr Gebhardt. His last words were from Heydrich senior's opera, *Amen*.

'The world is just a barrel-organ which the Lord God turns Himself.
We all have to dance to the tune which is already on the drum.'

CHAPTER 27
'WHEN THE BLOOD CREEPS'

London, 1942

Marks

Leo Marks pressed his fingers to his temples. He clenched a pencil between his teeth. The sequence was twenty-four characters.

79 39 AR 59 WH 93 5Y 41 G8 21 S4 O6

His eyes narrowed on the fifth letter-pair, 'WH'. He brought 'WH' together with the adjoining pair, '93'.

'WH93.'

He closed his eyes. Words – four letters – beginning WH?

What? When? Whip? Whim? Whom?

'9' had to be a vowel: 'A' 'E' 'I' 'O'. He could discount 'U'.

He looked at the first pair of numbers: 79. If '9' was a vowel, '7' was almost certainly a consonant. The letters and numbers spun round his mind like a fruit machine. Based on alphabet frequency, the winning letter for '9' was 'E'.

7E 3E AR 5E WH E3 5Y 41 G8 21 S4 O6

'5' was next to a vowel: 'E' and a consonant: 'Y'.

The fruit machine spun again.

If '5Y' was a single word, the 5 was either an 'M' for 'MY' or a 'B' for 'BY'. Therefore, the fourth pair '5E' was either 'ME' or 'BE'.

He ran both permutations. The first gave him:

7E 3E AR **ME** WH E3 **MY** 41 G8 21 S4 O6

He grouped the fifth and sixth letter pairs: 'WHE3'.

'3' was almost certainly an 'N', as in 'WHEN'.

7E **NE AR ME WH EN MY** 41 G8 21 S4 O6

If '5' was 'M' then looking at the first pair, '7E', the only option for '7' was 'B'.

BE NE AR ME WH EN MY 41 G8 21 S4 O6

He smiled. The '1's even looked like capital 'I's.

BE NE AR ME WH EN MY 4I G8 2I S4 O6

The 'G' and 'O' were hiding in plain sight.

BE NE AR ME WH EN MY 4I G8 2I S4 **O6**

The 'I' in the adjacent to group to 'S' was a giveaway.

BE NE AR ME WH EN MY 4I G8 2 **IS** 4 **O6**

The remaining numbers had nowhere to run.

BE NE AR ME WH EN MY **LI GH TI SL OW**

He regrouped the letters.

'BE NEAR ME WHEN MY LIGHT IS LOW'

Bingo! What would Tennyson have said? He looked at his watch. Forty-two seconds. *Child's play.*

*

Marks left St Paul's before the war. The High Master gave some parting words.

'You've proved almost unteachable, Marks. But have by all accounts an exceptional mind. Whatever you do in life, don't lay it on too thick.'

Marks went away, hands in pockets. *Don't lay* what *on too thick?*

A career in Marks & Co. awaited. Books were in his blood. And he had cracked his father's secret coding system as a child. There was, however, a rude interruption. War. Sooner or later, the cannon would come looking for its fodder. Marks's parents awaited the postman's footsteps with silent dread. Leo was the apple of their eye. One day, an envelope arrived marked 'War Ministry'. Mrs Marks collapsed into a chair and cried through an entire box of tissues. Mr Marks senior sat in grim silence.

'Our only son!' cried Mrs Marks. 'Our only s-s-on.'

Mr Marks held her hand. Her hand clenched and unclenched as if in spasm.

'Leo will be all right,' said Mr Marks.

'How do you know?' said Mrs Marks, burying her face back in the tissues.

The die was cast. Marks would be joining a London regiment. Fate, however, had other plans. They came in the form of a competition in the crossword section of *The Times*. It looked simple. Entrants were asked to decode a series of twenty-four letter groups and send the outcome to *The Times*' offices, along with their contact details. Successful applicants had the chance to enter a competition for which there was a prize of £50. Leo Marks sent in his entry from Marks & Co.

A letter arrived back within a week. Three more codes were included for decryption – each more difficult. Marks sat on the same stool with the same pencil, his internal fruit machine turning code into text. The third code had taken over a minute, but nothing that came close to breaking into a sweat. After returning the answers, an invitation came to compete with other entrants one afternoon at Grosvenor House.

Uncle Abe squeezed Marks's hand before he left. He was a wizened fossil now, spending his days in a wheelchair in the corner of Marks & Co. His eyes were still bright.

'Remember the master pattern, Young Leo. Few look. But it is there for those with the eyes to see.'

The competition at Grosvenor House was different. The codes were on the nursery slopes of demanding. Decoding had to be done in less than two minutes. For Marks, however, he simply pulled the handle of his mental fruit machine once or twice and the plain text appeared. There were two men at Grosvenor House who made notes, but said nothing, either to themselves or the twenty or so competitors, who included an archaeologist from the British Museum who had worked on decoding the Linear B characters from the ancient tablet of Knossos.

Another letter came. It was marked '**Restricted**'. Marks's call for active service would be suspended pending two interviews related to national security. The first was carried out on the premises of Marks & Co. by Detective Sergeant Rush-Williams of Special Branch. Marks was required to sign a sheaf of documents, including the Official Secrets Act. There followed a further letter ordering Marks to catch the ten o'clock train the following Wednesday from Euston to an unheard-of town. Bletchley. He would be met at the station. On no account was Marks to discuss with anyone the time, place or contents of the interview.

A uniformed corporal met Marks at Bletchley Station. The corporal said nothing during the journey from the station to Bletchley Park. At Bletchley he was one of six undergoing a series of timed tests. Two of the six were women, one a physics undergraduate at Cambridge. The codes were more challenging. Marks had to stop the fruit machine now and again and do some thinking. On one occasion, he had to give it a kick. Each time, however, the correct letters came up like a winning row of cherries. He was interviewed by a gaunt naval officer, who put a number of terse ticks and crosses on a report. Marks would hear within a fortnight.

Uncle Abe scooped up the letter. It was marked 'Inter Services Research Bureau'. The letter inside was signed by a Brigadier Gubbins. Marks was required to report the following Monday for special duties. The address was not Bletchley. It was London: 64 Baker Street, part of the Ministry of Economic Warfare. Marks wondered why the ministry needed a codebreaker, but his thoughts gave way to a dam bursting.

'You mean Leo's not going to war?' said Mrs Marks, sobbing into Mr Marks's chest.

Fate smiled. Little did Ma Marks know.

*

The following Monday saw Leo Marks pacing down Baker Street. His curls were temporarily constrained under a bowler hat. He wore a pinstripe suit and carried a briefcase befitting an economist.

Inside the briefcase was a corned beef and pickle sandwich made by his mother, a slice of honey cake and an apple. He could not think what else to put in the briefcase other than two sharp pencils. At his mother's insistence, he added a spare clean handkerchief.

It felt like his first day at school. Butterflies were playing lacrosse under the pinstripes. He presented himself at 64 Baker Street at 08:30 sharp. The building was recent. It looked to Marks like the headquarters of a semi-reputable insurance company. Once inside, he was shown to a desk where he presented his passport. He was given a temporary pass by a uniformed constable. He was taken by an armed lance corporal to an office on the second floor.

Inside, the place had the feel of a militarized firm of stock-brokers. It echoed to the clatter of teleprinters and wire signals, as if equity prices were coming in from the London Stock Exchange. The difference was that the women collating information as it came over the wires were in uniform – Army and Air Force. The majority of men, striding, reports under arms, were also in uniform.

Marks was shown into a small office. He placed his briefcase on the desk and sat in the chair. The clock on the wall had a piercing tick. No one came. As the seconds carved further incisions into the air, his apprehension turned to boredom. He thought about his sandwich. And his apple. Then he thought about the test code that had led him to 64 Baker Street.

The plain text made imprints on his mind, like typewriter keys.

> *Be near me when my light is low,*
> *When the blood creeps, and the nerves prick*
> *And tingle; and the heart is sick,*
> *And all the wheels of Being slow...*

He did not know it at the time, but Marks had entered a world in which poetry was sometimes the thread to stop a person falling from the 'dark verge of life' into a bottomless void. He took out his pencil. What to do? There was a blank sheet of notepaper on the desk. *Now what if we were to put it into real code.*

The moment his pencil stabbed the paper, the door opened. It was an infantry captain. He was holding a long piece of teleprint. He was breathless.

'You must be the new chap.'

Marks stood. People sometimes said of Marks senior that it was difficult to tell whether he was sitting or standing. 'What we lack in height,' he would say, tapping his forefinger on his temple, 'we make up for with brains.' Young Leo was of the same build, with the same expressive nose and clever brown eyes. While Marks senior's hair had gone the way of many first editions, Leo had a head of curls that might have sheltered a family of starlings. The captain extended his hand.

'Owen.'

'Marks.'

'The new cryptographer?'

'So I understand, sir.'

'Do you know anything about what we do here?'

'Nothing.'

'I'm afraid I can't give you a rundown now. There's a panic on. What would help is if you could try and decode this? The girls have drawn a blank.'

Who were the girls?

Owen passed him a sheet of teleprint.

'It's just in from Norway and we need to signal back within eight hours.'

Norway? Before Marks could say anything, Captain Owen was gone. Marks placed the sheet of paper on the table and took up his pencil as a surgeon takes up his scalpel. The patient was a body of sixty-six letters of random code. Marks set to work. By the time Marks looked up, the hands of the clock had moved to one-forty-five. He was tired. And hungry. And no further forward. The fruit machine had jammed. He ate his corned beef sandwich and his slice of honey cake with utter despondence. He put the apple between his teeth and sat with his fingers pressed to his temples.

There had to be a way in.

He closed his eyes. As before, the figures rose off the page. First, he saw them running left to right. Then right to left. Certain figures started to pair off. The pairs would spin, then separate and spin off with other figures. It was like watching a Viennese waltz from above. He delved into the furthest reaches of his mind, straining for patterns, frequencies, clues.

Captain Owen put his head round the door at teatime.

'How's progress?'

Marks looked up.

'Slow, I'm afraid.'

A cloud passed over Owen's face. Marks could feel his time at the Ministry of Economic Warfare was going to be short. Owen shut the door. Marks took up his pencil. Somewhere, in the deepest cavern, there was a tremor. A faint echo. He grouped ten letters together. He ran more than a hundred permutations. Then the same again. The echo faded. The lead of his pencil almost fractured. Whatever this organization was, its codes were unbreakable. Or were they? Something triggered Marks to transpose the letters in reverse. Part of a word appeared.

'EAV'

Then part of an adjacent word.

'ATE'

This time, he went further into his mind than he had ever ventured. From the deepest cavern, two words appeared.

'HEAVY WATER'

What on earth was heavy water?

The message followed within the hour.

**THREE TONNES OF HEAVY WATER HAVE LEFT
VERMORK DESTINED FOR HAMBURG**

Owen returned. Marks handed him the message. Owen gave him a look that said, 'About bloody time'. Half an hour later, Marks was ushered into a larger room, which he discovered was the nerve centre of SOE's coding section.

'Come in,' said Owen.

There was another officer in uniform, who introduced himself by the name of Dancy.

'I see you broke the code eventually,' said Dancy.

'Yes, sir,' said Marks, looking ten years older.

'Thank you, Marks,' said Owen. 'Just one question. Where is the encryption key I left with you this morning?'

Marks looked blank.

'Encryption key, sir?'

'The key to break the code.'

'I am not sure you left me a key, sir.'

Owen looked at Marks. Then at Dancy.

'You mean you broke the code without the key?'

'Yes, sir,' said Marks.

Owen looked at Marks as if he were naked. All he could do was repeat the question.

'Sorry. You broke the code *blind*?'

'Yes, sir.'

Owen looked at Dancy.

'There's only one problem,' said Owen. 'That's impossible.'

*

A bespectacled woman entered the room and set down a tray of tea and biscuits. Marks sipped his tea while Owen and Dancy used the key to check Mark's decryption. They put down their pencils after fifteen minutes and looked at one another. Marks's earlier decryption was letter perfect.

'You'll do,' said Owen.

The following day, Marks was sent to see 'the Brigadier'. The looks people gave him on his way to the brigadier's office suggested that if he had a best foot, now was the time to put it forward. He was shown into a spacious modern office. There was a large map of Europe on the wall next to regimental photographs from the Great War and prints of Highland deer. Above the mantelpiece there were two crossed samurai swords. Clearly, thought Marks, economic warfare was a literal business.

Behind a neat desk sat a man with a clipped moustache, sparse hair, and eyes etched with the horrors of the Somme and Arras. Brigadier Gubbins was a soldier's soldier, hewn from the granite of Mull. The crossed swords over the mantelpiece were echoed in the crossed swords of his shoulder flashes. As Marks discovered later, Gubbins was born in Tokyo. The samurai swords were a gift to his father from the emperor.

Gubbins' authority, born of blood and sacrifice, was almost tangible. Marks had to resist saluting.

'Come in, Marks,' said Gubbins with a voice of undiluted Presbyterian.

He gestured to a chair.

'I gather you're the new cryptographer.'

'I believe so, sir.'

'Do you know what we do here, Marks?'

'Economic warfare?'

'Wrong.'

Marks shifted. The samurai swords glinted in Gubbins' eyes.

'Economists do not carry sleeve pistols, Sten Mark II silent submachine guns, cyanide capsules, radio crystals or commando knives.'

'No, sir.'

'Economists do not carry out nocturnal parachute drops into remote, unlit fields or receive ammunition drops at midnight.'

'No, sir.'

'Economists do not detonate bridges and railway locomotives.'

'No, sir.'

'Economists do not attack the enemy from behind and risk being summarily shot as spies.'

'No, sir.'

It was like being in the High Master's study, save for the fact the brigadier had a samurai sword within easy reach, not a cane.

'We are the Special Operations Executive, Marks.'

'Yes, sir.'

'We wage a different kind of war, Marks. An irregular one. But let me be clear. Operations run from this building are more hazardous than any carried out on the battlefield.'

'Yes, sir.'

'Mr Churchill ordered us to set Europe ablaze. And that is what we are doing – in France, Belgium, Denmark, Holland, Italy, Greece, Albania and Yugoslavia. And other places besides.'

'Yes, sir.'

'Our agents are only as good as the frequency and security of their comms. For agents in the field, it may mean the difference between life and death.'

'Yes, sir.'

'That's where you come in, Marks. I need a cryptographer of the highest calibre. Do you have the fibre, Marks?'

At St Paul's, Marks had been ahead of his fellow students and some of his masters. Even the recruiters at Bletchley thought Marks was one too many worlds removed. For the first time in his life, Marks could feel himself stepping up to a plate that was bigger than his mind. Two pairs of eyes met. The Celt and the Jew. Mr Marks senior used to say the lost tribe of Israel was hidden, scattered in the Highlands. An instinctive understanding pervaded the room. Marks felt the frisson of duty.

Gubbins rose.

'Welcome to SOE, Marks.'

*

Marks frowned. Something was wrong. Putting his finger on it was like putting a finger on a tomato pip. He had spent his first fortnight reviewing SOE coding procedures. Coded text from agents in the field went to SOE headquarters. Text that could not be broken in the first twenty attempts was sent to a group of female codebreakers in Grendon – the team Captain Owen referred to as 'the girls'. In some instances, it took the Grendon codebreakers up to a thousand attempts to decipher incoming traffic. *So the double-transposition system was temperamental.* There was something more troubling. The system required a poem key that was stored in the mind of the agent. *Anything stored in an agent's head was at the mercy of the Gestapo.* And once the enemy had the key, how would London know the agent had been compromised? The bluff and true checks were all very well, but not if the Gestapo were riffling for their pliers.

He imagined an agent tied to a chair as the pliers were put to use. He also realized he was SOE's greenest acquisition. After his first week, he was taken aside by a likeable man with a jovial smile. Under the outward bonhomie, Marks could detect a hard streak.

'Tread carefully here, old chap,' he said, inhaling a pipe. 'SOE can be an unforgiving place.'

'Yes, sir.'

Marks's expression did nothing to hide his unease.

'Tell you what,' said the man. 'Why not step into my office?'

He pulled something from a bottom drawer. It was a bottle of Scotch. Drinking in the building was forbidden, so he poured the Scotch into teacups.

'I'm pretty expendable,' said the man. 'So while I'm still here, why don't you tell me what's on your mind?'

Marks spent the next hour with a pencil in one hand and a teacup of whisky in the other, explaining why the poem code was insecure. The man followed every detail of Marks's exposition and asked incisive questions. By the time the night shift arrived, he needed no more convincing. He had, after all, a fine eye for detail. An eye that could pinpoint the perfect length of a woman's evening glove or the right shade of *charmeuse* silk for the shoulders of the *grandes dames* of Paris. Then, he managed the Molyneux fashion house in the French capital. Now he was the SOE agent Tommy Yeo-Thomas.

CHAPTER 28
'THE QUICKENING'

Occupied Paris, 1943

Suttill
Morel

HUGO BLEICHER was a middle-ranking Abwehr man with a hard-edged face and a threadlike mouth whose corners gravity made exceptional efforts to pull to the floor. He was clever, ruthless and calculating. Posing as 'Colonel Henri', he was one of the Abwehr's best spy-catchers. The agents he caught he handed over to the Gestapo without compunction.

There were two prizes of ultimate value. The circuit leader and the wireless operator. The King and Queen. Bleicher wanted both. And with them the board. Abwehr intelligence suggested an energetic circuit leader was at work in Paris. And he was building his network with determination and speed. Physical descriptions varied, but he was known to have honey-coloured hair, a clear gaze and, sometimes, an Errol Flynn moustache. Intercepted radio transmissions showed a substantial amount of traffic concerning the circuit leader, codename: PROSPER. The name of the leader and the network would always be entwined in Bleicher's mind. It had a ring. The Prosper Circuit.

Abwehr agents were now watching the movement of various pieces on the chessboard – a courier here, a safe-house keeper there.

326

They were pawns in the game, but Bleicher was shrewd enough to know that pawns had their uses. They would, in turn, lead him to the King and Queen.

For now, he would watch, listen and wait.

*

Prosper, real name Francis Suttill, was on the move. His forged papers presented him as François Desprées. His aide-de-camp was a dark-eyed woman, the SOE-trained Andrée Borrel, whose blood pumped with cold defiance. She was Suttill's main courier. She moved around Paris disguised as a Red Cross nurse. Suttill had met some spirited people in the nascent Resistance, but the courage and determination of Borrel was unlike anything he had encountered.

'She is the best of us all,' said one circuit member one evening over Armagnac.

Prosper made it a rule never to sleep in the same place for more than one night. The Prosper network was growing. Its strands were weaving themselves into disparate worlds. Academics at the Sorbonne and a lead professor at the agricultural school near Versailles. Painters, printmakers and a block of sculptors headed by a Monsieur Simon. Noblemen willing to allow their estates outside Paris to be used for arms drops. Communist rail saboteurs with oil-smudged caps and jagged derailment tools.

Sub-agents were being recruited, parachute drops organized, factions united. The network head had charisma and charm. He found a spark in people, and they went out of their way to help. He was as engaged at the bar of Le Boeuf sur le Toit drinking Chablis with patrons of the arts as in station basements drinking rough cider with communist rail saboteurs.

The network also placed significant reliance on two other women, Germaine and Madeleine Tambour. The Tambour sisters moved messages and equipment around Paris with their own reserves of considerable *sang froid*.

As the Prosper Circuit burst into flower, another circuit was waiting in bud.

*

327

Charles Lelong was a respectable Paris engineer. He left his apartment in the Rue Vineuse every morning at eight sharp and would return in the evening at six. His suits were well pressed, his face well scrubbed, and his eyes had the look of someone modest but dependable. He was the epitome of charm to his concierge, who turned a blind eye when the Monsieur entertained a certain lady at the weekends. Sometimes Monsieur was away on business and the concierge would collect the small amount of mail marked 'Lelong'. Monsieur never failed to return from a trip without something for the concierge – the odd bar of chocolate or packet of cigarettes. In wartime Paris, it was like manna from Heaven.

About several things, however, the concierge was in the dark. Charles Lelong was not Monsieur's real name. Charles Lelong was not strictly an engineer.

Charles Lelong was the former racing driver William Grover-Williams, also known as 'WW', the surprise winner of the 1929 Monaco Grand Prix. 'WW' was a sleeper agent of F-Section, SOE. Buckmaster briefed him to begin by keeping a low profile.

'You are my slow-burn fuse,' said Buckmaster. 'Take things gradually at first. Build a small, trusted network. Its time will come.'

WW's first task was to track down his long-time friend, a man familiar with burning rubber, Robert Benoist. The two men met at a bar near the Rue Vineuse. Robert was unable to conceal his delight, kissing his friend from Garage Banville days three times, then three times again. WW retained his Anglo-Saxon composure, but his heart almost beat through his chest at seeing Robert again. The last time was before the war. Benoist ordered two glasses of Ricard and the men went to a corner table.

'Why aren't you driving armoured cars in the dessert, WW?' said Benoist.

Grover-Williams smiled. There was a look in his eye that told Benoist everything.

'Let's meet where we cannot be overheard.'

'Tomorrow, my apartment,' said Benoist.

The two men met the following day. Grover-Williams trusted Benoist. He laid his cards on the table. Benoist looked ecstatic.

'I have been trying to organize things through various local networks in Paris. But we do not have access to weapons.'

'That is something with which I can help,' said WW, eyes averted, modest as ever.

The men spent the next hour making plans. A new network was born: the RACING Circuit. Benoist was its first recruit.

'There is someone else we need on board,' said Benoist. 'One hundred per cent trustworthy, with his own built-in crash helmet.'

Both men spoke at once.

'Georges Morel.'

*

As the Prosper network grew, Baker Street sent two gifts. The wireless operator Gilbert Norman and a man with the force and strength of a Mauritian wave: Joseph Antelme. SOE now had a clear channel to Paris. And the Prosper network gained an agent of such drive and ability that any person or object foolish enough to block his path was left bobbing in his wake like dazed flotsam.

For Hugo Bleicher, the spy-hunter, the men's arrival was also a gift. Antelme was clearly an important agent. Norman provided a keyhole at which to listen, through intercepted wireless traffic, to the activity of Prosper Circuit as it grew larger and larger.

*

Robert Benoist rang the bell of the concierge's apartment on Rue de la Harpe. The door was opened on the latch. Benoist could see a man in shadow, wearing a trilby. The man unfastened the latch and pulled open the door. For reasons known only to a few, Morel had had more visitors of late, but he was always pleased to see his old friend and employer.

'*Mon c-confrère*,' said Morel. '*Bienvenue.*'

Morel invited Benoist into his apartment on the ground floor. It had been a while. The walls of the apartment were still bare, enhancing the feeling of coolness. It was modest, but well ordered.

On the mantelpiece was a yellowing photograph of two young men looking at the camera with all the mischief of youth. Beside the photograph was a hip flask, dented in the centre. Benoist also noticed a glass on the table, holding a handful of wild flowers.

Morel located a small amount of real coffee, which he had been saving. He washed some axle grease off his hands and put the coffee pot on the stove.

'There is something I wanted to speak to you about, Georges. About *La Peste*.'

It was an allusion to the Occupation.

'An important confidence.'

Morel stopped. Time had etched the face of Georges Morel but he was, if anything, more handsome. He looked straight at Benoist.

'I would never b-betray a confidence, Robert.'

Benoist smiled.

'I know, Georges.'

The men sat down over coffee. Benoist described, in a lowered tone, WW's reappearance in Paris and the genesis of the Racing Circuit. With each word, Morel's eyes lit brighter. When Benoist finished, Morel placed his hand on his friend's shoulder.

'I pledge my life, Robert. Now it is your turn to keep a secret.'

*

Morel's life had changed. Just before the war, he went to see a film. *The Wizard of Oz*. He went three times. Tears ran down his face. The third time he sat alone afterwards, hands clasped, as the credits rolled. As he sat, hat low, he was aware of a presence. He looked up. It was a young woman with a tray of cigarettes. She looked like the woman Dorothy would become.

The projector light flickered on the streaks running across Morel's face.

'Makes even strong men cry,' she said. Her tone was warm. She knelt down, balancing the tray of cigarettes on her knees. She was nimble. She looked straight at Morel.

'Is anything the matter?'

Morel took out a handkerchief and wiped his eyes. The question was so at odds with his tears he found himself almost smiling.

'I'll be fine,' he said.

Her eyes were still narrow with concern.

'Suggestion,' she said, gesturing to the cigarettes. 'Why don't we steal a few of these?'

Morel found himself standing outside the closing cinema smoking a cigarette with the usherette. Her name was Zoë. Morel was old enough to be her uncle, but she seemed quite happy. In fact, Zoë's eyes were caressing his features with her eyes. She was trained to pick up every detail. He looked like someone who graced the silver screen in *The Awful Truth*: Cary Grant. Older, but a likeness.

At the end of the cigarette, something possessed Morel to ask the young woman to go for a drink.

'I could kill for one,' she said.

They found a bar with candles that flickered behind the windows. Morel ordered two Armagnacs. He removed his coat but not his hat. Zoë removed her felt cloche. Her dark hair played about her shoulders, setting off her cocoa-coloured eyes. She offered Morel another cigarette. Morel accepted. There was something about the woman that made him feel safe. It was now or never.

'You asked what the matter was,' he said.

Morel pinched together the top of his trilby and pulled it off. The flame of the candle froze. Zoë put her hand to her mouth. Morel looked up at the ceiling. He closed his eyes. For a moment he was on Dr Boucher's operating table, just going under. He brought his head back level, expecting to see an empty chair.

Zoë sat, affected but composed. Her eyes said: 'How did it happen?'

She placed her hands over Morel's. He could feel the heat. As the barman put away the last of the glasses, Morel traced the footprints of his life with the young usherette. Sometimes his words stuttered, but he reached the last footprint. She held Morel's gaze, never looking away. At the end, she gave his hand a squeeze.

She emptied her glass. Surely, thought Morel, her cue to leave. Instead, Zoë leaned forward.

'One for the road?' she said, with a smile that revealed two dimples.

Her story unfolded. She was an artist. She was studying sculpture at the École Nationale Supérieure des Beaux-Arts. She was a studio assistant to a sculptor called Octave Simon. She worked nights in the cinema to make ends meet. Dishing out cigarettes in a dank cinema was not her life's ambition. As she spoke, Morel could detect an energy in the woman opposite. The way she sat, talked, moved. Something irrepressible. A force in the human machine as powerful as a Bugatti.

'I am also politically active,' she said, dragging on a cigarette. 'But that is a story for another time.'

Another time? To Morel, the words dripped like honey.

Rain drummed on the windowpanes of Morel's apartment when, the following morning, Zoë and Morel awoke entangled. She kissed the metal of his head. She rose, took one of his shirts from a wardrobe, and made coffee. Morel sat up in bed and put on his trilby. Zoë walked back, Morel's shirt almost reaching her calves, with coffee on a tray. She stroked his cheek.

'Hats off in bed,' she said.

'Zoë' meant 'life'. Zoë was, as Morel discovered, a life force all of her own.

The woman he first met wearing an usherette's white gloves and pillbox hat was freer than the ocean and wilder than fire. She proved to be a talented sculptor and, as it transpired, a communist. Convention had tried to smooth away the corners of Zoë as she was growing up in Lille. Convention found itself sprawling on the floor. She drank, smoked, wore long black culottes and, Morel knew, was no stranger to men. She asked to sculpt Morel naked. Morel sat for her in Octave Simon's Rive Gauche studio. She looked at every part of him as if he were a creation of wonder, down to the ridge where the metal of his plate met his existing skull. She took up her chisel and, as the shadows elongated, brought stone to life. Or was it, she thought, life to stone?

Sometimes she would spend the weekend at the Rue de la Harpe. Then disappear for weeks.

'I ask you only for one thing,' she said. 'Freedom.'

Morel wondered how her desire for freedom sat with her communism, but he saved his words. Instead, he enjoyed the whirlwind of cigarette ash, communist pamphlets, sculpture fragments, and wide-eyed talk about strike pickets, rallies and debates with communist intellectuals.

The outbreak of war was a call to arms. Doctrine against doctrine. Zoë volunteered as a courier, moving between communist Resistance cells forming around the outskirts of Paris. Then she became a lookout for a group of rail saboteurs derailing German troop trains before they reached Paris.

One afternoon, she appeared at the Rue de la Harpe, grimy and exhausted, and soaked in the bath for two hours.

'God, I needed that,' she said, wrapped in a bath towel, twisting her rope of chestnut hair.

As she lay back on the pillows, her towel fell away.

'Well, don't just stand there, Georges,' she said, drawing on a cigarette.

When they recovered their breath, she stroked Morel's head.

'Sooner or later, *mon petit*, I am going to need to ask for your help.'

It was then that the visitors started. Zoë would sometimes knock on the door in the middle of the night with a tough-looking, unshaven rail saboteur.

'He needs hiding for two nights before we can get him out of Paris.'

People left letters and packages to be collected by others. Fugitives turned up, tired and hungry, on the run from the German authorities. 'Zoë sent me,' they would mutter. 'She said it would be okay.'

Before Christmas the previous year, a man knocked on the door at midnight and collapsed in the doorway. He had been shot in the shoulder. Morel was no stranger to gunshot wounds. He propped the man up and applied pressure with his palm before wrapping the man's shoulder in a bandage. He went in search of a doctor two streets away, who he knew would not ask questions.

As the Occupation continued, Morel learned, through Zoë, about the nascent Paris Resistance. Resistance groups in communist Gennevilliers and Clichy-sous-Bois. Resistance groups within the Sorbonne. Resistance groups known as 'circuits', organized, funded and armed by the British. Zoë's sister, Juliette, was working for one of the latter. Morel caught other fragments – names, drop-zone locations, radio broadcasts with coded messages. Zoë had forged links between the rail saboteurs and the head of Juliette's network. His codename was Prosper. Apparently, even the communists looked up to the head, an Ivanhoe sent from England. There was someone else Zoë mentioned. A key force, she said, known as 'Le Prof'.

As Morel was drawn into the Resistance world, he found himself busier and busier. Fixing the motorbikes of the communist saboteurs. Patching up wounded fighters. Sheltering agents on the run. His apartment became a hub for clandestine meetings – a motley collection of communists in blue workman's jackets, academics with pipes and, once, Prosper himself along with his courier, Andrée Borrel, dressed as a nurse.

War had killed his brother, Fabien, and left Morel with a tin head. War was now bringing life back into his veins. Zoë was the catalyst. The fire of regeneration kindled in the eyes of Georges Morel.

A message arrived from Zoë after a month's absence. There would be a meeting the following Wednesday. The utmost security was required. Could Georges make the arrangements? Someone important was coming. Zoë arrived at the Rue de la Harpe in the late afternoon. She was wearing fawn corduroy trousers fastened with a man's belt. She looked tired. Her hair was loose and smelt of diesel. Morel ran her a bath. She emerged with her hair tied back and wearing a necklace – a present from Morel. They started to prepare. Morel brought extra chairs into his apartment and set out some wine and black-market salami. He would keep a lookout while Zoë answered the door. She knew, after all, who was invited.

By eight o'clock there were ten people in Morel's apartment, including two women both armed with revolvers. They were waiting for the eleventh. At 8:30 there was a knock at the door. Zoë showed a man into the apartment. It was 'Le Prof'.

He looked an academic, from the crinkle of his thinning grey hair to the horn of his black Le Corbusier spectacles. Behind the spectacles was a pair of intelligent, humane eyes. Eyes that had witnessed horror and revelation. Eyes that turned the acts of the dead into narrative. Le Prof was not a tall man, but he had presence. Everyone in the room stood when he entered.

As Morel opened the wine, his own mind was turning like a corkscrew. There was something about Le Prof. Something familiar. If he believed in reincarnation, he would swear he had met him in a past life. He looked again at the man's face. Morel almost dropped the bottle. The visitor was older. But it was him. He walked up to Le Prof and removed his hat. The men looked into each other's eyes. An artillery barrage sounded across time.

It was Professeur Marc Bloch.

Morel stood to attention. His salute was automatic.

'Sergent Morel reporting for duty, *mon Capitaine*!'

*

'You are full of surprises, Georges,' said Benoist.

'I try,' said Morel, smiling.

Benoist had never seen him happier.

'I will do anything and everything you need for the new circuit,' said Morel.

'I never had any doubt, Georges.'

'One question, R-obert. Does anyone else know about the Racing Circuit?'

'Just you, me and WW.'

'Good.'

There was a pause.

'And one other,' said Benoist. 'My brother Maurice.'

'We are all brothers now,' said Morel.

'I will return soon,' said Benoist. 'We need to start planning.'

*

Morel switched on the radio in his apartment and moved the dial through the hiss and crackle to the Radio Londres frequency. Heads crowded around, straining their ears.

'*Christophe est allé à la pêche*' – 'Christopher has gone fishing.'

'*Tante Amelia fait du vélo en short*' – 'Aunt Amelia cycles in shorts.'

'*Il est temps de cueillir des tomates*' – 'It is time to pick tomatoes.'

'*Clémentine a perdu une dent*' – 'Clementine has lost a tooth.'

'*J'adore les chats Siamois*' – 'I love Siamese cats.'

The last message sent a ripple around the horseshoe of listeners. Some clapped. Morel could feel Zoë's hand tighten around his palm. The arms drop for the following night was going ahead. The arms would be dropped north of the Rambouillet Forest and hidden behind a false wall in an outbuilding in Robert Benoist's estate in Auffargis. Juliette, Zoë's sister, was going as part of the reception committee. Morel would do the driving.

The following evening, a Moon Squadron Lysander flew low enough over Rambouillet Forest to skim the trees. Six canisters were dropped before the plane veered away, its fuselage glinting silver in the moonlight. The moon did not just bring arms. It brought agents. And in numbers.

Agazarian, a resourceful former airman, now a wireless operator. Déricourt, a former French aviator with equal quantities of swash and buckle. F-Section's Clark Gable. Tommy Yeo-Thomas, formerly of the Molyneux fashion house.

As agents dropped from the sky, agents on the ground went on working like bees. The Prosper Circuit and the Racing Circuit continued to expand – new worker-bees swelling the Prosper hive close to bursting. Paris was now teeming with F-section agents.

The sky – silent witness to everything – pondered a collective term. A swarming of agents? A gathering? In the end, the sky chose a different word. *Quickening.* A quickening of agents. One was yet to leave England. The sky rumbled a warning. With each day, the Abwehr's knowledge of the networks was increasing. And no SOE circuit was immune from treachery.

CHAPTER 29
'THE QUARTERMASTER'

London, 1943

Marks

The muffled chime of midnight padded down Baker Street. Marks sat alone, surveying the ammunition unfurled across his desk. His eyes narrowed beneath his curls. There were few wartime commands, he thought, that sent warriors into battle armed with *poems*. SOE was the exception. Before being dropped into occupied Europe, each agent had to be kitted out with a poem. The poem became the frequency for the agent's broadcast to London. Without the frequency, London would hear only hiss. The frequency itself would be set by five 'keywords' chosen from the poem. An 'indicator group' of five letters indicating which words were being deployed would precede each message. The message would then be coded using the keywords from the poem. Each agent's poem became part of their identity. Some felt the words as if they were an extra pair of hands.

Marks was Quartermaster. SOE's Keeper of Poems. The week before insertion into the field, an agent had to attend a mandatory code briefing with Marks. At the briefing, Marks would add the final polish to the agent's transposition skills. Then it was a question of matching the agent with the poem. *What made the agent tick?* The Quartermaster worked on instinct. He disappeared into SOE's stores and from the arsenal of verse he would reappear with what he considered the most suitable weapon. The agent examined the poem like a sniper inspecting a rifle – testing the sights, checking the barrel, caressing the trigger. Most of the time, agent and weapon became fist in glove. On occasion, Marks had to return to the stores and select a different weapon.

In his first few months at SOE, Marks briefed a spate of F-section agents. One was a friend and mutual confidant: Tommy Yeo-Thomas. Marks was extra anxious to ensure Tommy was properly equipped. He had discovered that under the bonhomie of a one-time purveyor of silk to the *grandes dames* of Paris, Yeo-Thomas suffered bouts of leaden depression.

For Quartermaster and agent, the weapon of choice was obvious. His old friend, Lord Tennyson.

Be near me when my light is low,
When the blood creeps, and the nerves prick
And tingle; and the heart is sick,
And all the wheels of Being slow.

Be near me when the sensuous frame
Is racked with pangs that conquer trust;
And Time, a maniac scattering dust,
And Life, a Fury slinging flame.

Be near me when my faith is dry,
And men the flies of latter spring,
That lay their eggs, and sting and sing
And weave their petty cells and die.

Be near me when I fade away,
To point the term of human strife,

And on the low dark verge of life
The twilight of eternal day.

After the briefing, Yeo-Thomas smiled and told Marks where to
find his 'medicinal' supply of whisky while he was gone. Marks
might need the odd dose of medicine.

For the compartmentally minded wireless operator Agazarian,
Marks went to the back of the SOE stores and pulled out 'Cargoes'.

Quinquireme of Nineveh from distant Ophir,
Rowing home to haven in sunny Palestine,
With a cargo of ivory,
And apes and peacocks,
Sandalwood, cedarwood, and sweet white wine.

Stately Spanish galleon coming from the Isthmus,
Dipping through the Tropics by the palm-green shores,
With a cargo of diamonds,
Emeralds, amythysts,
Topazes, and cinnamon, and gold moidores.

Dirty British coaster with a salt-caked smoke stack,
Butting through the Channel in the mad March days,
With a cargo of Tyne coal,
Road-rails, pig-lead,
Firewood, iron-ware, and cheap tin trays.

For Antelme, who brought the force of an ocean wave into SOE,
Marks pulled down an anthology of poems by Baudelaire. The first
verse of '*L'Homme et La Mer*' made the book pitch and roll.

'*Homme libre, toujours tu chériras la mer!*
La mer est ton miroir; tu contemples ton âme
Dans le déroulement infini de sa lame,
Et ton esprit n'est pas un gouffre moins amer...'

Free man, you will always love the sea!
The sea is your mirror, where you see your soul
In the infinite unrolling of its swell,
Your mind is no less rancorous an abyss...

For the dashing Henri Déricourt, the F-Section Clark Gable,
another Baudelaire poem caught Marks's eye.

'*Sans cesse à mes côtés s'agite le Démon;*
Il nage autour de moi comme un air impalpable;
Je l'avale et le sens qui brûle mon poumon
Et l'emplit d'un désir éternel et coupable...'

At my side the Demon writhes forever,
Swimming around me like impalpable air;
As I breathe, he burns my lungs like fever
And fills me with an eternal sinful desire...

The role of Quartermaster was a natural fit for Marks. He had
been born into words. As a cryptographer, he turned gibberish
into words. Now, as Quartermaster, he armed agents with words.
Sometimes, he painted a blank canvas with his own words. A phrase
here, an adjective there. He weaved the words around his encryption workings like a chain of daisies. Sometimes the daisies wept
with longing. *What to call these word paintings?* Marks reached in
his mind for the right word... Poetry? Had SOE created the war's
first poet-cryptographer? A quartermaster who forged his own
weapons. Marks looked at his most recent impressionist haze of
words and gave a fleeting smile.

Marks signed himself out and walked, bowler hat tilted at the
stars, south along Baker Street. The buildings were blacked out,
windows staring blind into the night. The only echo was Marks's
footsteps on the pavement. He wondered whether the tumult in
his head and heart would wake the bomb-weary city. His head felt

as if it was being gnawed by a plague of rats. As for his heart, it fluttered like a murmuration of starlings.

The rats. They spread doubt. Every time Marks reappeared from SOE's armoury, the jaws of doubt gnawed at his mind. What if the weapons he was handing out were faulty? Or at least inferior? While invisible, anything lodged in the agent's memory was capable of extraction by force. Was SOE providing the Gestapo with bait? Whenever he thought of the consequences, he shuddered. For a moment he was back at school. One of the few masters he respected was the historian, Mr Cook. 'Never accept the received view on anything. If something is so, why is it so? Test it. If it fails the test, replace it with something better.' Then Uncle Abe came into his mind, eyes twinkling. 'Not everyone can depict the master pattern,' came his voice, 'but it is there for those with eyes to see.'

A plan formulated in his mind. He would continue to arm agents with poems. But he would also test the entire system – line by line, verse by verse… If a master pattern showed it endangered agents, he would take action. He operated from a warm office in Baker Street. Captured agents were in the hands of the Gestapo.

The starlings were a different matter. A month earlier, Brigadier Gubbins had sent Marks on a visit to rally the codebreakers of Grendon. SOE's 'Station 53a' was based at Grendon Hall in Buckinghamshire. Coded wireless traffic that could not be broken after twenty attempts was dispatched to the all-female military team at Grendon. Most were recruited from the First Aid Nursing Yeomanry, whose motto was 'Undefeated in Difficulties'. Some of the coders had broken 'mutilated' code on the thousandth attempt. Marks had devised a system to penetrate mutilated traffic more quickly. A breathy report came back from the Grendon Commandant that made Marks chuckle. *Mr Marks your consummate skills have reduced penetration time by up to thirty per cent.*

Marks arrived at Grendon Hall on a drizzly Tuesday morning with a briefcase containing a miniature chess set, paper with blank squares, two sharp pencils and a salt-beef sandwich. Grendon Hall looked like his idea of a girls' boarding school. Its neo-Jacobean windows were suitably draughty, its arches suitably pointed, its exterior suitably forbidding. The coat of arms above the entrance should, thought Marks, have been two crossed hockey sticks under a ribbon-tied boater. The interior smelt of cabbage and disinfectant and Marks imagined the inhabitants' underclothes were regulation bottle green.

Half an hour later, SOE's cryptographer found himself in what was once the billiard room. It was no ordinary alcove. Marks reckoned it was the size of a cinema, illuminated by three ceiling-height stained-glass windows. It served as the assembly room of Station 53a. Marks walked on to a podium. Seated before him were forty young women in uniform, SOE's army of codebreakers. The title of Marks's address was:

'There Is No Such Thing as an Indecipherable Message.'

He looked at the upturned faces of forty female codebreakers. Marks had never considered cryptography to be the most seductive part of the war, but the women sat in rapt attention and made him feel, for once, like an Apollonian Spitfire pilot. Marks gave well-chosen examples of Station 53a being 'Undefeated in Difficulties': codebreakers attacking mutilated codes through the night to find epiphany at dawn. He recalled instances of codebreaking that had saved lives. The end of his talk was met with rapturous applause.

Marks took questions from the audience. As the meeting dispersed, a few of the codebreakers queued to ask more informal questions. One was blonde. She wrote down his pearls of wisdom in an exercise book. Each time she looked up, she shone her eyes on Marks as if he were a rare animal. It was after the blonde closed her exercise book and walked away, looking over her shoulder, that the ground under Marks's feet started to shake. It was the codebreaker behind. She stood with Cleopatra-black hair, animated dark eyes, olive skin and cheekbones of the Hebrew goddess Asherah. She introduced herself as Ruth. Her uniform accentuated her slimness and had the shoulder flashes of a lieutenant. Marks watched her

tongue dart behind her nectarine lips as she asked several percep-
tive questions. Marks could hear himself answer but his head was
spinning. Words his father once imparted were ricocheting around
his skull.

'When women of the faith are beautiful,' warned Mr Marks
senior, 'the game's up, my son. Resistance is futile.'

Marks was standing and falling at the same time. Resistance
was futile.

The commandant's assistant came over while Marks was trying
to keep his words in the right order. Would Mr Marks like to join
the commandant for sherry before lunch? Marks stumbled out
an affirmative. As the assistant wandered away, he turned back to
Ruth. He took a breath.

'I'm wondering if you ever, erm, come up to London on leave?
I might be able to give your questions a fuller answer.'

Ruth smiled.

'Are you speaking in code, Mr Marks?'

Marks could feel the heat move across his face.

'If I am right in thinking you are asking me out, Mr Marks,
then I'm told there is the occasional train from Aylesbury to
Marylebone.'

It was the weight of his briefcase that stopped Marks from
toppling backwards.

He withdrew some squared paper and a pencil. As he put
pencil to paper, the lead broke. Ruth laughed. Marks delved for
another pencil and wrote down his details. The letters were shaky
but legible.

'Until next week,' said Ruth, tongue darting behind her smile.

It took three sherries with the commandant for Marks to
regain his equilibrium. On the train back to London, he stared
out of the window. Starlings were fluttering in his heart. All he
could see was Ruth.

*

Beaulieu, 1943

Noor

The full moon was approaching. The next batch of F-Section agents was undergoing final preparations for their drop. One was a harpist. The night before she left Beaulieu, Noor Inayat Khan sat cross-legged beside her bed. She closed her eyes and began the descent. She glided like a manta ray to the sea floor of her mind.

She heard a voice. She turned. A man in a gold robe was sitting between two columns. His eyes were open, his mouth closed.

'What is your *Sankalpa, Bābouli?*'

Her answer came.

'My *Sankalpa* is to shorten the war, Papa.'

'Your *Sankalpa* is the arc of your life, *Bābouli*. Will you follow it, even into peril?'

'Yes, Papa.'

A look of radiance shone from the figure's face.

Then he was gone.

*

Marks

Marks sat reading the file on the agent he was due to brief. The agent's details were intriguing.

Gender: Female.
Codename: MADELEINE.
Education: Sorbonne.
Former occupation: Children's author.
Original unit: WAAF.
Agent status: Wireless operator.
Proficiencies: Morse code, pistol marksmanship, unarmed combat.
Special attributes: Harpist.
Religion: Sufi Muslim.

Next of kin: Amina Begum (mother).

Her name was Noor Inayat Khan. Marks's cryptographer's instincts were piqued. She was a puzzle. It was time to assemble the pieces. He gathered his sandwich and apple and strode down the steps of 64 Baker Street. His bowler hat was tilted back and he could feel sun on his face. He walked south towards Wigmore Street. His step was light. The starlings were still fluttering. As he walked, he pictured Ruth's face, upturned, laughing.

Ruth had come to London on leave. Marks took her to see *Casablanca* at the Film Theatre in Leicester Square. When Sam turned to the piano in the final scene to play 'As Time Goes By', Marks moved his palm over Ruth's. She wrapped her fingers around his hand as if it were his heart. He took her to dinner at Umberto's afterwards and Carlo, the ancient maître d', ensured the Chianti came from a dusty bottle with a cork. The scenes of Arcadia on the wall were faded but to Marks the meadows and trees burst with colour. He imagined lying down in an Arcadian field, looking up into Ruth's face. The pair walked back to Marylebone Station together, oblivious to the bomb rubble. At the barrier of Platform 2, as the train erupted with smoke, their lips met and their codes were broken.

They met whenever Ruth could escape on leave. She had studied archaeology at University College, London. She had done a PhD on deciphering Linear B. She could hold her own with Marks on any subject from poetry to cryptoanalysis. Marks even dared to think what they would do after the war.

He walked up the steps of 84 Charing Cross Road. The familiar bell went. The shop still opened during the war, though many of the more valuable manuscripts had been moved into the basement or away altogether. Marks found Frank, the general manager, packaging a collection of books on rare birds to be despatched to General Alanbrooke at campaign HQ in North Africa. Frank's knowledge remained undimmed.

'Greetings, Young Leo. What brings you in on this bomb-free Tuesday?'

'I'm looking for works by a children's author named Noor Inayat Khan.'

Frank squinted.

'Noor Inayat Khan. Yes. A book of children's stories came out under that name in '39. Did well, I seem to remember. Twenty Jātaka Stories...? If you wait there, I'll have a look.'

Frank disappeared. Marks looked around. The bookshop held so many faces. His father's, Mr Cohen, Aleister Crowley 'the Wickedest Man in the World', and of course the beautiful, bookish Doris. Young Leo was in the shop in December 1938 when a man in a homburg, with a beard and a thick Austrian accent, rapped on the door. He asked what books were stocked on psychology.

'We've enough Freud and Jung to open a clinic,' said Mr Cohen.

The man smiled as Mr Cohen took him up to the first floor. He came down with a pile of books half an hour later.

'Could you have these delivered to my address?'

'Certainly,' said Mr Cohen. 'Those should keep you on the straight and narrow.'

The man handed him a card. The address was overshadowed by the name.

SIGMUND FREUD

Frank reappeared with a book. *Twenty Jātaka Tales* by Noor Inayat Khan. A line of animals walked along the cover. A lion, a hare, a horse, a swan, an elephant, a monkey and a deer.

'Well done, Frank,' said Marks. 'The old magic lives.'

Marks took up position on the stool by the till and opened the book.

'1. The Monkey-Bridge'

A giant-like monkey once ruled over eighty thousand monkeys in the Himalaya mountains. And through the rocks where they lived streamed the River Ganges before reaching the valley where cities were built. And there where the bubbling water fell from rock to rock stood a magnificent tree.

Marks read on. It was the story of an exquisite fruit that fell accidentally from a tree into the Ganges and flowed all the way to the City of Benares. There it found its way into a fisherman's net. The fruit was so beautiful and unusual that the fisherman presented it to King Brahmadatta. The King tasted the fruit.

'It was laden with fruit so wonderful that none could be compared to them, and the sweet winds of the mountain gave them the sweetness of honey.'

The King asked his woodman what tree bore such fruit. The woodman said it came from a rare tree in the neighbouring valley. The following day the King assembled an entourage to journey in search of the tree. The tree came into view the following night. It stood in the moonlight, its golden fruit glittering through the leaves. Shadows moved on the branches. *Monkeys!* said one of the guards. King Brahmadatta gave the order that at first light the monkeys should be shot and the tree stripped of its fruit. Overhearing the King, the Chief of the Monkeys decided upon a plan. He plucked a reed from its root and fastened it around his foot. He fastened the reed around another tree and suspended his body to make a bridge. He told all eighty thousand monkeys to escape along his back. The King awoke to see the last of the monkeys run to freedom over the Monkey Chief's body. It was the last straw. The final monkey broke the Chief's back. King Brahmadatta was astonished. He ordered the Monkey Giant to be brought to the ground, clothed in yellow raiment, and given water.

The Monkey Giant lay dying.

He walked to the tree and asked the Chief of the Monkeys why he would give his life to save his subjects.

'O King… I am their chief and their guide. They lived with me in this tree, and I was their father and I loved them. I do not suffer in leaving this world for I have gained my subjects' freedom. And if my death may be a lesson to you then I am more than happy. It is not your sword which makes you a king. It is love.'

The Chief of the Monkeys closed his eyes and died. Tears ran from the eyes of King Brahmadatta. The King ordered that a temple of pure white be built where the Chief of the Monkeys died. The King went on to rule his people not with a sword but with love.

Marks sighed. Was SOE really intending to drop the author of The Monkey-Bridge into occupied Europe?

*

Marks was at his desk in Baker Street when there was a knock at the door. A bespectacled secretary in a cardigan put her head round the door.

'Agent Khan is here for your twelve o'clock, sir.'

'Thank you, Ester,' said Marks, shuffling squared paper. 'We may as well get started.'

A young woman was shown into Marks's office. It was her gaze that struck him first. Marks had never seen eyes of such serenity. They stared out from an exotic face under fine eyebrows. The agent could have passed for Italian or even Lebanese. If Marks was not mistaken, there was an aura about the agent whose hands plucked at the harp and turned Morse code into music. As well as deflecting armed attack.

She wore a neat suit with the brooch of a bird on her lapel. Marks could detect an aroma of jasmine. She extended her hand.

'It is so very kind of you to see me, Mr Marks.'

Her voice was educated, with its own quiet serenity. She pronounced the word 'very' with the shadow of a 'w' over the 'v'. The shadow cast back through time to Tipu Sultan, the Tiger of Mysore.

'I gather you are going in the next full moon.'

'That is what Colonel Buckmaster has said.'

'Splendid,' said Marks. It was a word his father used when he was not quite sure what to say. 'Perhaps the only agent to play the harp.'

Noor sat with her fingers interlocked and smiled.

'I am not sure there will be much time for music, Mr Marks.'

'Perhaps not. I gather you have completed the coding course.'

'Yes, sir.'

Marks looked at her reports. She excelled in Morse code but was an average coder.

'The most important thing before you go into the field is to ensure you are happy with your poem.'

'Yes, sir.'

'Would you permit me to make a suggestion?'

'Of course.'

It was the hour of the Quartermaster. Marks descended into SOE's armoury. Instinct told him where to go, deep into the labyrinth. He returned with a book so dusty the cover was obscured. Marks took out a handkerchief and exposed the author's name, Farid ud-Din Attar. As he wiped the cover it revealed a congregation of birds, their heads cocked as if listening to a sermon. Noor could see the title.

THE CONFERENCE OF THE BIRDS

Her heart quickened.

'When the birds of the world gather to decide who is to be their sovereign...' began Marks.

'...the Hoopoe, the wisest of them all,' continued Noor, 'suggests they should seek the legendary Simorgh.'

'You know better than me the Seven Valleys the birds must cross,' said Marks.

He lay open the book. Noor knew each of the chapters.

The Valley of the Quest.
The Valley of Love.
The Valley of Knowledge.
The Valley of Detachment.
The Valley of Unity.
The Valley of Wonderment.
The Valley of Poverty and Annihilation.

Marks read from the narrative.

'When the birds hear the description of these valleys, they bow their heads. Some even die of fright. But despite their trepidation they begin the great journey. On the way, many perish of thirst, heat or illness, while others fall prey to wild beasts, panic and brutality. Only thirty birds make it to the abode of Simorgh. In the end, the birds learn that they themselves are the Simorgh. The name Simorgh in Persian means Thirty ('Si') Birds ('Morgh'). They come to understand that the sovereign is the sun that can be seen reflected in a mirror. The birds that look into that mirror will behold their own image.'

Noor sat. The silver bird on her lapel felt as if it were twitching. Marks read a section of verse.

~

If Simorgh unveils its face to you, you will find

~

That all the birds, be they thirty or forty or more,

~

Are but the shadows cast by that unveiling.

~

What shadow is ever separated from its maker?

~

351

Do you see?

~

The shadow and its maker are one and the same.

~

He marked the passage and handed it to Noor. She mouthed the words as she read. Then she placed the book on the table and closed her eyes. She opened her eyes and quoted the verse, word for word. Her eyes shone as she spoke.

'I am going to circle five words to make the key,' said Marks. 'The first letters of each word will become your indicator group.'

Marks wrote out the coding key at the top of the squared paper and a twelve-word message in plain text.

THE DROP WILL BE NORTH OF PARIS AT THE NEXT FULL MOON.

Noor split the letters into groups of two and started to code. Marks watched her fingers, a deft but firm grip of the pencil. He watched her transposing the letters, one by one, until they were all in code. She was focused, although something in her eyes did not look comfortable.

She handed the squared paper over for cryptographic scrutiny. Her coding contained several errors of significance. Marks sensed the problem. Distortion of the truth. He pointed out the errors. Noor bit her lip.

'If the letters are not coded properly, it means the letters are telling London a lie.'

Her eyes widened.

'Each letter is a soaring bird. Or a monkey that has to cross to safety over the Chief Monkey's back.'

Her eyes widened further.

'You've read my book, Mr Marks!'

'I have.'

Something shifted.

'I promise that I will lead every monkey over the Chief's back.'

'Let's meet again tomorrow at the same time.'

Noor left. She had such an elegant walk, thought Marks. He sighed. The rats were back, creeping along his arm. He was planting a seed in her mind that the Gestapo might one day try to extract. The thought still nagged. Should SOE be sending the author of The Monkey-Bridge into the Inferno? Unless her coding was perfect, he would recommend she remained.

The following day, Noor returned. Everything about her spoke of purpose.

Marks gave her six passages to code. She took up her pencil and started work. Twenty minutes later, six passages were in code. Marks looked over the codes. Something, please *Yahweh*, to prevent her going. Her coding was perfect. With any other agent, this was cause for celebration. In Noor's case, it made Marks's heart sink.

'What about your bluff check and true check?' said Marks.

'We were taught about both at Beaulieu. A bluff check means the operator is transmitting freely. Inclusion of the true check means the operator is transmitting under duress.'

'Correct.'

Noor smiled.

'But who knows how one's mind works if it all kicks off? So I am going to give you a system that is unique to you. If you transmit a message that is eighteen characters long, it means you are operating under duress.'

'Eighteen?' said Noor. 'That's my lucky number.'

'Mine too,' said Marks. 'It's the code for life.'

*

Marks signed off F-Section's only harpist as code-ready. He frowned. A quartermaster handing out weapons that might explode during handling? It was time to put on his surgeon's gloves and take a scalpel to the entire poem-code system.

'Never accept the received view on anything. If something is so, why is it so? Test it. If it fails the test, replace it with something better.'

The system was devised shortly after SOE was formed. The rationale was that the agent did not have to carry encryption keys. Memorized poems were invisible. That was fine if the enemy did not have saws, pliers and truth serum. The other problem was that mistakes might be made if an agent was transmitting at speed in difficult circumstances. There was also the problem of 'Morse mutilation' – sooner or later, a message would be transmitted that was indecipherable. Why? Because, mused Marks, the agent was in a hurry or made a mistake coding the message into Morse. Or worse, the agent was transmitting under duress. That was why so many messages required the coders of Grendon.

The messages became known as 'Indecipherables'. The fate of a truculent Indecipherable was painful dissection by the coders of Grendon. Each country section had their fair share of Indecipherables. Some were worse than others. Agents in Rome sent the highest number, and Marks imagined them coding after lunch on the Via Condotti. Agents in Greece were another culprit, no doubt sunning themselves under the Cretan sun and splashing in the wine-dark sea. There was, however, one anomaly. Holland. Since the first SOE agent was dropped into Holland, all messages had come through loud and clear. No agonizing dissection at the hands of the Grendon coders. It was a clue to catch the attention of even the most preoccupied detective.

Marks looked at the messages coming back from the Dutch agents. As he read, he could feel his blood creep and his nerves prick. Some agents had been killed, according to surviving agents, during the drop. Others had succumbed to illness. The most senior agent, responsible for building up a Dutch underground army over months, was killed in a shoot-out with German soldiers the day before he was recalled to London. And with all this going on, the surviving agents had broadcast for nine months without a single mistake. Apparently.

The words of Tennyson echoed. The Dutch agents were on the low dark verge of life. Captured. The Abwehr was using their radios to spoon-feed Baker Street a *stroopwafel* of false intelligence. If there was a Eureka moment in Marks's life, this was it. Marks fed a sheet of paper into his typewriter and tapped out the title.

INSECURITIES OF THE SOE POEM CODE

He typed into the small hours. It was a report of which the high master of St Paul's would have approved. Factual. Analytical. Critical. He included a complete breakdown of all messages received from Dutch agents since the first drop in 1942. At the end of the section, he added a footnote in pencil with a view to erasing it later.* He wrote on until the fingers of dawn spread over Baker Street.

A plan formulated in his mind over the next few days. It was vintage Marks, but it was not without its risks. He would feed the Abwehr some of their own *stroopwafel*. Before leaving for a meeting in Duke Street with the French government-in-exile, he left instructions for a message of sixty-four characters to be transmitted to Agent Boni in Holland. Sixty-four seemed as good a number as any from No. 64 Baker Street. The message was an intricate concoction of gobbledygook. An Indecipherable. If the Abwehr were controlling Boni's radio, how would they deal with something unexpected? The ultimate spin ball. Marks smiled as he imagined the looks on the Abwehr's faces.

That weekend, Ruth dropped a bombshell. She was being transferred to Canada for six months to train a new unit of codebreakers in Toronto. It was an order. As she placed her hand over Marks's, she bit her nectarine lip and a tear streaked from the corner of her eye. She would be leaving within a week. Marks could feel his heart twist. Providence propelled his hand into his pocket. His hands shook as he tore out a piece of paper. He wrote out a message in code. Ruth took his pencil and, in the candlelight of Umberto's,

---

* Will this report be too detailed for the PILLOCKS who read it?

started to decipher. By the time she had deciphered the message, she was blushing and a shy smile was pulling the corners of her lips.

She wrote a message back in code. Marks had deciphered it before she stopped writing. His heart was breaking and singing all at once. He took Ruth to Marylebone Station. The guard's whistle broke their embrace. Ruth waved from the train. As the train shunted away, she was engulfed in steam. Marks walked home, hands in pockets. He was going to have to become a man of the world PDQ. That was Gubbins-speak for *Pretty Damn Quick*.

The following day, Marks slipped out of Baker Street and took a taxi to Hatton Garden. His father's first cousin had a jewellery business. Since the war began, Uncle Leonard had been doing a brisk trade in wedding rings – some for less permanent use than others.

'How long do you need it for?' said Leonard Sachs of Einhorn & Sachs.

'Just a week,' said Marks.

'I may have just the job,' said the jeweller, opening a bottom drawer.

Next stop, the barber's shop on Clerkenwell Road. Marks's curls lay in a ring round the chair. As the barber dusted the back of his neck, the question came with a Neapolitan lilt.

'Anything for the weekend, *signore?*'

On this occasion, Marks said yes to the discreet envelope.

He returned to Baker Street via an imposing Victorian building in Russell Square.

'A room for you and your wife?' said the receptionist at the Great Russell Hotel. Marks was apprehensive, but the man did not bat an eyelid. The place was teeming with servicemen and their sweethearts in wedding rings on loan from Hatton Garden.

Marks remembered Ruth's hand in his as they walked through the marble colonnades. His pulse was racing. Hers faster. Marks ordered two gin rickeys at the bar, but his hand was shaking so much he had to use a straw. There were muffled thuds in the distance. An air-raid siren wailed. A tide of people streamed down the main staircase, spilling out into the square and heading for the Underground. A man and a woman swam against the tide.

He turned a key. Lights from anti-aircraft batteries made the curtains flash silver. He lay her down. Her nectarine lips swelled.

'Let the bombs fall,' he whispered.

*

'The chief wants to see you,' said Captain Owen, poking his head round the door. There was something in his expression that made Marks think it was not a courtesy call. Marks entered Gubbins' office. It was obvious that something was wrong. Tennyson's line re-echoed.

When the blood creeps, and the nerves prick.

Gubbins sat in silence. The samurai swords on the wall glinted. The crossed swords on Gubbins' shoulder flashes sharpened in response. The brigadier held a memo in his hands. His face was pale, his words glass.

'Sit down, Marks,' said the brigadier. 'The answers you give me will be the truth, the whole truth and nothing but the truth. Do you understand?'

'Yes, sir,' said Marks.

'SOE message Number 59 transmitted to Dutch agent Boni in 64 characters was indecipherable. I have reason to believe it emanated from you. And that it was deliberate.'

The samurai swords glinted, as if preparing for execution.

'Guilty,' said Marks. 'Both charges.'

His heart was in his boots, but he held Gubbins' glower.

'And since when, Marks, do members of this organization act outside their orders?'

'I had reason to believe Agent Boni has been captured.'

'Did you, Marks?'

Gubbins was a small man with large lungs.

'DID YOU?'

'Yes, sir,' said Marks.

'Did you deign to share your theory with anyone, Marks? Or did you just go on a frolic of your own?'

'I did not share my theory, sir. But I drafted a report.'

'You drafted a report?'

'I did, sir.'

'And where is this report, Marks?'

Marks found himself racing through SOE headquarters like a hare on amphetamine. He returned, report in hand. As Gubbins scanned each page, brow taut, Marks remembered he had left in the footnote. Gubbins looked up after turning the final page. The room was silent, save for breath.

'As regards the pillocks who might read this report, this pillock would observe that far from being too detailed, it's not detailed enough.'

'Yes, sir,' said Marks.

There followed a dressing-down. Marks could have been a subaltern in the Great War who had gone over the top without his pistol. It went on for a full five minutes, each word cutting like flying glass. Marks was wise enough to say nothing. When the rocket looked like it had reached its zenith, Gubbins' tone changed.

'Next time, Marks, think beyond yourself. You may even be on the right track. I will be asking Captain Owen to undertake an independent investigation into the security of all our Dutch agents. But make no mistake, Marks. Another performance like this and you will be emptying the potato peelings of the Catering Corps.'

'Yes, sir,' said Marks.

There was a glint in Gubbins' eyes as Marks withdrew.

*

Marks kept a low profile for the next three months. Rumours went around SOE that he had done something so bad it was good. It gave him an unexpected cachet. Marks said nothing. He concentrated on his codebreaking. A penance. He made himself invaluable to both SOE and Grendon Hall, whatever the hour. He played chess against himself over lunch and did what he was told. Whenever he looked out of the window, he saw Ruth's face, her nectarine lips beckoning.

On a crisp blue afternoon, a letter arrived addressed to Leo Marks Esq., c/o The Ministry of Economic Warfare, 64 Baker Street, London NW1. It was written in a clear hand. The stamp was Highgate, London.

It was from Ruth's father. Each word ached with pain and dignity. It was the writer's sad duty to pass on that Ruth had been killed in a plane crash. The transport plane in which she was travelling crashed after taking off from Toronto Airport. There were no survivors. There would be a funeral as soon as her remains were repatriated.

Marks sat blinking. His eyes were beyond crying. His stomach tightened as if clenching a bullet. The starlings fell, one by one. He opened his notebook and took up a pencil. The words flowed straight on to the page.

The life that I have
Is all that I have
And the life that I have
Is yours.

The love that I have
Of the life that I have
Is yours and yours and yours.

A sleep I shall have
A rest I shall have
Yet death will be but a pause.

For the peace of my years
In the long green grass
Will be yours and yours and yours.*

---

* Copyright required [this isn't a footnote, but a reminder to obtain permission]

CHAPTER 30
'DINNER IN MADRID'

Valladolid,
Spain, 1943

Canaris

A thin beam of light cut the gloom in the Iglesia de San Pablo. A figure knelt, eyes closed, silver head bent. His palms were joined, fingers interlinked. The church was silent save for the whisper of his prayers. The last time he was in Valladolid he was pursuing Abwehr interests in Spain at the height of the Civil War, disguised as a Dominican monk, Guillermo. This time he had no need. The head of the Abwehr wore a pale linen suit. He remained open, however, to any guidance from above.

There was good reason. Admiral Canaris was now fighting a war on two fronts. The previous month he had received two top-secret intelligence reports for the eyes of Admiral Canaris only. The first was from an Abwehr agent inside the Vatican. The other was from an informant within the SD. An elite Gestapo detachment was on its way to Rome. Their mission was complex yet simple. To kidnap the pope. The ransom? Nazi domination of the world. And it was unlikely Hitler was ignorant of the plan.

On receiving the reports, Canaris sat with his face in his hands. The Nazis were not just ruthless. They were mindless. And Godless. Canaris oversaw the transmission of an immediate warning to a staunchly Catholic Italian general. The Vatican's Swiss Guard were alerted and His Holiness was evacuated.

Germany faced an enemy from within and without. From within: the man with the black nosebleed and his Gestapo coven. From without: the prospect of invasion. Sooner or later, the Allies would muster in England and sweep across the Channel into France. From France they would move east. It would be the opening of the war in reverse. This time Berlin, not Paris, would be surrounded and suffocated. Which front would Canaris attack first?

That evening, Canaris returned to Madrid. He dined alone in the Gran Hotel Inglés. The irony of the name was not lost on the admiral. He drank a Torrontés, cold and crisp, and closed his submariner's eyes. His thoughts pulled him downwards. Downwards through the currents deep behind his eyes.

He was moving. Moving through the night waters of the Mediterranean at a steady six knots. He could hear the familiar hum of the diesel engines as Unterseeboot-34 slipped through the currents like an electric eel. He could feel the air again, hot from the six-cylinder diesel engines and humid, like a sea-going jungle. *U-34* had picked up a scent. He took position in the control room behind the gyrocompass, flanked by his first officer and navigator. He glanced at a chart and called out his orders, calm and precise, like a surgeon in theatre.

'Torpedo room. Prepare bow torpedoes.'

He looked at his wristwatch.

'Two minutes to target.'

'One minute...'

Kapitänleutnant Canaris relinquished *U-34* to take command of the pioneering prototype, *UB-128*. In 1918, under Kapitän Klasing, *U-34* went down with all hands. In the years that followed,

Canaris often saw, before sinking into the depths of sleep, *U-34*'s crew wandering the seabed like lost phantoms.

His thoughts bobbed back to the service. The realization of the present felt like a rent in his side. As a naval officer in the Great War, his cause was the empire. The cause he now served was spawned from the bowels of Lucifer himself. The man with the black nose-bleed was a direct threat to Man and God.

By the end of dinner, Canaris was the only guest in the cool of the art deco dining room. A young man entered the room at ten-thirty. He walked over to the table. He was fair for a Spaniard.

'*Está ocupado este asiento…?* Is this seat taken…?'

The men spoke until midnight over coffee and port. When the bill was presented, it was the younger man who insisted on paying.

'With the compliments of Sir Stewart,' he said.

Canaris smiled.

'Please return my compliments. I look forward to our speaking direct.'

The two men stood and shook hands. The younger man left. Canaris sat for a moment in thought. *The duty of a patriot is to protect his country from its government.* Whatever the danger to his own life, he knew it paid to start at the top. Especially when dealing with someone who considered the Admiral a potential caretaker leader if Germany sued for peace. 'Sir Stewart' was Sir Stewart Menzies, head of Britain's MI6.

CHAPTER 31
'THE PICNIC'

Angers, France
1943

The words crackled over the radio.

'*Jasmin joue de la flûte*' – 'Jasmine is playing her flute.'

London was calling.

A crackle of excitement spread around the dinner table. Four agents would be dropped the following night. The Resistance group huddled in Monsieur Linville's basement went into immediate action. Within twenty-four hours, everything would be assembled. Torches, batteries, blankets, bandages, binoculars, petrol, Sten guns, revolvers, coffee, Armagnac, several bottles of Chinon and – most important of all – a corkscrew.

*

London, 1943

Noor

The following afternoon, Vera Atkins collected Noor from Orchard Court in Portman Square, where F-Section maintained an opulent art nouveau flat with a black-tiled bathroom. The pair drove away in a dark 4-litre Alvis that SOE agents called 'the hearse'. Atkins wore a grey-blue skirt, a bomber jacket and a WAAF cap. Noor declined the constant offer of Lucky Strike cigarettes as Atkins drove south-west out of London through country lanes watched over by wheeling hawfinches, out towards the Surrey Hills. From Surrey, the fields grew a deeper emerald and the hedgerows taller as the car headed into West Sussex. By late afternoon, the black Alvis entered the restricted grounds of RAF Tangmere. The base was home to No. 161 'Special Duties' Squadron. Tangmere was one of two Moon Squadrons flying agents in and out of France.

There was a dinner that night at Tangmere Cottage, close to the base, where SOE maintained two French chefs on permanent rotation. Atkins ensured the candle wicks in the seventeenth-century dining room were trimmed, the china was warm and the elaborate Gallic dinner a far cry from wartime rationing. With each tick of the agents' watches came the sound of increasing activity on the airfield. RAF ground staff were making last-minute checks to the engines while the chosen pilot and navigator underwent their final briefing. When the carriage clock above the mantelpiece struck ten, the agents could hear the sound of the Lysander's propellers.

Before she left, Noor went into the library, a womb-like room with low beams and a crackling fire. Set out on the table were various current books and magazines. One of the books had the title *Remarkable Women*.

In the frame of the door, Noor could see the outline of a woman in a flying jacket.

'Final checks,' said Atkins.

She conducted a complete search of Noor, looking at the labels of her clothes, and the contents of her handbag and purse. She even inspected her hair clip.

'If the reception committee is friendly, don't forget to bury your pistol.'

Atkins left unsaid what to do if the reception committee comprised the less friendly Gestapo. Then there were the pills. Atkins unscrewed the gemstone on Noor's ring. In the hollow was a purple pill marked '**BN**'. She re-screwed the gemstone.

'Remember, the purple pill will give you six hours without sleep.'

Benzedrine.

She passed her thumb over a button on Noor's coat. The button slid open as if two coins were pulled together by a magnet. Inside was a white pill with red letters on both sides.

DANGER!
KCN

'You know what the white pill is for.'

Noor nodded.

'I do.'

'K' – *Potassium.*

'CN' – *Cyanide.*

'It will take about twelve seconds,' said Atkins.

She squeezed Noor's hand and smiled.

'And for heaven's sake, Agent Khan, don't get the pills mixed up.'

*

Occupied France, 1943

Noor

The navigator spotted the lake north of Villevêque from eight thousand feet. It glinted like a silver shilling in the moonlight. He strained his eyes through his goggles at the fields beyond. It was faint, but visible. An inverted 'L' south of the village, demarcated by electric torches.

Flying Officer Bunny Rymills eased the nose of the Lysander into descent. The needle on the altimeter flickered and began to fall. Seven thousand feet... six thousand feet... five thousand feet... An experienced Moon Squadron pilot, Rymills silenced the engine at four thousand feet and allowed the Lysander to glide towards the 'L'. The torches became landing lights as he levelled the aircraft on approach. The plane came to a juddering halt on the grass.

A fuselage door opened. A ladder dropped. The agents descended – three women and a man. One of the women agents wore a green oilskin coat. Tight in her palm she held a silver bird with a ruby eye. The contents of her handbag included a hand-kerchief, a powder compact, and a loaded Webley Mark IV .38 calibre pistol. The agents stood in a huddle together as the torches approached, glowing like fireflies. They could hear French voices, animated and relieved. One of the voices belonged to F-Section's dashing Henri Déricourt.

'*Bienvenue, tout le monde,*' he said, flask of Armagnac outstretched. The flash of his eyes was visible in the moonlight. He wore a black sweater under a rough corduroy jacket. An SOE-issue pistol was tucked into his belt. He looked the archetypal *Résistant*.

Standing in a muddy field north-east of Angers, Noor was back on French soil. Once in the safety of the reception committee, the first thing she did, as per her orders, was to bury the Webley pistol. It could be retrieved later. Of all accessories, a loaded firearm was the least easy to explain. Her radio would be dropped separately.

The Lysander was airborne again within fifteen minutes. Bunny Rymills smiled as he headed north into the dawn. It had been a textbook insertion. He was looking forward to bacon and eggs. And a good dollop of HP Sauce.

*

Jeanne-Marie Renier stepped off the Angers train at Paris, Gare Montparnasse. She wore a nondescript jacket and skirt, scuffed lace-up shoes and a burgundy hat that had seen better days. She carried a handbag and a small case with toiletries and a change of clothes. Jeanne-Marie Renier was a children's nurse with a degree in child psychology from the Sorbonne. Her father was an itinerant philosophy lecturer who had died in India just after the Great War. Her mother, Ora, was an American who had fled France for the US in 1940. In 1941, Jeanne-Marie had married a French civil engi-neer from Angers. Her wedding ring was scuffed like her shoes. She had come to Paris to visit a sick cousin. She was unlikely to stay more than a few days.

Madame Renier walked towards the barrier. German soldiers stood behind the ticket collectors. The soldiers would stop and question particular passengers. She presented her ticket at the barrier, willing her hand steady. It was clipped by a railway guard. As she moved forward, one of the soldiers blocked her path.

'*Papiers!*'

An internal voice said: 'Always find and follow your breath.' She centred herself. She fished in her handbag and pulled out a well-thumbed *Carte d'identité*. The soldier looked into a pair of dark, serene eyes and back at the *Carte*. The young Unteroffizier had no idea that the passenger's hatpin was tipped with a fast-acting toxin. He returned the *Carte* and tilted his head towards the exit. She walked through the concourse. Jeanne-Marie Renier had made it to Paris. It took a full five minutes for her pulse to settle.

Jeanne-Marie Renier was the name on the forged *Carte d'identité*. Her codename was MADELEINE. Her real name was known to Colonel Buckmaster and Vera Atkins. The same Vera Atkins who stood alone on the runway at Tangmere watching the Lysander as it flew, like a moth, at the moon. As she waved, she crossed her fingers and her heart for Noor Inayat Khan.

*

The best instructors at Beaulieu could not have prepared Noor for occupied Paris. As she walked on to Rue Pasteur, she found it difficult not to stop with disbelief. The city was a Renoir leached of all colour. The remaining spectrum was an aperture between black and pavement grey. Black snared the eye on the swastikas flying from every official building and the Iron Crosses pinned at the necks of the soldiers. Grey proliferated in the shop windows, tired and empty, and in the faces of war-weary Parisians. It was the monochrome of Occupation.

She headed on foot along the Rue Émile Zola. A column of German soldiers was marching in the opposite direction. She crossed the river and continued west along Rue Mirabeau until she found the corner of Rue Erlanger. She walked a short way into Rue Erlanger until she found Number 40, a handsome stack of stone and wrought iron. She took a breath and rang the bell for the apartment on the second floor. There was a buzzing sound. Noor pushed open the heavy front door. The inside was cool and silent. She ascended the stairs. She knocked on the door of the apartment on the second floor. It seemed to echo through the building.

The door was opened by a young Frenchman with a cravat and cigarette.

'*Entrez.*'

Noor stepped into the apartment. It had once been grand and there were books everywhere.

'Password?' he said.

'*Y a-t-il des moineaux dans ce quartier?* – Are there sparrows in this neighbourhood?'

'*Juste quelques pigeons de temps en temps* – Just the occasional pigeon.'

There was a pause.

'Field name?'

'Jeanne-Marie Renier.' She showed her *Carte d'identité*.

'Codename?'

'MADELEINE.'

The man extended both hands.

'Henri Garry. Codename PHONO. We have been expecting you.'

He turned and called into the apartment. A woman appeared.

'Marguerite, *ma fiancée.*'

The woman gave Noor a warm embrace. Her clothes smelt musty despite the scent of rosewater.

'Please,' said Marguerite. 'You must be famished.'

Noor had been too nervous to buy anything. She had not eaten for twelve hours. Soon the apartment filled with the aroma of black-market eggs whipped into an omelette. Noor ate every bit of the omelette and tried not to gulp at her *thé*. She could feel her energy returning. Marguerite returned to the kitchen to make some more tea for everyone. It would, she knew, allow both agents to talk.

'So,' said Henri Garry, 'London has blessed us with a wireless operator. As a female transmitter you are, I believe, the rarest species of all.'

Garry gave a rundown of the situation in Paris. The largest network was the Prosper Circuit. In one month alone, the Prosper Circuit had carried out sixty-three separate acts of sabotage and derailed a fleet of German troop trains.

There was a number of subcircuits. There was the Racing Circuit, run by former racing drivers, that specialized in sabotage. There was the Satirist Circuit, run by the sculptor Octave Simon, comprising *artistes résistants* specializing in subversion and prop-aganda. Garry himself ran his own subgroup, the Cinema Circuit.

'In due course I will try and put you in touch with Prosper himself, though he is harder to track than a white tiger. I will also arrange contact with a key Prosper agent, codename RENAUD.'

He sucked in a gulp of smoke.

'You will like them both.'

Noor had been briefed about the Prosper Circuit at Beaulieu. Prosper himself, Francis Suttill, had admirers on both sides of the Channel. And few in F-Section had not heard of the Mauritian millionaire, codename Renaud. One female F-Section agent described him as an eye-melting demigod. Noor tried not to look anxious. Her training had drummed in that she was to limit her contact to as few people as possible. The fewer spokes in the wheel she came across, the safer the wheel. Garry appeared to read her thoughts.

'Paris is starved of wireless operators. The few we have are shared like precious gemstones.'

Noor could not help liking the attractive young Frenchman with the cravat. Monsieur Garry excused himself and went into the kitchen. The couple exchanged looks. Noor was not what they were expecting. And for such a dangerous mission. Marguerite mouthed the words *très jeune* – very young. Garry took his fiancée's hand.

'We're desperate,' said his eyes.

*

Henri and Marguerite decided that Noor should stay the next few days in Rue Erlanger. Marguerite made up the spare bed and even found a small bouquet of flowers for a vase on the bedside table.

The last time Noor was in Paris, she had been a writer living in the Quartier Latin. Now she had a Benzedrine tablet screwed into her ring and a cyanide capsule concealed in her coat button. Radio crystals were sown into the hem of her skirt and her hatpin was tipped with a toxin that could cause instant paralysis. The ripple of Debussy over the harp strings was now the monotone tap of Morse. The arc of animals from the *Jātaka Tales* now roamed under the airwaves of a Mark II radio transmitter.

She went to sleep thinking of a flock of birds flying over the Seven Valleys. The journey was perilous. Only a handful would make it to the abode of Simorgh. Just at the point of sleep, Noor heard a voice, and it elicited an opiate calm.

The river that flows in you also flows in me.

At eight the following morning, Noor entered the dining room. Henri and Marguerite were sitting together at one end. Henri rose and gestured to her to join the breakfast table. There was a figure sitting with his back to the door. His sheer stature made it look as if he was sitting on a child's seat.

'Before breakfast,' said Monsieur Garry, 'there is someone I should very much like you to meet.'

The man rose and turned to Noor. The first thing that struck her was his unbound physicality. His collar and tie looked out of place, as if worn by a hulking Mauritian stag. The seams of his suit looked precarious, like the stitches of a wound about to open. His chestnut hair was slicked back, his chocolate eyes pools of eager sincerity. Noor felt the F-Section agent's description of him as a demigod was, if anything, an understatement. She had to stop her hand riding up to her mouth. He extended a firm, capable hand.

'Codename Renaud,' he said. 'Welcome back to Paris.'

The 'back' suggested he had been briefed on her life before the war.

He drew up a chair. He might have been moving a matchbox.

'Please,' he said.

He pushed her and the chair to the edge of the table. Noor could feel his heat.

'There is much to discuss, Agent Madeleine, but not before one of Marguerite's legendary black-market omelettes.'

The quartet ate a breakfast comprised of black-market eggs and, for those who wanted it, *saucisson sec*. Noor noticed Antelme's appetite. He ate like a man who was chopping wood before dawn. The pleasure he took from his breakfast made her smile. As breakfast drew to a close, the doorbell rang. Henri and Marguerite tensed. Antelme reached inside his jacket, not for his wallet. The voice over the intercom had a strange lilt. Henri's shoulders relaxed.

'*C'est l'Irlandais.*'

Marguerite went to put on some coffee. There was a knock at the apartment's door. Henri Garry opened it to what looked like a starved bird of prey wearing a washed-out mackintosh and a polka-dot scarf.

The words had come to him as he walked up the stairs and his lips betrayed traces of a writer's smile.

- The Tuesday Scowls
  - The Wednesday Growls
    - The Thursday Curses
      - The Friday Howls
        - The Saturday Snores
          - The Sunday Yawns
            - The Monday Morns
              - The Monday Mourns

Irlandais, whose real name was Beckett, entered the apartment. He handed a package to Henri. He took a wordless seat at the breakfast table and took out a notebook. He wrote looking over the round black spectacle frames that rested halfway down his beak. Noor's mind was searching. She had seen that face before. The gaunt cheeks, the ice-blue eyes, the riven brow. And the polka-dots on his scarf that turned out to be moth holes. It was Paris 1939. The fellow scribbler in the Rive Gauche café. She smiled to herself.

There was something reassuring about the company of writers, even if this one was as talkative as a brick.

Irlandais was a courier for several Resistance circuits. The package was to be his final delivery. When he returned to his apartment later that morning, he found the flowerpot on his balcony had been moved to the far end. It was an emergency signal from the concierge. The Gestapo had been. *The Thursday Curses...* It was a cue to leave Paris or *The Friday Howls* would be his last. That evening, Irlandais bought a one-way ticket to Avignon and resumed his writing from a hayloft in Roussillon.

Marguerite spent the morning putting together what scraps she could find for a wartime picnic: chopped potato, rough mackerel pâté, a triangle of Camembert past its first flush of youth, half a dry baguette, a thermos of ersatz coffee and an emergency bottle of Beaujolais. Antelme borrowed Henri's Renault Novaquartre, which the latter had filled with bootleg fuel. Antelme placed the picnic basket in the boot. Marguerite lent Noor a scarf of red roses on a white background. As Antelme switched on the ignition and Noor tied the scarf over her head, it felt like an outing to the Bois de Boulogne. The difference was that both carried forged *Cartes d'identités* and concealed cyanide capsules. Noor carried a codebook concealed inside a copy of *Elle*. Antelme carried a Liberator pistol under his jacket.

They drove west towards Grignon. The Renault was spacious, but Antelme managed to look constricted behind the wheel. As the outskirts of Paris gave way to open fields, Noor imagined Antelme breaking free from the car, the stag turning back one last time before clambering over rocks up into the distant mist. As they drove, Antelme told Noor of his home in the Indian Ocean where pink pigeons held their parliament in the branches of ebony forests while Mauritian flying foxes leaped from tree to tree; where rusa stags stood like lighthouses on the cliffs watching the sun melt into the ocean; where hawksbill turtles scuttled over the sands of Saint Félix towards the moonlight on the water. Before his recruitment to F-Section, he had been a sugar planter.

Noor spoke of Moscow, London and Paris – her girlhood in the House of Blessings, her Sufi mystic father, her harp, her days at the Sorbonne. Before the war she had been a children's writer. When the war was over, she wanted to return to writing. Meanwhile, she yearned to go back to Suresnes.

'One day we will go to the House of Blessings,' said Antelme.

The conversation turned practical.

'While your transmitter awaits delivery, I am going to arrange for you to use one that has already found a home in Paris.'

As the car approached Grignon, there were signs for the École Nationale d'Agriculture. Antelme turned through a pair of imposing stone gates and drove along a gravel drive. The École was housed in the seventeenth-century Château de Grignon. The pink-brick château, set among orchards, meadows and lakes, might have been home to the grandest *seigneur*. There, the scions of some of France's oldest families learned the mysteries of crop rotation and animal husbandry. At the rear of the château were various outbuildings and a legion of greenhouses. Antelme parked the car and showed a pass at the entrance. The porter looked furtive. Noor and Antelme were ushered through the château to the rear.

'*Conservatoire Numéro Cinq*,' said the porter before turning on his heels.

The outline of a figure was visible in the middle of a row of conservatories used for practicals. Antelme gave three taps on the glass. It was a pre-arranged signal. The door was opened by a man of about thirty with sleek black hair. He looked as if someone had tried to assemble a matinée idol under pressure. His face just missed handsome. One side of his moustache dropped like a black caterpillar with a sagging tail. A strand of black hair kept falling loose on his forehead, no matter how often he smoothed it in place. He extended a hand to Antelme and then to Noor.

'My codename is ARCHAMBAUD. Welcome to F-Section's little haven in the country.'

His French had a hint of English. It was Gilbert Norman – and one of the only wireless operators active in and around Paris.

'Let me show you some of the plants we grow in here.'

Norman led Antelme and Noor to a corner of the greenhouse. Concealed behind a shelf of tomato plants was his SOE transmitter. The antenna lead was coiled in a circle on the ground behind a flowerpot.

'When I make transmissions, I slip the lead through there.' He indicated a point in the conservatory's wooden foundation that looked like a mouse hole.

'I take it on occasion to that tree over there,' he said, pointing, 'and tie it to one of the lower branches before connecting the antenna. Once the broadcast is finished, everything comes back into the greenhouse.'

It was decided the rest of the conversation should take place away from the college outbuildings. Antelme took the picnic basket from the car and the trio walked deep into the grounds. They found a bank by a small lake where they could not be overhead. Antelme laid out a tartan rug and Noor set out the picnic. Birds scattered into the sky as Antelme uncorked the Beaujolais. Under the dappled light of the tree, a trio of F-Section agents tucked into a picnic as if the war were a thousand miles away.

At the end of lunch, Norman sat, supporting himself on his elbow, while he sipped the last of the Beaujolais.

'I hate to lower the tone,' he said, 'but I am going to have to talk shop.'

He gave a wry smile.

'In occupied Paris, the wireless operator is the mouse. The friendly Funkabwehr – otherwise known as the Radio Defence Corps – is the cat. The Funkabwehr sniff out clandestine radio transmissions. The toms on the ground are the radio direction finders known as "D/F". There is a dedicated D/F platoon based in Paris tracking frequencies from 20 to 300 megahertz. Believe me, they know what they're doing.'

Noor sat cross-legged, eyes and ears alert.

'What they don't teach you at Beaulieu is this. The D/F move around Paris in delivery vans. The man wearing a beret and striped top delivering baguettes could be a D/F with a hidden stethoscope, listening out for radio signals. The D/F can also shut down the city's radio mast. Once there is radio silence, isolated signals can be detected quickly and easily.'

'Like a light shining during a blackout,' said Antelme.

'Spot on,' said Norman. 'They say a hungry D/F patrol can find the location of a clandestine broadcast within twenty or so minutes of the signal first being intercepted.'

Noor narrowed her eyes.

'What it means is this,' said Norman. 'Try, if possible, to stay on air for no more than twenty minutes. And stick to Beaulieu's training manual when it comes to changing – where possible – the location of each broadcast. Just remember that during any broadcast the D/F may be on their way.'

Noor could feel the deft fingers of fear surround her heart.

'It's not impossible,' said Norman with a smile. 'I'm still here.'

After the picnic, the trio walked around the grounds discussing the plans of the various circuits in the weeks ahead. It was clear Norman was overworked, whatever the bonhomie, transmitting messages on behalf of most of the F-Section agents in Paris, not to mention the circuit heads and their deputies. Before Noor and Antelme left Grignon, Norman suggested a meeting with Professeur Balachowsky. Balachowsky was on the staff at the École Nationale d'Agriculture. While many lecturers made their distaste for the Occupation clear, Professeur Balachowsky was an active *Résistant* who had arranged – with a quiet nod from the principal – for Norman to use the grounds of the École for SOE agents to make clandestine broadcasts. Both knew the risks to everyone in the École. Neither, however, was prepared to watch the war from the sidelines.

The meeting took place in Balachowsky's office late in the afternoon amid the paintings of Aubrac, Simmental and Tarentaise cattle. Professeur Balachowsky's secretary, Anne-Sophie, set out the best china, some fresh milk from the school's dairy and a pot of tea.

'*Comme en Angleterre,*' said Balachowsky, gesturing Noor to the table. Noor took the jug of milk and poured a dash into the bottom of the cup. She filled the remainder with tea. As the tea reached the brim, the professor frowned inwardly. He did, however, agree to obtain a pass for Noor to allow her to come and go from Grignon as a student. It was also agreed that Noor should make her first broadcast to London as afternoon lectures ended. There was no time like the present.

As the sun began to set over Grignon, Noor took her codebook and accompanied Norman to the conservatory. Norman located the antenna lead behind the flowerpot and passed it to Noor through the mouse hole. Noor took the lead some fifty paces, as if laying an explosives cord, to the tree pointed out by Norman. She tied the end of the lead to one of the lower branches and affixed the aerial. She returned to the conservatory. Norman had pulled the transmitter from the tomato plants. The transmitter sat like an instrument awaiting its player.

Noor opened her codebook. She wrote out five letters chosen from her poem to act as the key. She wrote out the message in plain text. For her first message, she added the Morse code on the page. She placed the receiver arm under her index finger and in the hot, earthy air of the conservatory, began to transmit. A harpist's fingers were alive once again. As Gilbert Norman kept watch, he became a one-man audience for a cantata in Morse. He gasped inwardly at the rhythm and inflection as she tapped out the code. She was fast.

ARRIVED SAFE. MOVED TO PARIS. LINKED WITH
PHONO AND RENAUD. USING ARCHAMBAUD'S
TRANSMITTER PENDING DELIVERY.
INSTRUCTIONS AWAITED. MADELEINE.

The message was well over eighteen characters. Eighteen characters spelt danger. Mr Marks would know she was not transmitting under duress. His words echoed in her mind. Eighteen is the code for life. Noor put on a headset and waited, crouching. Silence. Then after several minutes came music that surpassed Bach and Mozart. A series of dots and dashes coming over the airwaves, far but near.

London was calling.

Noor took up a pencil and transcribed the Morse. It was a series of apparently random letters. Noor set the letters into rows, with the five keywords at the beginning. She began the transposition sequence. From the random letters, like rays of sunlight, came the plain text.

MESSAGE RECEIVED FROM MADELEINE.
TRANSMITTER WILL ARRIVE NEXT WEEK.
LOCATE PROSPER FOR IMMEDIATE ORDERS.

There was a pause. Noor thought London had signed off. Further pinpricks came over the airwaves.

— —.— —.— — —.— —— —..— ....—.—.— ...— — —.. -

MAY GOD KEEP YOU

Noor suppressed a tear. She rose and handed the message to Norman.

'First blood,' he said with a smile.

It was not the way she would have phrased it, thought Noor, but she could not help her feeling of elation. She had contacted London from the field and London had replied.

Agent Madeleine was operational.

After the transmission, Noor and Antelme went to say good-bye to Professeur Balachowsky. It was while Noor was leaving that her codebook dropped from inside the magazine. Balachowsky stooped, retrieved the codebook, and looked at the writing on the first page. He handed it back to Noor.

'*Un instant*,' he said, gesturing Antelme to wait outside.

Balachowsky turned to Noor. His expression was good-natured but exasperated. Fear haunted his eyes.

'We are under occupation,' he said, as if the last word was one syllable. 'I am not sure you fully understand the consequences.'

He raised his palms to the ceiling. His caution was well placed, as the professor was later to discover when a detachment of Gestapo arrived outside his office the following month. Noor's elation evaporated.

'If your codebook fell into the wrong hands, the whole École would be rounded up.'

He managed a weak smile.

'One other thing. The French add milk to their tea at the end. You put yours in at the beginning. A tiny matter. But enough to arouse suspicion. I don't want you getting yourself arrested over a *thé*.'

On the journey back to Paris, Noor sat quiet and pensive. Regret had turned to anger. Self-anger. How could she have been so careless? She swore inwardly it would never happen again. Antelme did not try to fill the silence. He drove east, his thoughts a kaleidoscope of different patterns.

That evening, Antelme took Noor to meet others at a black-market brasserie on Rue Thouin. Noor remembered the street from her Sorbonne days. Henri Garry and Marguerite were already there. There was a woman called Zoë with eyes of passionate intensity, whose dark hair smelt of diesel. Next to her was a quiet man whose face was overshadowed by a trilby hat. Next to Antelme sat a woman known simply as La Coquine. She was Noor's antithesis. She was blonde and curvaceous, with a low-cut *chemise*. Ruby lipstick had left its trail around her bud-like mouth and her nails gleamed with the same redness. She exhaled smoke from her cigarette through her nose during dinner. Noor noticed how she clung on occasion to Antelme's sleeve. The dinner was convivial, but with a frisson of peril. The table might have been reserved under the name 'Paris Résistance' and there was concern that Déricourt was late. But then, as La Coquine observed with a drag of her cigarette, men are always late. As dinner wore on amid the smoke and muted laughter, Noor remembered the look La Coquine had given her earlier. Unmistakable. La Coquine had her red-nailed hand on Antelme's shoulder and turned with a flick of her hair to Noor.

'*Ne touchez pas*,' hissed her eyes.

*

The man sitting in the faded mackintosh in a café two blocks from Rue Thouin was known sometimes as 'Colonel Henri'. Other times he was known by his real name, Hugo Bleicher. Bleicher was used to sitting alone. Few would willingly approach a man with threadlike lips and a permanent scowl. He remained, however, the Abwehr's best spy-catcher in Paris.

The door to the café opened. Bleicher looked towards the door. It was him.

The man approached the table. He was carrying a newspaper. Bleicher gestured him to sit, without a word.

'Your copy of *Le Monde*,' said the man.

He passed the newspaper across the table. Bleicher could feel the slim package inside. Had he opened the package and spread the contents out on the table, he would have looked like a poker player spreading a hand of aces. Names, addresses, dates, drop-zone locations. There was some original documentation straight from Baker Street and a photograph.

'There's a new radio operator in town,' said the man.

He put his thumb in his broad leather belt and with his other hand drew the lapels of his heavy corduroy jacket together.

'A woman.'

Bleicher raised his eyebrows. It was not, however, a total surprise. A rumour had reached him from another source that was, if anything, even closer to the action. Bleicher sipped his *bière blonde* and drank in every part of her description.

'I have to go,' said the man. 'I'm late.'

It was a cue. Bleicher placed his hand in his pocket. A smaller package awaited in darkness, tied with a rubber band. The man extended his hand. For all the man's swash and buckle, Bleicher knew all traitors were the same. As the men shook hands, the bundle of notes switched from palm to palm.

'Au revoir,' said Bleicher, a smile dying on his lipless mouth.

CHAPTER 32
'CONSERVATORY NUMBER FIVE'

Occupied Paris, 1943

Noor

It was hot. The train carriage was airless. The passengers shared each other's sweltery breath, but they were alone. They wore the monotone expression of Occupation. Bored resentment. Noor sat opposite a man in his sixties with brittle grey hair, false teeth and a funeral suit. Only the beads of perspiration collecting on his temple marked him out from a waxwork. There was an older woman across the aisle reading a book, her crucifix hanging limp from her neck. Opposite was a young mother holding a newborn wrapped in muslin. The baby had a heat rash, its forehead and nose speckled the crimson of wrath.

Noor sat looking out of the window with practised nonchalance. She fanned herself with her copy of *Elle*, her handbag resting on her lap. Her dress was a cast-off of Marguerite's with faded purple primroses, a slim belt and a frayed collar. The dress held two secrets: the coded messages on folded rice paper sewn into the hem and the scratched button on the right cuff holding a cyanide capsule. The needle securing the bow of her soft straw hat was tipped with a fast-acting toxin.

The train alighted at a scruffy, nondescript station with a name that was nothing if not optimistic: Gare-de-Plaisir, Grignon. The sun beat down from a savage sky. The air was thick, its prayer for a breeze unanswered. As Noor walked towards the École, she could feel her dress beginning to cling. A rivulet of perspiration coursed down her neck. At the gates of the École she presented her pass in the name of Renier. The courtyard within offered no shade. As she walked through the grounds, the heat was leaching the colour from the École's surroundings.

Noor made her way to the fifth conservatory behind the bell tower and tapped three times on the door. A bicycle was resting against the glass. Gilbert Norman opened the door. He stood framed in the entrance, wiping his brow. There were dark patches radiating from his shirt like ink on blotting paper. He ushered her inside. It was several degrees hotter under the glass. The marrows panted in silence. The leaves of the tomato plants dripped on to the earth. Condensation gambolled in rivulets down the glass. The conservatory was running in its own sweat.

The pair moved to the corner of the conservatory. There was a battered leather suitcase on the ground, almost the same colour as earth. Norman had replaced the transmitter behind the tomato plants from an earlier broadcast. He had received three messages from London, which he was in the process of decoding. Under his smile, Norman looked tired. The veins in his neck stood proud. Noor pointed to the hem of her dress and made a sign. Norman handed her a penknife and looked away as Noor flipped back the hem of her dress and cut the stitching. She handed a sheaf of messages to Norman on folded pieces of rice paper. With a needle and cotton from her bag, she restitched the hem.

Gilbert took the messages and placed them in his wallet. He finished decoding the earlier messages – all for Prosper – and committed them to memory. He took the antenna cord and wound it in circles around his shoulder like snake coils of twine. He placed the transmitter and cord into the battered leather suitcase. In the past, he would have camouflaged the transmitter among vegetables and straw. Experience had taught Norman that it was easier to admit being a black marketeer and to use a large roll of francs to divert prying eyes.

Norman tied the suitcase to the back of the bicycle, affixed the aerial to his belt and set off with a wallet full of messages that, if he ran into danger, he would swallow. Noor reassembled the tomato plants. She walked outside into the shade of a beech tree from where she would keep a lookout on the conservatory. Norman had given her a bottle of Vichy water. She spread out her copy of *Elle* and put the bottle to her lips. The water flowed into her system like a stream coursing down a dry riverbed. As the sun cast dappled light on the grass, an SOE agent gave an involuntary sigh. Her shoulders loosened. She thought of the garden in the House of Blessings, Amina in a straw hat training roses while her brothers climbed in the trees. She could see Inayat smiling at his desk in his study overlooking the garden and a thorn from the rose stem pierced her heart. Then the familiar words echoed, and she smiled.

The river that flows in you also flows in me.

Almost two hours later, she heard the clatter of Norman's bicycle. Norman looked drenched but relieved. There had been no roadblocks and he had sent all his transmissions. The messages on rice paper, once transmitted, had dissolved on the end of Norman's tongue. The two returned to the greenhouse and replaced the transmitter among the tomato plants. The transmitter cord lay circled on the earth like a sleeping serpent. Once outside the conservatory, Norman locked the door with a rudimentary padlock. They decided to return to the centre of Paris on different trains.

Before leaving, Norman took Noor to a former hunting lodge in the grounds. It was where Professeur and Madame Balachowsky lived during term time and spent the occasional weekend. They found Madame Balachowsky at work in the kitchen. The older woman smiled and wiped her hands on her apron. Would the pair like a tisane before returning? It was clear from the open cookbook and the array of knives, chopping boards and saucepans that Madame Balachowsky was planning something sumptuous. One of the benefits of association with the École was the ability to obtain produce beyond the reach of ordinary Parisians.

'Lunch will be at two tomorrow,' she said. 'Come for one.'

She smiled and tucked a strand of grey hair behind her ear.

'We are expecting the usual suspects and a few others besides.'

*

Macalister counted the seconds to impact.

THREE

TWO

ONE

Thud!

His boots hit the earth at thirty miles an hour. His torso hit the soil like a dummy. The ground spun from horizontal to vertical. He lay, winded and dazed. He had, however, survived the jump. His parachute was fluttering grey-white in the moonlight. Another, smaller, parachute was flapping fifty feet away. He saw lights moving behind a hedge. He remained horizontal and reached for his pistol. He propped himself up on his elbows, pistol in hand, trigger finger curled.

The lights grew closer.

'*Faucon!*' shouted a hoarse voice.

It was the password. Macalister stood, replaced his pistol, and started gathering the strings of his parachute. A moment later there was a friendly pat on his shoulder. It was the same hoarse voice.

'*Bienvenue à Val-de-Loire.*'

The voice belonged to an unlikely looking *Résistant:* a small wiry man with a toothbrush moustache and horn-rimmed spectacles. His men were already gathering his parachute. Macalister pointed to the other parachute, its lines twitching.

'*Ma radio.*'

The leader, whose name was Culioli, gestured his men towards the second parachute. Macalister started scanning the next-door field.

'Don't worry, we picked up your friend a mile south. He's with others from my group. Bruised but okay.'

The new Canadian F-Section agent smiled. So far so good. Macalister was reunited with a fellow Canadian named Pickersgill in an isolated farm building. Both agents considered the *saucisson sec*, cut with a penknife, the chunks of baguette and the rough Pinot noir was in every sense a midnight feast.

At dawn, the committee head ordered a search of the fields to ensure all remnants of the parachute drop were hidden. As the officers awoke, the group were joined by a woman in her forties with wiry grey-black hair and humane, alert eyes. Her codename was JACQUELINE. She was an SOE agent trained at both Wanborough and Beaulieu and the first female agent to be sent to France.

Under Jacqueline's supervision, Macalister's transmitter, fresh radio crystals and correspondence for Prosper were loaded into a battered Renault. Jacqueline used some strips of gingham to make the transmitter look like a lunchbox. It was rudimentary, but time was short. SOE remained critically short of radio operators and the messages for Prosper were urgent. With Culioli at the wheel, she took the front passenger seat. The two Canadians sat at the back.

It was their first morning in France, and Macalister and Pickersgill had to quell their excitement. Training was over. This was real. Finches hailed the early morning as the car drove towards Dhuizon. The sun was rising into a cobalt sky. A breeze sent a wave through cornfields vanishing into the distance. After twenty minutes, the Canadians in the back began to relax. Nothing could spoil such a beautiful morning.

The road narrowed. Around the next bend there was a small queue of cars.

'Roadblock. Damn!' said Jacqueline.

Culioli looked in the mirror. A car had come to a halt behind. There was no way to turn.

'Whatever your cover stories,' said Culioli, looking over his shoulder, 'I hope for all our sakes they're good.'

Minutes later, two German guards stood one on either side of the Renault, both with Alsatians.

'*Papiers!*' said the first.

Culioli and Jacqueline handed over their *Cartes d'identités* with a disinterest at odds with their pulses.

'Where are you going?'

'We are taking lunch to friends on the other side of Dhuizon. It's a cousin's birthday.'

Pickersgill shifted on the back seat. One of the dogs snapped. Something was wrong. The second guard leaned in to the driver.

'Open the boot.'

*

The blow came from nowhere. A backhand slap. Pickersgill winced. It was more of a shock than anything.

'Tell the truth!' shouted the Gestapo officer, his blue eyes glowering.

A Vichy policeman sat in the corner of the hut by the roadside, making notes. He rose and whispered something into the Gestapo officer's ear.

'Why do you speak French like a Canadian?'

Culioli's words echoed in Pickersgill's mind. 'Whatever your cover story, I hope it's good.'

Pickersgill stuck to his cover story, though he could feel perforations appearing with each question. Sand in the hourglass was spilling through tiny apertures, and he could feel the grains diminishing. He had been in France for less than twelve hours. Things were not looking good. The Gestapo kept returning to his accent.

'WHY DO YOU SPEAK FRENCH LIKE A CANADIAN!'

While a second backhand slap struck Pickersgill's face, Culioli and Jacqueline sat in mute desperation in the front of the car outside. The search of the boot had been cursory. The Germans were more interested in the two passengers in the rear. Had there been a leak? As they sat, waiting for the two Canadians, Agent Jacqueline went over the contents of the boot in her mind. A radio, fresh radio crystals and correspondence that threatened to expose Prosper himself.

If they sped off, Macalister and Pickersgill would never be heard of again. They waited, each second cutting another groove into the constricted hearts of Culioli and Jacqueline.

Jacqueline looked sidelong at Culioli.

'Are you carrying cyanide?'

Culioli shook his head.

'One capsule between two is the worst of all worlds,' said Jacqueline.

A grim smile passed over Culioli's lips.

There was a commotion as two guards came running from the hut.

'*Raus!* – Out!' shouted the first.

Culioli looked round. Both guards had their machine guns pointed at the car.

He and Jacqueline knew too much. They could not be taken alive, even if it meant abandoning the Canadians. He turned the ignition key, released the handbrake and hit the accelerator. The battered Renault bolted forward, a momentary Bugatti. Culioli could hear the machine guns open fire. The back windscreen shattered. A bullet hit Jacqueline in the base of her skull. Her head plummeted forward. She could feel blood running down the side of her neck. Time slowed. She saw everything from eyes looking horizontally from the dashboard. Her vision went from double to triple. She could feel her life leaving, yet as the car surged forward towards the wall of a farm building, she remained alive.

The wall appeared to rush at the car. Culioli closed his eyes as Death extended its hand. He felt the force of the Renault as the vehicle hit the brickwork. The car hit the wall at an oblique angle, the bumper taking most of the impact. The front left wheel buckled, forcing the car to a scraping halt. Culioli was, amid the smoke from the engine, bruised but alive. Death had snatched back its hand. His thumbs seized on the buttons on Jacqueline's coat, searching for the hidden cyanide. Jacqueline's eyes were open. Culioli thought she was dead until she whispered the word '*Ourlet* – hem.'

By now, the barrel of a machine gun had smashed the window and was pointed at Culioli's temple. Another machine gun was pointing over the slumped head of Jaqueline. Culioli was pulled from the vehicle, coughing and struggling. Jacqueline could feel a hand holding her collar but her body refused to stand. She slumped like a ragdoll. One agent was alive. The other was in the shadow of the Reaper's sickle. And the treasures in the Renault that lay smoking on the road were the Gestapo equivalent of the tomb of Tutankhamen.

*

The lunch table was set out under an overhead vine. Dappled light fell on a wooden bowl of *salade niçoise* dotted with fresh radishes, a tray of roast aubergine and endive, and a saucepan of bubbling *coq au vin* courtesy of two of the École's roosters. Next to the saucepan sat a plump, full-moon Brie surrounded by a constellation of white goat's cheeses. Cellar-cold bottles of Alsace dripped in the sunlight. A dash of cassis rested in the bottom of a dozen glasses. The Alsace muddled with the cassis, making a Kir of watery violet. A breeze fanned the faces of the guests as they raised their glasses of Kir to the safe return of Prosper from touring arms dumps in Normandy and to welcome SOE's most recent wireless operator.

'*Nom-de-code MADELEINE*,' said an assembly of voices.

Noor stood smiling in the same dress of faded primroses. Around her neck was a printed Chanel scarf that fluttered like a prayer flag.

Next to Noor stood Antelme, the broad-shouldered Mauritian, wearing a blue suit with an open white shirt. The turn-ups of his trousers rested on a pair of moccasins. His ankles were bare. Late in the afternoon, the moccasins would be kicked off as Antelme splashed through the weeds of the largest lake in the École's grounds and plunged into the mirror-cool water. Next to Antelme stood Prosper. It was the first time Noor had met the head of the circuit. There was something unmistakably chivalrous about the Englishman, who took Noor's hand and looked into her eyes with radiance and purpose. Prosper was slighter than Antelme but Noor could not help but notice his even features, clear brow, honey-coloured hair and neat moustache. He wore a pale linen suit and walked with the insouciance of a fielder in a village cricket match. Rumour was that people would stand between him and the barrel of a Mauser to protect the knight with the green eyes and honey-streaked hair. Next to Prosper was Andrée Borrel. She was not dressed, this time, as a nurse. She wore a faded yellow dress, her hair tucked under a straw hat tied with a white bow. She looked younger, thought Noor, the girl showing through the woman. Attentive to her glass was Gilbert Norman, his dark hair falling, as he poured the cassis, into a truculent comma. Dr Vanderwynckt, principal of the École, and Madame Vanderwynckt completed the party. The principal had given tacit approval for the École to be used by SOE, though at night he stared into the blackness, imagining what would happen if the activities were discovered. Under his panama hat, his eyes maintained a weary sparkle.

The party sat. As the *coq au vin* was served in the vine-dappled light, Monsieur Balachowsky patrolled the table with a bottle of cooled Beaujolais. There was a toast for Madame Balachowsky, tumblers held up in a ruby circle to the sun. By the time the Armagnac came out with fresh figs and cream, laughter was carrying across the grounds of the École.

No one passing would have known it was a lunch for key members of the Paris Resistance.

After lunch, while Prosper was in animated discussion with Professeur Balachowsky, two pairs left to walk in the grounds. Borrel and Norman. Noor and Antelme. The latter pair stopped at a lake, where Noor sat under a willow. She closed her eyes as Antelme kicked off his loafers and unbuttoned his shirt. She heard several strides and a loud splash. When she opened her eyes, she saw water roll off Antelme's back as his head turned and his palms sliced the water. After thirty yards he stopped, shaking water from his hair, the laughing Mauritian stag, head turned up to the sun.

*

As the sun blazed Armagnac-gold over Grignon, Hugo Bleicher was examining the haul of sparkling treasure delivered by motorcycle despatch from the Gestapo. It had arrived while he was still eating his *Leberwurst*. He slid his tongue across his thin lips as he inspected the haul. There was a transmitter, a miniature sarcophagus of current SOE engineering, and a royal flush of radio crystals. Then there was the correspondence. Letters addressed to agents by their field names in plain text. There was also a series of addresses. Bleicher spent an hour sifting the correspondence and writing in his notebook. The last jigsaw pieces of the Prosper network were falling into place. And at the centre of the picture was the face of Prosper himself, radiant and determined. He spoke to an empty office.

'Prosper – your time is approaching.'

Two parallel threads lengthened. It was the closest Hugo Bleicher came to a smile.

*

That night, Noor lay in bed, tired but with a butterfly heart. Her last thought, as her dreams circled, was of the water coursing off Antelme's back before he stopped and shook his laughing head, drops of water flying from his hair.

That night, Antelme lay in bed in the neighbouring *quartier*, tired but with a butterfly heart. His muscles had the languid vigour that came with swimming. His eyelids fell as he descended into a dream vortex. He dreamed he was standing in the Mauritian shallows, shaking the sea from his hair. He walked up the beach, following the trail of shells to the wooden beach house, once pink, now bleached like a sugared almond licked by the sea. The inside was a single room, walls and ceiling slatted like a saltbox. The jaws of blue marlins and bull sharks were suspended, yawning open, from the wall opposite the shutters. A wooden fan hung from the ceiling, slow-revolving like a gramophone record stalled to a moan. The rough-hewn bed in the corner lay under a wooden frame, with mosquito nets hanging down like a veil. Behind the veil he could just make out the shape of a woman's head, jet-black hair spilling around a white frangipani slipped behind her ear. Her cheek was resting on a raised knee. Still slippery from the ocean, he walked to the tumble of mosquito nets and with bronzed hands drew the veil apart. The girl with the frangipani behind her ear had the face of Noor Inayat Khan.

CHAPTER 33
'THE KNOCK'

Occupied Paris, 1943

Suttill

The paraffin lamp in the attic in the 16ème Arrondissement flickered behind folded shutters. Gilbert Norman sat at a desk poring over an array of *Cartes d'identités*. His clandestine transmitter rested between his feet. Andrée Borrel sat opposite, filing the *Cartes* from the same batch. In keeping with the last Occupation diktat, the photographs had been changed to profile. Updating the *Cartes* in question represented two weeks of work by Sergeant Redknapp, SOE's finest forger. In each case they gave the holder's name, date of birth and their address.

One was for Prosper himself, in the name of Desprées. Norman looked at the *Carte*. Sergeant Redknapp had surpassed himself, even down to the colour and width of the thread that ran down the crease in the middle. Prosper in profile looked more like Erroll Flynn than ever – honey-coloured hair swept back from a clear brow and a perfect profile. Norman could feel a stab of envy.

Borrel stood. She walked over to the single gas hob and put on a pot of black-market coffee. It was going to be a long night. The gas from the hob rose with a hiss. She rejoined Norman at the table. As the hiss grew louder, Norman and Borrel sat oblivious to the detachment of Gestapo assembling in disciplined silence in the street below.

*

Bleicher sat in his office staring at the wall. He too was drinking coffee, the bitterness combining with the remnants of *Leberwurst* in his mouth. The montage opposite was expanding. In the centre was Prosper. Radiating outwards were names – planets revolving around the sun. In the immediate ring were Borrel, Prosper's aide-de-camp, and Norman the wireless operator. Then Joseph Antelme, Henri Garry and Octave Simon, heads of the Prosper subcircuits. Octave Simon's right hand was a woman known only as Zoë. There were two racing drivers involved in a subcircuit concerned with sabotage: Robert Benoist and a British agent thought to be called Grover-Williams. There was an agent by the name of Tommy Yeo-Thomas who had evaded capture twice. The Gestapo code-named him the White Rabbit and put a two-million-franc bounty on his head. There was a Resistance leader called Culioli and his accomplice, an SOE agent code-named Jacqueline, now with a bullet in her skull. There was Professeur Balachowsky from the École Nationale d'Agriculture – a place of learning the Gestapo would soon be showing a great deal of interest. There were two further radio operators. One was a former actor named Rake, though he was believed to have left Paris.

The other was a woman. She was known only by her codename: MADELEINE.

Further names expanded into the galaxy. At the bottom were two sets of initials. The first was 'H.D.' Bleicher had to tread carefully with Henri Déricourt. Déricourt was understood to be serving a variety of different masters, and if handled incorrectly was more dangerous than a grenade. The second was 'M.B.' 'M.B.' was a different matter altogether. One thing was for sure. It was time to roll up the Prosper network.

*

There was a knock. Borrel looked up. Norman felt inside his jacket. Empty. His pistol was in Grignon. Neither agent was carrying cyanide. There was a further knock. Both agents could hear a low growl outside the door, followed by an urgent bark. The Gestapo seldom carried out arrests without a pair of Alsatians.

'*Ouvrez la porte!*'

The accent was German. The knocking became thumping.

'*OUVREZ LA PORTE!*'

The thumping grew harder.

'*O-U-V-R-E-Z L-A P-O-R-T-E-!*'

The room echoed to the sound of shattering wood as a battering ram smashed the lock. A jackboot kicked the door inwards. Framed in the doorway were a group of Gestapo in their trademark black leather coats. Two at the front were straining to control their Alsatians. Norman and Borrel stood frozen. There was nowhere to hide the *Cartes*. They were strewn across the table like cards in an illegal poker game. One card, Borrel knew, was an Ace. It had the cover name and, worse, the address of Prosper himself. There was a pile of other Aces, Kings and Queens.

The soldier at the front unleashed his Alsatian. A streak of black and gold lurched across the room, fangs bared. Its teeth found Norman's forearm. They gnawed at his elbow, piercing his skin through his jacket. As the Alsatian's jaw locked, its fangs dug into the bone. The more Norman moved his elbow, the more the Alsatian turned its head and tightened its grip. Another canine streak flashed across the room. The Alsatian hit Borrel in the chest with such force it knocked her to the ground. She crossed her wrists to stop the dog tearing at her throat. The Alsatian gnawed at one wrist then the other. It was seeking the prize – her windpipe.

An order was shouted, as loud and abrupt as the Alsatians' bark. The dog handlers moved forward, collaring their Alsatians. The leader of the operation, Hauptsturmführer Oberhauser, had orders to bring in two live prisoners, not ribbons of flesh hanging from bone.

Norman and Borrel were handcuffed. Sub-machine guns were pointed at their heads while the apartment was searched. Fifteen minutes later they were being marched down the steps of the building with Mauser pistols trained at the base of each of their skulls. The commotion had woken other residents. Some stood by their front doors, expressions ranging from defiant to disapproving. Borrel caught the eye of an older woman in a nightdress making the sign of the cross.

It was the moment of dread. Each step down was a step closer to Gestapo hospitality in one of the most feared buildings in Paris. Each step was another butterfly in the stomach whose wings turned to lead.

Soon, Norman and Borrel would be shepherded at gunpoint across a notorious threshold. Gestapo headquarters: **84 Avenue Foch.**

*

Sturmbannführer Kieffer reclined on his chair. He lit a cigar and put his boots on the desk, right over left. His left boot obscured the face of the woman in the portrait opposite. She was a coquettish eighteenth-century beauty. Kieffer's focus, however, would be required elsewhere. He stretched for a decanter and poured himself a glass of Armagnac. As a black Mercedes moved towards Avenue Foch with two captured agents in the back, he spun the golden liquid into a vortex.

Life at 84 Avenue Foch was Kieffer's conundrum. On one hand there were the Sturmbannführer's grand living apartments on the first floor, with the chandeliers reflected in the polished parquet and the floor-to-ceiling windows veiled with lemon silk. The carved four-poster bed in the panelled bedchamber, draped in the same lemon silk, felt like a horizontal throne. And while Frau Kieffer remained with their daughter in the relative safety of Baden-Baden, the Sturmbannführer wondered if anyone would blame him for testing the strength of the bedposts with the *poulets de luxes* who were willing, in return for a little magnanimity, to engage in some spirited *collaboration horizontale*.

On the other hand, there were the basement rooms converted into cells and the rooms set aside for 'preliminary questioning' and 'enhanced interrogation'. There was the iron bath shunted into the interrogation chamber that even Kieffer struggled to imagine was to keep the prisoners clean. There were the cases of instruments brought into the building by Dr Winkler, the Gestapo medical officer, which Kieffer had difficulty believing was for the prisoners' health. And there were hand-operated drills and different sizes of pliers, which Kieffer had trouble convincing himself were for renovations. As for Dr Winkler's sourcing of two in-patients from the Sainte-Anne Psychiatric Hospital to become his assistants, Kieffer had to look the other way. Both men, an Algerian and an Albanian, Dr Winkler considered psychiatric rarities.

'They have the capacity', said Dr Winkler, wiping some spittle from the corner of his mouth, 'to inflict pain without remorse. *Kein Bisschen* – not a bit. Remarkable.'

Dr Winkler had ordered a series of electrodes.

'Malik and Bled will be experts before the end of the week. Electricity is the Holy Grail.' Winkler's smile was almost audible. 'It leaves no visible trace.'

Kieffer found Dr Winkler, with his bald-onion head and eugenics theories, beyond tiresome. At the same time, everyone in the Gestapo was a higher servant of the Reich. Were there limits? What Kieffer found awkward was the sound of muffled screams from the basement when he was with a *poulet de luxe*. It was difficult not to notice, and once or twice a *poulet* would look searchingly into his eyes. Afterwards, Kieffer had sat on the side of the bed thinking of Frau Kieffer and his daughter and felt his stomach contract. On several occasions he had sent a message down to the basement for Malik and Bled to go home for the night.

Sturmbannführer Kieffer regarded himself as the conscience of the building. Kieffer decided who came through the portals of 84 Avenue Foch. Kieffer decided who should be released. Kieffer decided who should be transferred to Gestapo headquarters in Berlin. Thereafter, their fate was out of his hands. He was only the gatekeeper. Or so his conscience said.

Kieffer showed genuine surprise at the fear in the eyes of those prodded over the threshold of 84 Avenue Foch. And the eyes of those he encountered at the theatre and the ballet as he drank in the remnants of Parisian culture under occupation. He seemed oblivious to the impact of the silver *Totenkopf* skull staring eyeless from the centre of his Gestapo cap.

*

The roll-up of the Prosper network had been planned for weeks. With Oberhauser heading the operation, Kieffer knew matters were in the hands of an enthusiast. Oberhauser was tall, blond and broad, with a formless, fleshy face and blank blue eyes. The back of his head was shaved bare. The contrast between his blond hair and black uniform unsettled even Kieffer. Rumour had it that as a student at Freiberg, he had challenged a fellow undergraduate to a duel. The latter had made the cardinal error of insulting Hitler.

'I took out the man's right eye,' said Oberhauser. 'He was Yugoslav scum. If it wasn't for the umpire, I would have run the blade through his putrid throat.'

Oberhauser had learned the art of interrogation at the feet of Hauptsturmführer Barbie while on detachment to Gestapo head-quarters in Lyon.

'It was quite a learning curve,' he told Kieffer and Winkler over dinner, his teeth reddening as he chewed a forkful of steak *onglet*.

He wiped his fleshy mouth on a napkin. A thin streak of red stained the linen. The conversation turned technical. At the mention of Resistance child prisoners, Kieffer held up his palm.

'Can I invite you to discuss the technicalities in my absence, *meine Herren?*'

Oberhauser would put his proficiency with 'technicalities' to good use with two high-value pieces of the Prosper jigsaw. They decided that the preliminary questioning would be handled by Kieffer. In the event of non-cooperation, Oberhauser would undertake the enhanced interrogation – with any required techni-cal assistance from Malik and Bled.

*

Kieffer sat behind a desk in the interrogation chamber. The surface of the desk was bare. Each drawer, however, contained a secret. The skill of the interrogator was which drawer to select and when. It was a game of cat and mouse and there was no question who would win.

Gilbert Norman was brought into the room. Kieffer stood.

'Welcome to Avenue Foch, Monsieur Norman. Or would you prefer me to use your codename, *Archambaud?*'

Norman tried not to gulp. *How on earth?* He was pushed on to a chair that was riveted to the floor in the centre of the room.

'The one thing of which you must be sure: we know everything. Everything. The sooner you decide to co-operate, the more likely your stay here will be comfortable. If you are unwise enough not to co-operate, your stay here will be uncomfortable. Not just for you but for Mlle Borrel, who is the courier to a man known as François Desprées, codename Prosper. The SOE's very own Sun King.'

They knew about Borrel, and worse still, Prosper.

Norman retained his outward composure. Inside, his heart was falling through a trap door.

'Let me show you something,' said Kieffer.

He opened a drawer. He took out the *Carte d'identité* in the name of Desprées.

'That is Prosper, is it not. Real name Francis Suttill?'

Norman said nothing.

'You must know something about this *Carte d'identité* because it was found at the apartment where you were arrested.'

Kieffer smiled.

'The *Carte* is the tip of the iceberg, Monsieur Norman.'

From a different drawer, Kieffer took out a typed list. It was a list of names and Paris addresses. In some places, the SOE codenames were also given. It was a long list. And accurate. Kieffer opened a further drawer. It was a map of Paris and the environs. Marked with 'X's around the periphery of the city were known drop-zone locations.

'Do you still prefer not to co-operate?'

There was silence. From another drawer, Kieffer withdrew a document. The address at the top said 'Inter Services Research

Bureau' with an address of 64 Baker Street, London. They were F-Section orders signed by Colonel Buckmaster. The orders were recent. Norman could feel the pace of his heart as it fell into the void.

'Any gaps in our knowledge are small and insignificant. You will be able to assist by giving us your full co-operation.'

The interrogation room next door was different. There was an iron bath against a wall. On the opposing wall was what appeared to be an open coffin. There were portable gas rings on a sideboard and a kettle. On a table in the centre of the room were syringes. Next to the syringes was an open case of medical instruments, including surgical saws and pliers of differing sizes. There was a drill and a row of welding electrodes connected to a power source.

The difference between the chair in the first interrogation room and that in the second was that the latter had leather straps on the arms. Norman was pushed into the chair. Malik, eyes expressionless, fastened the straps. In the background, Norman could hear the hiss of a kettle. SOE orders were to hold out for the first forty-eight hours. By Norman's calculation, he had been at Avenue Foch for less than four.

*

The last thing Norman saw before he lost consciousness were the blank blue eyes of Hauptsturmführer Oberhauser. The bloodstains on his black Gestapo uniform were almost invisible.

*

The night duty officer at Grendon Hall picked up a coded transmission from Norman's radio the following evening. It was sent to the decryption pool. Miss Pickering, who decoded the message an hour later, pressed the red buzzer. Other codebreakers formed a circle. Miss Pickering was trembling. According to the message, the Prosper network was collapsing. Norman himself had evaded capture. He warned that all agents still at liberty should shelter in their safe houses.

Miss Pickering darted over to the index of previous messages from Norman. The style of the message was different, though that could have been down to atmospheric conditions. There was something more troubling. The 'true' and 'bluff' checks were missing. Grendon Hall forwarded the message to SOE as priority 'Zulu' traffic.

The senior signals operator in Baker Street was just going off duty when the message arrived. The junior signaller said the message omitted its true and bluff checks.

'Send an immediate rebuke,' said the senior signaller as he put on his hat to leave.

The sermon received on Norman's blood-smeared radio caused a skitter of smirks among the listening Gestapo.

'You have forgotten your double security check. Be more careful next time.'

*

The dominoes of the Prosper Circuit started to fall. They crashed in a jagged line that led to the highest value piece in the set: Prosper himself.

Kieffer was all smiles when Suttill was frogmarched over the threshold of 84 Avenue Foch. Berlin would be delighted. His gilded nest in the first-floor apartments was secure.

'So good of you to come and see us, Mr Suttill.'

As Prosper was led down to the interrogation cells, Kieffer returned to his study. He poured himself a cognac and sat at his desk with his boots on the table. The brandy was a way of muffling the sounds that came from the basement. A second brandy chased the first. He looked up. The eyes of the woman in the portrait opposite radiated something beyond disgust. Kieffer looked away. Suttill's arm hung limp and broken. He had given his interrogators nothing, save a concise lesson in dignity.

'Never let your opponent sense your fear,' his pupil master had told him on his first day at court.

Kieffer sent down for a progress report. The prisoner refused to co-operate. Perhaps, thought Kieffer, it was time to call off

Malik and Bled? Otherwise there would be nothing left of Prosper to interrogate. Kieffer felt nausea in the pit of his stomach when he attended Prosper's cell. The man who had crossed the threshold of 84 Avenue Foch was no longer recognizable. Yet he remained able to speak.

'*Donoghue v Stevenson [1932]*, House of Lords judgments, page 100,' came a clear voice. 'Court split 3-2, Lords Atkin, Thankerton and Macmillan in the majority. A case that turned on a drowned snail in a bottle of ginger beer. Now who would have thought that, Herr Sturmbannführer?'

Kieffer could feel the nausea spreading. He tried to sound as calm as Prosper.

'Mr Suttill. Your suffering will end if you furnish us with the location of all weapons caches held by the Prosper network. Your co-operation may save the lives of other Prosper agents.'

Prosper's look of quiet contempt made Sturmbannführer Kieffer stand and leave. Kieffer could feel his eyes follow him out of the interrogation chamber, along the corridor and up the stairs.

Two members of the Prosper Circuit still eluded Kieffer's grasp.

Joseph Antelme, codename Renaud.

Noor Inayat Khan, codename Madeleine.

CHAPTER 34
'THE RELUCTANT DIVA'

London, 1943

Buckmaster
Atkins

Buckmaster dug his nails into his palm. The skin split. Blood ran down his lifeline into his cuff. He took a handkerchief from his pocket and squeezed it into a ball. The muscles in his forearm tensed and contracted. He had tried to cry. He was beyond tears. The fall of the Prosper Circuit was like the roof of 64 Baker Street crashing through each floor into the basement. It was the largest of all SOE networks and it was linked to an array of sub-networks. With the arrest of Prosper, SOE's sun had been extinguished over Paris.

Buckmaster thought of Suttill strapped to a chair in the basement of Avenue Foch. Waves of nausea pitched and rolled in his stomach. Vera Atkins put down the tray of tea. She walked over and opened his palm. The blood-smeared handkerchief rolled on to the floor. She held his palm in hers, stilling the tremble. The tea was cold by the time she rose.

'It's a disaster on every level,' said Buckmaster.

Atkins knew enough to say nothing. There was a knock at the door. A transmission had arrived from a member of the Juggler

402

Circuit, still operating in Paris. Two agents connected to Prosper remained at liberty. Codenames: Renaud and Madeleine.

'Antelme and the Khan girl,' said Atkins. 'Thank God.'

'We need to get them out,' said Buckmaster.

Atkins lowered her voice.

'Agent Khan is one of our only remaining pairs of eyes. Without her, we're blind.'

'Blind is better than dead.'

*

Occupied Paris, 1943

Noor
Antelme

Noor was standing in a telephone booth around the corner from Rue Erlanger. On the floor next to her feet was a bulky, scuffed leather suitcase containing her radio. On the phone, Henri Garry broke the news. Prosper was ill. The word 'ill' in Resistance circles meant only one thing. Arrested.

Noor gripped the receiver. She felt faint. The heat inside the booth was wrapping itself around her face like a flannel. A familiar voice echoed.

In times of strife, always find and follow your breath.

She invoked *adham pranayama* – three deep breaths into her diaphragm. She thought of Prosper in Grignon. His clasp of her hand on first meeting. His clear brow, honey-streaked hair and neat moustache. Everything about him radiated decency. And he was now in the hands of the Gestapo.

'Archambaud and Denise are also ill,' said Garry. It was a reference to Norman and Borrel. 'Others are falling ill by the day.'

Noor shut her eyes.

'You need to lie low and get a message out that you are not ill. I will make arrangements for you to contact Renaud.'

Her heart jumped. *Joseph!*

'He's all right?'

403

'Yes. But he will be high on the wanted list.'

Having jumped, her heart sank.

'I am going to give you details of a fixer for various circuits. Codename PAPILLON. Papillon will arrange for you to lie low.'

'How can I trust Papillon?'

'Two reasons. The password I am about to give you. And instinct.'

The line hissed.

'There is something else,' said Garry. 'Marguerite and I are getting married. We would love you to come to the wedding.'

Noor's heart rose again.

'*Félicitations!*'

'*Merci, Madeleine. Restes en garde.*'

*

That afternoon at four o'clock Noor was sitting alone in the Café des Siciliennes on Rue Thouin. The silver bird given to her by the SOE librarian was pinned, wings folded, to her lapel. The café's colour had been drained by the war. The once-red banquettes were now a smudged watery rose. The tables were dry and warping in the heat. The mirrors reflected their un-wiped dust. At Noor's feet was the suitcase carrying her radio and a change of clothes. She was unarmed, though her hatpin was tipped with poison. Her powder compact contained two cyanide capsules.

It will take about twelve seconds.

Her thoughts were interrupted by footsteps, heavy and assured. She looked up, expecting to see a man. Instead, it was a young woman in blue overalls. Her chestnut hair was unwashed and she carried an aroma of diesel. The freckles under her eyes were joined with axle grease. She looked like a woman in a Shakespeare play disguised unconvincingly as a man.

'*Absinthe verte ou thé à la menthe?* – Green absinthe or mint tea?' said the blue overalls.

'*C'est un peu tôt pour l'absinthe* – It's a little early for absinthe.'

The woman sat.

'Codename Papillon. We met once before. You may call me Zoë.'

She had said a handful of words. Yet there was something in the tone of her voice that struck Noor, and the level of her gaze. Strength and capability. And behind her tired eyes, bravery and passion. Could she be trusted? Noor's instinct was that Papillon was less butterfly, more lioness.

'I am connected to a number of groups in and around Paris and I am also a railway specialist.'

Noor recalled from training at Beaulieu the critical role of the rail saboteurs.

Zoë looked around the empty café. 'My sister was part of the Prosper network but we managed to get her out to Normandy.'

There was no clue as to the 'we'.

'*C'est un désastre*,' said Zoë. 'But we continue. I shall be helping you with safe houses while the dust settles. I am also charged with connecting you with Renaud.'

Noor's heart rose.

'You will need to be extra vigilant with the contents of your suitcase. There has been a spike in activity by the signal trackers. Your passing baker's van may have a stick of Funkabwehr agents among the baguettes.'

Noor's gut instinct told her she was in safe hands. Her heart began to calm.

'I would rather not stay anywhere for more than two nights.'

'Make it one night,' said Zoë. 'And we will have to do something about your appearance.' Noor looked quizzical.

'*La Peste* will have your description.'

*

Her first night was spent in the Place Malherbe overlooking the Rue de Rome. Zoë advised against transmitting from the roof. There were rumours of increased Funkabwehr activity in the 8ème Arrondissement. She fell asleep in a strange bed a dream's distance from the Église de la Madeleine.

The following night, Zoë arranged for Noor to sleep in an apartment block on the Boulevard Richard Wallace north-west of the 8ème. Noor arrived in the early evening with her battered leather suitcase. The concierge took her to a room on the top floor. He gave her the key without a word, looked into her eyes for a moment and descended the stairs. The day was cooler and Noor could feel, after a night in Malherbe, her energy returning. The most pressing issue was contacting London. She had been off air for more than forty-eight hours just as Prosper collapsed. It was imperative to contact Baker Street.

After dinner in a small café around the corner, Noor went to her room. From her suitcase she extracted the silver coil. She wound the antenna around her arm, like an African bracelet that started at the wrist and ended at the elbow. Bracelet on arm, suitcase in hand, she walked downstairs and into the garden.

The garden was an abandoned courtesan. Her borders were unkempt and the branches of her trees were overgrown. Yet white agapanthus still grew from her beds and red bougainvillea still clung to her walls. Noor took a chair from one of the tables and placed it at the foot of a tree towards the back of the garden. She started to unspool her bracelet around the lower branches. As she stood on tiptoes to reach a higher branch, she heard a click from behind. She turned. Standing behind her, the black of his uniform leaching into the darkening sky, was an SS officer.

*

WW, the sleeper agent, awoke. The ignition key was about to bring the Racing Circuit to life. By now the network included WW, Robert Benoist and Georges Morel and their occasional courier, code-named Papillon. Morel identified the first drop zone in Rambouillet, where he used to scramble his motorcycle. It was part forest and within reach of Benoist's estate in Auffargis. Torches of the circuit members provided landing lights for a Moon Squadron Lysander making a low pass over the adjoining wood. The first drop of a single canister was the *hors d'oeuvre*. The *plat d'entrée* was delivered a week later – six canisters, all recovered. When the canisters were moved to Auffargis and opened, the circuit's headlights shone full beam. Sten guns, pistols, plastic explosives, detonators, incendiary devices. There were also medical supplies as well as chocolate, cigarettes and – rarer than fire opals – tinned peaches. The fruits of the drop were hidden in a covered well on the Benoist estate.

Further drops continued. In one, the Lysander discharged human cargo: a wireless operator by the name of Dowden. It was the Buckmaster seal of approval. The Racing Circuit was under the starting gun. By midsummer, the number of weapons in the Auffargis estate had outgrown the well and colonized a false compartment within the stable block.

The Racing Circuit was accelerating. Just as the needles spanned across the dials, a car on the same team veered across its path and burst into flames. The word PROSPER was just visible on the side of the burning wreck. To make matters worse, the Funkabwehr picked up a repeat transmission signal in Méry-sur-Oise. This led to Dowden, the new radio transmitter, falling 'ill' amid a hail of gunfire. Another wireless operator on the ground in Paris, Agazarian, was lured into a Gestapo trap and taken straight to Avenue Foch. There was only one wireless operator left in occupied Paris. Her codename was MADELEINE.

*

The click was the Gestapo officer's heels. Noor turned.

Always find and follow your breath.

'*Bonsoir,*' she said, as if butter would not melt.

'*Bonsoir, Mademoiselle,*' said the officer, gripping the peak of his cap. 'I am wondering whether I can render you any assistance?'

Noor put her palm to her breast and became a coquette.

'That is most kind, officer. I was trying to listen to some jazz, but my radio antenna is broken. So I thought I would rig something up in the garden.'

'*Typisch* – Typical. May I?'

He extended his hand. Noor took his fleshy palm and stepped down from the chair.

'*Erlaube mir* – Allow me.'

The Gestapo officer placed one, then two leather boots on the chair.

'Would the branch above be satisfactory?'

'The higher the better.'

For the next several minutes, Noor watched as a Gestapo officer trailed the antenna of her SOE transmitter. She had to bite her lip. She was suppressing a querulous nervous laughter that threatened to spill in peels on to the flagstones.

The officer dismounted, bowed, and was gone.

Noor remained in the garden, calming her pulse. She went back inside and asked to borrow the concierge's radio. She spent the next half hour listening to jazz on Radio Paris under the tree. After the programme she retrieved the antenna, returned the radio and ascended the stairs, heart still thumping.

Next morning, as the sun rose over Paris, Noor left the building with her suitcase. By eight it was already strong. She took a bus back to the 8ème. After breakfast in a café near the Église de la Madeleine, she went to the telephone booth at the rear. The reassuring voice of Papillon came on the line. When Noor caught up with Zoë later that day, she recounted the incident with the antenna. It was the first time Zoë's eyes showed fear. She placed her hand on Noor's.

'That could have ended badly.'

'I know.'

The other issue was that she had to transmit to London.

Zoë smiled.

'I know a place you will be undisturbed.'

In the late afternoon, just as the sun's glare was losing its anger, Noor was shown through the door of an apartment of discreet grandeur in the 7ème Arrondissement. The marble in the hallway gave a welcome coolness. The interior was painted in dove greys and duck-egg blues. The walls of the ground floor opened into various pastoral dreamscapes by Watteau. The paintings on the stairs leading up to the first floor showed women with lower necklines and a sporadic glimpse of calf. The paintings on the first floor made Noor draw breath. Around her, young women were moving from room to room in silk dressing gowns, each with a different coloured peacock on the back. They had one thing in common. They were breathtaking. The atmosphere crackled with anticipation. The painted eyes of the woman wearing only pearls in the far portrait glinted.

Zoë led Noor through a gilt passageway into a room of hellfire red. At a polished Louis XVI table sat a woman who had seen the passing of almost eighty winters. Her dress was of the finest *charmeuse* silk and her cameo brooch of aquamarine and white was discerning. Her pearl-white hair was held in place by mahogany hairslides more polished than the table. Her regal grey eyes were hooded. She had an air of worldly wisdom. Her face retained some of the beauty that had compelled men to duel over her before the Great War.

'I am Mademoiselle Pelletier,' said the woman. 'Welcome to our house.'

Her expression was inscrutable, her tone businesslike.

'Beatrice will prepare a room for you on the top floor. What happens in this house stays in this house. War is a complicated business and this is not my first. The safest place for you in Paris at the moment is in a house for the exclusive use of top-ranking German officers.'

Noor's eyes widened.

'The one door the Gestapo will not enter is the one through which the German High Command file to seek their evening's entertainment.'

Noor discovered that the 'house' was a regular stopping point for escaping agents. And that Mademoiselle Pelletier was a source of significant intelligence for the Juggler Circuit. It was a dangerous game, thought Noor, but the hooded eyes of Mademoiselle Pelletier remained inscrutable.

Noor was taken to one of the bedrooms. The sheets were ivory silk. The drapes were grey damask. The ottoman was sheathed in red velvet. The prints on the walls showed eighteenth-century Parisians at their most eager to proliferate. A silk nightdress was laid out on the bedspread. Noor lay on the bed. Her hair fell over the pillow-silk. The chandelier above was made of blue Murano glass, cutting the light into diamonds. *Was this real?* She closed her eyes and allowed herself an hour's sleep. By early evening, the front door chimes were clamouring. She could hear the intermittent popping of champagne corks on the first floor. A volley of corks followed by flurries of high- and low-pitched laughter. An hour later, bursts of song came and went like guttering candles. Louder laughter was followed by the sound of dancing on parquet led by a jazz trumpet.

As the heels of the German officers spun on the parquet, Noor seized her chance. She took her suitcase and slid through the attic window. She stood on the balcony, enveloped in a Paris night. The scent of jasmine from a neighbouring balcony clung to the air. Across the city, Le Stryge, the gargoyle perched below the south tower of Notre Dame, sensed a pulse. Le Stryge picked up what Kieffer and others dancing in the 7ème failed to sense. Or see. A harpist climbing barefoot up a lead gully leading from the window to the roof. She dragged a suitcase along in her right hand. Any loss of balance and Le Stryge would shield his eyes: she would fall eight storeys on to the boulevard. Le Stryge's shoulders heaved with relief when she found a ledge. From there the harpist coiled a spool of silver around a chimney stack.

Noor crouched with a coded message on her lap. She opened the suitcase and set her transmitter to eight megahertz. She placed her finger over the Morse key. An *allegro* of dots and dashes pricked the Paris air. Another impressionist painting in monochrome unfurled. Once the message was complete, she took a match to the painting. Burnt fragments of the coded message vanished in the wind. Her transmission was picked up by the listeners at Grendon Hall and forwarded post-haste to SOE. From the coding room at Baker Street, it was taken straight to Leo Marks.

Marks sat with his hands in his curls, dissecting the transmission from Agent Madeleine forwarded from Grendon. Marks closed his eyes. The letters from the coded version passed through the prism of the keyword and descended, one letter at a time, into plain text. His heart swelled. Noor's coding was perfect – and she had used both safety checks. He cautioned himself. That was assuming Noor was transmitting freely. He cross-referenced the message with previous Madeleine traffic. The language and the syntax matched. And the message was less than eighteen letters. He thought of Noor in his office, her eyes radiant. He muttered lines from the *Tefilat Haderech* – the prayer to protect the traveller from peril.

A return message was waiting in the event of contact from Madeleine. It came straight from Buckmaster. The return volley made Noor's eyes widen. It was too dangerous, came the transmission, for Madeleine to remain in Paris. She would be withdrawn on the next Lysander. Meanwhile, she should keep out of sight.

Le Stryge was aware of two bright brown eyes staring, indignant, into the Paris night. Noor felt the wind caress her face. She heard a familiar voice.

What is your Sankalpa Bābouli?

To shorten the war.

That night, she lay swathed in a Yokohama silk nightdress. The sound of the jazz trumpet was fading. She heard footsteps in the corridor, some heavy, some light. The door opened to the adjacent room. Noor's ears picked up a noise. It sounded like a belt whipping a cushion. The sound came again, followed by a man's yelp. An expectant pause gave way to a rhythmic thumping. A woman's voice began to escalate like Mozart's Queen of the Night until the aria crested into a scream. The male contribution sounded like something from the orangutan enclosure of Vincennes Zoo.

As Noor lay on the pillow, she thought of the librarian's entreaty to the women agents at Wanborough. *What a piece of work is a man!* The answer, thought Noor with a sleepy nod, was a very strange thing indeed.

*

Buckmaster paced his office. His palm was still scabbed from hearing the news about Prosper. His head was stooped as he walked. To the outside, it looked as if he were still counting the threads of the carpet.

The conundrum was agony. Rake was not yet back in the field. Norman's radio was, by Marks's analysis, almost certainly under German control. Dowden was off air, presumed arrested. Agazarian was off air, presumed arrested. Noor was his only pair of eyes in Paris. He needed her more than any current SOE agent. Yet he had to get her out. Would she abandon her radio?

He continued to pace.

*

The Citroën 7 approached the checkpoint. There were three passengers. The man at the wheel wore a trilby, despite the heat. There was a woman in the passenger seat with chestnut hair, in a floral dress. The woman in the back had a darker complexion and wore a summer hat pinned with a flower.

'*PAPIERS!*' shouted the German guard at the checkpoint.

He looked at the *Cartes d'identité* with one hand while restraining his Alsatian with the other. Apart from the dog, he was alone. His fellow corporal had vanished into Pigalle the night before and failed to report for duty. The guard waved the car on with his free hand. He stood on the road, the Alsatian jumping at its collar, ignorant of the passengers and the cargo. Had the guard searched the woman in the front, he would have found a loaded Liberator pistol. Had he searched the suitcase on the back seat, he would have found a concealed radio transmitter. Had he sent the hatpin belonging to the rear passenger for analysis, he would have discovered it was tipped with a paralysing toxin. Zoë squeezed Georges Morel's thigh as the car picked up speed. The harpist in the rear breathed into the space between her collarbones. The flowers in

412

the hedgerows nodded as the Citroën sped past. The trio began to relax. Morel had packed the boot with wine and some black-market charcuteries. They were looking forward to a weekend at Robert Benoist's estate in Auffargis.

*

Zoë had introduced Noor to a familiar-looking man in the Café des Siciliennes the previous week.

He wore a striped shirt, braces, and a trilby, despite the heat. Under the lines, his face was still striking. When he looked towards Zoë, a bashful smile crossed his lips. There was something Noor saw in his eyes: courage and suffering. Noor's heart stopped. Time somersaulted. She had seen him at her school gates! Then he wore a chauffeur's cap, which he never removed. Yes, Morel had been chauffeur to Falinne's family in Suresnes. Noor almost burst into tears as memories of life in the House of Blessings surged through her heart. She steadied herself. That was another time. Now Morel, he told her, was part of the Racing Circuit. In addition, he fixed up the motorcycles of the communist rail saboteurs and allowed his apartment to be used for Resistance gatherings. His old room in the attic was sometimes used as a safe house. Morel approached the bar, leaving Zoë and Noor at the table. Zoë leaned forward.

'One person whose loyalty you will never have to question. He lost his brother in the last war, and half his scalp.'

Hence the trilby.

Noor looked over at Morel. He was speaking to the *patron*, the suffering under his hat concealed.

*

Robert Benoist greeted his guests with the bonhomie of a *seigneur* easy on his own turf. The grandeur of the main house had faded and the outbuildings rambled at will. Yet the sons and daughters of the house always returned to the jaded manor by the woods with its dusty family portraits, sloping passageways, uneven floors, unpolished trophies and sepia photographs of duck shoots from before 1914. The house worked its scruffy charm on all who came to visit, the fields beyond unfurling behind warped window frames. Behind the main house was a walled garden with a raft of flagstones in the middle that moss and wild flowers threatened to engulf. Above the garden were vines even older than the house, which cooled the garden and made the sunlight dapple.

Benoist invited his guests to the walled garden for a glass of Saumur from a bottle so dusty the label was unreadable. The table was laid for six. It was clear from the way Benoist embraced Morel that they were close. He kissed Zoë with affection and extended his hand to Noor. With middle age, Benoist had turned into even more of a hawk. He was spare, the skin concave under his cheekbones, and his nose was a fleshless beak. His eyes were wide apart and moved with predator-like intuition. Benoist's outer casing disguised a disposition as warm as fresh-lit tinder.

'*Bienvenue, tout le monde!*' he said, popping the bottle of Saumur.

In the dappled light under the vine, they raised a toast. The Saumur was cellar-cold, with a zesty *pétillant*. For lunch, the party was joined by Benoist's parents. The father was, if it were possible, even more hawk-like than the son. The old *seigneur*, immaculate in a pale linen suit, extended a mottled hand to everyone. His handshake had a faint tremor. Next to Père Benoist was Madame Benoist, slight and elegant, wearing a muted floral tea dress and an emerald brooch. A set of pearls covered the skin around her neck. Their manner spoke of an old France. An old order. They treated their guests with a rare and unassuming *noblesse*.

Madame Benoist had prepared a *salade niçoise* with black-market eggs. The creaminess of the eggs, the bitterness of the black olives and the freshness of the lettuce hearts made all the guests smile. Noor sat next to Père Benoist. He spoke with dew-eyed pride about his son being an airman in the last war and his triumph in the 1927 French Grand Prix. Père Benoist patted his heart and jutted his chin towards Robert.

'*Coeur de lion,*' he said. '*Coeur de lion.*'

Noor sensed an unspoken secret around the table. Invisible but unmistakable. All those helping themselves to the *niçoise* were active *Résistants*. Everyone, Mère and Père Benoist included, knew the estate was a Lysander drop zone. Everyone knew a column of weapons was growing in the dry well. Everyone knew the stable block had enough ammunition to arm a regiment. The unspoken secret spun in the vortex of Sauternes served by Robert after *crêpes Suzette*. After lunch, the guests rose. Benoist smiled and promised Noor, with a wink, a surprise before sunset.

In the afternoon, Benoist and Morel disappeared into the garage for their favourite pastime: putting on overalls whose colour had long since disappeared and fixing up a pair of Type 35 Bugattis.

That afternoon, Noor walked in the estate grounds with Zoë. The bonds of trust had forged between two women at war. Zoë confided, though Noor knew, her courier work for the Racing Circuit. She was also part of the Satirist Circuit comprised of a group of *artistes résistants*, but they had lost their radio operator. The head of the circuit, Octave Simon, was – like her – a sculptor. She also helped various factions of communist rail saboteurs.

'*Agenda complet* – full diary,' smiled Noor.

'*Oui, un peu, disons* – just a bit.'

Zoë looked into the sky and narrowed her eyes.

'They say it is better to die on your feet than live on your knees.'

They walked on, arm in arm, and sat together under a beech tree by the banks of the river.

*

The party assembled for drinks in the drawing room before dinner. Père Benoist opened a bottle of pre-war Clicquot. As the champagne was being poured, there was the crunch of tyres on gravel. The visitor was expected. Benoist opened the door to a figure so imposing he blocked out the light.

'I never come empty-handed,' said the visitor, holding an impossible jar of *foie gras* and a tin of caviar. It was Antelme.

That night, Noor lay within the drapes of a Napoleonic four-poster. She had pinned the silver bird to her nightdress and she ran her finger over its small silver body. Noor gave the bird a name: 'Little Pteech-ka'. The bird's ruby eyes glinted in affirmation. Noor could not sleep. The horror of the Prosper Circuit's collapse was running through her mind. She thought of Prosper himself in the soundproofed basement of Avenue Foch. She thought of Norman and Borrel, their hands strapped to a chair. She continued to stroke the bird. She wanted, she admitted, to touch and be touched. Antelme had sat next to her at dinner, composed and reassuring. The summer heat suited him, loosening his belt and unthreading his tie. He sat at dinner with a white handkerchief in a blue suit and a white shirt open at the neck. The Racing Circuit was still intact, he said, as the evening breeze toyed with his hair. As was the Satirist and the Cinema Circuit. And two Prosper agents were still active, he said, with a squeeze of Noor's hand.

She wanted the sure-footed Mauritian stag to be with her now, to stroke his fur and run her fingers along the ridges of his antlers. Her ears were alert to any movement in the corridor. Only silence came. She carried on stroking Little Pteech-ka until a dream beckoned her across Lake Manasa, the floating flowers parting as the boat moved of its own accord across the water.

The following day, though Sunday, felt more businesslike. After breakfast, Benoist took Noor aside and asked her if she could transmit a message for Buckmaster. He would show her, he said, a suitable tree on the estate for her antenna. Noor sent Benoist's message, together with two messages from Antelme. Zoë said that when Noor returned to Paris, the head of the Satirist Circuit had a backlog of urgent messages.

Noor felt like a musician about to embark on a series of demanding concerts. The difference was that one slip of a key could lead to the Gestapo's own brand of music criticism.

That afternoon, Zoë filled a bathroom sink with water. The cracked ceramic seemed as old as the house. She placed a towel around Noor's shoulders.

'Right, Agent Madeleine,' she said, unscrewing a bottle of liquid that might have been dragon's blood. 'We need to do something about your hair.'

The wireless transmitter who returned to Paris had hair of war-faded red.

*

Hugo Bleicher was running the operation. He sucked the remains of *Leberwurst* from his teeth as he stared at a collage of documents. One was a copy of a letter written by Noor to her mother. The original had flown, with a batch of others, back to England on the last returning Lysander. Before the letter left France, it had been copied by Déricourt and passed to Bleicher. The letter made reference, among the usual ardent sentiments, to an address in Suresnes. Bleicher made a note. The House of Blessings.

Déricourt had also managed to obtain a photograph of Noor on an updated *Carte d'identité* that was dropped by incoming Lysander during the last full moon. Bleicher looked at notes taken from the interrogation of Gilbert Norman in 84 Avenue Foch. The interrogation, judging by the notes, had been conducted over a series of days. The notepaper had several dark flecks. The note-taker's shoe, as it happened, had left sticky patches of crimson along the corridor leading away from the interrogation chamber.

Of the radios under German control, one belonged to Macalister, the Canadian agent arrested the day after his drop. That gave Bleicher an idea. The arrest of Macalister and his fellow agent, Pickersgill, was known only to the Germans. As far as SOE agents on the ground were concerned, the pair remained at liberty. And looking – naturally – to unite with agents already in the field.

There were also reports from the Funkabwehr of transmissions from a radio broadcasting at eight megahertz in the 8ème and 17ème Arrondissements. The Funkabwehr could not ascertain if it was one or more operators. The operator(s) showed a high-level of security. The broadcasts were short, carefully worded and from different locations. Their radio traffic was increasing. So was the range of transmission points.

'*Spielzeit*,' said Bleicher out loud. 'Playtime.'

*

Paris was oblivious to the atonal concerts taking place around the city and the monochrome sound-paintings that sprang behind the eyelids of the performer. Paris was oblivious to the blisters on the heels of the musician as she moved, instrument in hand, from one urgent venue to another. Paris was oblivious to the baker's vans screeching round corners only to find an empty stage.

Every surviving circuit in Paris had a sheaf of urgent messages. There was already rumour of an allied invasion and Resistance networks were bellowing for arms and equipment. Noor moved through Paris like a reluctant diva with a clamour of hidden followers, her eye always alert to the concert acoustics – a place to wind her silver strings. Her concerts played around the Arrondissements and in the outlying districts of Montrouge and Levallois. The music varied from the familiar tones of drop-zone locations to new compositions on sabotage targets – including tank gearboxes and submarine parts – and *Cartes d'identités* needed for a group of downed airmen hiding out in the 5ème. And each time the musician attended a new concert, she had to lug an instrument as heavy as her Salzedo harp.

As for her sleeping arrangements, Noor awoke under a different ceiling every morning. Some high and airy, some low and smoke-stained, some classical, some art deco, some corniced, some plain. Each morning there was a different cup for the black-market coffee. Each morning there was a different mouth wishing her luck and a different hand waving her goodbye. Each morning the hand waving goodbye, once Noor was out of sight, would make the sign of the cross. One of those was a woman with sausage-like fingers, whose name was Renée. She waved but never made the Trinity.

Amid a packed concert schedule, there was a day of respite. Noor went to the wedding of Henri Garry and Marguerite. It took place in the church of Saint-Séverin where Noor used to rehearse as a student. To a passer-by, there was nothing unusual about the short, dignified service. There was nothing unusual about the beaming groom and the radiant bride. There was nothing unusual about the rice showered on the newly-weds as they ran down the steps of the church. The passer-by would not have known that all present were inner-circle *Résistants* drawn from a cross-section of Paris networks. The woman who caught the bride's bouquet was a wireless operator so active across Paris the Funkabwehr thought she was one of several. Baby peonies scented the air around Noor's face.

'*La prochaine!*' shouted a member of the Juggler Circuit.

Antelme was out of Paris that day. She imagined them both running through a shower of rice. A shy smile flitted across her lips.

The honeymoon was short. Next day, one of the well-wishers fell 'ill'. A racing driver and winner of the Monaco Grand Prix. WW. With his arrest, the front wheel had come off the Racing Circuit. Grover-Williams was a guest at 84 Avenue Foch. His host, Sturmbannführer Kieffer, welcomed him in person.

'So good of you to come and see me, Mr Grover-Williams. Or should I use your codename, SEBASTIEN?'

He had the same eyes as Prosper, thought Kieffer. Such misplaced decency. Pools of decency that reflected in the dark pools around the interrogation chair. And yet nothing Malik and Bled could do, even with their spanners out, loosened WW's cylinders.

Other pieces of masonry fell. A careless conversation by an estate worker on the Auffargis estate led the Gestapo to the rambling Benoist manor. Père Benoist stood at gunpoint on the steps as the Gestapo ransacked his estate. After fifteen minutes, there were shouts from the area of the well. When the first Sten guns were brought up, the Gestapo major struck Père Benoist with the butt of his pistol. Mère Benoist ran to her husband. She was struck by the open palm of Stabsscharführer Vogt. The front of a septuagenarian's white linen dress took on the colour of the roses that crowned the front door. Père Benoist was taken to 84 Avenue

Foch. After two days' interrogation he was transferred, his right eye the colour of aubergine and his left wrist hanging limp, to join Mère Benoist in Fresnes Prison.

Word reached Robert through Zoë. By the time Zoë had imparted the news, Benoist looked like a hawk downed by shot, flapping on the ground in agony. The thought of his parents, bones broken, in the dank cells of Fresnes made him burn with fury and despair. He called on a man he trusted more than his brother.

Georges Morel knew about pain, but the look in Benoist's eyes when he rang the concierge bell in Rue de la Harpe made Morel's heart crack like an engine block. He reached for the bottle of Armagnac he opened once a year on the summer solstice. He poured Benoist a large measure. Benoist chased away the liquid and slammed down the glass. Morel poured out repeat measures until his friend stopped shaking. Morel put his hand on his old friend's shoulder.

'You need to lie low for a few days.'

They decided Benoist would go to a safe house used by the Satirist Circuit. It was a basement room in the 10ème. There, Benoist stayed out of sight for two nights, unable to sleep or eat, while the Gestapo hunted a high-value bird of prey. By the third day, Benoist could stand it no longer. He left the basement to telephone the family lawyer. He walked, head low, along the Boulevard. Car brakes screeched. Footsteps clattered. A hand came down on his left shoulder. A barrel was pressed into his right flank, just below the kidney. Two men in plain clothes bundled him on to the back seat of a Mercedes 770. He sat, flanked. As the car sped off, Benoist was aware that pistols were trained on both his kidneys.

*

Noor lay on a camp bed in a second-floor apartment on Rue de la Faisanderie. She was within half a mile of Avenue Foch. She had made the journey to the waveless depths of her mind, yet on surfacing she could not sleep. Her ankle was blistered. Her hair felt stiff and dry. She had changed the colour twice since Zoë's intervention. She moved apartment so often that sometimes she awoke unable to recall which boulevard she was in, let alone which arrondissement. The circle that sought out her concert ability continued to expand. An agent working for De Gaulle's London government-in-exile was also asking for performances from the rooftops of Paris. Not only was she transmitting concerts to Baker Street, she was also playing for De Gaulle's audience in Duke Street. After lunch one day with Octave Simon, head of the Satirist Circuit, she had a feeling she was being followed. And every time she took to the airwaves, she could sense the Funkabwehr direction finders tracking her signal.

She stroked the silver body of Little Pteech-ka and thought of the House of Blessings. Of Inayat sitting in his study, writing. Of Amina trailing roses through the trellis in the garden. Of her brothers climbing in the trees. She imagined her harp, sitting in the corner of her bedroom. She imagined wooden Pteech-ka still lying on her bed. It was a risk, she knew. But the house in Suresnes sang like a mermaid, the colours of her childhood blurring into a Matisse.

*

Morel slid the box out from under his bed. His brother's birthday had not long passed and the Luger was freshly oiled. He turned his attention to the bullets. He polished each one in turn and loaded them into the magazine. He palmed the magazine into the Luger's grip. The bullets gave the gun its familiar weight.

It was loaded.

*

A woman with blistered heels and a heavy suitcase was walking along the Rue des Fleurs in Suresnes. The hair visible under her scarf, dyed three different colours in as many weeks, looked as frayed as its owner. When the sun's glare became too much, she shuttered her eyes with the sunglasses perched on her scarf. Sewn into the hem of her dress was a pair of type-348 radio crystals. Concealed between two halves of a button held together by magnetic force was a capsule marked 'KCN'. Atkins' words were now a comfort.

421

It will take about twelve seconds.

Noor was walking with her head down, eyes on the boulevard. She was aware of a rattling sound. Then the screech of bicycle brakes. Her veins pulsed with fear. She looked round.

'Noor!'

The word came from a woman rider. She looked the archetypal *femme française* in striped top and culottes. She was older than Noor, but her still gamine frame and face of amiable defiance gave the impression of someone younger. Her hair was cut in a short bob at odds with the threads of grey.

She was older, but it was her. Mademoiselle Monette. Her old music teacher.

Noor remembered the teacher who once wore her boyfriend's trousers rolled at the ankle and smoked Gauloises. She was not someone Noor imagined would have been high on a list of collaborators.

Henri Garry's words echoed in her mind. '*Restes en garde.*'

'*Que fais-tu ici?* – What are you doing here?' said Mademoiselle Monette.

There was surprise and delight in her voice. Noor smiled. She said nothing.

Mademoiselle Monette had been one of the most intuitive sight-readers at her *conservatoire*. She traced the notes in her former student. Dyed hair. Worn shoes. Heavy suitcase. Haunted eyes. This was no vacation. Another musician might have been slower to pick out the tune, but not Mademoiselle Monette. Her tone changed.

'If your commitments allow, perhaps we could meet for tisane later today? I would be pleased to do anything to help one of my best students. Anything at all.'

Her eyes glinted.

'Thank you,' said Noor. 'That would mean much.'

Noor could feel a dam of tears pressing behind her eyes. After arranging a rendezvous, she carried on down the Rue des Fleurs, suitcase in hand.

At a café on the Rue Diderot, two women sat drinking tisane. Both had thought twice about meeting. A heavy suitcase rested on the *fin de siècle* tiles. Apart from an elderly man an expanse of tiles away, they were alone. The older woman lit a Gauloises. She blew a smoke ring and leaned forward on her elbows. Her musician's intuition spoke.

'If they catch you, the consequences are unthinkable.'

Noor affirmed the statement with a blink.

'Where are you staying?'

Noor said nothing.

'If you don't have anywhere planned, you could stay with me.'

The roulette wheel spun in Noor's mind. To trust or not to trust? She chose blood red.

'It's too dangerous, M'mselle.'

The woman opposite placed her hand over Noor's.

'Henriette, please.'

'Henriette.'

'At least let me cook you something and run you a bath.'

The hunted look returned to Noor's eyes.

'If it helps, you can cut my telephone line before I cook,' smiled Henriette.

She exhaled a lungful of Gauloises. She turned her head just as Noor remembered.

Half an hour later, Noor lay in a rose-scented bath. A candle flickered on the windowsill. Her dress lay on a chair, the radio crystals and cyanide capsule in repose. She could smell the oregano that her former teacher was whisking into an omelette. She could feel the tension in her shoulders begin to evaporate with the steam. The pleasure of warm water lapping around the body...

'My family are active as well,' said Henriette over omelette from the best black-market eggs.

She took a sheet of music. In pencil, she drew a vertical line on the five-line stave. She made a short horizontal line on the middle line and a shorter one on the line above. It was the Cross of Anjou, the symbol of the Resistance. She rubbed out the cross and looked straight at Noor.

'My brother is an artist who shares a studio with a sculptor called Octave. It is not just chisels they keep under the floorboards.'

'Does Octave's surname begin with an *S*?'

'Yes,' said Henriette. 'One of the disciples.'

Octave Simon – head of the Satirist Circuit.

Noor's breath became easier.

'Will you stay tonight?'

'No, Henriette. It's too dangerous.'

'Where will you go?'

'Back into town. I just wanted to see a certain old house.'

'What about a bedroom facing a certain old house?'

Noor's eyes widened.

'Madame Prénat still lives in the house next door. Do you remember? It used to belong to your friend Falinne's family.'

*

From the roof of Madame Prénat's house, Noor could see the outline of the House of Blessings. The house was asleep. The garden was in darkness. She closed her eyes. She saw, under the cherry tree, a daughter with her arms around her father.

'I don't want you to die, Papa.'

'Every mortal will taste death, Bābouli. But only some will taste life.'

Her only companion in the darkness was a suitcase.

'Do not feel lonely. The entire Universe is inside you.'

Across Paris, Le Stryge detected a pulse in Suresnes. It was almost imperceptible. A teardrop on a roof tile. Noor sent a short *allegro* to London. Baker Street transmitted back by return. She was ordered to make urgent contact with Antelme. She was also required to meet two Canadian agents on Friday. The RV point would follow. Across Paris, there was another pulse. A radio pulse. The signal of a Mark II radio had crossed the screen of a Funkabwehr direction finder. It came from Suresnes. A baker's van stopped and changed direction.

That night, Noor lay in Falinne's old bed. Urgent contact with Antelme? *Was he all right?* Which Canadian agents? Was it wise to be so close to the House of Blessings? She reached down to feel her suitcase under Falinne's bed. Where were her radio crystals? Where was her cyanide? She lay on one side, then the other.

Le Stryge sensed a movement. A baker's van was moving through the 16ème Arrondissement. It was heading north-west. It had just turned on to the avenue Ingres. Ten minutes later it would be in Suresnes. Noor opened her eyes. Words from her Beaulieu training echoed. *If in doubt, get out.*

She moved around Falinne's room like a cat. If there was one thing being a wireless operator in occupied Paris had taught her – it was to pack fast. She tiptoed down the stairs, her arm straining to keep the suitcase level. As she reached the bottom stair, the baker's van was moving along Rue des Puits. A Paris night swallowed a harpist-with-suitcase. As she walked down Rue Carnot, a baker's van was moving the opposite way, one street parallel. Noor took a right, a left and another left. She knocked on a front door. There was a rustle inside. A voice came from within.

'*Qui est là?*'

'Henriette. It's me.'

*

The following day, Noor rang Papillon. Antelme was not ill, she said, but he was seeing Lizzie at the weekend.

'Lizzie' was SOE-speak for a Lysander.

Antelme was returning to London.

'He asked me to arrange a meeting for you both.'

The words 'you both' trickled like nectar.

Noor rang back after lunch. Antelme would pass by Suresnes the following day. Noor broke a rule. She stayed an extra night with Henriette. She paced around Henriette's drawing room while Henriette sat in a blue cloud of Gauloises.

'You told me once of your gift,' said Henriette. 'Does it still work?'

Noor nodded. Henriette sat at her upright piano, the cigarette suspended on her lower lip.

'When it comes to music – and music alone – the enemy have us beaten.'

Schumann's *Träumerei* infused the room. The colour behind Noor's eyelids went the gold of a Van Gough cornfield under sapphire.

*

Standing by railings surrounding the Suresnes Parc du Château stood a man and a woman. Both had eyes of dark umber. The man was broad-shouldered and *sportif*, with abundant dark hair. The woman had darker skin, her hair covered by a scarf. Her features were fine, her slimness exaggerated next to the man. At her feet was a battered leather suitcase. Together they could see the House of Blessings. Wehrmacht officers were reclining in the garden. One officer sat on the spot of the old cherry tree. The woman's hands loosened and tightened.

'I am being extracted at the weekend,' said Antelme. 'Buckmaster wants a personal debrief on the fall of the Prosper Circuit and the Racing Circuit going off the road. I will come back.'

He handed Noor a large roll of francs.

'Unforeseen expenses.'

Antelme smiled.

'There's something else. Baker Street want to pull you out too. Not because you aren't a one-woman Morse orchestra. Two months is a long time in the life of a wireless operator. You have survived longer than any other. No cat has more than nine lives.'

Noor looked towards the House of Blessings. For a moment, she saw a family in the garden. A Mauritian sugar planter sitting on a picnic rug next to a harpist-writer surrounded by laughing children.

'Noor?'

Her eyes blinked back to the present.

'There is a meeting tomorrow at Rue Erlanger with Phono. I have to go to the Citroën factory. No doubt Phono will have a logjam of messages.'

Phono was Henri Garry.

'In a week you will be back in London.'

Noor nodded.

'I know you can look after yourself. Just be careful with your ninth life.'

The dam behind Noor's eyes felt like it was going to burst.

'I will be fine, Joseph,' she said.

Antelme walked towards the station. After twenty paces he turned and waved.

Rue Erlanger was the first address Noor had stayed as an agent. It felt like a lifetime ago. Henri Garry and Marguerite were spending their honeymoon directing Lysander drops for the Phono Circuit. Another artist from the Satirist Circuit was present, along with Zoë. There were two railway saboteurs on the hunt for explosives. Noor was aware of Henri Garry's sister, Renée, moving in the kitchen. They decided that, after making a broadcast from a neighbour's roof, Noor would stay another night *chez* Garry.

Zoë was already thinking about Noor's safe house for the following night. She placed an object in the hand of the gruffer-looking rail saboteur and said something close to his ear. He nodded. The collection of people around Henri and Marguerite's dinner table that evening included members of the Phono, Satirist and Prosper networks. Renée paid more attention to Noor than she had before.

'Joseph seems fond of you,' she said at dinner.

Noor looked away.

'Such an attractive man.'

As she drew on her cigarette, Noor noticed her sausage-like fingers.

'Still, one can't always have everything one wants.'

*

One hundred thousand francs was the going rate for a high-value agent.

The roll was squeezed in a hand with sausage-like fingers as a pair of squat calves hurried away from 84 Avenue Foch.

*

The following day, the engine of a Sunbeam motorbike echoed in Rue de la Harpe. Morel knew the engine note. It belonged to one of the rail saboteurs. He walked into the street, his trilby shielding his eyes from the sun. The saboteur dismounted. He was a bear of a man, who wore his belt like a pirate. The saboteur asked how long it would take to check the brakes and tune the engine.

'A day or two,' said Morel.

'*Ça marche.*'

The saboteur extended a calloused hand. An object that felt like a thick stamp passed from palm to palm. In the cool of the apartment, Morel opened his hand. It was a double-folded note. The handwriting was Zoë's.

'Arriving this afternoon + 1. Prepare the attic.'

The letters B. E. were underlined at the bottom. Morel took a match to the note.

B.E. was her usual signature. '*Brûler ensuite* – Burn afterwards.'

Two women were walking down the Rue de la Harpe. One wore blue overalls and carried a duffel bag. The other wore a dress with two capsules concealed in the hem and carried a scuffed leather suitcase. Noor remembered Rue de la Harpe from Sorbonne days. Zoë rang the concierge's bell at the apartment halfway along the street. Morel opened the door. He smiled under his trilby.

'If you would like, I c-can help you with your suitcase.'

The question was phrased to give Noor the choice.

'That would be so kind,' smiled Noor.

Morel noticed that Noor had gone from slim to thin. There were dark circles under her eyes and her hair looked stiff and unnatural. They entered Morel's apartment. A Sunbeam motorcycle was mid-surgery in the vestibule, a helmet suspended from the handlebars. The building was deserted over the summer and no one seemed to mind.

Inside his apartment, Georges put on his last grains of black-market coffee and made a tisane for Noor. Noor looked around Morel's room while Zoë went to the top of the building.

On the mantelpiece was a photograph of two young men, both under twenty, against a craggy backdrop. The young Morel was easy to recognize, smiling into the camera under a tumult of black hair. The young man with his arm around his shoulder looked similar, perhaps a few years younger. Next to the photograph was a dented hip flask. There was an empty birdcage in the corner.

'I have prepared my old apartment on the top floor,' said Morel.

He looked at her suitcase.

'There is access to the r-roof if you need it.'

Noor gave a shy nod.

'And if any non-resident comes to the building, they will have to g-get past me first.'

After Noor put down her tisane, Morel took her suitcase and the two made their way up the stairs. It was cool in the building, but Noor's legs felt like lead. Without Morel, she was not sure she could have managed her suitcase. The strain of a life in the shadows was coming into the open – especially at the prospect of a Lysander back to London.

The attic room was bare but clean. The plaster on the wall remained the colour of a bruised peach smudged by an impressionist's thumb. Zoë had carried out a security check and put fresh flowers in a glass beside Morel's old iron bed. Noor lay on the bed before making her transmission.

The evenings were becoming cooler. As the sun set behind the buildings opposite, Noor climbed through the window on to the roof. Her suitcase felt like two Salzedo harps. She coiled the antenna around the nearest chimney and placed her finger above the Morse key. She surveyed Paris in the sunset and let out a breath. As she moved her eyes across the skyline they became level, for an unconscious moment, with the stone eyes of Le Stryge.

Le Stryge whispered the words of Napoleon. *Secrets travel fast in Paris.*

Noor returned to Morel's old room and placed her suitcase under the bed. There were no other hiding places.

*

Sunset gave into evening. One of the restaurants dispatched a tureen of *bouillabaisse* to a family in the Rue de la Harpe. Chunks of white cod simmered in the rich red soup as it was ferried along the street.

Morel was washing axle grease from his hands when there was a double thump at the door. The double thump became a series of single thumps. Something was wrong. Morel unlocked a box under his bed and removed a leather bag. He entered the vestibule. He took a seat behind the concierge's desk. He pressed a buzzer that opened the front door.

It was a sight of anticipated dread. Framed in the doorway was a bulky Gestapo officer, the black of his uniform blotting out the light. His face was young and formless, his eyes vacant blue. His hair under his cap was the colour of boiled corn. The Gestapo normally moved in pairs, but this officer was not prepared to wait. Morel could feel his heart beating outside his shirt. The officer thrust a photograph in Morel's face. It was Noor.

'*Wer ist das* – Who is this?' said Hauptsturmführer Oberhauser.

'I c-cannot help you,' said Morel.

'Really.'

Morel took a breath.

'I c-cannot help you. *Aucune idée* – no idea.'

'Our information from a reliable source suggests the woman in the photograph is a British spy hiding in an attic in this street. The penalty for shielding enemy agents is execution.'

'I realize. But I c-cannot help you.'

'We can do this the easy way or the hard way,' said the officer. 'Either you open the apartments on the top floor or you and anyone in the building will be taken for interrogation at 84 Avenue Foch.'

'*Un instant*,' said Morel. 'I will g-get the key.'

'Jetzt! – Now!'

In less than '*un instant*', the days of the life of Georges Morel telescoped into a single gesture. From a leather bag he pulled an antique Luger, polished and oiled on Fabien's birthday every year since 1915. Hauptsturmführer Oberhauser laughed.

'*Was ist das Relikt?* – What is this relic?'

Morel too laughed. There was a *crack*. Thirty years of pain propelled the bullet. A third eye opened under the Hauptsturmführer's cap. His body fell like a puppet, strings cut. Behind him, it appeared as if the waiter had thrown the *bouilla-baisse* against the wall. Morel crossed himself. He closed his eyes. Behind one eye was Fabien. Behind the other was Benoist.

There was a commotion in the street. Morel walked outside and calmed his neighbours. It was a bang from the exhaust of a motorcycle he was fixing indoors. Morel returned to the building. He had three priorities.

Noor.

The body.

The need to vanish.

CHAPTER 35
'THE REQUEST'

Occupied Paris, 1943

Noor
Morel

The attic room was empty. The scarf and sunglasses were gone. The suitcase under the bed was gone. Even the flowers on the bedside table were gone. As to Noor, there was no trace. Morel opened the window and climbed on to the rooftop. He saw only chimney stacks and a prowling cat. He cupped his hands around his mouth and shouted in a hoarse whisper.

'Madeleine! Madeleine!'

Nothing. He looked at his watch.

'If you can hear me, be ready to leave at 20:30. *Je reviendrai!* – I will come back!'

There was another cat on the roof, crouching behind a chimney stack. A cat down to her ninth life. The tone of Morel's voice suggested he was acting freely. There was something else. Morel noticed it too as he raced down the stairs. *No stutter.*

For the next fifteen minutes, every screw holding Georges Morel's head together oscillated with the sheer focus of his mind. First the corpse. Morel was no stranger to the union of flying lead and the human skull. He wrapped the head and torso in a dustsheet and dragged the body into an open area at the rear where the dustbins congregated. He tore up some cardboard boxes and laid them over the body. He removed his hat. His whisper was almost inaudible.

'*Que nous vivions ou mourions, nous allons au Seigneur.*'

'Whether we live or die, we go to the Lord.'

From his cleaning cupboard on the ground floor, Morel took a bucket and mop. Morel had always been a diligent concierge. Although time was short, he did a workman-like job of removing traces of the evening's *bouillabaisse*. Next, he took a screwdriver and fastened the engine casing back on the Sunbeam. He entered his apartment. Into a suitcase he threw a bundle of clothes, the photograph of himself and Fabien and the dented hip flask. From a small safe in the wall, he took the Morel savings and stuffed them into his wallet. He retrieved the Luger, clicked the safety, and tucked the gun into his belt. He put down his suitcase and ran back up the stairs.

'Madeleine,' he called across the roof tiles. 'We have to go! There is no time!'

From Morel's position on the balcony, he saw a head emerge from behind the chimney stack. A cat with one life. He climbed over and grabbed her suitcase.

'*Allons-y vite!*'

From his expression, Noor knew she had been right about the gunshot.

Back on the ground floor, Morel fastened his suitcase and Noor's to the back of the Sunbeam. There was something different about the way Morel moved, thought Noor – about Morel. A burden lifted. A Tin Man with a new heart.

'Here,' he said, passing her the helmet. 'Put this on.'

There was only one helmet. Noor looked up.

'Don't worry,' smiled Morel. 'I have my own.'

With a brush of his hand, Morel removed his hat. He stood, hatless in the half-light. The tin made a mute reflection. To Noor he looked, if anything, more handsome. The words of Rumi came into her mind. *A wound is where the light enters.*

Morel looked around the vestibule. He would not be returning. High on the south tower of Notre Dame, Le Stryge heard
thunder. It was the sound of a Sunbeam's engine revving from
inside a building in the 5ème. Le Stryge's stone ears followed the
sound. A motorbike burst like lightning out of an apartment on
the Rue de la Harpe.

*

Morel headed south past the Sorbonne, past the place du Panthéon
and right on to Rue Descartes. On Rue Descartes he crossed Rue
Thouin, passing the Café des Siciliennes on the corner. At Rue
Orlotan, Morel turned left a sharp left, right and left again. Noor
had one hand on Morel's hip, the other behind, keeping the suitcases from taking their own journey. As they burned through Place
Montague, Noor put her mouth to Morel's ear.

'Where are we going?'

'Emergency safe house,' said Morel.

Morel took a right, another right and a left on to Rue
Daubenton. The Sunbeam skidded to a stop. An imposing building loomed in darkness. The entrance had a distinctive archway,
surrounded by geometric stars that radiated into the Infinite.
Above the archway, a crescent moon held a star in suspension.
To the right of the entrance was a tower. From the summit of the
tower, a minaret speared the sky. The Grand Mosque of Paris.
Morel pulled the bell. There was a shuffling inside. A white-
bearded caretaker opened the door.

'The charity you give shall be your shade on the day of judgement,' said Morel.

'Give charity without delay for it stands in the way of calamity,'
said the caretaker.

He bowed. The intricate pattern of his prayer cap shimmered.

'*Entrez-vous,*' he said.

Noor took the headscarf from her suitcase. Noor and Morel
removed their shoes. They walked through a geometric cosmos of
zellij wall tiles into an internal courtyard where a fountain skittered

in the centre. From the courtyard they entered the enormous, empty prayer room. A vast dome opened above, inlaid with an infinite master-pattern of sacred geometry. The night sky leached through a rotunda of widows under the dome. Noor stood looking up into the Infinite as Morel and the caretaker spoke. As she looked down, her eye fell on a stone inscription from the Quran.

إن االله لا يثقل النفس بعد أن تتحملها .
'Allah does not burden a soul beyond that it can bear.'

The caretaker turned to Noor.

'Monsieur Morel has explained your predicament. Let the house of Allah give you shelter.'

Noor placed her hands over her heart.

The caretaker was no stranger to visitors. The war brought an unlikely variety at an unlikely hour. The rector of the mosque reminded the caretaker that the All Knowing moved in mysterious ways.

'He does not give you what you want when you want it. He gives you what He knows you need at the right time… And He has made you Gatekeeper for a reason.'

The caretaker slept on a mat by the door. For him, every visitor, day or night, arrived at the right time. Whoever they were, it was Allah's will. *Résistants.* Escaping agents. Downed airmen. Lost paratroopers. And those even more needful of Allah's protection.

As far as the young woman with the suitcase was concerned, he bowed and said she was welcome to stay as long as she needed.

The time came for Morel to leave. Under the infinite geometry of the dome, Noor and Morel embraced. The last she saw of Morel was a flash of metal as he stepped into a Paris night.

*

Morel walked around the corner into Rue de Mirbel. He made a telephone call to the head of the group of rail saboteurs in Clichy-sous-Bois. His words were carefully chosen. He had put an old

435

mattress out behind his apartment in the 5ème. It was essential the mattress was taken away before dawn. It would need cleaning before disposal. As to the whereabouts of a certain Sunbeam motorcycle – it would be parked outside the Gare Montparnasse with the ignition key under the front wheel. After hanging up, Morel reflected. *No stutter.* The Sunbeam sped north towards the station. The next day, Georges Morel would be back in Saint-Malo.

*

The police report on the body found on the railway tracks outside Paris was curt.

- Male, late twenties.
- Body damaged beyond recognition.
- Remnants of worn rail-worker's overalls found at the scene.
- Male suspected of jumping from the bridge at Charonne-Voyageurs then hit by a freight train.
- Suspected cause of death: suicide.
- Status of investigation: inactive.

As the report was being typed, the flames in a brazier a mile away were turning the last piece of Gestapo uniform into ash.

*

'*Excusez-moi*,' said Noor to the caretaker. 'I am going to need access to the highest roof.'

He looked at Noor, hand glued to her suitcase. The ways of the Form Giver were indeed mysterious.

'*Suivez-moi* – follow me.'

The caretaker picked up a lantern and together they walked through the courtyard with the fountain. In one corner was a carved wooden door. He took out a metal hoop with keys suspended. He took one of the larger keys and unfastened the lock. He took Noor's suitcase and led the way up the stairs. Each staircase was nine steps for the nine tenets of Islam. On the top step there was a platform and another staircase at forty-five degrees. The ascent continued, staircase by staircase. They were moving up the mosque's tower. They reached the zenith where the minaret began. The caretaker put Noor's suitcase down on the spot where the muezzin made the call to prayer.

'How long do you need?'

'Fifteen minutes.'

Noor sat under the tower's battlements and opened her suitcase. She coded a message and switched on her transmitter. The call to prayer that night was an incantation of dots and dashes. Stars came out where the dots pricked the sky.

Baker Street responded. The time and place of Agent Madeleine's R/V with the two Canadian agents was confirmed. One was the replacement wireless operator. Madeleine would be extracted in forty-eight hours by Lysander.

-... .. -.. - .-. .- -.-. .- .-. . ..-. ..- .-..

BE EXTRA CAREFUL

Noor switched off her transmitter. She heard footsteps. Shadows flitted across the wall. She froze. The footsteps reached the top. It was the caretaker with his lantern.

'Are you all right?' he said. 'You're shaking.'

'I'm fine,' said Noor.

He led Noor down the tower.

'I have prepared you dinner,' he said. 'And you can meet the others.'

The others?

The caretaker smiled. 'The Creator's house is open to all in peril.'

He took her first to the ablutions room for washing.

'*Suivez-moi*,' he said. He took Noor along the edge of the prayer hall and opened another wooden door at the end.

He took Noor's suitcase and, lantern swinging, led her into a basement chamber. All her trust, she realized, was in the hands of a stranger with a white beard. Noor inhaled as they reached the far end of the chamber. The caretaker took out another, smaller key.

'Stay close,' he said.

Behind the door was a low passageway formed of rock. For a moment, Noor wanted to turn around and run.

Always find and follow your breath.

She could hear the muted sound of voices. The passageway opened into an underground cavern. The cavern was the hub from which a fan of passageways radiated. Set out in the middle of the cavern was a scarlet rug. At the edge of the rug were ceramic *tagines*, each on a gas ring. A mound of *khobz* bread stood on a plate. A silver Arabian teapot flickered in the light of lanterns that marked the corners of the cavern.

The unusual setting was matched by an unusual circle. Seated cross-legged on the floor was what Noor thought must be a Jewish family. The father was gaunt, tieless with his shirt buttoned to the top. The mother had hollow eyes and black hair that was brushed on one side and tangled on the other. An infant slept beside her in a blanket. The infant's grandmother and aunt had been at home, she discovered, when the Gestapo knocked, and were taken away in only the clothes they wore. A message went out to the parents to go into immediate hiding. Next to the Jewish couple sat Minerva, an American author and friend of Miss Beach from the Shakespeare and Company bookshop. A monograph Minerva had written about the Occupation had put her on a Gestapo blacklist. Next to the woman sat a man with hair that, in the lantern light, looked the colour of burnt gold. He wore a civilian suit with a grimy silk scarf round his neck. The way he sat, as if at tea with his grandest relatives, made Noor sense he was English. Something about him looked familiar. He sat in profile. Once or twice he turned face-on. Noor could make out his right ear was missing. The skin between his missing ear and his cheek looked like it had been pressed with a red-hot coal. He was in evident pain, but he stood for Noor.

'Percy de Vere,' he said. 'Bomber Command.'

He extended a hand.

'Rather blown off course.'

*

A woman carrying a suitcase entered the Café Le Colisée on the Champs-Elysées. She was wearing a cloche hat with a hatpin. She walked through the café to the cloakroom at the rear. She and the attendant exchanged passwords. The woman with the suitcase and a silver bird on her lapel asked if two men had arrived with the codenames Bertrand and Valentin. The attendant jutted her chin at two men sitting at a corner table. Between the two men was an empty chair. Noor walked over and asked if the chair was free. One of the men half-stood.

'Please,' he said.

Noor had met various contacts in Paris who she knew by code-name alone. The two unremarkable-looking men in their early thirties did not arouse any particular suspicion. Bertrand did most of the talking. His French was hard to place. He was the replacement radio operator. He seemed less keen to talk megahertz than setting up a new circuit in Normandy. Bertrand was also interested in acquiring her safe-house address before she returned to England. The meeting ended with Noor giving Bertrand details of transmission spots around Paris and the telephone number of Henri Garry of the Cinema Circuit. Like all meetings, she kept it brief. She warned the men to be extra vigilant. The Gestapo continued to make arrests by the day.

Noor left the café, suitcase in hand. Soon, she thought, she would be free of her suitcase. *Hide or bury?* She thought of waking up in the same bed without the blanket of fear. She thought of evenings without skittering over roof tiles with her transmitter. She thought of Buckmaster and Marks at 64 Baker Street. She could almost see the expression in Antelme's eyes as he saw her and broke into a run... A strange, almost manic euphoria started to imbue her spirit as she walked. Her heavy suitcase felt, for a moment, light as a violin.

On Noor leaving the table, Bertrand and Valentin made notes of the meeting and recorded a detailed picture of Noor's appearance and coat. As she left the café, a man with his face behind a copy of *Le Monde* folded his newspaper. Another man on the opposite side of the Champs-Elysées put on a pair of sunglasses. Both were converging on the same target.

The real wireless operator, Macalister, was nowhere near Paris. Noor had been speaking to two men, bilingual in French and English, in the pay of the Gestapo. Bleicher, running the operation, decided against an arrest at the café. That would be too obvious. In any event, the Gestapo wanted to see where London's elusive harpist was going on a warm Parisian October day.

Noor walked. To her eyes, splashes of colour in the drained Renoir were returning. The burgundy of a woman's beret. The purple of a bougainvillea entwined around the entrance of a florist. The pink of a ribbon around a box of *pâtisseries*. The weather was still balmy. She felt as if she were back at the Sorbonne, carrying a Salzedo harp instead of a Mark II transmitter. Soon she would be enveloped in the mauve vibration of the Lysander's propellers.

She cut through Rue Marbeuf. On the wall of a kiosk, she saw a reward for 200,000 francs for information in connection with the disappearance of a Gestapo officer last seen in the 5ème Arrondissement. Her heart quickened. As she walked, she felt a presence. The ruby eyes of Little Pteech-ka glowed warning-red. A man carrying a copy of *Le Monde* was matching her pace. Another man in sunglasses was visible in the reflections in the shop windows. Was it her imagination? She recalled the last transmission from Baker Street. *Be extra careful.*

The brachial nerve in her right arm twitched. If necessary, she would use the hatpin tipped with a fast-acting toxin. But in broad daylight it was a risk.

Noor spotted three mannequins in a shop window. Each wore a winter dress. One held a handbag. Noor entered the shop with her suitcase. Two men together would look out of place in a women's boutique. She took a coat from the rail. She looked over her shoulder as she was led to the changing room. One of the men was visible between the mannequins. He glanced at the door and back at the shop window with the look of a man weighing up whether he should enter.

Noor entered the changing room. She heard footsteps on the shop floor. Then muffled voices. A man questioning a woman. Panic rose in Little Pteech-ka's eyes. The conversation stopped. Footsteps approached the changing room. There were six cubicles. One had its curtain drawn. The man carrying the newspaper muttered a few words before ripping it open.

The cubicle was empty. In an alley behind the shop, accessible via a basement lavatory, a woman with a scuffed leather suitcase was moving with the stealth of a cat with no remaining lives.

Noor walked west. Papillon had arranged the safe house on Rue de la Faisanderie for Noor's last night. The safe house felt the same as it had done when she stayed there weeks before. The only difference was the pistol Papillon had placed under the mattress. *Juste en cas.* She decided to stay put for the rest of the day. *Be extra careful.* As evening fell over Paris, Noor took her suitcase up the steps of the apartment to the door at the very top that gave access to the roof. The moon was already shining as the stars began to open. An ideal guide for the Moon Squadron pilots, thought Noor, as she opened her transmitter. She placed her finger over the Morse key and tapped out a coded message. She had made contact with the two Canadian agents. Baker Street responded. Congratulations were due to Agent Madeleine on her successful mission. There followed information about the drop zone for the Lysander the following night. She would be travelling back with two male agents. *Stay vigilant.*

As Noor was transmitting, a baker's van one street parallel picked up her signal. It was clear. It chimed with the information from Bertrand in the Café Le Colisée and conversation overheard by a woman with sausage-like fingers. The Gestapo had details not just of the apartment building but the apartment itself. Second floor on the left.

Noor looked at the Paris skyline. She saw a parade of faces. Antelme, Prosper, Norman, Benoist, Henri and Marguerite Garry,

Mademoiselle Monette, Papillon, Morel. The full intensity of the mission would take time to process. Yet she had survived. And she had followed her *Sankalpa*. The sinews in her shoulders allowed themselves a brief respite from the tension. As Noor sat looking at the moon, Le Stryge picked up an almost imperceptible pinprick in Rue de la Faisanderie. He strained his ears. It was the sound of a hook-pick inside a keyhole.

*

Buckmaster was pacing his office in 64 Baker Street. His head was stooped, his hands behind his back. The head of F-Section looked, as always, as if he were counting the threads in the carpet. He was calculating the hours until Agent Madeleine was extracted by Lysander. He planned to travel to RAF Tangmere to meet her in person. A Parker pen lay encased in velvet in a box on his desk. For an agent who wrote children's stories, he could think of no better gift.

*

Noor came down the stairs, suitcase in hand, just as it started to rain.

She turned the key in the lock.

She entered the apartment.

She put the suitcase down on the parquet.

She took off her coat.

She was about to take off her cloche when frisson spread across her skin.

There was a silhouette in the hallway.

A shadow.

It was the outline of a figure.

Papa, the shadows!

A man burst from the bedroom doorway.

It was the man from the street with the newspaper.

'*Bougez pas!* – Don't move!' he shouted.

Little Pteech-ka's eyes flashed.

'You're under arrest.'

He was French.

'Do not resist. I am to take you dead or alive.'

442

His hand lunged at Noor's throat.

To the man's shock, a forearm moved into his line of sight.

It moved with such speed the man saw only the hardening of a blur.

The next thing he saw was an open palm.

The cartilage of his nose cracked.

The man stood, his mind and body still processing.

Crimson dripped from his nostrils on to his shirt.

Noor turned and lunged for the front door.

'*NON!*' shouted the man.

A bloody palm slammed the door shut.

The Bishop's words echoed.

Everything is a weapon.

Noor spun like a dervish.

Jutting from her index and third finger was a key.

As she whirled, the key sliced the man's wrist.

An arc of red spurted.

The man became a fountain of pain and fury.

He also felt a rising panic.

What would the Gestapo say if he failed to subdue a woman half his size?

He lunged again for her throat.

This time he felt a hand on his wrist and a hand on his forearm.

A set of teeth bit down in between.

His fingers convulsed as the teeth crushed a radial nerve.

As Noor's teeth clamped, she felt for her hatpin.

Her cloche was smooth – where *was it* when needed most?

All the life force in Noor told her she could not be taken alive.

She felt for a button on her dress.

The two halves of the button were magnetic.

She thumbed the top half across.

A pill marked **DANGER! KCN** bounced over the parquet.

Cyanide.

Noor knelt to catch the pill.

The man groped to the side of this belt.

It was his last chance.

He stood, blood dripping from his nose and wrist.

In his hand was a Gestapo-issue pistol.

He spoke with white anger.

'Sit down on your hands or I will shoot.'

When Stabsscharführer Vogt and his Gestapo colleague entered, they had to goose-step over the pool of blood in the hallway. The sight that greeted them made both men blink. The man holding the pistol had blood on his mouth, chin and shirt. His right hand hung limp, also dripping with blood. He had a pistol trained on the head of a slim female sitting on the floor, uninjured. He held the pistol in his left hand. The tremble in his arm was magnified in the tremble of the barrel. His breathing was forced. He looked like he might collapse at any moment. Powder from a crushed cyanide pill was mixed with some of the blood.

'*Danke*,' said Vogt. 'We will take matters from here.'

He glanced at the man as if he were a waiter who had set down an overcooked *gigot d'agneau*.

Noor was bundled into a Mercedes 770. The driver slammed the boot. Inside was her transmitter. Rain pelted on the windows. She sat between two Gestapo. She could feel their heat. A pistol was jabbed into each of her kidneys.

High above Paris, streaks ran down the face of Le Stryge.

The car pulled up outside 84 Avenue Foch. Noor was taken over the threshold clamped between the two Gestapo. The entrance had the same grandeur as Mademoiselle Pelletier's *maison* in the 7ème Arrondissement. While Wehrmacht soldiers in Mademoiselle Pelletier's house sought pleasure, the Gestapo in 84 Avenue Foch sought information – by any means. While the women in Mademoiselle Pelletier's house fluttered like butterflies, the men in 84 Avenue Foch reminded Noor of beetles. Men with beetle-black uniforms. Men with shiny beetle-black caps. Men with expressions radiating all the humanity of shell-cased insects.

There was something in the atmosphere. Phantom traces of colour. The colour of screams from the basement that still clung to the air. A colour-scape of deceased screams.

Sturmbannführer Kieffer flicked the non-existent dust from his shoulder. He straightened his SS cap in the mirror. He smoothed his eyebrows with a manicured finger. He wanted to look his best to receive such a high-value agent. And a woman, to boot. And surely the defences of any woman would be no match for a striking Sturmbannführer, immaculate in his favoured black?

He sat, waiting.

There was a knock.

'*Komm herein!*'

Two pistols nudged Noor into the room. Kieffer stood. He looked at her, three-quarter face. It was, a photographer once told him, his most flattering angle. He made an almost imperceptible click with his heels. He removed his cap to reveal hair trimmed and parted in Noor's honour.

'So good of you to come and see me, Miss Khan,' he said. 'Or should I call you Agent Madeleine?'

Noor stood silent.

'Please, Miss Khan. The Gestapo has not lost its manners. Won't you be seated?'

A Louis XVI chair was proffered.

Noor sat. Kieffer looked at the slight woman with badly dyed hair. So this was the famous Madeleine, he thought. The invisible Morse diva.

'You don't look very dangerous,' smiled Kieffer. 'But then again you have just put one of my agents in hospital.'

Defiant eyes, noted Kieffer.

'I want to make your stay with us as pleasant as possible. The person who dictates your treatment here is you, not me. Everyone breaks eventually. Personally, I do not wish you to come to harm. But in making your decision you should be aware that we know everything.'

445

Kieffer smiled.

'Prosper has been a guest of ours. So has WW, codename Sebastien. And the pair shuffling forged identity cards. We know about every circuit in Paris. We know about the armoury at the Benoist estate. We know about the soon-to-be-arrested Henri Garry and his charming wife, Marguerite. We know about Antelme codenamed Renaud on a temporary visit to London. We know all the drop-zone locations. We can even tell you the field where a Lysander was going to be collecting you tomorrow evening.'

Silence pervaded the room. Kieffer opened a drawer.

'As for you, Agent Madeleine, I even have your most recent letter to your mother. "Darling Mama, I trust with all my heart that this letter reaches you safely and please do not worry about my being away..." Shall I go on?'

Always find and follow your breath.

Noor's chest rose and fell. She cleared her throat.

'Herr Kieffer,' she said. 'I have a request.'

Her tone was quiet, assured. In all the time Sturmbannführer Kieffer had dealt with suspected agents, no one had ever made a personal request.

'How can I assist?' he said, turning three-quarter face.

'I should very much like to have a bath.'

Le Stryge's stone ear was cocked. From 84 Avenue Foch, he heard the unexpected. Laughter. Kieffer poured himself an Armagnac. He spun the sun-coloured liquid into a vortex.

'Miss Khan. How can a gentleman refuse a lady a bath? But before I agree, you must swear on everything that is sacred to you that you will make no attempt to escape. Should you do so, your experience in the building will be very different.'

'I swear.'

It was, Noor thought as warm water lapped around her body, one of her more unusual experiences of the war. The Gestapo had even provided bath salts. There was nothing in the top-floor bathroom save a towel. A guard sat outside. She looked at the bathroom window.

Promise to tell the truth always and never to lie.
Three things cannot be long hidden, said Lord Buddha.
The Sun, the Moon and the Truth.

Le Stryge picked up a sound above Avenue Foch. It was faint, just perceptible. The sound of bare feet on roof tiles.

CHAPTER 36
'THE SECOND CROSSING'

England, 1943

Buckmaster

Buckmaster waited, moonlight casting his shadow on the grass. In his breast pocket was a coffin-shaped box containing a gold Parker pen. Propellers purred in the distance. Buckmaster looked into the sky. A Lysander flew from the face of the moon. The plane descended and came to rest on the runway. The propellers sputtered and halted. The rear door opened. A ladder dropped. Buckmaster's heart soared as the first agent descended. Then the second. Both men. There was a pause. Where was the third? *Retrieving her things, surely?* The ladder retracted. The passenger door slammed. The plane taxied towards a warehouse.

No Madeleine.

Buckmaster dug his nails into his palm. It started to rain. He stood, head down in the moonlight. Water poured off his trilby as fresh blood seeped down his palm. Some raindrops found their way into his shirt. He drove back from RAF Tangmere alone. The headlights of the SOE Alvis lit the raindrops. The Parker pen felt as if it were leaking. Was it the rain, he thought, or the tears of a pen crying for its writer? As he drove, he told himself there were a hundred and one reasons why Noor might have missed her flight. It happened all the time. The two returning agents said the plane had waited an extra forty minutes for Madeleine. The Moon Squadron pilot had risked a court martial for each minute. As a German patrol came within earshot, the pilot had no choice. Bursts of machine-gun fire came from the ground as the Lysander flew at the moon.

He imagined Noor strapped in a chair in Avenue Foch. He slammed the brakes. Outside the car, he put his head between his knees. He convulsed. The bitter taste remained in his mouth for the rest of the journey.

*

Occupied Paris, 1943

Noor

The moonlight that cast Buckmaster's shadow also cast the shadow of a figure on the roof of 84 Avenue Foch. Noor moved like a cat, hands and feet padding over the tiles. She reached a chimney stack and paused. She peered over the edge of the building. Eight floors below, cars moved in contrary motion down Avenue Foch. One slip and the only thing between her and the unforgiving boulevard was a white bath towel.

Always find and follow your breath.

She kept moving. From the chimney stack, she navigated a low rampart that divided Number 84 from the adjoining building. Anything to distance herself from the House of Black Beetles. She continued to pad, palm-sole-palm-sole. Until something happened that neither she, nor the black beetles, anticipated.

Le Stryge looked up into the sky. Shadows were crossing the moon. Paris erupted in a cacophony of sirens.

Bombers.

The cars in Avenue Foch stopped as the occupants dived into the nearest air-raid shelter. Noor heard the purple hum of Lancaster and Blenheim bombers. Their target was German missile dumps south-east of Paris.

Why did Bomber Command have to choose *that moment* to put occupied Paris on full alert?

Noor lay flat on the tiles. They were cold.

The thumps on the bathroom door grew louder. The guard shouted. Wood splintered as he kicked the door open. The bathroom was empty. The curtain flapped next to an open window. An alarm rang within the building. Kieffer ordered the area within a mile of 84 Avenue Foch to be cordoned off – bombers or no bombers.

Noor found a fire escape ladder. The rungs dug into her bare soles. Of all the SOE training, nothing had prepared her for descending a fire escape at night next to Gestapo headquarters during an air raid wearing nothing but a bath towel. A chill wind chased around her towel as she descended.

Always find and follow your breath.

She dropped on to the boulevard. With one hand holding up her bath towel, she broke into a run. The boulevard was cold and rigid underfoot. Noor passed the odd stranger. Some looked quizzical. Some concerned. Others looked away. In occupied Paris, it was sometimes better not to know. She ran into Rue Pergolèse. She could hear running footsteps. She made for streaks of lights on the pavement. The light came from shutters unfolded at the sound of the bombers. It was a brasserie. Noor threw open the door and ran inside.

The blast of the air-raid siren followed her in. Diners were crouched under the tables, staring up like wide-eyed children. She ran to the back. She descended a short flight of stairs. She darted to the left. The lavatory was empty. There was a window above the sink. As she climbed on to the sink, she heard footsteps.

The stone hands of Le Stryge tightened.

Noor pulled a catch at the top of the window. It gave way the length of a pencil. She heard footsteps outside. Noor turned her back to the window and jolted her elbow backwards. There was a crack. On the second jolt the window smashed. As Noor prepared to climb over jagged glass, three Gestapo entered the room. Three pistols were trained at her head.

'How dare you!' she shouted.

*

Of the suspected agents taken to Avenue Foch, none had crossed the threshold twice. The second time Noor was bundled into the entrance was with a black leather trench coat around her shoulders. There was no urbane meeting with Sturmbannführer Kieffer. She was taken straight down to the basement. As she was led down the stairs, the phantom traces of colour grew more vivid. The deceased screams that hung in the air were not long dead.

She was taken to an interrogation room. There were only three pieces of furniture. A desk with locked drawers and a chair. In the middle of the room was another chair. Each piece of furniture was fused to the floor. The room was windowless. There was a bare light bulb in the middle of the ceiling, caged behind mesh. A small air duct lay hidden behind a vent at the top of one wall. Apart from a metal door leading to a tiny, windowless bathroom, the walls were bare.

Noor stood barefoot on the floor. It was concrete and painted a colour somewhere between crimson and black. One of the Gestapo sat at the desk and unlocked a drawer. He withdrew a piece of a paper and started writing. He drew a line at the bottom of the document and added a date.

'Sturmbannführer Kieffer does not take kindly to those who break their promises. This document is an undertaking that you will not, if allowed to leave this room, try to escape again from the building. Please sign at the bottom.'

He proffered a pen.

'*Nein, danke.*'

'As you wish,' said the man. His tone was flat. He had encountered resistance before. The only question was the time between confrontation and capitulation.

'We will meet again tomorrow, Agent Khan. I suggest you try and get a good night's sleep. Tomorrow promises to be a long day. *Schlafen Sie gut, Fräulein.*'

High above Notre Dame, the stone eyes of Le Stryge stared into the void.

Noor sat on the concrete floor, hugging the towel around her knees. The cold of the floor leached the heat away from the soles of her feet. No blanket. No pillow. No bed. She was also aware, after the adrenaline subsided, of a gnawing hunger. Her SOE training echoed in her mind.

Try and keep track of time.

Try and hold out for the first forty-eight hours.

Remember your two weapons: your cover story and your dignity.

By Noor's calculation, it was around nine at night. Every hour she divulged nothing would be a personal victory. She made a mental note. Nine p.m.

Le Stryge felt nine muted strokes of the bell of Notre Dame.

Zero hour.

Noor pressed her forehead against her knees and closed her eyes.

She saw a garden in Suresnes. It was summer. Inayat was sitting by the window, writing. Amina was trailing roses through the trellis. Her brothers were climbing in the trees. She and her sister were sitting on a picnic rug. Between them was a plate of shell-shaped madeleine cakes. She took one of the madeleines and, like Proust before her, dipped it into a cup of golden tea…

She wanted to feel the cushion of Inayat's beard and the softness of Amina's cheek. She wanted to feel the grass underfoot of the garden of the House of Blessings. She wanted to fly with wooden Pteech-ka, skimming the water of the Seine and upward through the towers of Notre Dame. She wanted to be walking along the beach of Saint Félix next to Antelme. She opened her eyes. The blank walls of the interrogation chamber felt closer. She was in a room from which there was no escape. She felt the tightening panic of a trapped animal.

Always find and follow your breath.

She inhaled into her diaphragm. Exhaled. Inhaled. The breathing calmed her pulse. She stayed in the foetal position. As her face burrowed between her knees, it happened. Internal implosion. Her harp strings snapped, one by one. Her frame heaved and juddered. Noor could hear the orange of her own sobs. Tears rolled down her face and dropped on to her towel. A voice came.

There is a sacredness in tears.

They are not a sign of weakness but of power.

After a time, the tears stopped rolling. The sobs ceased. Noor felt a sense of relief. She was still alive, she told herself. She was unharmed. And she had given nothing away. She closed her eyes. It was time to descend. Down through the churn of the waves, through the stilts of light under the surface, through the darker, stiller water, down to the sea floor of her mind. She came to rest on the bottom, her thoughts slowing in the undercurrents. Her pulse dropped and her breathing slowed. There she stayed, the cacophony of her thoughts quietening, until it was time to return to the surface. As she was about to ascend, she heard a voice. She used her third eye to look inward. In faint outline, she saw the figure of a man in gold. His white beard swayed in the currents. His eyes were open, twin apertures radiating back into infinity.

'Love is fearless in the midst of the sea of fear.'

Papa!

Noor reached out. Her hand passed through water. She ascended. The room felt bigger, less oppressive. Perhaps a heating system had come on: the floor felt warm. She felt a strange calm. *Keep track of time.* Noor reckoned it was around eleven at night. The adrenaline in her body was leaving. Her chin fell on to her chest. She tumbled into a deep, unexpected sleep. Her head bobbed up several times during the night and she opened her eyes. Other than that she had slept, she thought, for around eight hours.

The key turned in the lock. Noor's heart jumped. Two objects were set down by an unknown hand. It must, she thought, have been around eight in the morning. By the door was a piece of baguette wrapped in a paper napkin. To Noor's amazement, there was butter in the middle. Next to the baguette was a mug of watery tea. Of the breakfasts Noor had had during the war, this was the most welcome. Every crumb of baguette and every drop of tea disappeared. Half an hour later she heard footsteps. Not shoes. Boots. The key turned again. The same black beetle from the previous night entered the room.

'I trust you slept well, *Fräulein*.'

The Gestapo presented a piece of paper. Noor could make out a word in German at the top.

DIE AUSSAGE.

She knew it was German for 'STATEMENT'.

'Your interrogation will be as long or as short as you want it to be. If you wish to co-operate, it will be short. If you wish not to co-operate, it will be long. It's that simple. The choice is yours. Not mine.'

Noor said nothing.

'Let's start with your name.'

Silence.

'Everyone knows their name, *Fräulein*.'

Silence.

The officer put down his pen.

'This could become a painful process,' he said.

A familiar voice sounded in Noor's head.

'Promise to tell the truth always and never to lie.'

In war, Papa?

Noor drew a breath.

'My name is Jeanne-Marie Renier,' she said.

'Jeanne-Marie Renier. And what is Jeanne-Marie Renier doing in Paris?'

The black beetle wrote. He seemed to be taking down her words verbatim. He looked up from time to time. His expression was, if anything, bored.

'Yes,' said his eyes. 'Let's have your cover story in all its glory. Then the work will start.'

After what seemed to Noor was almost two hours, the black beetle put down his pen.

'Read through the statement, and if accurate, sign it. I will record the date.'

Noor read the statement. It was her cover story, courtesy of a Gestapo pen. She signed. The officer folded the statement and left.

After an hour, the key turned again. It was the same black beetle, this time with a suitcase. He placed it on the desk. He clicked the catches. It opened to reveal a Mark II radio.

'Why did you have this transmitter with you when you were arrested?'

'You were not present at my arrest. I have never seen this suitcase before.'

'Please do not insult my intelligence, Agent Khan.'

'Please do not call me Khan when my name is Renier.'

The officer looked at the ceiling.

'Those who play games with the Gestapo always lose.'

He left with the suitcase.

*

An invisible hand placed a bowl of soup on the floor for lunch. She had been in Gestapo custody for around sixteen hours. There was a period of silence after lunch. Mid-afternoon, the key turned again. A prison blanket was left on the floor with a prison uniform folded on top. The uniform looked like a pair of hessian pyjamas. She was a prisoner, as if it needed confirming. Noor sat on the floor in hessian stripes.

Silence. She closed her eyes. Her captors were in no hurry, it seemed. No doubt a strategy to instil fear. Noor's mind wound forward. She saw herself strapped to a chair. There were three men in the room. Her head was tilted at the ceiling. Her body was convulsing. She put her hand over her heart and found her breath. Her mind paused a few moments in the stilts of light then dropped straight to the sea floor.

A voice came.

Why do you stay in prison when the door is wide open?

Noor's forehead puckered.

455

The door is locked.

After a silence, the voice returned.

Is it?

Noor opened her palms.

I am trapped!

The voice retorted.

Become the sky. Take an axe to the prison wall. Escape!

She opened her eyes.

The ceiling began to unfold into a cobalt sky. Clouds vanished into mist. As the sun's rays started to appear, the key in the lock turned. Two black beetles entered.

'Sturmbannführer Kieffer has read your statement. He does not wish to be responsible for the steps that will be taken to unlock the truth.'

Silence.

'The choice is yours, *Fräulein.*'

The key turned in the door. As she sat in silence, Noor could hear faint signs of activity in an adjacent room. Furniture sounded like it was being rearranged. And there was something else she could not determine. It sounded like the distant placing of cutlery.

The silent hours continued. Noor went back to the sea floor of her mind.

There was another turn of the key.

An invisible hand placed a bowl of soup on the floor. It must, she thought, have been early evening. She had been in Gestapo custody for almost twenty-four hours. She had given the black beetles nothing except the fog of deception. She had to hold out another twenty-four hours. She closed her eyes. A familiar voice came.

What is your Sankalpa, Bābouli?

To shorten the war.

High on the south tower of Notre Dame, Le Stryge's stone eyes looked towards Avenue Foch. From his stone mouth, a whisper dispersed on the wind.

'Fear no evil. For I am with you.'

Noor lay in her hessian stripes under a prison blanket. She made her towel into a makeshift pillow. When she closed her eyes the spectres crowded, the hoods of their cloaks pulled over their hollow eyes. She had seen those eyes before. They stared out from the iron skulls pinned on to the caps of the Gestapo. Each spectre had a name. Fear. Trepidation. Dread. Their shadows loomed over the prone prisoner. Noor put her hands over her eyes.

Papa, the shadows!

A voice spoke.

Never lose faith, my Dear Heart.

Miracles dwell in the invisible.

When she opened her eyes, the shadows had fled. Sleep followed, sporadic like the patches on her prison blanket. She dreamed that wooden Pteech-ka was sitting on her wrist, ruby eyes glistening. Pteech-ka spoke.

'Fear no evil. For I am with you.'

*

The key turned in the lock. An invisible hand left a baguette and some watery tea. Morning. She was exhausted. The tea felt like acid and the bread like rock. She forced herself. She had to hold out until evening. She closed her eyes. A voice came.

In the blackest of your moments, be without fear.

The key turned in the lock. The butterflies in Noor's stomach turned to lead. She stood.

'This way please, *Fräulein*.'

The voice returned.

Move, but do not move the way fear makes you move.

Noor was led into an adjacent room. A chair sat in the centre, with leather straps on the arms. Next to the chair was a table that contained an array of syringes and what looked like dental equipment. There was also a soldering iron connected to a power source. Against the wall was a tin bath. A wooden duckboard stood next to the bath like a prayer mat. The bath was full. Noor could see pieces of ice floating on the surface.

Always find and follow your breath.

There were three men in the room, one in black uniform.

'I am Dr Winkler, a physician with the counter-intelligence branch of the SS,' said the bald black beetle.

'These are my assistants.'

He pointed to two men in shirtsleeves. Noor looked at two sets of dead eyes.

'The work we carry out is a sacred duty. A duty to a power of such unutterable greatness we are privileged to be its servants.'

He smiled.

'I am going to ask you, without an unseemly struggle, to take the throne.'

Move, but do not move the way fear makes you move.

Noor moved of her own accord to the chair. One of the assistants buckled leather straps around her wrists.

'Now, *Fräulein*. I would like you to help me with some questions.'

He smiled again.

'I have a range of devices at my disposal to help you answer.'

He picked up a soldering iron. The tip glowed red.

'Fire precedes water.'

He jutted his chin at the bath.

'Every human has a name, Agent Khan. I wonder whether you would be good enough to tell me yours?'

There was a pause. A voice spoke, quiet but assured.

'My name is Jeanne-Marie Renier.'

There was a crackle as the soldering iron met a woman's skin, and a smell of burning. To Dr Winkler's surprise, there was no scream.

'I am going to ask you that question again.'

There was another crackle. But no scream.

*

Sturmbannführer Kieffer sat in the chair in his study two floors above. The Parisian coquette on the wall glowered at him with undisguised contempt. He found himself reasoning with her painted eyes. He had his orders. And besides, the woman in the basement was a dangerous agent who had tried to escape. The portrait's lip appeared to rise into a snarl. Kieffer looked away. He imagined his own daughter, twenty years on, in the hands of Dr Winkler. A shudder went through his body.

He stood. There was an eerie quiet from the basement. Where were the sounds of interrogation? There was no question of going downstairs himself. Dr Winkler would report to him at lunchtime. He pulled his collar away from his throat. He was perspiring.

*

Noor's head was thrown back.

The vein in her neck stood proud.

Her vision was blurred.

She was counting the seconds.

Tick tock.

The sound of a clock.

Loud and clear.

Always near.

Measuring.

TIME.

Invisible.

Always moving.

Never still.

Time for what?

A time to kill.

A time to heal.

A time to love.

Was time a line?

Was time a wheel?

Was time everlasting?

Where, now, were the hands of time?

Was it time to look back…

…and descend the stair?

Noor reached the lowest stair. And fell.

She fell into a void of beetle black.

Her head hung forward.

Dr Winkler had nothing to show for his morning's work.

He looked at the slumped head. He took her pulse. Yes, she was alive. Why did she appear not to suffer pain? It was a conundrum to consider over *Bratwurst* and potato dumplings.

*

The void cleared.

Noor was in a room.

Her hands were strapped.

She was alone.

Burning hung in the air.

Pain guided her eyes.

She looked away.

A voice came.

In the blackest of your moments, be without fear.

She closed her eyes.

She descended through the stilts of light, through the waves that churned fragments of cinder down into the stiller waters of the deep. She came to rest on the sea floor of her mind. As she sat, a circle formed.

Tiger

Elephant   Hare

Horse   Lion

Deer   Swan

Monkey

Each animal spoke in turn.

'Fear no evil. For I am with you.'

Beyond the circle, Noor could make out the edges of a gold robe.

There was a turn in the lock.

The animals scattered.

460

Noor returned to the surface.

She was no longer in a chair.

She was kneeling.

Someone was roping her hands behind her back.

'After fire, water,' said the bald black beetle.

The hand at the back of her head was well rehearsed.

Noor felt a jaw-like grip around her neck.

Without warning, her head was submerged in water so cold it stung.

Dr Winkler noted the agent's clavicles as they spasmed.

Such fine bones, he thought.

At his signal, a hand pulled her head up by the hair.

'We were discussing your name, Agent Khan.'

Noor heaved breath into her lungs.

'Jeanne-Marie Renier.'

Splash.

Back into the stinging water.

This time, she was submerged for longer.

Dr Winkler noticed her scapulae.

He considered the shoulder blades an anatomical masterpiece.

They looked most magnificent when taut.

He gave a signal.

Noor's head was pulled from the water.

She heard violent heaving.

Where from?

She was, for a moment, looking down from the ceiling.

The heaving came from the mouth of a woman kneeling, hands tied, her head just above the water.

'I was asking, *Fräulein*, about your name.'

Silence.

'Jeanne—'

The water closed over her head.

Immersion.

She counted the seconds.

461

Forty.

Fifty.

SIXTY.

Tick tock.

The sound of a clock.

Loud and clear.

Always near.

Measuring.

TIME.

Final seconds.

Hands.

Moving across a face.

Towards.

An infinite

Respite.

A time...

A time.

To die.

*

High above Paris, Le Stryge's stone eyes looked into the sky. Le Stryge's stone palms were open in supplication. *God in whose name men built Notre Dame.*

Reveal yourself!

*

Dr Winkler noticed the scapulae had stopped fluttering.

She must, he thought, be entering the hinterland.

Timing was everything.

Noor opened her eyes underwater.

In the blur she saw Inayat.

His eyes were shining.

His hands beckoning.

You are not a drop in the ocean

You are the entire ocean in a drop

An arc of water flew backwards as a hand pulled her hair.

A moment later, she could feel her face on the cold floor.
She heard whimpering.

Was it her?

Or the tiger lying beside her, fur soaking, face contorted?

*

'The agent is extremely stubborn,' said Dr Winkler over drinks that
evening. 'But she lives.'

Noor sat on the floor of her cell. There were dark patches on
her prison top and two of her harpist fingers hung limp. But she
was alive and, after forty-eight hours, had given nothing away. A
strange euphoria spread through a wracked body. The next objec-
tive. Alerting London.

*

England, 1943

Buckmaster
Marks

Dots pricked the air over Grendon Hall. Dashes cut grooves. It
was a message from Madeleine. Miss Pickering pressed the buzzer
under her desk. Other radio operators gathered around as she transcribed the Morse.

MY CACHETTE IS UNSAFE

There was euphoria. The message was sent to SOE flagged 'Zulu':
emergency traffic. There was a knock on Leo Marks's door. Marks
looked up from under his curls.

'Message from Madeleine. Came through from Grendon two
minutes ago.'

'Thank you,' said Marks.

He thought of Agent Khan sitting in front of him a few months
before. Such serene eyes. He cleared his desk and sharpened a pencil.

It was time to dissect a message. He took his pencil and positioned it on the page like a surgeon with a scalpel. Ten minutes

later, Marks had been through the Morse twice. There was something, however, that made Marks's stomach clench. The message was eighteen characters. *Eighteen*. The number Marks had given Noor to transmit if she was captured. Marks looked again at the message. *My cachette is unsafe*. Was Noor telling London she was captured but for London to play along? Was she luring the Gestapo down a blind alley?

He took the codes up a floor and knocked on a door that said 'COLONEL BUCKMASTER'. Buckmaster squinted at the paper.

'Are you sure she's been captured?' said Buckmaster.

'As sure as the nose on my face,' said Marks with a grim smile.

The bags under Buckmaster's eyes had developed bags. The capture of any agent added another rock to his shoulders. The capture of Noor felt like a lead diving bell.

'Madeleine must be an agent of the most extreme self-possession,' said the Chess Master. Marks was about to begin a game of chess in which the two opposing armies were comprised of Dots and Dashes. As play commenced, Marks had to give the impression Noor was transmitting freely. His opponent had to play the same way. Radio chess. How much did the other player know? How much was he beginning to reveal? How many sacrifices would be offered? What was the endgame? Marks rolled up his sleeves. First move.

'Where is your current cachette?'

Response.

'RUE DE LA FAISANDERIE.'

The location of Noor's arrest. Marks squinted. The Germans probably knew that anyway.

'What cachette are you moving to?'

'57 RUE VERCINGÉTORIX.'

Any address could have been given, thought Marks. So play opened. The Chess Master was competing in a game that would unfold over weeks and into months. He thought of Uncle Abe, eyes twinkling over the chessboard. The stakes were different. A single mistake could compromise a captured agent or worse, an entire network. It made his hand tremble but not his brain. As he mulled his moves, his mind was calculating ten different permutations of strike and counterstrike.

As for tactics, the old skills died hard.

- Frontal assault
  - Flank attack
    - Pincer movement
      - Siege
        - Attrition
          - Stealth incursion
          - Subterfuge
        - Supply-line disruption
      - Tactical withdrawal
    - Counter-attack
  - Endgame

Marks waged war on every front. In the open. By night. Behind enemy lines. Play went back and forth, each side trying to elicit how much the other knew. Black was played by Noor's transmitter, white by SOE. Black Pawn to C4: when was the next arms drop? White Knight to F6: the following full moon. Black Knight to F3: Where? White Bishop to C5: Angers. Black Pawn to G6: Was it safe to proceed? White Rook to A4: No, the drop should be aborted. Black Queen to D7: Why...? The messages from Noor's transmitter haunted Marks as the game developed. It was as if a woman cleared her throat to speak – and from her mouth came the voice of a man. Yet throughout the match he felt the presence of Noor, sabotaging where she could, the German game – a fleeting clue as to his opponent's battle orders, a nudge of the enemy's King into danger. His instinct – that Agent Madeleine continued to wage war as a captive – was correct.

Marks played on, his needlepoint focus never wavering. Until Buckmaster accepted that it was beyond doubt that Noor's radio was under German control. SOE transmissions to Noor's radio slowed to a trickle. The opposing player eventually broke cover. Yes, it was all a game. The final transmission commended Baker Street on a most interesting tournament. The Gestapo now had no further use for Agent Madeleine in Paris.

'*So lange, Herr Marks.*'

*

Occupied Paris, 1943

Noor

Kieffer received a communiqué direct from SS headquarters in Berlin. Agent Madeleine would follow Prosper and the others for further interrogation in Germany. Kieffer looked at the painting opposite. The portrait had been replaced with a landscape.

CHAPTER 37
'THE HISTORIAN'S PEN'

Montluc Prison,
Lyon, 1944

Bloch
Morel

Professeur Bloch sat under the window of his cell, writing in his notebook. There was nothing that focused a historian's mind more than knowing he was to be executed the following day. The notebook had started as a letter to his son, who asked all those years ago why he was a historian. *What's the use of history, Papa?* It was, he admitted, a fair question. Whenever Bloch had a few spare minutes, he would add to the letter. The letter turned into a book. Now it was a book that would never be finished. But while there was still time, Le Prof's mind continued to search.

He closed his eyes. It was October 1915. He surveyed the world from his trench. Machine-gun posts stood at intervals in a sea of churned-up mud pockmarked with craters and flanked by rolling hills of barbed wire. In the distance, an artillery barrage was beginning. A smudged orange glow rose over the horizon. In the sky above, two enemy planes were looping and spinning in a courtship of death.

On the same field, five hundred years before, the French and English armies faced each other at Agincourt on the morning of St Crispin's Day, 1415. Royal standards of blue and gold fluttered behind opposing lines. The lines met. Lions and unicorns on the knights' shields locked with rival swans and griffins. Sparks flew from the clash of longswords. Lances slammed through breastplates. Maces crumpled helmets. Arrows darkened the sky, thudding through armour, sending knights wheeling and pounding on to the green field of battle.

What had changed? The weaponry. Half a millennium on, mankind still made war. And hunger for war did not stop in 1918... Man without history was, he thought, like a man without a memory. 'History', he wrote, 'is neither watch-making nor cabinet construction. It is an endeavour towards a better understanding.' A better understanding of what? His pen resumed.

'*Misunderstanding of the present is the inevitable consequence of ignorance of the past.*'

He was to be shot the following day because his executioners were ignorant of the past. Naming the word gave him a grain of comfort. He knew what his executioners did not. They were ignorant.

*

In the cell next to Bloch lay Georges Morel. He cupped the back of his head in his hands. He could feel the ridge where his scalp became tin. He could feel Dr Boucher's rivets. His pain would soon be gone. Like Bloch, Morel was to be shot the following day.

The metal that encased his mind drew the deep-buried thoughts like a magnet. He thought of his earliest memory. The night his mother entered his room with a doll wrapped in a christening blanket. She lay the doll down in a cot. When the door closed, Morel crept over to look through the wooden bars. The doll lay still, eyes closed. The doll breathed! Morel reached out to touch the doll's face. The doll's two eyes opened, blue and blank, and closed. Two decades later, Morel would see a third eye open before Fabien fell back into his arms.

He remembered the picnics on the beach outside Saint-Malo. The warmth of the towel his mother wrapped around his shoulders. The strength of his father as he carried a towel-clad brother under each arm towards the family car. He remembered the dining room *chez Morel* where he sat with a straight back and a stiff collar and listened to grace. He remembered his mother's embrace the day he set off for war. He remembered his mother's face after his operation. He remembered his mother sitting in an armchair before she died with a yellowing photograph of himself and Fabien as young men on her lap. He remembered the day he met Zoë, crouching with a tray of cigarettes in the cinema after *The Wizard of* Oz. He remembered Zoë standing in one of his shirts in his bedroom. *Hats off in bed.* He remembered her, chisel in hand, sculpting every groove of his head. He remembered her animation at the meetings of *Résistants*. He remembered the day one of the rail saboteurs telephoned. There had been an explosion. The charge went off prematurely. *She was our bravest.*

Zoë. The word for life. The butterfly with the heart of a lion. And now she was dead. What fear could death bring? Life had taken his scalp. Life had taken Fabien. Life had taken Benoist. Life had taken Zoë. Life was about to take his *coeur.* Would life take his courage? It would not. The next day Morel would walk, tin head held high.

*

Bloch's name had found its way on to a Gestapo hit list. Had he stayed in Paris, he would have ended up in 84 Avenue Foch. He moved south to Lyon, where he presented himself to a local Resistance group. At first the leaders did not know what to make of the short, grey-haired gentleman with round glasses, a suitcase full of books, and a cane. What use was an ageing historian?

'This much use,' said Bloch as he removed a semi-automatic pistol from inside his belt. From his coat pocket he withdrew an eight-round magazine. He jolted the magazine into the grip of the pistol with an upward flash of his palm.

'I survived the First Battle of the Marne and the Battle of the Somme.'

He opened his briefcase.

'I also carry these.'

From a hidden compartment he withdrew two rusting possessions. The Croix de Guerre and the Légion d'Honneur.

'You are full of surprises, Monsieur,' said the Resistance leader.

'Strictly speaking, it's retired Capitaine,' said Bloch with a smile.

He was, as the *Résistants* discovered, a crack shot and seemingly impervious to danger. For a man who had spent the Great War eating from a mess tin to the whistle of artillery shells, small arms fire was just an *aperitif*. Bloch, with his spectacles and watch chain, had the perfect cover of a historical archivist. An archivist on the move. Within months, 'Le Prof' had become a regional leader, organizing existing supplies and writing propaganda. Through a contact in SOE's Spruce Circuit, he was able to call in arms drops by Lysander. The canisters of Sten guns that fell from the sky by moonlight cemented Bloch's position.

As operations expanded, he needed a trusted aide-de-camp. Word travelled through Resistance wires north to Saint-Malo, where one Georges Morel was considering his next move. Paris was too dangerous. He was thinking about Tours. Then came the call to join his old commander in Lyon. It took Morel less than ten minutes to pack a suitcase. He travelled hatless, his heart thumping with purpose.

Both men took rooms above a dressmaker's in the Rue des Quatre Chapeaux. Morel, bareheaded, smiled when he first saw the name of the street. It was from Rue des Quatre Chapeaux that important Resistance operations were planned. A radio operator attached to the Spruce Circuit taught Bloch coding. Le Prof transposed a variety of secret Resistance documents into code. He also allowed the radio operator to use the roof of the building for short broadcasts. One evening, the operator asked if he could hide his radio in Bloch's room. Le Prof waved his hand.

'*Bien sûr, mon brave.*'

Next day, as the sun beamed through the window of Bloch's room, Bloch and Morel were poring over a map with rings marked for air drops courtesy of Baker Street. They heard a clatter of boots on the narrow stairs. The door splintered with the kick of a Gestapo boot. There was a blur of black and tan as two Alsatians streaked across the floor, finding the forearms of Bloch and Morel. In Bloch's room, the Gestapo found the air-drop map, a sheaf of coded documents and, most incriminating of all, a concealed wireless transmitter. As Bloch and Morel were led away, the woman in the dressmaker's placed a large roll of francs in her apron.

*

The two men were taken to Gestapo headquarters in the Hotel Terminus. Bloch was tied to a plank and submerged head first through a crust of ice into water so cold it made his consciousness float away. Morel was tied to a chair. The Gestapo in charge gave him the option of talking or having his tin scalp prised off with a crowbar. Dr Boucher's rivets, it turned out, might have welded together two parts of a Bugatti. Instead, they used the crowbar to test the strength of Morel's ribs.

Neither talked.

The pair transferred to Montluc prison, where Bloch almost died of broncho-pneumonia. His dying wish was for more paper. The historian wrote his way out of the pneumonia's grasp. His cell was littered with page after page in his clear, elegant handwriting. When the key in his cell was turned the final time, he was mid-paragraph.

'In a word, in history, as elsewhere, the causes cannot be assumed. They are to be looked for...'

*

Twenty-four prisoners were handcuffed and taken from their cells. They were grouped under armed guard in the well of the prison. One group included a boy of sixteen who happened to be upstairs at an address where *Résistants* were found hiding. An SS Sturmbannführer read a proclamation. The penalty for the actions of those assembled was execution without trial. Shouts of '*Vive la France!*' echoed from the cells above. The prisoners were marched out of the prison gates. The boy walked, head down, between Bloch and Morel. He turned to Bloch.

'Do you think the bullets will hurt?'

Bloch looked at the boy with the tenderness of a father holding his first child.

'*Mon garçon,*' he said, 'it will be less than a mosquito bite.'

Morel looked over at Bloch, smiling. They continued to march along the River Saône towards Saint-Didier-de-Formans. It was a day to taunt the soon-to-depart. The sky was Monet blue. The grass was vivid emerald. Flowers, the earth's laughter, scented the way as the men passed. Spring sang in the song of birds. The sun shone through the trees, dappling the light on the heads of the men as they marched. It was a world away from the necropolis of mud and bone that encircled his trench thirty years before. Bloch recalled a saying by Dostoyevsky.

'Beauty will save the world.'

He had a strange feeling that it would. An unexpected calm suffused his body.

The men were split into lots of four. Each quadrant of men was marched towards a post.

Machine-gun fire. Fall of four.

Machine-gun fire. Fall of four.

Machine-gun fire. Fall of four.

Machine-gun fire. Fall of four.

Machine-gun fire. Fall of four.

Bloch was in the last group, with Morel and the boy. They were marched in front of a post. The earth underfoot was dark. Bodies lay scattered on the ground, some still twitching.

'Fall in, Sergent,' said Bloch.

'*Oui, mon Capitaine!*' shouted Morel.

Morel and Bloch stood to attention either side of the boy. The metal of Morel's head glinted in the sunlight.

'You will feel nothing,' said Bloch to the boy.

As the machine gun cracked, Morel saw his brother's face. Fabien was smiling.

Morel and Bloch fell together, each with an arm around the boy.

CHAPTER 38
'N + N'

Pforzheim Prison
Germany, 1944

Noor

Noor crouched in the corner of her cell. It was underground. A small amount of light leached from the top of the coldest wall. The only furniture was a metal bed and a metal bucket. Her hands were bound by a metal chain. Her feet the same. A third chain linked both. The chains were so heavy she could not lift her hands to eat. A warder spooned turnip soup into her mouth twice a day. Stray hairs often floated on the surface. Once she almost choked on a button.

Alone, it took her fifteen minutes pushing with the soles of her feet and using her back to edge up the wall to stand. Once standing, she moved around her cell like a deep-sea diver. The weaker she became, the more she forced herself to stand and move twice a day. At night, she crawled up on to her bed and lay twisted, the chains on her feet keeping her toes pointing at the ceiling, the chains on her hands keeping her wrists pointing at the wall. She had only one item of clothing. A thin cotton dress. On the back of her dress was sown a badge with two letters.

N + N

'*Nacht und Nebel* – Night and Fog.' It was a regulation dreamed up by Hitler himself for Nazi resisters. The full decree read '*Nacht und Nebel (Rückkehr Unerwünscht)* – Night and Fog (Return Not Required).' N + N prisoners were kept in solitary confinement, disallowed any type of communication and placed on the lowest food ration. Of all the letters stitched to a prisoner's clothing, N + N was a private invitation to the anteroom of Hell.

At least, smiled Noor to herself, they guessed one of her initials right. She was the first N + N prisoner to arrive, handcuffed and shivering, at Pforzheim prison.

It was winter; 1943 was coming to a bitter end. She was led to an underground cell. Cell 1. There she was shackled.

When the key turned in the door of Cell 1, her incarceration began. An incarceration that began at the speed of a tortoise. And slowed. An incarceration indifferent to weekdays and weekends. An incarceration indifferent, at first, to the names of the months or even the seasons. The rhythms of her life were dictated only by the opening of her cell door twice a day. Strict orders were given that no one should speak to her, even the warder who fed her soup.

She knew every part of her cell. Where the floor joined the wall and where the walls joined the ceiling. She knew every contour and spring of her metal bed and every chip of paint on the steel cell door. It was a perfect cube. On her first morning, a voice came.

Wherever you stand, be the soul of that place.

She sent regrets to Master Rumi that she could not stand. She would, instead, be the soul of that place from her shackled position on the floor. The soul of her cell. She looked at every corner. How could she be the soul of her cell without keeping it immaculate? Sometimes she would slide her foot across the floor to wipe the dust. Back and forth, back and forth. Her cell needed to be presentable for visitors. Visitors.

Her enduring guest was TIME. The guest with revolving hands. The guest who spun seconds into hours. Hours into days. Days into weeks. Weeks into months. Time's hands were everywhere.

Hands spinning alone. Hands spinning around faces. Hands spinning on the walls. Hands spinning in the air.

- Time.
  - Never.
    - Stopped.

Time allowed her to see the colour of every piece she knew by Bach, Vivaldi, Mozart, Handel, Ravel and Debussy. Time allowed her to make an inventory of every person she had ever met. Time allowed her to relive every moment she had spent with her family. Time allowed her, again and again, to run her finger from Antelme's head, down his face and on to his chest. Time, she told herself, was marching towards a point when her limbs were free and she would walk barefoot on the grass. She heard a whisper. It sounded like a locomotive.

Tick Tock
The sound of a clock.
Never to stop.
Never to stop.
Follow the hands.
The falling sands.
Never to stop.
Never to stop.
Follow the hands.
Their just demands.
Never to stop.
Never to stop.

The train that would one day take her away.

*

Other visitors came. When she shuffled her chains into the middle of the floor, they formed a circle.

Tiger

Elephant   Hare

Horse   Lion

Deer   Swan

Monkey

The visitors sat in rapt attention, as she read stories from *Twenty Jātaka Tales*.

Their favourite was 'The Swan Kingdom'.

'Many lakes there are in the world – blue lakes, green lakes, some with white lotuses, some with white swans sailing through, but none as beautiful as the Lake Manasa, for its water shone with all the colours of the sky. Miraculous flowers with large red cups of honey grew around its margins, and each day they dropped a little of their beauty in this lake.

In this kingdom lived sixty thousand swans...'

When all sixty thousand swans attended their homecoming at the end of the story, the animals pawed the air or flapped their wings. One day, Noor began the story of the Monkey-Bridge.

A giant-like monkey once ruled over eighty thousand monkeys in the Himalaya mountains...

When she looked up, she saw the eyes of all eighty thousand monkeys blinking as they listened. Noor told them of the MonkeyGiant who made his body into a bridge to save his subjects from being shot by King Brahmadatta's guards. At the end, the Monkey Giant lay dying, his back broken.

'Why,' asked King Brahmadatta, 'have you given your life to save your followers?'

'I do not suffer in leaving this world for I have gained my subjects' freedom. And if my death may be a lesson to you then I am more than happy. It is not your sword which makes you a king. It is love.'

477

When Noor read the final sentence, the monkeys clapped and somersaulted.

In a blink, they were gone. She was alone again, on the floor of her cell, where her leg irons had made a ring of sores around her ankles. She had given up trying to raise her wrists. She had grown weaker as the clock hands moved. The warder had to hold her head when feeding her soup. Like an infant, thought Noor, head thrown back as she swallowed the soup. When she closed her eyes, she was on the hearthrug by the fireplace in Moscow. Amina was rocking her while feeding her honey *blinis*. When she opened her eyes, she was shackled in a prison cell wearing a badge saying 'N + N'.

Her other visitor was almost as constant as Time. Noor sensed him in the air.

Their dialogue was constant. When she shuffled in her chains to face the dim light from the coldest wall, she heard her voice and his.

'Why do we die, Papa?'

'Death is the greatest gift to the living. Without death there cannot be new life. And besides. You can only die once.'

The ultimate gift? Her forehead puckered. She did not want to die.

'What path do you imagine the Divine Weaver is planning for your life, Noor?'

'Papa. I wish to be an anchoress.'

An anchoress. An anchoress, said her teacher, kept a vigil for humanity. Many died on the spot where they prayed. She did not want to die. Inayat's words returned.

'A life of self-sacrifice is the hardest path of all. But as Master Rumi teaches us... What you seek is seeking you.'

She thought of the Monkey Giant who saved eighty thousand followers.

I do not suffer in leaving this world for I have gained my subjects' freedom.

A faint smile crossed Noor's lips. She heard Inayat's voice again.

'What is your Sankalpa, Bābouli?'

'My Sankalpa is to shorten the war, Papa.'

'Your Sankalpa is the arc of your life, Bābouli. Will you follow it, even into peril?'

'Yes, Papa.'

Tears fell from Noor's face. She could not tell if they were joy or despair. Life had called on her to be an anchoress. She had answered her vocation. Now she was shackled. Did she have to die?

As the invisible clock hands ticked in Cell 1, Noor's mind always returned, while her body was shackled, to the riddle Inayat left in the House of Blessings.

It is so close you cannot see it.
It is so profound you cannot fathom it.
It is so simple you cannot believe it.
It is so good you cannot accept it.
What is it?

*

Noor was unaware but the eye that looked through the spyhole into her cell one night was different. It belonged to a prison guard from a farm on the edge of the Black Forest. He was the youngest of four brothers. He was not yet twenty, with freckles on a bovine face and close-set eyes. At school he would be called to the front of the class and made to stand by the blackboard. The teacher gave him a piece of chalk and asked him to spell 'matchbox'. The boy shrugged.

'Ich weiß nicht – I don't know.'

'Streichholzschachtel,' screamed the teacher.

He took the boy by the shoulder and bent his head over his desk.

'Dummer Junge! – Stupid boy!'

The cane snapped once.

'Dummer Junge! – Stupid boy!'

The cane snapped twice.

The class laughed.

'Dummer Junge! – Stupid boy!'

The name stuck.

'*Dummer.*'

He overheard other members of the family whispering.

'He's just not right.'

'He's a runt.'

They made him angry. Someone would pay. The boy spent his time with dogs, cows and pigs. Animals didn't call him '*Dummer*'. On duty at night, the boy looked into Noor's cell. She lay shackled on the bed. A woman tethered like a dog. Someone needed teaching a lesson. The following week, he sat outside Noor's cell. One leg was straighter than the other. He was alone. No one could see the metal bar protruding from his trouser leg. He turned the key in the cell door. Noor opened her eyes. She tried to sit, but her chains were immoveable. She saw a shadow move on the wall. The shadow was holding a bar. She looked again. Two bars.

Papa, the shadows!

The bars came down.

Papa, the shadows!

There was a crack.

Papa, the shadows!

And a spark.

Papa, the shadows!

Another crack.

Papa, the shadows!

Another spark.

Silence.

The shadow disappeared.

Noor's chains were broken.

*

Noor shuffled off her irons. Tears fell on her wrists and ankles as she rubbed the skin. She stood, uncertain as a newborn foal. She walked. Her walk became a skip. Noor danced unshackled around her cell as if she had discovered movement for the first time. She threw her arms out and arched her back like a diver. She placed her

cheek against the wall and her palms high over her head. She made
a series of arabesques and jumps. She knelt on the floor with her
arms outstretched. She made a series of poses Inayat had taught
her in the House of Blessings.

The Lion.

The Cat.

The Cobra.

The Eagle.

The Scorpion.

The Firefly.

The Monkey.

The Warrior.

At the end, she lay in blissful exhaustion on the floor.

The Corpse.

As she lay, her limbs unshackled, a line of the riddle came into
her mind.

It is so simple you cannot believe it.

A key in her mind turned.

Papa.

Is it freedom?

*

When the warder came to feed her soup, Noor reapplied her shackles. If she sat cross-legged, her leg irons looked like a tangle of
chains. She put her hands in her lap in the thin folds of her cotton
dress. The advantage of being fed by the warden was that she only
had to move her head. At night, she slept as if chained. She and the
broken chains shared their secret.

Other differences to the life of the N + N prisoner in Cell 1
appeared in a dream-like procession.

Time was turning the seasons. Slowly at first, she noticed the
hours of daylight, discernible from the tiny aperture above one
of the walls, were lengthening. Then, as if it were notes come
direct from the pen of Wolfgang Amadeus Mozart, birdsong.
Birds in the world of trees and flowers were singing of spring.

481

She imagined wooden Pteech-ka circling her cell, wings flapping, ruby eyes shining.

'A bird,' said Inayat once in the garden, 'does not sing because it has an answer. It sings because it has a song.'

She recalled Inayat's gift: *The Conference of the Birds*.

~

If Simorgh unveils its face to you, you will find

~

That all the birds, be they thirty or forty or more,

~

Are but the shadows cast by that unveiling.

~

What shadow is ever separated from its maker?

~

Do you see?

~

The shadow and its maker are one and the same.

~

Shadows.

Her fear had flown.

Birds were singing.

Another key turned in her mind.

It is so good you cannot accept it.

Papa!

Is it music?

The second change was the almost imperceptible sound from the wall by her bed. It was as if the wall's heart was beating. Sometimes it came during the day. Sometimes during the night. It was so faint Noor thought it was her imagination. Then she would hear the faintest heartbeat again. When she put her ear against the wall, it would be gone.

Noor dreamed again of Suresnes. She was sitting in the garden, lying on a rug. It was summer. Her eyes were closed. She heard the percussion of a woodpecker. Short taps, interspersed with longer taps. It was a message.

. _ _   ....   . _ _   . _ _ _ _ _   . _   . . .   . .   . _ .   . .   . _ .   . _ . . .   . _   . _ _ . _ . _ _

WHAT YOU SEEK IS SEEKING YOU

Noor sat upright. Was she losing her mind? Someone in the next-door cell was trying to communicate in Morse! No doubt using a heel of a hand on a wall three feet thick. The next morning, Noor used all her strength to bang a message on to the wall.

. _ . _ . . _ . _ _ _ _ _ _ . . _ _ .... . . _ .

'Are you there?'
Silence.
Then heartbeats that were almost inaudible.

_ . _ _ . ....

The heartbeat replied yes! Noor's heart leaped. The conversation in Morse took days, if not weeks. The woman in the next-door cell was a Jewess from Lyon whose husband had been murdered by the Gestapo. She was a Resistance wireless operator. Who was the prisoner in Cell 1? Noor's SOE training died hard. Safety first. 'Nora Baker. RAF.' It was too dangerous to say any more. Or it could be a trap. But the feeling of a fellow human in the cell next door gave her succour while the hands of Time revolved.

The final change was the hum of purple. Noor noticed the increased regularity of the movement of aircraft overhead. In particular, the purple hum of the Blenheim bombers flying at night. She knew the hum like her own voice. She thought of the crew with their flying jackets, goggles and maps. Unknown to Noor, one of the airmen to fly over Pforzheim prison was a squadron leader with one ear missing and a once-white evening scarf around his neck. They had met in the cave under the Grand Mosque in Paris.

Percy de Vere. Bomber Command. Rather blown off course.

Bomber Command. 'She never had a chance to say goodbye to her friend Joan from Bomber Command. For a moment she was on a picnic rug with Joan, surveying the Oxfordshire countryside from Boar's Hill.

'What do you want to do after the war?' said Joan, sitting, hugging her knees.

'I want to have children. As many as I can.'

She placed a hand over her womb. A tear fell to the floor of Cell 1 and exploded. Then she told herself, like the clock, to keep going.

Follow the hands.

Their just demands.

Never to stop.

Never to stop.

There was something that the N + N prisoner, locked in a cube with planes passing overhead, was unaware of. The increase in RAF activity was the precursor to an event that would change the course of history.

*

The Normandy landings were about to take place five hundred miles away, yet Noor could sense something was changing. The purple hum of Blenheim and Lancaster bombers was audible almost every night. And Time, the guest with the revolving hands, seemed to be telling her something.

'As I turn,' whispered Time, 'so turns the tide.'

Was it possible even to think of peace instead of war? Of the door to her cell bursting open and airmen from Bomber Command carrying her away? Of a tiger, a hare, a lion, a swan, a monkey, a deer, a horse and an elephant wandering free? Of eighty thousand monkeys racing down the corridor and climbing into the trees of the Black Forest? The thought was so ecstatic her mind dizzied itself as thoughts spun like the heads of whirling dervishes. Faster and faster... She came close, once, to passing out just at the thought of blissful deliverance.

It was, she knew, also a race against her guest with the revolving hands. The ration of turnip soup was taking its toll. She had always been slim. Now her bones were beginning to protrude, and the pangs of hunger had been replaced by periods of light-headedness. If Bomber Command were going to fly her away, they would have to have an urgent conversation with Time.

One morning, the warder came in to feed her soup. Noor sat on the floor as usual, swathed in her chains. As she tilted her head back, she thought she might faint. The wall opposite was falling backwards. Her vision blurred. She heard the shake of a chain. Her arm had made an involuntary jolt. The metal cuff of the chain fell open. The warder's eyes widened. She looked at Noor as if she were a witch. The warder was a heavy woman, but she ran from the cell with unexpected speed.

As she lay on her bed that night, the shackles on her hands and feet were locked tighter than the jaws of a ferret. She was beyond crying. She stared at the wall with eyes staring at a hinterland long past despair.

A life of self-sacrifice is the hardest path of all.

What were the limits?

Time had turned for a slow week when her cell door opened at an unusual time. Two guards entered. They turned the key in her chains with wordless disinterest. Her hand irons were replaced with handcuffs. She was taken to the commandant's office. The new commandant had left his deputy in charge that morning. The deputy spoke as if he were passing the time of day.

'You have two visitors. You will be taken to them shortly.'

He wrote something in a ledger. As he looked up, Noor could see unease in his pupils.

She was shown into a separate office. Two men were standing. Her stomach turned. Two black beetles. The first of the men sounded businesslike, even cordial.

'We are from the Karlsruhe Gestapo. Do not alarm yourself. The commandant has given orders that you are to be physically unharmed.'

Noor stood in silence. The second spoke. 'We have orders to ascertain further information about you and other members of the Prosper network.'

The prisoner from Cell 1 had been interrogated at Pforzheim before. That, however, was by Abwehr officers. There were raised voices at times, but she had not been ill-treated. After 84 Avenue Foch, it was like being interrogated by schoolchildren. This was different.

'The same rules as Avenue Foch apply,' said the first beetle. 'Your interrogation can be as difficult or easy as you want it to be.'

He smiled.

'Do you wish to co-operate?

Silence.

'I thought so.'

A chair was brought.

'Pray be seated.'

Noor sat.

She looked at the clock. It was midday. She could hear one of the black beetles walk behind her.

'This is for your own safety,' he said.

A black blindfold was tied. She could feel the other beetle tying her feet.

She could hear furniture being moved, as if the room were being rearranged.

She heard footsteps as both men left the room. Then footsteps as they returned. Something was different. The next moment, she was being lifted. Both Gestapo noticed she was the weight of a child. She was placed into a container. It was fresh-cut wood. She heard the swing of a hinge. The lid of the container closed with a thud. She could hear a click. It sounded like a padlock.

'Do not alarm yourself. The lid has enough perforations to allow you to breathe.'

He set his stopwatch. Agents who were shut in a coffin always talked within the hour. Sometimes minutes. Noor lay still.

A life of self-sacrifice is the hardest path of all.

The full horror took hold.

She was in pitch darkness.

She could not move.

Her hands were beneath her body, the metal of the handcuffs cutting into her wrists. The adrenaline of animal panic flooded her system. Her throat tightened.

Papa!

Papa!

A familiar voice came.

In times of strife, Noor, always find and follow your breath.

She found her breath. It was fast, like a hunted fox. The voice returned.

Adham pranayama: abdominal breath.

She breathed deep into her diaphragm. Twenty breaths, perhaps thirty. Her pulse began to calm. Inayat had told her once of Buddhist monks who would seek Enlightenment by being cast into a living statue. The statue was open only at the mouth, where the monk would breathe before finding earthly Nirvana. Compared to a statue, she told herself, her container was airy.

It was time to descend. Down through the churn of the waves, through the stilts of light under the surface, through the darker, stiller water. Down to the deepest sea floor of her mind. She came to rest on the bottom, her thoughts slowing in the undercurrents. Her pulse slowed further. There she stayed, the panic giving way to composure.

How long was she submerged?

Time's hands continued to revolve, but at what pace?

Tick tock.

The sound of a clock.

Loud and clear.

Always near.

Measuring.

TIME.

Invisible.
Always moving.
Never still.
Time for what?
A time to kill.
A time to heal.
A time to love.
Where, now, were the hands of time?

On the sea floor of her mind, she picked out a figure in gold. His beard billowed in the currents. His arms were outstretched. His hands were beckoning. His face was serene.

A time to love.

Noor stayed on the sea floor, oblivious to the hands of time. She must have dozed for a while, as she was jolted from a strange, opiate sleep. She heard shouting in German. Men were arguing. It was impassioned. She could hear what sounded like a fist coming down on a desk. She could pick out a few of the words. '*Nacht und Nebel*', one voice kept saying. '*Verboten!*' boomed another. *Verboten* – Forbidden. What was forbidden?

When the hinge turned on the lid of the coffin and Noor's blindfold was removed, she saw the face of the commandant staring down in horror. He raised her himself. He was muttering words of contempt.

'*Wir beugen uns in Pforzheim nicht vor Gestapo-Methoden* – We do not stoop to Gestapo methods at Pforzheim.'

He summoned a guard to unlock her handcuffs and untie her feet. She was walked through his office. The deputy commandant was standing looking at the floor. There was no trace of the Gestapo. The clock on the wall said four-thirty. She had been in the coffin for four and a half hours. It was strange, but Noor felt she wanted to comfort the commandant, a man who must have been in his seventies. She was not sure if she had ever seen an expression of such injury.

When she returned to her cell, Noor found a mattress on her bed and a sheet embroidered with roses. There was a book propped against the wall: *Grimms' Fairy Tales*. She was not re-shackled. That evening, a man in chef's whites entered her cell and set down a tray on the floor. It was an omelette, still warm. In a metal cup was apple juice.

Cell 1 felt the size of the Albert Hall. As for the omelette, it was ambrosia itself. The weeks that followed saw an improvement in the prison fare. Bread came with the turnip soup, sometimes with butter. She ate unshackled. The real feast, however, was the book. The stories were in German, but she was able to pick out the narrative. Rapunzel. Rumpelstiltskin. Hansel and Gretel. Cinderella. The Pied Piper of Hamelin. She read and reread every story. There were even illustrations. She found herself coming back to Rapunzel, the maiden locked in the tower.

'*Rapunzel, laß deine Haare, runter daß ich rauf kann.*'

She remembered the rhyme from her childhood.

'Rapunzel! Rapunzel!

Let down your hair

That I may climb your golden stair.'

She felt her own hair, dark and unwashed. But still part of her. Who would climb her hair and break open the door to Cell 1? Time, the enduring guest, was silent. Its hands continued to revolve. Day into night. Night into day.

Tick Tock

The sound of a clock.

Never to stop.

Never to stop.

Then, on a morning no different to any other, the warder told Noor she would be leaving the following day by train. Her heart's first response was to swell.

The train to take her away. She spent the day remembering every part of her cell. Her prison and her home. How could she feel wistful about the place of her incarceration? One thing made her smile. The packing. Apart from a book of fairy tales, she had no possessions.

The following morning, her cell door opened. She was taken to the commandant's office. The silver-haired commandant stood. His eyes spoke of resignation. He asked her to keep the book of fairy tales. She was given a coat and taken to a waiting Mercedes. Inside were three black beetles.

It was, to anyone, a strange party of travellers that boarded the train at Pforzheim station. Three SS officers were escorting a gaunt young woman with dark skin and radiant eyes. She was handcuffed to one of the SS, her N + N prison uniform partially visible under the coat.

The train was heading for Munich. The four sat together, Noor by the window handcuffed to the soldier on her right. The other two sat opposite. Others in the compartment looked away. The stare of the death's head from the Gestapo cap was enough to keep the eyes of the local civilians averted. They and their clothes looked grey, like the Parisians under occupation, but without the simmering defiance. She noticed the date on a newspaper. It was October 1944. At first, she thought the date must be wrong. The full extent of Time's stay in Pforzheim was revealed. She must have been there for ten months. She had, of course, no idea that the allies had invaded Europe.

Her Gestapo escorts on the train were civil, if curt. One even went to the buffet to bring her a sandwich of pumpernickel and cheese and a tisane. On the table next to the pumpernickel was Noor's one possession. A book of Grimms' fairy tales. Noor looked out of the window. The fields on either side were lush and verdant. Seeing flowers and trees after ten months in a windowless cube was like witnessing a miracle. Birds wheeled over a copse by a lake. The Swabian mountains rose, majestic, to the south. There was, thought Noor, so much beauty in the world.

She felt a strange oneness.

A voice came.

Love is the bridge between you and everything.

She smiled. The train arrived at Munich. The party were met by a large black Mercedes. Noor noticed the road signs the car was following. It was a place of which she had never heard.

DACHAU

*

Canaris

The man with silver hair and deep-etched parentheses framing his upper lip lay in his concentration camp cell. His nose was broken. On the back of his prison uniform were the two letters 'N + N'. Admiral Canaris had been sentenced to death. His request to be shot was rejected. He was waiting to be hanged.

In July, a high-ranking German officer had placed a bomb in a briefcase within feet of Hitler. The officer left the room. The bomb detonated. Hitler's stenographer was killed instantly. Others were blown through a window.

Three died within hours. The Führer survived. Seven thousand arrests followed and almost five thousand executions. Canaris escaped the initial finger of suspicion. He was, however, associated with the key conspirators. As investigations continued, one conspirator confessed to Canaris being their 'spiritual instigator'.

There followed seizure of Canaris's diary. Some of the passages, although oblique, were used as evidence against the admiral. He was tried and convicted by a summary SS court. The judge, a silhouette in front of an oversized swastika, pronounced the verdict. The SS had turned its fury on the Prussian. As the judge fulminated, Canaris remembered his words to Heydrich.

'Your people and my people will always be different.'

Canaris marched with a ramrod-straight back as he was led away.

*

The night before his execution, the Prussian eagle tethered in Canaris's mind took flight. Back in time flew the eagle. Back over the chop and swell of the admiral's life. Back to the place where it happened. First, he saw himself standing on the deck of the *Dresden*. He could feel the bitter spray of the Chilean Sea. The same sea that sprayed his back as he rowed away from Quiriquina Island on the *Impávido*. He was ashore, a fugitive in a *chupalla*. Next, he was moving through the Andes with his guide, Maicu. Then alone. What drove him to continue after his guide turned back? Was it madness? Maicu's replacement was *soroche* – altitude sickness. *Soroche* brought dizziness and an *explósion* behind his eyes. When Canaris looked again at the sky, he was lying on his back. His limbs were lead. Snow was settling on his eyelids. He heard the shriek of an Andean condor as his focus slipped from white to black.

After a time, his eyelids fluttered open. The sky was gone. He was lying on a bed of llama pelts. His mountain furs lay over his body. His boots had been removed. His feet felt supple, as if washed and anointed. Beyond his feet, a wood-burning stove blazed orange. The air smelt of roasting pine nuts. There was a faint trace of caramel. His eyes traced the black and brown contours above. A cave? A hut? That moment, he realized – he was not alone.

Six feet away was a man sitting on the earth. He wore a pale alpaca tunic. His arms were wrapped round his knees. His hair fell about his shoulders. He had a narrow, unlined face and cinnamon eyes. He looked both concerned and calm. Maicu? No, Maicu's face was broader, eyes blacker. The man did not speak, though his eyes radiated affinity. In the firelight, Canaris noticed small indentations in his forehead – as if a *tapaculo* chick had left a trail.

Where had he seen that narrow face and those forgiving eyes before? And those indentations? The marks of a Crown of Thorns? *It couldn't be...*

*

Canaris was taken naked to the scaffold. As he stood in the wind, he was for a moment standing at the conning tower of *UB-128* as it sped into Kiel harbour. Figures hovered above the water. His wife and daughters. Ernesto, the cook from Quiriquina Island. Elvira

Talamantes. Rear Admiral Behncke. Klasing, his aide-de-camp. The Kaiser himself, hand upon sword, epaulettes glittering. There was also a group of nameless Jews he had helped evacuate from Holland. The women waved. The men saluted. Last, he saw the man in the Andes cave, hair about his shoulders, marks upon his forehead. The radiance of the man's eyes warmed his naked body. He was not alone.

The noose tightened around Canaris's neck. His vision blurred. He could hear his breathing, fast and hoarse. Dots appeared behind his eyes, as the tableau of a dying man became an impressionist painting of charcoal-grey flecked with obsidian. The dots coalesced and darkened into a smudge of Goya-black. He heard a sound, as if a sack of coal was thrown from a truck. He was on the ground. It was him. Naked but alive! His vision came into focus. He was seeing the world from the perspective of a fallen climber. Had the man in the Andes cave intervened? He rolled on to his back, lying on his bound wrists.

A voice snarled in his ear. 'A traitor must feel death not once but twice.'

Canaris stared into the sky, bound and naked. The narrow face from the Andes cave reappeared. This time a crown of thorns encircled his head. Streaks of blood ran down his forehead. Minutes rolled past as the clouds darkened. A strange peace descended on the naked admiral. The noose tightened once more. He felt his head being lifted. His breathing became hoarse again, but slower. As his vision blurred, he saw the man's face a final time. The thorns around his head burst into roses. Their eternal red deepened into a crimson sea. Then endless black.

In his cell afterwards, the guards found two messages written in blood.

Auch wenn ich durch das Tal des Todesschattens gehe
fürchte ich nichts Böses, denn Du bist bei mir.
Even though I walk through the valley of the shadow of death

I shall fear no evil, for You are with me.
Ich habe aus Pflicht gehandelt.
I acted out of duty.

*

Dachau, Germany
1944

Noor

The metal gates were opened by a sentry. The Mercedes pulled up outside a low entrance building with a black tower extending from the roof. Beyond the tower, the skyline was pierced by a tall, smoke-blackened chimney. The arrival of a prisoner with a party of SS was unusual. Inside the administration building, one of the SS officers uttered the words *Nach und Nebel*. They acted as a catalyst. A medical officer made a cursory examination of Noor's teeth and scalp. Her height was taken. It was over in minutes.

From the administration building she was taken to a set of inner gates guarded by sentries. The words '*Arbeit macht frei*' were visible within the ironwork. *Arbeit* – Work. *Frei* – Free. Work would make her free! Perhaps work outdoors in the forest? Anything not to be shackled in a cube… The sentries opened the gates. Noor was escorted into the camp, still handcuffed to one of the SS.

As she walked, the world of Agent Madeleine intersected with a world so removed from the norms of human existence that she wondered if the SS had put a hallucinogen in her tisane. The camp was surrounded by a high electric fence interspersed with watchtowers from which guards trained machine guns. Guards with pistols patrolled the spaces between rows of long, low barracks. Everything was leached of colour. The rainbow had been replaced with four shades: black, charcoal, rat-brown and pigeon. The meadows of greens, whites and violets under the Swabian mountains might have belonged to a different planet.

A column of figures was marching in her direction. The column was surrounded by barking Alsatians. Guards used the butts of their rifles on the backs and shoulders of the marching figures. Noor could not, at first, compute what she was seeing. The figures were in uniforms and caps that had once been striped. They were filthy. The figures were from a medieval depiction of Purgatory. Walking skeletons, dead-eyed, heads cropped. It was impossible to tell the men from the women.

If they had been human once, they were now something else. Who were the living dead? The majority wore yellow triangular badges. Some wore badges of faded pink. Others green. The column marched in unison until someone at the back fell. One of the Alsatians leaped on to the figure's chest and started to tear at its throat. The figure lay, unmoving. An SS guard walked over with a pistol. Noor shut her eyes. The shot echoed. The column continued minus one.

Had she walked through iron gates into another world's hell? She was escorted to a block with the letters 'N + N' on the door. She was led down a dim corridor and placed in a cell. There were wrist- and hand-irons on the floor. The SS officer released her wrist from the handcuffs, and with his colleagues clapped her in irons in the cell. One said '*Guten Abend*' as they left.

The cell was less than half the size of the cube in Pforzheim, but there was a window. She sat on the floor and wrapped her arms around her knees. Her body was riven with involuntary spasms.

Always find and follow your breath.

She breathed deep into her diaphragm. Inhale. Exhale. Inhale. Exhale.

Time turned only twenty minutes before she heard activity outside. She heard the marching of boots and shouts. She heard a volley of shots. Then single, deliberate shots. She put her hands over her eyes. What poison had Humanity drunk?

There was further movement outside. Then quiet. She sat, eyes wide. Something was tugging her sense of smell. It smelt like horsehair mattresses were being burned. Burning hair. Whose hair? A thought began to writhe in the pit of her stomach. The chimney she had seen on the way into the camp was leaching smoke. The smell changed. It had a carnal note. The smoke from the chimney became darker and thicker.

Noor was about to scream when an SS guard entered her cell. She remembered the same manic look in the eyes of Dr Winkler in Avenue Foch. These eyes swung in all directions. Wild. His cap was tilted back on his head. A smell of sweat and spirits followed him into the room. He looked at the woman on the floor with deranged contempt. He threw his head back and laughed like a hyena. He knelt on the floor so that his eyes were an inch from Noor's. She could smell his whisky breath.

'*Nach und Nebel*,' he said, as if naming her. '*Nach und Nebel*.'

He clamped his hand around her throat and started to squeeze. Noor turned her head to the ceiling. Her vision was blurring. The squeeze strengthened. Time, the enduring guest, slowed. She had known it slow before.

TIME.
Final seconds.
Hands.
Moving across a face.
Towards.
An infinite
Respite.

He released his grip. The ceiling came back into focus. The SS guard started to walk around the room in a circle. Round and round, like a deranged circus animal. He stopped and laughed again. And then it started. The blows. They had a sequence.

Kick. Slap. Punch.
Kick. Slap. Punch.

Noor could see herself from above. A woman in shackles on the floor. A large man above her using all the force of his fists and his boots. How many blows could the body endure? As they continued, it felt as if they were raining down on another. Her mind began to stray. She heard a voice. A conundrum.

It is so close you cannot see it.

How close? So near it has no distance to travel. The eye cannot see the eye. Or can it? What is all around us that we cannot see? Air? Emotion? The Perfect Constructor? The answers could be infinite... Time prompted her choice. A key turned in her mind.

Papa.

Is it awareness?

As her mind wandered, something entered her line of sight. Something moving. Something gold. Noor strained her eyes. Wherever the black moved, the gold followed. She squinted. The gold was the outline of a figure. The figure sat, cross-legged. Moments later, he was sitting in another part of the cell. His eyes were closed, his brow rucked, his face taut. His lips were moving at speed. Noor recognized the infinite colours of the *Zikr*. The face she would recognize anywhere. An opiate calm infused her body.

Kick. Slap. Punch.

Kick. Slap. Punch.

The blows made a field of sunflower-yellow and orange behind her eyes.

She thought of the missing line.

It is so profound you cannot fathom it.

Her thoughts soared. Up on the wings of Pteech-ka. Up towards the towers of Notre Dame. Up past Le Stryge. A key turned in her mind. She smiled.

Of course.

She was about to answer when a voice came.

Wherever you stand, be the soul of that place.

She had to stand. Within a ring of crimson, she summoned all her strength.

She pushed with her soles. She was half standing, her chains straining.

The guard's eyes swivelled.

Was the prisoner *defying* him?

The rage of his eyes met radiance. He drew his pistol. The radiance intensified. He looked away. A voice came.

Allah does not burden a soul beyond that it can bear.
The last sound Noor heard was a gunshot.
The colour was sapphire.

*

The guard left.
On the floor lay a body.
Above the body, Divine Breath swirled.
From the breath came the whisper of Master Rumi.

This is love:
To fly toward a secret sky
To cause a hundred veils to fall each moment.
First to let go of life.
Finally,
To take a step without feet.

*

An Encounter

At the end of her days, a woman stood high upon a cliff overlooking the shore. She stood hand in hand with her Guardian Angel, gazing back over her life.

At the far end of the shore, she saw an image of herself as an infant at her mother's breast. So began the path of her life, two pairs of footprints in the sand, the woman's alongside the Angel's.

The path of her life unfolded in images that appeared, suspended above the waves, as they traced her days along the shore.

She saw herself – asleep on a hearthrug in Moscow, at her harp in the House of Blessings, at school in Suresnes, at the Sorbonne, at her writing table in the 5ème, at attention on her first day in uniform, at her transmitter as MADELEINE on the rooftops of Paris.

She saw herself in a sealed basement room, in a cell chained and, in another cell, lying on the floor.

The woman looked at the shore. She could see the two pairs of footprints walking in tandem from the start of her life.

They walked together, side by side.

At the end of her life, when her body was overrun by black beetles, she saw a lone set of footprints in the sand.

The woman turned to her Guardian Angel, her face riven with pain.

'Why did you forsake me when I was captured, tortured and shackled?'

A pair of devoted wings enveloped the woman.

At those times in your life,
said the Angel,
You could not walk.
So I carried you.

EPILOGUE

Noor is barefoot.

The grass under her feet is lush.

She is standing on a path in a forest.

Around her: a tiger, a hare, a lion, a swan, a deer, a horse and an elephant.

A wooden bird with ruby eyes is soaring.

The trees erupt with eighty thousand monkeys clapping and somersaulting.

In the distance is a man in gold, arms outstretched.

A single monkey drops from a tree.

The monkey takes her hand.

And leads her towards the golden man.

Who sings her true name.

Bābouli.

In addition, this book is dedicated to:

Uday Khemka
('the Earth's Protector')

And to the memory of:
Noor Inayat Khan (George Cross, Croix de Guerre)
1914–1944

The author warmly invites readers who have enjoyed this
book to leave a review on Goodreads.com and/or on his
author website. 'Those who honour me I shall honour.'

barnabyjameson.com

DRAMATIS PERSONAE

SOE = Special Operations Executive
Noor Inayat Khan: writer, SOE, codename: MADELEINE.
Inayat Khan: Sufi mystic, father of Noor.
Amina Begum: American mother of Noor.
Count Tolstoy: Moscow friend of Inayat and Amina.
Georges Morel: WW1 veteran, French Resistance.
Fabien Morel: WW1 soldier, Georges' brother.
Marc Bloch: WW1 veteran, French Resistance, historian.
Dr Daquin: WW1 doctor.
Lieutenant Robinson: WW1 pilot.
Sanjay: wounded WW1 soldier.
DS Rush-Williams: Metropolitan Police Special Branch.
Wilhelm Canaris: German Imperial Navy, head of the Abwehr,
    German Military Intelligence.
Ernesto: prison cook, Quiriquina Island, Chile.
Elvira Talamantes: Estancia Santa Isabel, Argentina.
Franz Tauber: head of the German Trade Legation, Buenos Aires.
'Treasure' (Doris Richards): enchantress of Balcombe Street.
Mrs Morgan: duchess of Balcombe Street.
Mademoiselle Pelletier: mentor of Balcombe Street.
Milton: attendant of Balcombe Street.
General Bertram Page: WW1 officer, patron of Balcombe Street.
Falinne: Noor's school friend.
Mathilde: school tormentor.

Henriette Monette: Noor's music teacher.

Leo Marks: chess prodigy, SOE cryptographer.

Mr Marks Senior: Leo Marks' father, owner of the antiquarian bookshop at 84 Charing Cross Road.

Mr Cohen: Marks Senior's business partner.

Uncle Abe: Leo Marks' great-uncle Abraham.

William Grover-Williams ('WW'): racing driver, SOE, codename: SEBASTIEN.

Robert Benoist: racing driver, French resistance.

Tommy Yeo-Thomas: manager of Molyneux in Paris, SOE.

Miss Beach: owner of Shakespeare & Co. bookshop, Paris.

Francis Suttill: barrister, SOE, codename: PROSPER.

Andrée Borrel: French Resistance, Suttill's courier and ADC.

Lionel Redknapp (aka Anthony Buckley-Chubb): forger, SOE.

Joan: Noor's friend from the WAAF.

Ruth: Leo Marks' girlfriend in WW2.

Captain Jepson RN: SOE recruiter.

Captain de Wesselow: SOE, Wanborough Mannor.

'The Bishop': SOE unarmed combat instructor.

Maurice Buckmaster: head of SOE French ('F') Section.

Vera Atkins: Buckmaster's Aide-de-Camp.

Brigadier Gubbins: head of SOE.

Reinhard Heydrich: SS, 'The Man With the Iron Heart'.

Gabčík. Kubiš and Valčík: SOE-trained Czech agents.

Percy de Vere: Bomber Command.

Joseph Antelme: SOE, codename: RENAUD.

Henri Déricourt: SOE, French Resistance.

Zoë: French Resistance, girlfriend of Morel in WW2 codename: PAPILLON.

Gilbert Norman: SOE, codename: ARCHAMBAUD.

Professeur Balachowsky: École Nationale d'Agriculture, French Resistance.

Henri Garry: French Resistance, codename: PHONO.

Marguerite Garry: fiancée of Henry Garry.

Renée Garry: sister of Henri Garry.

Octave Simon: sculptor, French Resistance.

Culioli: French Resistance.

Jacqueline: SOE agent.

Macalister: Canadian SOE agent.

Pickersgill: Canadian SOE agent.

Rake: SOE radio operator.

Agazarian: SOE radio operator.

Dowden: SOE radio operator.

Hugo Bleicher: Abwehr spy-catcher.

Sturmbannführer Kieffer: SS, 84 Avenue Foch.

Dr Winkler: SS doctor.

Hauptsturmführer Oberhauser: SS.

Stabsscharführer Vogt: SS.

Author's Note:
CODENAME: MADELEINE is inspired by real events.
While most of the characters bear the names of real
people, their stories have been fictionalised.

Read an exclusive excerpt from
the next book in the series:

CODENAME: GOD-GIVEN

PROLOGUE

Demarcation Line,
Occupied France, 1942

Rake

Rake approached the checkpoint.

A one-time doyen of the West End stage, his role on this occasion carried a danger altogether more pressing than a lukewarm review in *The Illustrated London News*. The consequence of fluffing his lines was a bullet. And not from a stage pistol. He faced summary execution as a spy.

Armed German sentries stood behind a storm-cloud of barbed wire. One held an Alsatian, straining at its leash. It snarled, baring teeth the colour of lightening. Rake remembered the dog-bite he received as a child: the clamp of canine incisors piercing the scaphoid bone in his right hand. He tried not to shudder.

He advanced. In his left hand was a forged *Carte d'Identité* in the name of 'Denis Rocher.' In his right hand was a battered leather suitcase in which his SOE-issue radio crystals were hidden. If they were discovered it would be the final scene in the life of a one-time matinée idol. He willed both hands to stop trembling.

'*Bonjour*,' he said, a little louder than anticipated.

He presented his identity papers with the stage-smile of a man whose heart was beating like a sledgehammer. The guard looked

509

at Rake's identity papers and back at his face. The Alsatian's barks became more excited. Rake could feel his palm moisten around the handle of his suitcase. A trickle of sweat coursed down his spine. The guard looked again at the *Carte d'Identité*, narrowing his eyes. Rake could hear the blood pumping in his ears. The guard snapped like the leaping Alsatian.

'*Öffne deinen Koffer!* – Open your suitcase!'